"Who am I holding? Are you an angel?
Are you real? Have I gone crazy too?
What are you, Bea?"

She leaned back to see the question in Virgil's eyes. The ring of his arms supported her. "I'm a woman."

She kissed him gently on the mouth. "Do you want to do this?"

"Do what? Kiss? Yes."

"No you jerk, not just kiss. Not just jump in the sack either. I mean this. This. The hugging and quiet little kisses. Lobster dinner and candlelight. You know . . ."

She extended her hand and waved it back and forth, taking in both of them and all of the unexplored and unexplained that lay between them.

"Because," she said, "I want to. With you. Do you know, Virgil? You were the last thing I saw dying on that sidewalk. You, and your voice. I . . . I felt something when I heard your voice. I want to know what that feeling was. I want to find out the rest of it."

"AMBITIOUS. . . . ROBBINS DOES
WRITE WELL . . . and succeeds in
keeping readers interested."
—*Booklist*

"A GOOD READ."
—*Java*

HarperChoice

Souls to Keep

David L. Robbins

 HarperPaperbacks

A Division of HarperCollins*Publishers*

HarperPaperbacks
A Division of HarperCollins*Publishers*
10 East 53rd Street, New York, NY 10022–5299

This is a work of fiction. The characters, incidents, and
dialogues are products of the author's imagination and are
not to be construed as real. Any resemblance to actual events
or persons, living or dead, is entirely coincidental.

ISBN 0-06-109791-8

HarperCollins®, ®, HarperPaperbacks™
and HarperChoice™ are trademarks of
HarperCollins Publishers Inc.

Cover illustration © 1999 by Joe Burleson

A hardcover edition of this book was published in 1998 by
HarperCollins*Publishers*.

First HarperPaperbacks printing: June 1999

Printed in the United States of America

Visit HarperPaperbacks on the World Wide Web at
http://www.harpercollins.com

❖ 10 9 8 7 6 5 4 3 2 1

For Tom Kennedy and Gary Green,
two long-standing friends and benefactors
who—depending on your perspective—
get a lot of the blame or credit for me.

and

In Memoriam

For Sam Robbins,
Carol Robbins,
and Moose.

Though I speak with
the tongues of men and angels
and have not love,
I am become but a
sounding brass
or a clanging cymbal.

1 CORINTHIANS 13:1

They say of an amputee that he
remembers his leg.
Well, I remember this girl.

JOHN STEINBECK
SWEET THURSDAY

Souls to Keep

1

"HELLO. Top Hat Escort Service."

"Yes. I'd like to make an appointment."

"Alright. That's what we're here for. What can I do for you?"

"I . . . uh . . . could you . . ."

"Yes?"

"Could you tell me what it is you . . . I mean, I . . ."

"Sir?"

"Yeah?"

"Let's do it this way."

"What."

"How about I run down our list of services for you. Then you pick something you'd like. That's the way we usually do it."

"That's better."

"Yes it is. Let me ask you a few questions first. That okay? Nothing personal, just some preferences."

"Okay."

"Okay. This is the Top Hat Escort Service. We have several items for discriminating adults to choose from. First, are you calling just for you or for a party?"

"A party? What do you mean?"

"You know, like a bachelor thing."

"No. Just for me."

"Alright. You want a dancer or an escort?"

"I don't know. What's the difference?"

"Simple. An escort will go out on the town with you—dinner, a play, whatever. You pick up the tab. A dancer will come to your home or office or wherever you say within reason and give you a private dance. If you want it in a motel, you arrange for the room."

"I see."

"Which one sounds good?"

"A private dancer's a bit much. That's not . . . it's not what I was looking for. You know?"

"You don't have to explain, sir. Just pick."

"Could I get maybe an escort I could go out dancing with? Up in Marathon or Miami?"

"Yeah, of course. All our escorts are dancers too."

"Oh."

"Now let me tell you what we got for you. Our signature service is called The Top Hat. This is first-class all the way. Evening gown, stilettos, zircons, the whole nine yards. Very classy, very chic. Only our best girls."

"Uh-huh."

"You can take 'em anywhere. People's eyes are buggin' out. You understand."

"I get it."

"You wanna go dancing, go. No extra charge."

"Alright."

"Next is our most commonly requested service, what we call The Fedora. This is a little less formal than The Top Hat. More like the tailored business-suit look. Executive kind of thing, if that's your taste."

"Uh-huh."

"Then there's The Panama, where we send you a Hispanic lady. Lovely. Latin. Great dancers. The best. Or maybe you want what we call The Ten Gallon, in case you don't feel like friggin' around with all the dresses and jewelry, you just want a gal in a pair of jeans and boots, you know, just knock around. And finally, in case maybe you'd like something else, you know, something out of the mainstream. What I'm saying is maybe you want us to send you over a male escort, there's our Brown Derby."

"No. No. Jesus."

"Just asking."

"I understand. No. The, uh, The Fedora."

"Alright."

"How much is that? Is a Fedora?"

"One fifty."

"Will she be, you know, pretty? I'd like it if she was attractive. For one fifty."

"Sir, I'll have her waiting for you to pick up in

the lobby at the Ramada on North Roosevelt. You don't like what you see, just get back in your car and keep driving."

"Alright."

"What night?"

"Is tonight too soon?"

"Right now is not too soon. You want tonight, we'll go seven o'clock. The Ramada. Have one red rose in your hands. She'll be in the lobby."

"Who do I ask for?"

"No names. You don't ask for nobody. She'll approach you. Otherwise you could walk up to the wrong woman and catch yourself a smack. It happens. Seven o'clock. If you pick her up, you pay her."

"Alright."

"Pleasure doing business with you. I'm sure we'll talk again."

"What time do I have to have her back?"

"You never done this before."

"No. I'm married."

"Yeah, well, don't feel bad. Lot of guys step out once in a while, it helps their marriages. Don't worry about what time. She ain't a pumpkin. Have fun."

Beatrice had stripped down to her fishnets, pumps, G-string and tassels when her four o'clock tried to touch her.

He reached out a big mushy white mitt. She slapped it away.

"Hey!" he bellowed.

"Shut up," she said. "You paid to watch. Watch."

"Come on. What is this?"

"This," she swiveled her hands down herself as if showing off a new refrigerator on a game show, "is a dance. This," she executed a quick pirouette on one spike, "is what you ordered."

He sat back in the motel room chair. "Is that all I get?"

Hands on hips. Pelvis in a circle rotating to the music from the portable player on the dresser.

"From me it is."

"Naw. Jesus." His eyes were glommed on her belly button. "Naw, Bea. You're killin' me."

He spread apart his knees and held out his arms. Beatrice thought of Humpty Dumpty. The rod behind his zipper was plain; the creases in his baggy, fat man's suit pants were like arrows pointing at his crotch.

"Christ, I can't put up with this."

Beatrice stepped left and stepped right, the imagination leaching out of her movements.

"Baby, please." He pointed with both hands at his bulge. "Come on. At least give me a blow job."

Beatrice stomped one heel. She whirled to the boom box and snapped it off. Her brown hair curtained her face; she swept the strands away with an angry wrist.

"Look, maybe we're not communicating. I told you I'm a dancer. That's what you ordered, that's what you're getting. I am not going to touch you or allow you to touch me. You want something else, call 'em back and make other arrangements."

The fat man lifted his eyebrows. He kept his legs wide as if to show Beatrice that his staff was so engorged and powerful he could not close his legs.

"Yeah," he said, "that's easy for you. But what am I gonna do with this?"

She collected his coat off the bed. She tossed it at him, over his lap. "Buy a goat."

He didn't move. The coat lay across his legs. His knees and arms were still open.

"Come on, Bea. Look, how about another fifty?"

"How about you hit the bricks. Show's over."

"Seventy-five."

"Out."

She opened the bathroom door and reached around for her bathrobe. She put it on and belted the terry cloth tight.

"Then gimme my money back." He indicated her purse where his two fifties had been folded and stashed when he'd first come in the room.

"You want your money back? Fine. You gimme back my twenty-five years of hanging around greaseballs like you."

"Aw, c'mon Bea. Just a hand job. That's all."

"That's all?" Beatrice shuddered at the thought of another unloving, demanding, paying penis. She'd been shuddering a lot lately, and this was finally the john and the penis she was tossing back out on the street where they came from.

"You got more nerve than a bad tooth," she said. "Out."

He rose from the chair and slid on his suit coat deliberately. He shot his cuffs and pulled his tie up under his pink pillow of chin. "I paid for the room. You gotta leave too."

She answered with a stare.

"You think you're so hot," he said.

She kept staring.

"Well, little lady, you're not. You're a forty-year-old bimbo past her prime. You ain't righteous and you damn sure ain't too good for me."

She moved to open the door. He stepped out into the garishly carpeted hall.

"No," she said sweetly, "you're right. Nothing's too good for you."

He turned as she closed the door. She put her smile in the remaining gap.

"And that's just what you're getting. Nothing."

The door clicked with its solid and heavy motel door fit. She heard him mutter walking away, "You can't do this to me."

Beatrice dropped her head to her chest and drew a deep breath. She whispered, "Fuck."

She took off the robe, laid it on the bed and stepped out of the three-inch heels down to her five-foot five. She peeled down the hose, skimmed off the G-string and spit on her fingertip to melt the glue from the tassels over her nipples. She piled all the clothes on the made bed in a stack of black and scarlet. Naked in the mirror, she lifted her head and thrust out her jaw. No double chin. She'd read in a magazine that the key to beauty was a strong jawline. Hers was like an anvil, without a hint of jowl. She felt her abdomen for flatness, ran a probing touch along the tendons of her groin muscles, inspected the curve of her hips. Her breasts were firm, all naturally hers. She paused to admire them with something almost like nostalgia, remembering the looks on more than two decades of men's faces when they'd been allowed to get close to these, not getting their eyeballs or hands full of stiff pontoons but the real wondrous things. Lots of the other Top Hat girls had fake boobs. But these two globes in the mirror with the red eyes of twin Jupitersi were her advantage and pride. Those other girls wore cheap outfits to show off their hardware, cleavage popping up like bread in a pan. Not Beatrice. She dressed tastefully, understating the effect of her uplifted chest and so underscoring it. She always made sure by her posture that the other girls knew hers were real.

Beatrice dropped her hands to her side. She, naked, motionless in the mirror, without the skimpy outfit, without the writhing and music and the man, stood free of the yoke of her beauty, was only beauty pure. A white virgin of the eye.

She turned on the shower and put up her hair while the water warmed. She wasn't a forty-year-old bimbo past her prime. She was forty-two. And if this body was past its prime, why was the fat man so eager to pay a hundred to see it dance and an extra seventy-five to touch? She had a seven o'clock pickup tonight here at the Ramada. She planned to call Top Hat and tell them what happened with the fat creep john, tell them not to take his calls again, then take a nap, then dress. Tonight was a Fedora. Bimbos didn't get The Fedoras. A Fedora was good work, good money. The company only had four girls who rated a Fedora, and only two who did The Top Hats. She'd brought along her favorite ensemble, a khaki mid-thigh business suit, narrow at the waist, referring the beholder's gaze upward.

She slipped under the water and closed her eyes. She put the stream on her cheeks, hot down her neck and front. She stood a long time like that and let the shower cry for her, something she would not do for herself.

The streetlight turned green. A passel of tourists walked in front of Virgil's bumper and he had to wait. This time of the evening, the dinner hour, brought tourists swarming out of their hotels and B&Bs daubed in pastelled frippery like reef fish cruising around Key West's Old Town in search of eateries and happy hours and patio music.

He looked at the colors and saw them as he always did, with the quiet jealousy of a man who'd in his lifetime had the colors taken away.

He tattooed his fingers on the steering wheel. Enough, Virgil thought. He tapped his horn to tell the stragglers to get back on the sidewalk.

He turned from Whitehead onto Truman which would become Roosevelt and he'd be at the Ramada by seven. Ellen was out for the evening at an Old Town Merchants Association Meeting. The kid Woody was closing up the shop.

Virgil pulled into the Ramada parking lot five minutes before seven. Not for the first time he noticed how much the Ramada resembled a prison building, a flat-faced square of brick walls and white paint. The dark vertical creases of the curtains in all the windows looked like bars. He'd been thinking about prison all day on this the anniversary of the girl's death. Lynn was her name. Would have been her name today, people calling her Lynn right this minute maybe if he hadn't run her over in the water that day. If. Eight years ago today. Everything in his life over that span had happened because he'd killed that girl.

To taunt him, as so much did, a speedboat churred past on Garrison Bight across the street heading to open water to do some sundown water skiing. Virgil saw a beer bottle tip up. Too weird, he thought, to see that right now, today, even though in another part of his brain he knew a speedboat full of people sipping beers was something you saw everyday.

He wiped his hands across his face until the sounds of the real power boat and the one in his head, the one still echoing from eight years ago, had faded. Parked close to the building, he looked through the windshield into the high brick wall of the Ramada and was struck by the old closed-in

feeling. He shook it off. He took up the single red
rose and fingered a thorn, pressing his thumb
onto the point. It smarted but he stopped before
he broke the skin.

Seven o'clock. He walked into the motel lobby.
The jacketed desk clerk saw him and his red
flower held up like a schoolboy's apple then looked
back down to his paperwork. Other employees
and passing guests saw him and went about their
business. People moved in and out of the lobby.
No one appeared to be waiting. He sat on a cool
leather sofa and laid the rose across his lap.

Five minutes he sat. No woman looked to be
expecting someone. No one sashayed up to him
and took the rose and breathed to him *Let's go*.

He lifted the flower from his lap and wondered
how slowly the thing must be dying without
water. The rose cap was unfairly red, provoca-
tively velvet; against his will it flung him into his
memory, into the warm ocean with the blood, a
cumulus of red around him.

A well-dressed woman exited a taxi; Virgil's
ribs squeezed. A man got out behind her and they
walked past his sofa laughing. He glanced at his
watch. Six minutes after seven. This isn't going to
bring her back, he thought. It's not going to bring
anything back.

He left the rose on the sofa. He looked at his
watch one more time to pretend for the desk clerk
that he had an appointment elsewhere and
hurried from the lobby. The light, warmth and
humidity of Key West outside the air-conditioned

motel hall were not restorative to his mood. He strode fast across the parking lot, the clicks of his heels on the tarmac going *tsk, tsk, tsk*. He opened the car door and flung himself in, slamming the door. He gripped the wheel with both hands. Virgil sat still, glaring at the road, the sidewalk and the paths of his life that had brought him there.

Beatrice woke late, with only ten minutes before The Fedora. She sprang off the bed, muttering, "Shit, shit, shit." She tore for the bathroom.

Makeup, she thought, groping for the light switch but clicking on the bathroom fan instead. "Shit." She flipped on the light and unzipped her cosmetics bag.

Seven minutes later her eyes and lips were jewels and her hair was combed out and bound into a French twist. She put on onyx and leopard earrings, silver bracelets, two opal rings and an old silver, heart-shaped locket. Beatrice took a few seconds in the mirror for appraisal and blew herself a kiss. Quickly she perfumed her pits and crotch, elbows and neck. White Wonderbra, black panty hose and she was going to be only five or six minutes late.

She slid open the closet door. The suit hung alone in the closet, a tawny sheath. She'd had the outfit tailored to make it slinky-tight but still scrupled. She laid it across the bed and set the shoes in front of it.

Beatrice was famished. If the john had the one

fifty for a Fedora, he had the twenty bucks to spring for lobster too.

She finished dressing. The suit traced her form nicely. Beatrice measured herself against her clothes: So long as they fit, she was holding her own. She buttoned the blouse down to the cleft in her breasts then changed her mind and secured one more button. She spritzed more perfume on her neck and opened the door, dropping the room key into her purse.

Seven minutes after seven. She checked the bun of her hair in the elevator. The doors slid apart and she stepped into the Ramada lobby.

The room had nobody waiting for a Fedora. Hawaiian shirts flitted in and out. Cleated preppies hefted golf bags from an open Cadillac trunk in the driveway outside the front door. A Cubano maid pushed her cart of cleansers through to another hall. The lobby was suffused with the expectant energies of dusk, plans for the evening under way, the chandelier sharing light with the last wash of day.

Was the john late? Beatrice doubted it. In her experience the kind of men who paid for a woman's company tended to be punctual. Typically they'd had their fill of disappointments in their lives, that's why they finally turned to hiring affection by the hour. They expected that their money ought to make events go right at least for that one evening and this usually meant, among other things, on time.

The teenage clerk caught her eye. She smiled

at him and saw the red rose abandoned on the sofa.

She strolled to the sofa and sat beside the rose, leaving it alone on its cushion. She arranged her hands in her lap and talked to the flower quietly.

"Let me guess. You got cold feet. A friend of your wife's walked into the lobby. Maybe you just decided you hadn't sunk this low yet."

She lifted the rose and brushed the petals under her nose. She filled her lungs with the aroma, the final good thing of the waning day.

She laid the stem across her lap and fingered a thorn. She watched a chubby couple in matching sweat suits—foreign tourists did that the most—bustle out for dinner or to take in the sunset street carnival at Mallory Square and wondered, Why couldn't The Fedora have stayed just another minute or two? This rose was left by a man who couldn't go through with it. Always, Beatrice met only the men who could.

Or had he left the rose on the sofa as a bait, to draw her to it while he hid and watched? She knew the rule for johns at Top Hat: You don't like what you see, you keep going.

She looked around the room again fast, maybe catch a look at someone hightailing it out the back door.

No one.

She was tired and deflated, looking as sharp as she did and having no one to parade in front of. Add to that the pang of rejection. Add to that the lost income for the evening. She considered call-

ing the office to maybe grab a last minute
appointment but for sure it wouldn't be a Fedora.
She was geared up for a Fedora and she wanted
to dance wearing clothes tonight. Oh, well, she'd
had a good week already. Even without tonight
she'd clear maybe seven hundred. All told, she'd
had a good run in this business, had worked on all
sides of it. Twenty-five years of living on her
looks; a quarter century was a good career in any
line of work. She had a few thousand bucks stashed.
Maybe tonight's no-show john was a sign. Maybe
she should consider moving back to Miami, even
Dallas again, take a typing course. She still had
some straight connections left in those towns.
She'd make a killer secretary. Maybe so.

After five more minutes of idle waiting on the
sofa holding the rose, Beatrice carried the flower
to the registration desk. The clerk looked up. She
set the room key before him. He blinked, grinning, a young blush coloring his cheeks beneath
his dimples. He had a pimple on his chin and
rubbed it to hide it.

"Call me a taxi, hon. Will you?"

The boy laughed nervously and picked up the
phone. Beatrice carried the rose out through the
glass doors to wait on the curb. She opened
another button on her blouse to let some air into
the outfit. A man hurrying by smiled at her.

She leaned against the column of the awning,
brushing the rose under her nose. She sighed.
"Shit."

Within seconds a white limousine with tinted

windows moved in the parking lot. The car pulled beside her. The passenger side front window slid down. There behind the wheel was the rooster-chinned jerk from that afternoon's private dance.

He leaned across the leather seat to see up to her on the sidewalk. He nodded before he spoke. Look at me, I'm in a limo.

He said, "Hey."

"I told you," she said. Her voice made him squint. His tie was still pulled up tight. "No."

"Look. I borrowed us a limousine."

"You borrowed yourself a limousine, mister. Not me."

"I brought you more money."

"Whatever you got on you, it isn't enough."

"I called Top Hat. They said it was okay."

"No, they didn't. I've got a seven o'clock and they know it."

"Yeah?" The fat man hoisted himself out of the car. He waddled around the hood to stand on the curb next to Beatrice. He made a show of glancing up and down the sidewalk. "So? Where is he?"

"It's none of your business. He's coming. He got held up."

"I'll bet. Where'd you get the rose?"

"He sent it."

"He just sent one? I'll buy you more."

"One's romantic."

"Okay. I'll buy you one. Jesus."

"Look, you need to go. He'll be here in a minute. He's a very big guy. Bad temper."

"Bring him on."

She lowered her eyes, exasperated. "Just go, will you?"

"Honey, come on. I got this big car. I got more money than your seven o'clock."

"He's got an appointment. You don't."

"Make me one."

"No. He's got manners. You don't."

"You telling me no? With the car and everything?"

"That's right, genius. No to everything."

"That's no, then, right? You're saying no."

"No for now. No forever. No. Got it?"

"Then you got an appointment."

"Yes I do. You figured it out. Good-bye."

"Good-bye."

The fat man reached under his coat, behind his big waist to the back of his belt. He pulled out a silver .45 automatic and aimed it at Beatrice's face.

He cocked his head.

Beatrice—it didn't make sense to look away from the gun but she did—shot her eyes to the street, the passing cars, searching for the john, the Fedora with whom she should have been dancing or ordering lobster by now. He would drive up right now, a big well-mannered guy with an armful of roses. He'd save her.

She brought her eyes back to the dark tunnel of the gun aimed between her brows.

She said, "No."

He lowered the pistol to her chest. For the few

moments the gun had been pointed at her head, she believed he'd just been trying to scare her, make her shit her pants or beg forgiveness and climb into the limo. Now, she knew.

He fired. It felt like fireworks in her chest, exploding colors of bang, terror and pain.

Beatrice was hammered back onto her rump on the warm sidewalk, her hands never raised from her sides.

Noise and blood sluiced in her ears but she could hear traffic screech. The fat man stood over her and fired twice more into her chest, each bullet for Beatrice less horrible than the one before.

He lowered the smoking gun. She looked up into his spilling chins.

"Told you," he said. "You can't do that to me."

The fat man turned away hard and a second later the limo chugged away from the curb. Beatrice, her head on the concrete, smelled the exhaust.

The bullets that had crashed their way into her chest were swamping her senses. The sidewalk moved sideways, her stomach flipped, her lungs filled with fluid. The bullets were inside her, they were amok and she couldn't stop them. She watched with melting eyes a blur run across the parking lot. It was a man; he scrambled right up alongside her and stopped hard, waving his arms to regain his balance as if at the lip of a cliff. He said, "Oh my God." He wore nice shoes, Hofheimer loafers, cuffs on his khakis and a leather belt. She tried to lift her gaze further to his

face but her eyes were glopping downward like
eggs poured out of their shells, they felt liquid
along with the blood streaming out of her. The
man came to his knees and her vision wandered
past his face and she thought he might be handsome, it was hard to focus, but he had dark hair
and that strong jaw the magazine said to look for,
but that was all she could tell, her slippery eyes fell
back down to his bent knees and the pressed
khakis. Then he spoke and his voice was gentle, so
sorry. He said as much. "My God. I'm sorry." He
touched her hand, the hand clutching the rose.
"That's the rose I brought," he whispered, as if
she, terribly wounded, could not even bear the
weight of words. "Oh my God, lady, I'm sorry."
He pulled back his touch.

Her Fedora. He was here, he hadn't left. He
hadn't stood her up.

Beatrice blinked to stop her roving focus. She
wanted to see his face. Her mouth went slack with
the effort; it hurt but she knew it was her last hurt.

The motel door flung open. The young clerk
ran out from behind his desk shrieking. The boy
galloped between her and her Fedora, his knees
and sneakers eclipsing him. She saw her Fedora's
ankles straighten, he stood. She watched his nice
shoes step back while the clerk howled at her stu-
pidly, "Are you alright?" She did not answer.
More people—she saw more shoes—rushed out
through the doors, also crowding and shouting.

"Call someone, quick!" the clerk yelled.

"*You* call someone!" someone screamed back.

"Oh, yeah," the clerk sputtered, "that's right."
He ran back inside. Her Fedora's shoes were
gone.

Beatrice blacked out.

Virgil parked in front of the shop. With the car
sitting still now and no wind rushing past his open
windows, he heard his breath in his nose, in and
out, scraping like a lumberjack's long saw. He
blinked—for the first time in several minutes, he
thought—and relaxed his hands on the steering
wheel. They were stiff, reluctant to open.

He blew out breath. "Whew."

She'd been shot. Right across the parking lot
from him.

He hadn't seen the first shot but he'd heard it
and watched her drop, saw the fat guy shoot her
twice more, pointing the gun down at her calmly
like he was watering her out of a can. Virgil froze
in the front seat of his car, then the fat bastard
drove away in a white limo and Virgil snapped out
of it. He ran across the lot, not knowing what he
could do for the woman except stand next to her.
Then he saw the rose. This was his date. His
Fedora.

He got out of the car and walked to the shop
door. Overhead the old wooden sign, carved
twenty years before by Ellen's father, caught the
dusk's last petals of light. The sign read: PAINT &
THINGS & PAINTED THINGS—ART SUPPLIES/GALLERY.
Virgil had never met Ellen's father or mother.
Ellen was running the store by herself .when he

first walked through this door four years ago accompanied by a county deputy sheriff. He was a felon then, convicted of involuntary manslaughter; he'd served most of his time and the county was trying to reinsert him to society through work release. She had signed up with Offender Aid and Restoration as a business volunteer through the Key West Chamber of Commerce. She was twenty-six then to his thirty-two. Blond, cute. A cheerleader's earnest face, blue eyes looking always for something to root for. Pale, which in Key West revealed that she worked inside too much. Mom and Dad had died in a car crash five months earlier on Seven Mile Bridge heading out to dinner on Marathon. Some tourist had been gazing too long at the sunset off the span and drifted into them head on. On his first visit to the shop she caught some fancy inside his chest like a nail snagging his shirt, a twitch he didn't trust because, after all he'd been in jail for four years without any womanly company at all, so how hard could he be to charm? But he smiled at her and she gave back the smile brighter than he'd sent it, polished and returned in the manner of a trusted neighbor who borrows your good silver. She offered him and his deputy some Cokes out of the fridge in the back. She showed Virgil how to miter cut and assemble metal frames, how to choose and fit mats. She walked close to and around him; she was confident, sharing her store and her skills. She moved with precision, orchestrated and decisive, the way Virgil liked people to

move, like numbers. She smelled nice beside him
at the workbench. Clean, a busy and honest smell,
with that tang of reliability you note in a reputable
garage. He had no problems with the tools; his
first two years inside, before he became a trustee
and was set to work in the commissary keeping
the books, he'd done machine work. He took one
look at her bookkeeping and pronounced he could
make it simpler, he could handle it and the stocking both. He smiled more at her. Now she nodded
back, a sober mien. The officer related to her that
Virgil had been a CPA before the accident, with a
big firm in Fort Lauderdale. She bobbed her head
slowly and sadly but with no trace of pity and
repeated the letters "CPA" as though a prisoner
with letters to his name must surely have suffered
some tragedy. Then she brightened at Virgil. No
one had gazed on him so calmly in his entire life
and he was stirred between his legs. The deputy
returned him to the halfway house, then brought
him back to the store the next day and left him.
Virgil told her right off that he'd killed a girl up in
Fort Lauderdale, a boating accident. He was sorry,
every day he was sorry. She offered him a job.

And here he was, four years later, but sometimes he felt he might just as well still be back in
prison. Virgil slid his key into the lock, not expecting to see Woody, the kid who helped out at the
shop.

"Man," Woody said, "what are you doing
here? What is it, seven twenty?"

"I guess." Virgil closed the shop door.

Woody arranged the bag in the trash can beneath the counter.

"Geez, man, you're fast. You know, that's part of getting old. See, if you were still a young dude like me you could go all night." He straightened and pumped his fist up and down like a piston. "Bang, boom, bing . . ."

"Shut up." Virgil moved behind the counter and sat on the stool. He set his chin in his hands.

But Woody would not shut up. Woody had too much to say, always. His father had left when Woody was six. The boy joined a street gang when he was thirteen. At sixteen, he had a fully-blossomed narcotics problem. He'd bought and sold drugs, injecting the profits, then held up a convenience store in Tampa with a .22 pistol and got sent up as a juvenile, first to detox and rehab for six months then for two years to a state farm outside Orlando surrounded by flatland, cattle and reptiles, Disney over the horizon. Now he was eighteen with a high and wasted IQ and believed that he'd lived hard and fast and was already a man. He was spending his last five months of incarceration in the same halfway house and the same Florida Work Furlough Program that had brought Virgil to Key West four years before. Two months ago, Virgil offered Woody a job at their art supply store. Ellen had objected at first.

"I think I worked out alright," he answered her, "and Woody served two years less than me."

"But I was young then. Mom and Dad had

just died, I didn't know how to run the store. You were just what I needed at the time."

"At the time."

"Oh Virgil," she'd said, grimacing, "don't be so sensitive."

Virgil liked the boy. After the first month Ellen accepted that Woody was a good worker and a positive community service credential for her shop and so took pains to introduce him whenever a member of the Chamber or Junior League visited the store. She began to mother him and Woody let her, working her. He was a manipulator, a con's skill. But tonight after the shooting Virgil wanted the boy to be quiet.

Woody kept on. "What'd she do, stand you up? No way, man, those bitches are getting paid, they can't stand people up. You should've waited. What'd you do, leave after five minutes? She's a chick, man, they're always late. Go back over there, she's waiting. I mean, she's on the *payroll*."

Virgil shook his head. He could not say, "She's dead." His hands were tired. He didn't want to hold everything that would spill out of Woody if Virgil told him she'd been shot dead. He decided right then he would tell no one.

He asked instead, "Woody, can you give it a rest?"

"No. Know why?"

"Please?"

Woody ignored him. "Because," Woody jumped up on the counter and plopped his bony blue-jeaned fanny near Virgil's elbows and head. Virgil had to sit up out of the way. "I keep telling you, Virg, we're simpatico. We're brothers. We both been in stir. We know what it's like inside there, man."

Virgil lamented into his palms, "Why do I tell you my business . . ."

"Because, man," Woody pounced again with a reply. "You talk to me because you still got this wild Woody child inside you. When you talk to me, you're talking to him."

"No, Woody, that's not it. I talk to you because you know if you blab one word to anyone you're fired and it'll ruin your work release."

"Big man," Woody said. He looked down on the crown of Virgil's head. "You ever think about getting one of those hair weaves or something? You're getting kind of thin here."

"No. Now give it a rest."

"You ought to. I would if it was me, man. I'd do it. I'm never getting old."

Virgil eyed the boy. Skinny, long arms and legs folding like a jackknife, his jailbird crew cut, Woody's naive confidence behind every word. Virgil wished the opposite for him, that Woody would see himself grow very old.

"I don't know." The boy jumped off the counter. "Maybe she got a good look at you first and hid until you left."

Woody paused. He picked at his fingernails.

"Why'd you want to do it? I mean, Ellen's alright."

"Yes she is."

"That wasn't cool."

"No. It wasn't."

"So why'd you go to the Ramada?"

"You wouldn't understand."

"Why? 'Cause I'm eighteen?"

"Yes."

"Oh, right." Woody sneered and kicked his legs. The table under Virgil's elbows swayed. "Let me ask you a question. You ever point a loaded gun to a man's head? Have you? I have. Put it right there, man, and told him to open the cash register or I'd paint his brains all over the gum rack. Yeah, okay, I know you killed someone and all but that was an accident, you didn't even see her. What I'm talking about, you know, is being ready to really do it. That changes you, man. It's like you're God for that one minute. And once you see things like God, even for a second, you see like Him for the rest of your life. So fuck you, I'm eighteen but I understand, okay? Don't tell me I don't understand. Fuck you."

Virgil left Woody at the counter. He walked to the back through the gallery to shut off the lights.

No, he thought, Woody doesn't understand, wouldn't understand. How can you explain to a teenager what this is like? To have everything, a place in the world, enough time and money, and feel busted flat anyway. To be like some stupid, uncooperative plant, watered, pampered, placed on a sunny windowsill, and still wilt. What could he tell Woody about having something dear once but losing it along the way of years, letting the dear thing slip away not because you didn't adore it but because you were weak and forgetful and so didn't keep the dear thing safe. And you look for your lost treasures—whatever baubles they were, your faith, your luck, your passion, your love for your woman—you look for the misplaced dear things everywhere, even in the wrong places at the wrong times, even at the Ramada.

Virgil entered the gallery and stopped. Two rocking chairs held down the center of the room, each bearing a small brass plate memorializing that they had once belonged to Rico and Margaret, Ellen's late mom and dad. Virgil had begun to dislike as tourist kitsch the paintings Ellen selected to sunbathe under the gallery's track lighting. He despised them a lot tonight, the evening of the anniversary. Every one of them was rooted in hues of blue, violet and ocean green. Dolphins, whales, schooners, sea foam, twisting dun nights. Dolphins frozen in their play. Ships straining under full spinnakers but motionless. Waves poised on the brink of breaking but never rolling. Clouds pasted on skies without wind, flags crinkled and never snapping, a lighthouse beam staring forever at one spot into the inky storm. These were not portraits of action or freedom as they purported. Despite the achievement that they were lifelike, they were in truth the opposite of life. They were single frames filched out of life's film. They were life imprisoned.

Virgil continued through the gallery to the panel box. He flicked off the lights and turned on the alarm. Night had fallen outside; the shop was bathed in neighboring neon.

"Come on," he called to the boy waiting in the shadows, "I'll give you a ride back to your cell."

Virgil's hands flew over the piano keys. His fingers were fast, blurrily expert. The keyboard held no mystery to his instinct. His confidence and power were in each of the thousand tapping touches. The music soared, some kind of music; it might have been classical, he could never be sure.

Virgil called these dreams "excellence nightmares." His subconscious had conjured up several in the past month; just five nights ago he'd played the trumpet with his fingers leaping on the valves like fire on a log. In other recent dreams he'd played the harp, the cello and the trombone. He'd also mustered up two steamy sex dreams where his abilities were, as they had been with the musical instruments, prodigious.

Virgil woke. The room was swollen with dawn, windows open, curtains loitering on the rising trade breeze. The screens were down for the bugs. His wife, buttressed on an elbow, stared at him.

He asked, "What was I doing?"

She drummed her fingers on the bed sheet, limning the keyboard.

"Well," he said, "that's better than the trombone."

"Virgil?"

"Yes?"

"What's going on?"

"Nothing. I'm just having some nightmares."

"Musical nightmares."

"Yes."

"I'm sorry, but that just doesn't sound like a nightmare to me, playing an instrument. I've said this before. You don't even play an instrument. Doesn't that strike you as a little odd?"

"Ellen, they're dreams. Everybody's dreams are a little odd."

"Not mine. I never have nightmares and I have never heard of anyone who plays music and calls that a nightmare. I always have nice quiet dreams where I don't wake you up thrashing all over the bed."

"Good for you."

She made a displeased huff.

He raised a hand off his stomach. "What do you want me to say?"

Ellen made no suggestion.

"They'll stop," he said.

"When what happens?"

"I don't know."

She turned her head to look at the scarlet numerals on the clock. She asked, "Can you go back to sleep?"

"I'm fine."

Ellen patted his forearm. "I know."

She bounced onto her side facing away from him. When she'd settled, much of the early sunlight spilling in the window did not make it past her hips rising off the mattress, the sheet cascading far down her backside into the pool of shadow she cast on the bed. The dip in the springs from her side rolled Virgil toward her. He fought the incline and leaned away. He curled on his side, regarding her form. A bug hit the screen.

He could not drift back toward sleep. He never could after the dreams. They left him hollow. Others, Ellen probably included, might feel exhilarated after fantasies of extraordinary musical skill or gymnastic sex but Virgil compared his waking reality with his dreams and so could not get back to sleep on the morning following the anniversary and the beautiful white arm on the bloody tarmac.

He brought his hand up to his brow and rubbed. Across the bed, the unplayed instrument of his wife lay blocking the rising sun.

2

WHEN Beatrice got her first look at Virgil, she had not been dead long.

She lay in an intensive care unit on the second floor of St. Joseph's Hospital. Ten hours earlier doctors had performed emergency surgery to halt the hemorrhaging. Two bullets had ripped through a lung, the third nicked the pulmonary artery. Then this morning buzzers went off beside her bed. An alarm flashed in the hall at the nurses' station. The machines made more noise than Beatrice did. She took a last breath and let it out. She unclenched her fists and damp palms and eyes flung open like springtime shutters. From her round mouth, her soul swept into the room.

Beatrice floated to the ceiling to look down on her body. Tubes up her nose, tubes in her arms, pale bloodless face, breasts holding up well even lying there a corpse. She was glad to be shed of her body. She paused to look into the hardening pools of her eyes; they were the green of all her years. They were the sweet-pea eyes of a little girl in Baton Rouge, of a feisty young gal with sugary hips in Dallas making a name for herself as an exotic dancer, of a lonely woman in Miami bartending and dancing in low-rent clubs, and finally the sad traveled eyes of the handsome lady at the end of the world in Key West. To the emerald eyes of all her years, Beatrice said So long.

A young nurse hurried into the room. She seemed confused. Her hands shot to her mouth. Quickly she pulled herself together and laid her palms on the chest of Beatrice's body. She shoved hard then raised her fist and struck the corpse twice in the sternum.

"Leave her alone," said Beatrice.

An older nurse came in. She moved beside the bed and laid a tender hand under Beatrice's wrist. She set the wrist down.

To the young nurse she said, "Leave her alone."

Beatrice said, "Thank you."

Outside, the early sun kept its promise to Key West. Beatrice gazed out the hospital window at palm trees and cacti, beach and shadows, brick and painted wood, tourists and locals, sunglasses and hats. A palm frond scraped over the window pane. Someone down the hall greeted someone. The nurses left the room. Beatrice on the bed, Beatrice on the ceiling, was alone.

She floated, stuck there like a child's helium balloon.

She gazed about, looking for some reason to be frantic or afraid. She found none.

Then without warning, without falling from the ceiling, she felt solid, the sudden grasp of gravity.

She saw a nice-looking man sitting at a table reading a newspaper. The man looked at her.

She asked him, "Who are you?"

Only in a flash, the space of a heartbeat, then he was gone and she left the hospital ceiling.

Clatter seemed to be the ballad of Ellen's body. She forged it around her like a katydid rubbing its wings, pots slamming in the sink, dishes rattling on the Formica table, fingernails on the coffee cup, her chair sliding on the tile floor, drawers pulled out and pushed back, the popping toaster, toast scraped over her plate. Virgil erected the newspaper between his quiet world and her cacophony but she raided around his perimeter.

Headlines declared the shooting outside the Ramada last night. An unidentified woman, name withheld. Three bullets in the chest. The man plugged her in the parking lot and drove away. There were some witnesses and descriptions of a fat guy in a suit and a big white limo. Good, Virgil thought, if there were other witnesses he could feel better about staying out of it. The woman's in the hospital, critical. Virgil put his tongue behind his lower lip and looked into his lap.

Ellen talked.

"Today, we need to finish that museum job.

They've waited for two weeks and I'm out of
excuses. If we can have them framed and out the
door by Friday, I can keep them happy. Alright?
Now, what are we going to do about Columbus
Day?"

Clatter at home, in the store. Firm footsteps,
hurry from point to point, overly strict with
Woody, overselling the customers even after
they've paid and are headed out the door, calling,
"Come back and see us," straightening stock on
the shelves, pictures in the gallery, busy, busy.

". . . I'd like us to have a sale. Ten percent off
in the store, fifteen in the gallery."

Virgil scanned the international news. He
glanced up for a moment at Ellen, house frock,
coffeepot to the sink, water on, rinsing, swirling,
water off, faucet squeak, water poured out, pot on
the counter. She said, "Are you listening to me
behind that paper?"

"Yes, of course."

She continued. "Now. We've got some sale
banners from last Christmas in a box down in the
basement. We can put them up in the windows
out front."

Ellen's voice paused as if to think very hard
about her sales strategy.

Virgil lowered his paper.

She quizzically asked, "Who are you?"

He did not answer.

She blinked. Her lids stayed down a moment,
then popped back up. She said, "And I also think
we should put an ad in the Sunday paper."

Virgil asked, "What did you say?"

"I said I want to have a Columbus Day sale. I swear, you listen to me sometimes as if I weren't talking at all."

"I heard you. You were talking about the sale and then you asked me who I was."

Ellen ran a sponge over the counter. "Why would I ask you that? That's a silly thing to say."

"You stopped talking for a second. Then you said, 'Who are you?' Then you kept talking about the sale."

"I don't think so."

"Yes you did."

"Virgil, I may have been thinking 'who are you' because I wonder sometimes if you're really my husband who ought to be helping me at the store as much as I need. You don't seem very enthused lately. Is something the matter?"

"No."

"You're sure? If I've done something to upset you, we can talk about it. Now is a good time to talk about it before we go into the shop."

"No, I'm fine."

He waited.

"I'm always here for you to talk to."

"I know."

"Well," she continued, back on track, "I think I would know if I'd actually said, 'Who are you,' out loud. Don't you think I would know what I said?"

"Yes."

He waited again. Why couldn't he just let it

go? She wanted him to reach out to her, give things names, fit them into words and make them finite so they could deal with them together. She always wanted to help. Help him, their customers, the community. She's always good. So why aggravate her?

"But you said it."

"Well," she threw the sponge down into the sink, "if I did say it, I take it back. I *know* who you are. I'll handle the sale by myself like I have to do everything else. You just show up, alright? And if it's not too much trouble, please get the museum's framing done by Friday. Will you do that much for me?"

She stepped from the counter to the table in one stride, swept up her dish and glass and set them with a brittle clink into the sink. Virgil marveled they did not break. She went upstairs.

Virgil set down his paper. Overhead, from the bedroom, sounds of Ellen filtered through the house. Dresser drawers opened, floorboards creaked, footfalls thumped, water gushed through the old pipes. Virgil washed the dishes while the big house thundered under Ellen.

Virgil gazed at the ceiling, on the other side of which his wife showered and reigned.

"Miz Sting?"

"Yes, sir?"

"You are the prettiest young thing these eyes have seen in years. Did you know that?"

"No, sir. Thank you."

"You and me are gonna stand Dallas on its head."

"That'd be nice."

"Now, would you do an ol' boy just one kindness?"

"What might that be? And please call me Bea. If we're gonna be partners and all."

"Yes. Alright, Bea. Would you mind if I could get just one up-close-and-personal look at that little act of yours? Not the whole thing, of course, but maybe the middle to the end?"

Beatrice put down her purse and stood from the leather chair. The lawyer across the desk from her stood to shut the blinds of his office windows which looked out onto an alley. He pushed her chair out of the way for more floor space, sat on the lip of the desk and lit a cigarette.

She crossed her arms over her chest, hands at shoulders, as if already naked and demure.

"I don't have my proper things, you know. My slit dress and silk scarves."

The lawyer dragged on the cigarette. Smoke came with his words. "I can get the idea."

"Sometimes I wear a hat."

He reached into his desk and tossed her a battered New York Yankees cap.

"That help?"

"I need my music."

The lawyer dragged on the cigarette, considering. Then he thumped the flat of his hand against the desktop in a rhythm.

Boom-ba-ba-*boom*, ba-ba-*boom*, ba-ba-*boom* . . .

She said, "Uh-huh."

Beatrice tugged on the bill of the cap and struck a sideways pose. She pulled one strap off a shoulder. Shifting her weight to one leg, she pulled down the other strap.

A light erupted so brightly it made her wince. It was hot, she felt it on her bare skin. Smoke cut strata through the spotlight. Beatrice undulated her belly and shoulders and the red tassels on her fine breasts spun like propellers, the sequined G-string chafed her crotch. She bent down to a man in a ten-gallon hat beside the runway waving a twenty and let him tuck it in at her spangly waist. More men in string ties, others in business suits, waved more cash.

"Miz Sting! Here you go, girly-girl! Come on over here. Sting me, missy! Sting me!"

A Japanese man in a starched collar with a hundred dollar bill in the air caught her eye. She strolled lazily to him, turned around and wiggled her powdered rear in his face, performing her trademark Bea Sting. She said "Bzzzzzz," while the Japanese man tucked in the bill.

The room applauded and hooted. The spotlight grew smaller and smaller until it wriggled in a flame held in the hand of a man lighting her cigarette. She clinked her glass against his but the drunk man on the next barstool jostled her, spilling her whiskey sour on her dress.

She howled, "Hey asshole, watch it!"

A rough voice answered. "Shut up and spread your legs. You know the drill."

The light waved beside her face, a flashlight in a Miami policeman's grip. Hands searched her armpits, waist and pockets.

"When you gonna learn, Bea?"

The flashlight swelled and chased the steaming night into afternoon blue but stayed warm against her neck. What sounded like applause was the lapping of the Mississippi against a bank. Her old daddy grinned while she held up a three-pound catfish on her line.

"Well, I'll be. You have caught dinner."

"I did, didn't I."

"Yes you did. Yes, indeed."

"I know how to clean it."

"It's awful messy."

"I ain't afraid."

"Well, alright. Hold it up, let your mama see it. Hey, Dee! You see this here? Look what your daughter caught."

"I don't want her to see it."

"Aw, let her look. She'll be proud of you. Hold it up a little higher. Them clouds get in the way sometimes. Hey, Dee!"

"Daddy, do they eat dinner in Heaven?"

"I don't know that one. Ask me another."

"Can mama really see us?"

"Well, I'm sure she can."

"You even think she's looking?"

"Beatrice. Be nice."

"Can she hear us, too?"

"I reckon."

Beatrice lowered the fish. She gazed up at the

cloud's lit backside until the sun crawled around the edge of it to blaze in her face. It did not make her look away but caressed her eyes.

"Hey, mama," she spoke up to the light, "I caught this all by myself. See?"

She turned to her father. "Daddy?"

"Yes, child?"

"Does mama see everything we do?"

When the sun is encased in a burly cloud on a callous day. When a beam shines through a rip in the cloud to make one brilliant girder of light. That is where Beatrice sat.

She looked into the honeyed face of a beautiful young man. His wheat hair was cropped short, flat-topped.

"You know," he drawled, "I've been a guide maybe a dozen times now. And I have never yet seen anyone sit down."

Deep dimples set off his grin, devilish for an angel. A white robe hung from broad shoulders to big bare feet.

"Shoot," he continued, "I didn't even know you *could* sit down. Thought you'd fall through or somethin'."

"Go ahead," Beatrice said, "take a load off."

"I reckon I can." He nodded, looking up the golden way to the light. "Guess there's no rush. Though, you know, I always figured for some reason there was."

He folded lithely beside Beatrice.

"So," he said, looking about his crossed legs as

if for a weed to chew on, "how come you're sittin' here? Aren't you ready to move on?"

"Nope."

"Darlin', you're dead. You're not gonna get a lot readier."

"I want to go back."

"Uh-huh. I don't think that's gonna happen."

"Then I'll stay right here."

The young man considered her. He lifted a hand. An oval image appeared at his fingertips. Beatrice's supine body was in the image, covered with a sheet on a gurney in a silver elevator. The elevator doors slid apart and she was wheeled into a white room. The four walls were tiled with rows of square enameled doors.

"That's the coroner's office." He pointed. "Someone'll be comin' along to claim your body but I suspect it ain't gonna be you."

Beatrice looked away. He closed the image.

She said, "No one'll be coming."

He put his arm across her shoulders and squeezed. The hug was hard, real.

"Well then, it looks like it's Potter's Field for you."

Beatrice hung her head. "Oh, shit."

He leaned into the hug. "It's okay, go ahead. You can cuss. Watch. Oh, shit. Damn hell. There, see? Nothin' happened."

He tousled her hair like she was a little girl.

"Hey, it's alright," he said, "I know how you feel. I got me a Potter's Field too."

The guide laughed and scooted on his robe a

pace away from her to talk loudly. She wanted to cry but could make no tears.

"I got me one body buried in Manchuria, I was a warlord over there. Took a spear through the back, some dirty sumbitch got me from behind. But man, what a shindig that send-off was. Flags and cannons and a thousand horses. Then another time I drowned in a flood in Argentina. I was just an Indian kid and they never found my body. Gator got me. Once I was an old woman who died of a puff adder bite in Bangladesh and my family wrapped me up in a shroud and floated me down the Ganges. Lemme tell you, I was one swollen up carcass, but I was a Hindu and had already disavowed earthly vanity, so it was okay. And of course there were others, but I wanted to tell you about the Potter's Field time. I was this hobo, see? Died of exposure in a coal car in Missouri. What was I thinkin'? It was damn January out. Ignorant is what it was. Anyway, I'm buried in Joplin. Ain't that a kick in the shorts? Never even been in Joplin before and that's where my body winds up."

He chuckled. Not lives and deaths, but jokes with good endings.

Beatrice asked, "What about your last life?"

"Oh," he said smiling, pulling his knees to his chest, enjoying the tale before he told it, "this last one was a pip. It was the life you get when they want to reward you. It was the best."

"What did you do?"

"I hit eighteen home runs in sixty-five World

Series games. I won twelve World Series in my first fourteen years in the bigs. I hit for the Triple Crown in 1956. I was the biggest star on the best team of the last century. But you know what? Even with all that, I stayed pretty much a bumpkin. I was a humble sort. I did my home run trots with my head down. I'm proud to say I was a damn loyal friend. I had one hell of a big funeral. No cannons and horses, but it was on TV."

"How about your family? Your personal life?"

He shifted, not uncomfortable but just changing gears.

"Well, alright, yeah, that was a sticking point. I might have had a little letdown in some areas. Drinkin' and such. Fact is, I was so taken up with being a role model for everybody in America with a bat and a glove that I kind of overlooked my own kids. It's funny but it's true, what goes around comes around. In the end, all my high livin's what got me. Liver failure. Cancer. Shoot, if I'd known I was gonna live as long as I did, I'd of taken better care of myself."

"So what are you going to do now?"

"The usual. I'll go hang out in the light for a while, recharge my batteries, then get back in the game and try 'er again. I'll probably end up a preacher's wife next time. That ought to learn me."

"So why'd they send you to me?"

"Someone said you were a Yankees fan."

"I'm not. I wore a Yankees cap in my act for a while."

"Really?"

The guide drew up his shoulders with pride. "Any special reason?"

"Yeah."

"Well. What was it?"

"You'll think it's tacky or dirty or something."

"Maybe. Is it funny?"

"Kind of."

"Then tell me."

"Well, sometimes if I had a big tipper beside the runway I'd lean over and whisper to him the letters on the hat meant Not Yet. But if the guy was a jerk, I'd tell him it meant Not You."

"Hey, that's alright. I never heard that one before."

"Not much to it."

"Well, that's good enough, ain't it? You had a Yankees cap."

"That's why they sent you? I had a Yankees cap?"

"Yup. That's what it looks like."

"Don't you think that's lame?"

"Maybe, but after sixteen lifetimes you learn to roll with things."

She turned away.

"Look," he said, "I'll admit it's not the best of reasons. We checked around and, to be honest with you, we couldn't find anyone who meant much to you during your life. Or you to them, for that matter. You didn't exactly let a lot of people get under your skin. So I'm afraid the Yankees connection is it, lame as it might be."

"I moved around a lot."

"We did consider sending your mama or your daddy out to you but, well, we figured you'd . . ."

"I don't want to talk about them."

"Alright, okay. Looks like we figured right."

She moved her hands to cover her eyes. "What, did you think now that I'm dead I'd be glad to see them or something?"

The angel plucked at his robe. Softly he said, "I don't know."

"What do you mean you don't know? You're an angel. You're supposed to know."

"Sweetheart, angels know a lot about life. That's kind of the irony of it all. We gotta wait till we're dead to understand living. But the ways of Heaven? That's only known to one."

He touched her shoulder. He waited, then kindly said, "We're doin' the best we can by you here, kiddo. Maybe you could work with us a little bit?"

She lowered her hands to look up with blinking eyes.

He asked, "Are you coming with me? Beatrice?"

She ran a finger under her nose. She wanted it to be wet and melancholy but it was dry. She asked, "Have I . . . have I had other lives?"

"I'm sure you have. But you won't be able to remember them until you accept the light. That's the way it is. That's the accumulation, the business of your soul."

"Can I do that thing you did? Can I see back into the world?"

"Yes." He sighed. "But there are limitations on you if you won't come into the light."

"Show me how."

Again he lifted his hand, nodding at her to copy him. Beatrice held up her palm as though balancing a ball. The air wavered as it does above a hot radiator, then spilled. In the rift, an image appeared: a man, wrapping brown paper over something flat, a painting.

"What is this?"

"I don't know."

"Why am I seeing this? Who is it?"

The guide said nothing.

"You gotta know," Beatrice pleaded, "you gotta tell me. I don't know what's going on."

"I said there'd be limitations if you stay on the path. Not knowing what's going on is the biggest one. Come with me into the light. It'll be better than knowing. You'll understand."

Inside the image, the man turned his face.

Beatrice pointed. "Hey, I've seen that guy. Before, at the hospital. And something else . . . somewhere . . ."

She felt a surge, a wave breaking at her back. The image flared to fill her vision. She said to the man, "Hey. Hey there, mister."

The man stared at her.

The surge passed.

The man continued to look right out at Beatrice. Then he stepped aside and a pair of woman's hands moved in to finish the wrapping and tape the brown paper down.

Excited, she said to her guide, "I think he heard me. Did you see that?"

"Yes."

She pressed his knee. "What's going on? Please tell me."

He covered her fingers with his, the angel's hand so young but also folksy and old, a grandfather's touch.

"There's nothing I can tell you."

He stood, smoothing the folds of his robe. Around him shone a corona. The light, moments ago far away, gilded his head.

He said, "I can only say this."

"What?"

"There's a plan, Beatrice. There always is."

She nodded. "Tell me one more thing."

"If I can," he said.

"In your last life, were you loved?"

Now the light spread over his shoulders and down his front, soaking into him like fire into a paper but where fire leaves behind only black this light left white and gold.

"Yes. I was loved. By millions."

"There, you see?" she said. "That's why you can go on ahead. But I can't yet. I didn't even have one."

"You are loved. Come with me."

"No."

"Try again. In another life."

"I'm not ready."

The light consumed him, all but his voice. "Be careful, Beatrice."

"Woody?"

Woody was in the storeroom. He called up front, "Yes, ma'am?"

"Will you please come here. Virgil and I would like a word with you."

The shop was empty of customers. Woody shuffled in. Ellen stood before the counter, hands joined primly in front of her skirt. Virgil sat on the stool behind the register.

Woody wore faded blue jeans lacerated at the knees and a black Harley T-shirt with the sleeves ripped away to show off his strong biceps. Ellen curled a finger to bring him close enough for her to pinch the fabric of his shirt. She drew in her lips and shook her head.

"Woody, this won't do."

"What won't do?"

"This. You dress like a bum."

"Miss E, everyone in my generation dresses like this. It's a sign of disaffection."

"Woody, please. I'm not that much older than you and I'm not disaffected. You don't see me wearing clothes that make me look like I just fought off a werewolf. Virgil doesn't dress this way. You've got to start looking nicer if you want to work for us. This store has been here for over thirty years, my family has lived in this town longer than that. We have a reputation to uphold. Isn't that right, Virgil?"

"Woody," Virgil said, "you stink."

Ellen jumped back in. "Well, we're getting ahead of ourselves but, yes, Woody, I also wanted to address your, um, your hygiene. You're growing into a man now, you're eighteen, and men need to be aware of their bodily odors. It's no one's fault, it's just the way men are built. Hormones."

Virgil said, "We'll get you some deodorant."

Ellen would not allow that. "Virgil, we pay Woody a fair wage. He can purchase his own essentials or how else will he learn?"

Virgil shot Woody a reassuring nod beneath Ellen's notice. Woody caught it and stayed cooperative with Ellen.

"Yes, ma'am."

"Don't they have showers at that halfway house? They did when Virgil was there."

She shifted her gaze quickly from Woody to Virgil, too fast for him to remove the scrunch of indignation on his face.

"Virgil, that slipped out. I was trying to make a point."

"It's alright."

Woody returned to Virgil the nod of support and solidarity.

"Anyway, Woody," she continued, "how do you expect to ever get a girlfriend dressing and smelling like that? Have you considered that?"

Woody grinned. "I guess I'll just have to find one who dresses and smells as bad as me."

"Oh," Ellen waved a hand before her nose as if the ragged couple were actually in front of her, "perish the thought. Now please go into the bath-room, take some paper towels, and scrub your armpits. And tomorrow, please wear more appropriate clothes to work. What you do on your own time is your business."

Woody smiled. Virgil had a ten dollar bill folded in his pocket waiting to slip the boy.

"Yes, ma'am." Woody went off to the bath-room.

"Well," Ellen said when he was gone, "I think that went well. Although you might have been a bit more supportive of me."

The shop door opened and a tourist woman in a big straw hat entered. Ellen said quickly to Virgil, "Oh, that's the lady who bought the light-house this morning. Go and take it down for me."

Ellen swooped to the customer. Virgil went into the gallery, took down the painting and carried it into the back to wrap it in brown paper.

Ellen came to check on his progress. "Are you done yet? She's in a hurry."

"One minute."

"Well, she's waiting so bring it out as soon as you . . ."

Ellen froze, her hands, her face, all her body and action went still as a stalk.

After a moment, she raised one hand in greet-ing. "Hey," she said. "Hey there, mister."

Virgil said nothing.

She froze again.

Virgil waved his hand in front of her face. Nothing.

Then she animated. She said, "Virgil, why are you standing there? She's waiting."

"Ellen?"

She ignored him.

"Please hurry up. Oh, for God's sakes, here. Let me finish, you take forever sometimes."

Deftly she folded and taped the craft paper over the painting. She hefted the package to the customer waiting at the counter.

"There you go," Ellen said. The lady and the painting went out the door. Ellen called after her, "Enjoy. Come see us again."

The door closed. Virgil came to the counter.

"You said something again."

Ellen pushed her hair behind her ears. She sat on the stool.

"What did I say, Virgil?" Her tone was a parody of patience. "What?"

"While I was wrapping the lighthouse. You said . . ."

"I *had* to speed you along. She was in a hurry. I told you that."

"Not that. You said, 'Hey, mister!' Right in the middle of asking me about the painting."

"I said 'Hey, mister.'"

"Yes. 'Hey, mister.'"

"I was hurrying you up with the wrapping and I suddenly said, 'Hey, mister.'"

"Yes."

"No, I didn't."

"Yes, you did."

"No, I didn't."

Woody came out of the bathroom. He raised his arms in triumph like a winning sprinter at the tape.

"Fresh as a daisy. C'mere, Miss E. Take a whiff. Just the way you like 'em."

Ellen turned away, disgust on her brow. "Oh, really," she said, "the two of you."

Business was slow in the afternoon. Ellen told Virgil she wanted to go home and take a nap.

"And please," she said leaving, "try to keep Woody out of sight of customers."

At the house, she closed her eyes for an hour.

When she woke, she took off her clothes and went into the bathroom to run the shower. She stopped in front of the mirror to put up her hair.

"Holy shit," groused Beatrice. "Look at this. How old can you be? Thirty and you look like this already."

Beatrice pointed into the image floating before her, at the mirror. "Honey, would you take a look at yourself? You've let it all go to hell. Look at your arms, you've got that worst kind of fat hanging under 'em. Like marshmallow cream. Ugh."

Ellen opened the mirror door to the medicine cabinet. Brown pill bottles lined the shelves. She grabbed them one at a time, read the labels and opened one to shake out three yellow orbs. She closed the mirror.

"I don't believe this," Beatrice grumbled. She swung at the side of the image as if to jostle an ill-working television set. "Don't take those, you twit! Go outside and get some exercise! Make yourself something healthy to eat! Oh, for God's . . . forget it. Go ahead, take 'em. Spend your whole damn day in bed."

Ellen stepped under the water, letting the stream pummel her back. Steam filled the shower stall.

"Why am I watching this?" she asked the silence around her. "Who is this chick?"

Suddenly Beatrice felt a forward acceleration as if she'd been shoved down a playground slide. She landed instantly in what felt like a mold, her face and arms and legs were slipped into a tight container waiting for her at the bottom of the slide.

Hot water prickled her backside.

"Oh my."

She was inside Ellen, in the shower. Alive. She whirled around. Hot water scalded her breasts.

"Yow!"

Without thinking, she stabbed for the faucet to turn it down.

Then she was gone.

"Ahhhhh!" Ellen screamed at the cold water, flailing her hands at the shower knobs.

"Ellen? I'm home. How're you feeling?"

"I'm in the kitchen."

She sat at the table in a bathrobe, her hair piled up in a towel turban. A cup of milky coffee and a pint of ice cream huddled in front of her.

Virgil sat beside her.

"Ellen?"

"What?"

"How're you doing?"

"I'm fine. What's the matter?"

"Nothing."

"The store okay?"

"Yes."

"You gave Woody money, didn't you?"

"Yes. He's a kid."

"We were all kids. The reason we grew into adults is because we learned to be responsible for ourselves. Woody has spent his entire youth either high on drugs or breaking who knows what laws. He needs to take control over himself the way we did. Believe me, you're not helping by babying him."

"Maybe he needs a break."

"Virgil, I know what you're thinking. Because you got a break, you need to pass it along to someone else who's in the same situation. That's fine. Understand, I have nothing against Woody, he's turned out to be a fine boy. But the two of you have nothing in common. When you and I first met, you were already a mature man who'd simply had an unfortunate incident in his life. I only helped you get back on the track you were already on before. I gave you only what you deserved. You did the rest."

She patted his arm and dug the spoon into the ice cream.

"I also love you," she said. "You know that."

She stuck the scoop in her mouth and put the top on the container. She spoke around the ice cream. "But Woody needs a firmer hand than you did. You know I'm right."

Virgil made no reply but waited for this unforeseen tack in the conversation to blow over. She returned the ice cream to the freezer.

He said, "I'm a little worried about you."

She sighed. "About what?"

"About these things you've been saying out of the blue. And you don't remember saying them."

"I haven't got the foggiest notion what you're talking about. This is all coming out of your head, not mine."

On the path to the light, Beatrice shouted, "It's me! Tell him it's me!"

Beatrice stood and backed away from the floating image. She willed herself into the vision, heaving her chest and stamping her feet. She flapped her arms. "It's me! It's me!"

"The hot water cut off today for no reason in the middle of my shower. Will you take a look at it?"

"Sure."

Beatrice realized she had no control over the image; she couldn't force or will her way in. She settled down before it.

Ellen said, "I'll change clothes. Then I'll start dinner."

"Alright. I'll take my shower."

Ellen went upstairs to the bedroom. She grabbed a denim skirt and a white cotton sweater from the closet.

"Bland," muttered Beatrice. "At least put on some perfume."

Ellen prepared pasta and poured sauce out of a jar over it. She put into the oven a premade garlic bread wrapped in foil and cut lettuce into a bowl. She set ranch dressing on the table.

Without warning, Beatrice—as though she were a grain of sand in the vortex of an hourglass—slid in. She flexed the hands, stretching the fingers as though to test the fit of new gloves. She breathed deeply the odors from the warming sauce and opened the oven to smell the bread. She expected to be whisked out of Ellen at any moment back to the lonely roost of her soul but somehow she lingered in the bubbling heat of the kitchen. Listening to be sure the husband was still showering upstairs, Beatrice ran her hands over the waist and rear of the woman, appalled at the flaccidity. The breasts were still firm—nowhere near as good as Beatrice's old ones, but not without their virtues. This used to be a good, pert little body, but the woman had let it go soft. Beatrice turned from the stove to take in the solid lines and comfort of the house, not just through the woman's eyes and ears as before, but now through her skin and nose. She touched a white ruffle curtain in the window, handled an antique rag doll in a wicker rocker, ran her fingertips over the smooth cool counter.

The pasta was being overboiled. Beatrice turned off the burner, grabbed a hot pad and ran a shot of cold water in the pot to stop the cooking.

She took up a wooden spoon in her left hand to stir the noodles.

Virgil came downstairs pulling on a T-shirt.

Beatrice turned to him. She nodded her approval.

"You're not bad looking up close."

Virgil stopped. "What?"

"I . . ."

Virgil moved to her. But Beatrice was gone. She left Ellen slack-jawed and staring.

He said, "Ellen?"

From the path to the light, Beatrice watched Ellen jump.

"Ah! Oh, my stars. Goodness, Virgil, don't creep up on me like that!"

He stepped back. "I didn't."

"You did. I never heard you coming. That wasn't funny. Now stop fooling about and set the table. Dinner's ready."

Ellen rattled her head and turned away from him to the stove, absently shifting the stirring spoon back to her right hand.

Virgil read for forty minutes. He set his alarm for seven in the morning and turned off his lamp.

Ellen was already heaved over on her side.

Virgil sat up in bed and looked out the open window. The waxing moon beamed straight down, the palm trees in the front yard stood on their shadows. Sounds of revelry from a bar around the corner coasted over the sill.

Virgil eased off the bed. He tiptoed to the

closet; grabbed a pair of jeans, a sweatshirt and sneakers; and slipped out of the bedroom. He went outside to sit on the front porch.

There is an odd tug to the stars over an island. Always the stars draw you outward, the way a fire draws you inward. When over land, their pinpoints carry you across more land that is solid, safe, known, but above an island the stars boost you out over a black depth, immense, shifting, a swallower of you and all that is solid, safe or known. The pull is keener because it is stranger. From the dark steps of the big house, Virgil felt the stars tug and he leaped in his heart up to them but tonight he felt leaden and the trillion lights could not lift him out over the ocean.

The neighbor's huge weeping willow swished and Virgil walked to it, past it, up Whitehead to Greene Street to Sloppy Joe's. The bar laid claim to the legacy of being Ernest Hemingway's favorite saloon in Key West. Tonight it was nothing for Virgil but the loudest and he wedged his shoulders in at the bar and ordered a beer. It was the first beer he'd tasted in eight years. He didn't stop to think beyond that because he would not have drunk it so he tipped the bottle up fast and took a swig. The beer stung his throat. His greed for it slaked quickly. He set the half-full bottle on the bar, laid three dollars beside it and walked through the noise and crowd to the door.

Outside, the smiling illustrated head of Ernest Hemingway beamed from a poster; his face had long been the logo for the bar. The head showed

only a frozen moment in the writer's life, a conge-
nial, manly one. The poster did not show the
hunting rifle propped under the chin or the top of
the skull blown off in Ketchum, Idaho, in 1961.
Virgil looked into the pen-and-ink crinkled eyes
and saw none of the end of the legendary author's
story. The drawing was just Hemingway. Whole,
happy Papa. Key West was one of his havens. He
had many. Many homes. Beautiful women. High
adventure. His friends, other strong men living
strong tales. And when his havens became his
prisons, when his body betrayed him to disease,
when his fame and stature no longer gave him rest
from anxiety and depression, when his palaces
became places to hide instead of enclaves to
gather his strength, when the world was no longer
Ernest Hemingway's movable feast, he took his
life the way he wrote, with suddenness and lean-
ness.

Virgil imagined that he felt what Papa might
have felt. Key West, a refuge surrounded by water
and night, jacketed in stars which finally would
not lift him, might have become for Hemingway a
prison. Except that Virgil knew intimately what
prison was and Hemingway did not. Hemingway
knew war and love but those things at least retain
some freedom for a man. Not prison.

A man out of prison—no, not "a man," not
some safe rhetorical being, but him, Virgil—after
four years served, Virgil out of prison sought
sanctuary. And he found it, fast. Even before he'd
cleared the halfway house, there was Ellen and the

shop on Duval. She—a talkative and stable girl—
became his boss, his caretaker, his apologist. She
had that sort of embracing nature, still had it, the
sort that gives advice, runs things, worries over
how to be helpful. He was obliged to her for his
restoration; she grew glad of his loyalty and attention. They became lovers, awkwardly at first. He
was only the third man she'd ever made love with,
each a quick affair for Ellen, one in high school
and again in college. None for him for four years
in a cell. Five months after meeting, two weeks
after his release from the halfway house and state
supervision, less than a year after her parents had
died on the crest of Seven Mile Bridge, she
became his wife. Virgil's four years of prison were
closely followed by four years of Ellen. And while
the prison years had stretched out like a straight
road, droning and similar, his marriage had been
a spectrum, starting out dark and uncertain, two
virtual strangers who believed they needed the
other to make them whole and bright and found
for a while that this was happening, moving with
hope and kindness into light. For the first two
years, Virgil's and Ellen's love was a ripening and
humid love under the constant Key West suns
and storms, tinting the shop and house even on
gray days with red laughter and pink, blushing
sex—conservative, level-headed sex, but Virgil
saw in his wife occasional sparks of liberation and
release he hoped would take flame. At least their
coupling was frequent. They worked beside one
another smoothly, divided labor easily, and held

hands on the sidewalk for the stroll home at the end of the day. They turned blind eyes and deaf ears to each other's flaws in belief that this was how to forgive. Nothing spectacular happened; they were married to each other and became married people. Each gave the other's life a sense of momentum, and they appreciated that. Then, sometime in their third year, beneath their notice (as it will), with the relentless round swelling of Ellen's hips and their bank accounts and their familiarity with each other, with the torpid movement of a minute hand which spins too slowly to observe but spins nonetheless, their union crawled back toward darkness, benighted by shades imperceptible until their relationship was so shrouded they could no longer see the original light from their early time. Days became unchosen routine, an evening's amorousness grew rarer as sex became associated with reward or ploy. The green excitement of life, the open road and plans the size and grandness of clouds, shrank to the size of the squares of a dull calendar. And so, today, every day, their life together was being buried under more and more blankets of household and business protocols, an intimacy of distance, until it was finally too dim for either of them to grope their way back to the other. They were traveling separate paths while on the same path. Without fault or effort, as naturally as they had once fallen in love, they were becoming again virtual strangers, as they had begun.

Virgil didn't think he could stop it. Perhaps

that was the prisoner in him, accustomed to waiting, accustomed to a sentence.

On the poster, Hemingway in his turtleneck sweater continued to beam and gaze straight ahead.

Virgil walked back inside. He ordered another beer, downed all of it, and then another.

He left the bar, slapped Papa on the nose, and walked toward home.

Two and a half beers. In about thirty minutes. The same he'd drunk on an afternoon eight years ago. How did he feel?

Not drunk. Able to walk straight. Able to drive a speed boat and spot a swimmer in the water.

But he knew that he was drunk. Legally. Just .002 above the Florida limit for blood-alcohol content. Just as he had been eight years ago. And he had not seen the swimmer in the water. What should have been only an ugly and unfortunate accident became vehicular manslaughter. What should have been a promising career and life for a budding CPA with a top Fort Lauderdale accounting firm became Virgil now under the impotent stars of Key West.

At the house on Whitehead Street he peed on the front grass so he wouldn't wake Ellen with a flush inside. He crept into the house, undressed downstairs, slipped up the steps and into bed.

He settled his head on his pillow. He looked up at the dark ceiling and imagined Hemingway's blood splattered across it.

Ellen rolled over.

"I'm sorry," he said, "did I wake you?"

She didn't answer. She laid her head on his shoulder. Without looking into his face, she brought her hand up from under the covers and let her fingertips play in the hair around his nipples.

Slowly, she traced the path of the hair follicles down his chest and over his stomach, her nails trickling, straying from the curling path to tickle in running legs over his belly, down the black ridge toward the elastic band of his underpants.

"Ellen, what are you doing?"

She shushed him.

He didn't know what to make of this sudden friskiness. He'd slid into bed only seconds ago in a funk, on the heels of his melancholic and secret walk into the flittings and carousings downtown. Now she had her fingertips at the border of his underpants. She lifted the elastic and stuck a finger in, exploring, peeking. The finger dove in and out, deeper each time and Virgil hardened. She brushed the back of the finger against him. She caught her breath, he did the same. Then, as if some taboo had been cracked so why not shatter it altogether, she wrapped her hand around him. She moved her lips to suck on his nipple.

"Ellen?"

Virgil's mouth and eyes went wide. She hadn't locked hands and lips on him like this in . . . his thoughts broke off.

She stroked him up and down. He blinked and puffed his cheeks and his face was like a clutch of big and little balloons, cheeks way out, eyes bulging, nostrils flared. Then he let out the breath, popping the bigger balloons, but his eyes stayed burst open and his brows were arched high. She continued, and in moments he throbbed. She stopped and squeezed hard. The spasm eased and she resumed climbing him and sliding down.

The second before he came, she plunged in her other hand and pinched his scrotum hard. He exploded inside his underwear, soaking the cloth so he did not feel the drippings.

"Oh," he breathed, flexing his buttocks and squirming his shoulder blades deeper into the mattress, "oooo."

That, Virgil thought, was damned unexpected.

And in that same instant, with his eyes closed and his body relaxing, his memory replayed a thousand recorded moments for him of how it used to be, he and Ellen hot for each other, buzzing around the big blue house stuck together like two dragonflies on a marriage that was an endless summer lake. He suddenly was disturbed by sadness that this present moment with his wife's hand around his pecker had indeed become unexpected, had become a treat for him on a restless night. But he snubbed the sadness. The beers he'd drunk seethed in his blood like surf and he decided to try being hopeful.

He released a generous sigh.

"Oh boy," he exhaled, "wow, Ellie."

But at her old nickname she did not lift her mouth to kiss him as he wanted, releasing him gently and generously into sleep with a kiss and so to seal away this something small and precious which had occurred out of nowhere, unbidden and promising—after what had been far too long a time between married people who claim and say they love each other. But promising what? Perhaps to again begin storing up those rare and small things only couples create, that grain which feeds their love in lean times?

Instead, at the nickname she fell asleep peculiarly, instantly, with her head on his chest and both hands down his pants.

3

THE next morning at breakfast, Virgil made no mention of the pleasure she'd given him the night before, nor of how oddly and quickly she'd gone from fondling him over the peak of a magnificent, pent-up climax to snoring. Ellen did not speak of these things either, oblivious, another clanking morning with her in the kitchen. She prattled on in her insistent way about her plans for the day at the shop. This was not what Virgil wanted to hear; he wanted words to signal that last night was a good omen, some midnight dove with an olive twig in its beak.

At the shop, Virgil did his best to keep close tabs on Ellen without getting in her way or alerting her. He watched to see that she remained her deft self while framing, ringing up purchases, locating supplies and helping customers. He listened to her greet familiar patrons by name should she forget one. He tracked her conversations with Woody and others to see that her words remained coherent and linear. He made a mess at the work counter to see if she would chastise him for it; he hid things to make her look for them madly as was her custom. He greeted one regular customer, an older gentleman who purchased fresh canvases weekly, by calling to him when he entered, "Hey, mister!" thinking the phrase might jump-start some curious response from her.

When the man had left with his rolls of new canvas under his arm, she motioned for Virgil to come to the cash register.

She said, "Come here."

Virgil pointed to himself in mock surprise.

"Yes, you. Who else? Come here."

Virgil walked over.

She held up a finger. "Number one. That wasn't a very polite way to greet that man. He's a very nice person." She held up another finger. "Number two. Do you think I'm an idiot? That 'Hey, mister' bit was weak. You can't trick me."

She stepped close, laying her chest on his. She put her left hand over his crotch.

"And number three." She squeezed his balls gently. "Don't look a gift horse in the mouth."

Virgil backed away. Her fingers stayed on his zipper until he was out of range.

"I've got to pee," she said. "Watch the store."

She swept away to the bathroom. Virgil stared after her. She closed the bathroom door.

In seconds, she screamed.

Virgil ran through the shop. Woody came out

of the stockroom. They met at the door.

"What was that?" the boy asked.

"Ellen's in the bathroom."

"I was just in there." Woody grinned. "I should've hung up a sign, you know, like, 'Stay Out.'"

"Shut up, Woody." He called through the door, "Ellen? Are you alright?"

"Virgil?"

"Ellen? I'm here."

"Virgil?"

He turned the doorknob. It was locked.

"Can you open the door? It's locked."

Her voice quavered. "I . . . what . . . I . . ."

"Stand back, okay? Stand back."

Virgil kicked the door. The bathroom lock, not made for heavy security, gave way. Woody applauded. Virgil rushed inside.

She stood at the sink. One hand was in her hair, the other reached for him.

"Virgil?"

"Yes?"

She held both arms out to him.

"What am I doing in the bathroom?"

"Stupid!"

Beatrice uncrossed her legs and rocked back. She balled a fist and beat it once against the golden way.

"Damn it! Stupid."

Yanking herself to her feet, she paced in front of the floating image, gesturing to it, the only thing to talk to here in the glow of the light.

"Why'd I have to take her into the bathroom? Alright, she had to pee, but Jesus, it could have waited! She can pee on her own time."

She threw up her arms.

"I know, I know, I should've stayed at the cash register or the workbench. But no, I had to make some big exit to the bathroom after grabbing the guy in the nuts."

She held her own head the way Ellen had done.

"Aw, Jeez, in the nuts. Stupid, stupid."

Beatrice focused again on the levitating image and sound. Ellen's eyes blinked, her vision was blurred from tears, her voice caught from fear. Virgil had his arms around her on the floor of the bathroom where Ellen had collapsed. The skinny boy Woody stood spying in.

"Something's wrong, Virgil," she whimpered. "You were right. Oh my God, what's the matter with me?"

"It'll be okay. We'll figure it out. It's something small, I'm sure. Just some blackouts. You'll be fine. It's nothing to worry about. Woody, get back to work."

Virgil held her. Supportive, strong, steady Virgil.

Beatrice cupped her chin in her hands to settle in and watch. She recalled what the guide had said. There's a plan. Always is.

The drive north to Miami that afternoon took three hours. Before they left, Virgil sent Woody

back to the halfway house and hung the CLOSED
sign in the shop door. Ellen took from her desk a
micro-cassette recorder and asked Virgil to record
any bizarre things she might say during the trip.
Virgil agreed to do it.

But he did not, for two reasons. First, he didn't
want to upset her any more than she already was.
She'd taken half a Valium just for the ride to the
hospital. If she were to hear her own recorded
voice say more things of which she had no recol-
lection, it might set off another blubbering jag.
Second, there was nothing to record. Ellen sat
glumly for the entire ride staring at the aqua skin
of the Gulf on the left, the Atlantic to the right.

At the hospital in Miami, they met at four
o'clock with Dr. Poondang Kithathanon, the neurologist suggested by their family physician in
Key West.

"Yes," he said, calling them out of their seats in
the waiting room, "yes, please to come with me."

In his office, the doctor sat first and quickly.
He was short and reddish brown, blending with
the dark leather of his chair. His small hands were
the mahogany of the desk.

Kithathanon looked up from his chair in obvious surprise that Virgil and Ellen still stood.

"Yes," he said impatiently, waving at the two
chairs in front of them, "sit, sit. Why do you want
to be standing?"

They took their seats. Advanced degrees from
the University of Rangoon, the University of
Mandalay and Michigan State adorned a wall. A

credenza was covered with statuettes of Buddhist gods shaped in wood or metal bearing the heads of elephants and eagles; bellies big as barrels; two, four, or eight arms.

"You are having visions?" he asked Ellen.

"No."

"Voices?"

"No."

"Then what, please?"

Virgil spoke. "Blackouts. She doesn't remember things."

The doctor shoved a hand at Ellen. "Why don't you let the lady answer for herself? She's the one who is sick with the problem, you know. My goodness, fellow."

Kithathanon prodded Ellen with a voice like a squeaky gate. "Yes? Please?"

"I say things. I do things."

"What things, please?"

"I don't know. Virgil knows them, not me."

"Yes, alright," Kithathanon pointed at Virgil, "you now."

Virgil lowered his head, rubbing his palms together. "Sometimes she says and does things that Ellen just . . . Ellen wouldn't do."

"Such as?"

Virgil knitted his fingers. Kithathanon waited, tapping his brown lips with a pen.

The doctor slapped his palm on the desk, insistent. "I am a physician, you know. People talk to me. I have a wonderful manner, I have been told that. You must talk freely."

At that, she slapped her own hand on the desk. "You want me to talk freely? Alright. You're a rude little dickhead. There. That free enough for you?"

Her hand was flat on the desktop, Kithathanon's hand pressed down too, as if together they were keeping the desk from floating away. They glared at each other.

Kithathanon surrendered the desktop to her. He tapped his lips more.

She pulled back her arm and elbowed Virgil.

"Virg, come on, don't leave me stranded here. He deserved that. Besides," she pointed at the diplomas on the wall and began to laugh, "how can you take a guy seriously whose first name sounds like 'poontang'?"

A temblor of mirth raked her ribs.

The doctor lifted his eyes to the ceiling.

"*Ay*, this again," he said. "Yes, yes, I know. Lady, you think you are the first to be making this joke? You want maybe me to change my name because it sounds like a bad word to you vulgar Americans. This is funny for you, a man's name?"

The laughter in her grew. She tilted from her chair over to Virgil, bumping his shoulder. Flushed and shaking, she gnawed her lower lip trying to control herself, waving her hands in front of her face as if to fan away bugs.

"Okay," Virgil whispered to her, now biting back his own laughter, "I get it. Calm down."

He looked up at Kithathanon's brown puckered face. He held out a hand to the neurologist. "Look, we're sorry. Ellen? Come on now. I'm sorry, doctor. Ellen, get a grip."

She stopped laughing abruptly. She stared straight ahead at the floor. After a moment she raised her eyes in shock and confusion.

"I . . . what? Did I . . . ?"

"Hmmm. Yes," Kithathanon said decisively, "I see what you mean." He touched a button on his phone. "Come in."

A nurse quick-stepped into the office.

The doctor stood and spoke to Ellen. "My nurse will take you to a change room." He shook a stern dark finger. "And behave, you."

The nurse took Ellen's arm to guide her from the chair. Crossing the room, Ellen looked back wide-eyed at Virgil.

Beatrice couldn't take her eyes from the image. If she did, she ran the risk of being injected—that's how it felt—into Ellen without knowing what was going on. Like missing a week of a soap opera.

Time never passed where she was, sitting on the shining way to the light. She tried counting to a million to get a sense of time but when she finished it seemed as though she'd counted only to ten. She never got tired or bored, her legs never ached from sitting, hunger and thirst did not visit. She observed Ellen's life unhaltingly through Ellen's eyes and ears until with no tingle or tip-off as to when it would happen or how long it would last, she lived portions of Ellen's life. She was inserted into the middle of sentences or actions which Beatrice then had to finish. And her stays inside Ellen had been growing in duration, beginning to last several minutes at a time.

So when Beatrice saw in the floating image the machine that Dr. Kithathanon was about to slide Ellen into, she did not look away, much as she wanted to, because she knew that would only make matters worse. And she did not sweat, though she felt the itch of nerves under her skin; apparently there was no sweating there on the path to the light.

Dr. Kithathanon was on the phone when Virgil opened his office door. The little neurologist gestured Virgil into the room with a fast hand, waving him down into the chair as if guiding a crane operator. With Virgil lowered into the seat, Kithathanon raised a palm to him.

"Yes, yes," he said into the receiver, "first thing. Yes, that is appreciated. Much appreciation. Yes. Good-bye."

He hung up.

"Your wife." Kithathanon waggled his small head.

Virgil sat forward. "Yes."

"Your wife's problems are not physiological, that much I can tell you."

"Good. That's good."

"Depends on what you are meaning by good."

"I mean she's okay?"

"Again, depends on what is okay for you. This

would not be okay for me. The MRI is telling me only what she does not have. No temporal lobe tumor. No lesion. That does not mean no problem."

Virgil shifted on the seat. "Did she . . . ? Something she did in there?"

"Come." The doctor led Virgil out of his office down the hall. They entered a door marked "Diagnostic Imaging."

In a dim gray room, the MRI resembled a massive lie-down hair dryer in an antiseptic beauty salon. Virgil imagined Ellen on the table.

Kithathanon gestured to the machine. "Normally, the MRI takes thirty, forty minutes. This wife of yours took an hour and a half."

Virgil did not ask why because Kithathanon did not pause.

"I ask if she is claustrophobic. If you are, I tell her, we will give you something before you go in, a Valium drip. No, she says. I am fine. Okay. We slide her in, she settles down. I turn around to go do my job somewhere else and—boom!—she starts kicking of the feet and yelling like we are sliding her head into a pencil sharpener. We sedate her enough for a rhinoceros. I'm telling you, fellow, this is some wife."

"Doctor, I'm sorry if she was . . ."

Kithathanon had already opened the door. Virgil hustled behind him to the office.

The doctor scribbled briskly on a pad as if scratching a lottery game ticket. He tore off the sheet and handed it across the desk.

"This is a colleague. A psychiatrist here in Miami. He will see you tomorrow morning and I strongly suggest you to see him. I am sure your wife is not sick. However, I do not know if she is not crazy."

Virgil waited in the hospital restaurant while Ellen's sedation wore off. In the lobby gift shop he bought a bouquet of daisies.

Just after 7 P.M., Dr. Kithathanon's nurse wheeled Ellen out of the elevator. Virgil handed down the flowers. She laid them across her lap tiredly. The nurse pushed Ellen outside the automatic doors where she stood from the wheelchair. The nurse gave Virgil a silent sympathetic look and rolled away into the hospital.

"Did you eat?"

"What I could keep down."

He drove them to a motel with a view of Interstate 95 and the settling sun over the flat tropical sprawl outside Miami. He put Ellen's flowers in a water pitcher. He called the halfway house to leave a message for Woody that the shop would be closed tomorrow. He stepped out on the verandah.

"In a little while I'll go down to the lobby and get us some toothbrushes." Ellen made no reply. He turned to look past the curtains into the room, at his wife on her stomach, shaking the bed with her big sobs.

He let her bawl. A light gust spread across his back. The daylight lowered. Virgil felt Gothic, standing on a darkening windy parapet, a lady in tears nearby. This was a romantic scene and Virgil knew the heroic role he ought to play. Rush to her, bend his knee beside the bed, take her hand, comfort her, smooth her hair and stroke her damp cheek. It's alright, m'lady, peace. Weep no more. But it wasn't alright and she *should* weep because she damn well might be out of her gourd and her husband, the tall gaunt man outside in the dusk, was afraid.

Listening to her cry, he wondered what he was afraid of. That Ellen would not be cured of her voices and blackouts? No, modern medicine was a great enough miracle to match most ailments. His fear was that he himself would go unhealed. That the woman there on the bed, the one who once might have taken away his guilt, had slipped away from the dock like an unwatched and untied boat. She was still within sight, but she had put to silent sea, unreachable because she could not turn around and he would not swim to her. Why? Why when it was all right there, crying and heavy and needy but right there? He was to blame. She was crazy now because she couldn't fix him anymore; he'd grown intolerant to her sort of castor-oil tonic for his ills: honest work, steady if unspectacular affection, a clean home. So, disappointed, she had become the one brittle and afflicted to take the focus and blame off of Virgil, that way to bring into their marriage healing of any kind.

"Virgil?"

"Yes?"

She sat up. The center of her face was swollen, a scarlet bull's-eye.

"Come inside. I want to talk to you."

He stepped in to sit in the chair next to the bed.

"Here." She patted the mattress. "I want to tell you what it's like."

He moved beside her.

"It's alright. You don't have to."

"I want to."

"Ellen, you're going to be fine."

"Virgil, may I please speak?"

He looked down to the bedspread.

"It's like I just blink. And when I open my eyes from the blink, it's some time later. I never know how much time. I look around for clues. Was it a second, a minute, ten minutes? And it's so sudden, Virgil. I never feel it coming."

"How often does it happen?"

"I don't know. It feels like it's getting more frequent. I don't always tell you after it happens, either. I just stay quiet if I can."

"I've noticed you've been quieter."

"Quieter than what?"

He hesitated. "You know, quieter."

"Quieter than usual? Are you saying I talk too much?"

"No."

"Yes, you are saying exactly that. Virgil, this is no time to pick at me. I need your support. This is a very trying experience for me."

"I support you, Ellen."

"Good. Now, we haven't really talked about it so tell me. What am I like when I'm . . . when I'm not here?"

"Ellen."

"Tell me. I want to know."

"I don't want to do this."

"Virgil, thank you, but please let me be the judge of what I need to hear. Now go ahead."

He sighed. "Well, you're okay."

"Virgil."

"You're just . . . not . . . completely you. I mean, you're okay, really, just not . . . totally you."

"You mean I'm what? I'm not totally me? What does that mean?"

"I mean you're just like yourself. Like you are regularly. You know, you laugh and cut up a little. Only, kind of more so."

"First you said I'm not me. Now you're saying I'm even more like me. You say I'm quieter and then you say I cut up."

"It's complex, Ellen. It's like you're another you. It's still you, just not . . . this you."

"Uh-huh. *This* you. Meaning me, right now."

"Yes."

"Uh-huh." She stared at him, suspicious. "And do you like this other me?"

"You're going to be okay. Don't worry about it."

Ellen paused, locked onto his eyes. Virgil leaned away; her eyes did not follow him. Her head became, for seconds, like a marble bust. And then her eyes found him again.

She said, "Well, you're right. No sense worrying about it till we know what's up. Right?"

She licked her lips, distracted, wanting something else to talk about.

"Anyway," she said, "screw that for now. You think they've got the Playboy Channel in this place?"

She bounded off the bed. Virgil had to steady himself from being bounced off the mattress.

From the top of the television she plucked a cardboard placard of channels available in the motel. She scanned it and flicked on the TV.

Turning to Virgil on the bed, she punched a fist in the air.

"Hey hey. We're in luck. It's show time!"

Beatrice started out fast, outpacing the sexy charades on the Playboy Channel. They were trying to develop a plot and Beatrice didn't care because she didn't know how long she would be in the body. But drawing Virgil to her, enveloping him in her arms and legs—they were beginning to feel increasingly like her own arms and legs and not this other woman's, especially using them now as she was, pulling him in, rubbing her heels on the backs of his knees, unbuttoning and unzipping herself and him—it was like dropping an anchor. The more he sighed and flickered his eyelids and went "ooh" and the more she purred, the more solid she felt inside these limbs on this bed of white and not the way of the light where she sat halfway damned and halfway blessed. This was all blessing. This was a man gentling a woman he loved, a woman whom he brought to climax three times with different hard and soft pieces of himself before he took his own satisfaction. These were arched backs that were a bridge and not just things bent, this was sharing, not buying and selling, oh, yes God, this was what love must feel like inside you and out.

Virgil marveled at her face. Her cheeks were puffy, her eyes red-rimmed and misty from crying only minutes before. But now there was laughter emanating from her. She was like rain on a sunny day, the incongruity of it. He had to grapple her off him, get her on her back and soothe her down with whispers and kisses on her body. She came quickly at first, and this was so unlike Ellen. It was a recall of the other Ellen of four—three, even two—years ago. Then she stroked the crown of his head, asking for another, and this too was like the old Ellen, wanting to receive and so in that way give to him, wanting sex to last to the end of their powers. He made her come wrenchingly twice more. Her flesh to his lips and fingertips was softer than it had ever been. He kissed and petted across a warm layer of fat but he believed the woman he felt beneath was still hard, still hungry for him.

Then she rolled him onto his back and settled on top of him. She squealed and made other sounds, including a strange *bzzzzz* that sounded like a mosquito, but she spoke no words. The two of them made the bed squeak and the headboard thump against the wall so that Virgil suspected they, for once, were that tacky couple in the next room at the motel; she did not stop self-consciously or giggle in embarrassment the way Virgil expected but grew in tempest and sent the bed ramming the wall with her hips.

Whoa! he thought, this is good! This is a sign. This happy energetic humping plus the quiet and enigmatic hand job she'd given him last night, these were portents, signals that maybe they had turned a corner, a U-turn in fact, heading back in the old and good direction. When his time came, spewing into her (some smokey woman inside the layer of fat felt his rush and heat, was it the old real Ellen, the one hiding behind all this flesh, the store, the big house, the ten percent sales and community service? His sperm was on the walls inside her, was it behind them that she existed, is this where he had to go to touch her?) he felt a tug of hope, heaving him upward with his semen, lifting him where the stars would not carry him the evening before. Are we back on track? he wondered. Yes, this is good.

Even so, while he clutched the sheets and strained to keep his heavy eyes open on her grinning red face, he wondered if her new and mysterious illness had anything to do with all this.

Virgil's head lolled back on the pillow. The motel blanket was on the carpet, the fitted linens were pulled out at the corners.

Again, he made the decision to be hopeful. He

cleared his throat and, playfully, made it comic, like the growl of a wild beast.

"Rrrrrr," he snarled up at her, "Ellie."

Her face fastened in its grin, but her eyes did not follow Virgil's when he sat up to his elbows under her to kiss her.

Then slowly, slacking the smile, she looked down past his face, down at the place where she and he were connected, where they were man and wife.

Her jaw dropped.

4

"COME in. Please,"

Dr. Lowe stood from behind his desk; Virgil guessed it was the man's desk though it more resembled a boulder of limestone.

The doctor was a spare, white column of a man. He indicated two formless chairs, which Virgil trusted were chairs though they might just as well have been two snowmen captured in mid-melt.

"Sit down."

The psychiatrist's entire office was this way, without angular points of reference. The room was round, no windows, drained of color, nowhere for Virgil's eyes to perch. Barring the doctor himself, every item was of a dissolving design. The phone on the boulder-desk was a milky dollop. Scattered statues brought to mind decomposing pillars of salt. The cream carpeted floor was level but the ceiling rollicked, somehow lit from within its folds.

Doctor Lowe gestured again at the chairs. Virgil and Ellen stepped tentatively into the room. The door closed with a colorless hiss behind them. With his black pants and blue denim shirt, Virgil felt like a cavity moving in on a child's innocent teeth.

They arranged themselves in the chairs. The cushions held him comfortably though Virgil could not figure how. Dr. Lowe sat, or seemed to kneel, for no chair back reared from behind his shoulders to receive him.

The man spread his hands—sunless chalky skin, alabaster shirt, hair not gray but snowy—and said, "I'm Dr. John Lowe."

His voice was sober, modulated. White noise. He raised a long finger and circled it beside his head as if making the sign for "Whoopee!"

"Let me explain my office. It's what I call a tabula rasa, a blank slate. Here, each of my patients is made to feel he or she is free to roam or explore wherever their thoughts take them. There are no preconceived ideas here, nothing to trip over or cling to, no pre-fashioned shapes or colors. Just open, free minds in an open, free atmosphere."

Virgil nodded. Dr. Lowe steepled his fingers under his chin.

Ellen said, "Thank you, doctor."

The psychiatrist opened his hands under his chin for one light and albino clap.

"Let's get under way, shall we?" He tipped the two joined hands at Ellen. "I have read Dr.

Kithathanon's report. Now give me yours."

Virgil listened while Ellen described her symptoms. Blackouts. Amnesia. Unpredictable onsets of strange behavior, including sex with Virgil in the motel the night before, of which she recalled only the aftermath which was principally making the bed and crying despite Virgil's entreaties that it had been wonderful and meaningful. Depression following the blackouts. Depression now, worrying that she was losing her mind. She interrupted herself several times to say, "You can ask Virgil," as if what she told the doctor was too fantastic, but Dr. Lowe did not ask him.

The psychiatrist did not move—his fingertips stayed glued under his chin—nor speak while Ellen talked. He did nothing to distract her while she ranged over many topics which Virgil didn't think relevant, including the store, her difficulty dieting, her dislike of cooking, some rich woman who'd snubbed her at a Key West Merchants Association meeting, even Virgil's dreams of musical instruments that he couldn't play in real life.

Dr. Lowe's fingers finally came apart, breaking some circuit of silence. "Ellen?"

"Yes, doctor?"

"I want you to look up at the ceiling. Keep looking up. Now let your eyelids close very slowly. Yes. Very good. I can see the whites at the bottom of your eyes. Yes, you'll do very well. Open your eyes. I should like to hypnotize you."

"Me?" Ellen perked up as though her name had been called at a raffle.

"Hypnosis may help us get past some psychic obstacles. Some pain in your past that you might have blocked out of your memory, which perhaps may even be causing these blackouts."

Ellen laid her hand on her breast. She turned to Virgil, smiling, honored to be recognized for her pain.

"Some pain in my past," she said.

Dr. Lowe indicated the couch on the far side of the room, a twisted padded chunk of driftwood on a white shag beach.

"Please go and lie down, Ellen. I would like Virgil to sit in the waiting room while you're under hypnosis. Will that be alright?"

"Fine."

Ellen walked over to study the couch.

The doctor instructed, "Your head goes there to the left."

Ellen placed herself on the couch. Dr. Lowe moved around the boulder to stand beside Virgil.

"Don't worry, old boy," he confided, "I just want her to speak openly right now. Without any pressure. You understand."

He patted Virgil on the shoulder and shoved off briskly.

"Lie there quietly," he called to Ellen. He opened the office door and a nurse led an intravenous bag and pole into the room.

"Doctor?" Virgil pointed.

"Oh, this is just sodium Amytal. A mild sedative. I'm going to give her a slight dose to help induce an hypnotic state. Nothing to fret about.

Standard practice. She won't remember a thing when she wakes up."

From the couch, Ellen asked, "Is that a truth serum?"

Dr. Lowe rolled the bag and pole toward her. "There's no such thing. No hypnotist or drug can make you speak against your will." He docked beside the couch. "But if you and I are going to dig down to the truths buried inside you, these are tools to make that easier for us."

Ellen glanced at Virgil in the doorway. "Hear that, Virgil? Truths buried inside me."

Virgil gave her a small wave back, like a father motioning to his daughter across the playground, go ahead, don't mind me, keep having a good time.

Dr. Lowe stuck Ellen's arm with the IV. The nurse closed the waiting room door behind Virgil. He took a seat on a cobalt leather sofa surrounded by four blue walls painted with cottony clouds. A large aquarium gurgled around restless fish.

"Relax," Dr. Lowe droned, "imagine your arms and legs are made of air. They are floating. You are getting lighter. Lighter. Feel the couch move away beneath you. You are rising off the couch. You are off the couch."

For several minutes, the doctor coaxed Ellen into lift-off and a holding pattern above the couch. As the drug and his lulling tone took hold, her responses devolved from Yes to Yeah, Uh-huh, and finally, Huh.

"Ellen?"

"Huh?"

"Ellen, I want to take you back to a time in your childhood. You are very young. Five or six years old. All the buildings are very tall. The cars are very big. The palm trees are swaying way over your head. You are so small, a little girl."

"Uh-huh."

"Where are you?"

"I was in the store."

"She grew up in their store." Virgil indicated the silently spinning cassette tape on the doctor's desk. Ellen, conscious, sat outside in the gurgling, sky blue waiting room while the doctor and Virgil reviewed the recording in his office.

Dr. Lowe shushed Virgil behind a vanilla finger.

Ellen began her recollections of her early life in past tense ("I was . . . ," "I went . . ."), then fell gradually into present tense ("I am . . . ," "I go . . . ," "We are . . ."). She first helped to stock the shelves at age seven. She rang up her first sale at nine, had her own keys to the shop by eleven.

Dr. Lowe punched the pause button.

"Virgil, I am certain about a few things. One of them is that your wife was robbed of her childhood. Her parents burdened her as a preadolescent with adult responsibilities and duties. She learned to be in control at an age when the rest of us were still learning to experiment."

"Well, you know," Virgil added, "she does like to . . ."

The psychiatrist held up a digit as if punching Virgil's stop button, then hit fast-forward on the cassette player to skip ahead in the session.

"Wait," he said, "that's not her problem. Yes, it might make her difficult to live with sometimes but it doesn't explain why she's developed a completely separate and distinct personality."

The words pressed Virgil into his chair.

"She what?"

The doctor consulted a legal pad. When the tape counter hit the scribbled number, he stopped and hit play.

"Here," he said, crossing his arms, "listen."

The doctor's voice. ". . . to tell me, Ellen. How does your mommy treat you?"

"She's great."

"She's kind to you?"

"Yes. We finger paint. We talk. She gives me pennies and lets me put them in the register."

"Where is she? Where do you see her?"

"She's in the store."

"Is she always in the store? Don't you see her at home?"

"She's . . . I . . ."

The tape was silent for many moments.

"Where is your mommy?"

"She's . . . I . . . I don't want to talk about her."

"Why not?"

The sound of Ellen snuffling back emotion. Clear on the tape, some bandage inside her had come undone and a tear wanted to seep from the wound.

"I don't need her. I don't need anybody to come get me. I'm staying here."

The doctor. "Staying where? Where are you?"

"They want me to come in. But I won't."

"Come in from where? Where are you?"

"I . . . I don't know. I can see the light."

"What light?"

Virgil asked the same question. "What light?"

Ellen: "The light."

"Where is your daddy?"

"I don't want to talk about him either."

"Where is he?"

"Leave him out of this."

The tape went quiet. Dr. Lowe uncrossed his arms. "Here I turned up the drip on the sodium Amytal IV. She seemed to be coming out of the hypnotic state. I needed to lower her back in."

Ellen: "We're fishing."

"Who is?"

"I caught supper, daddy."

"Where are we?"

"The river."

"That's good. That's a good-size fish."

"I'll clean it for us."

"Okay."

"Daddy?"

"Yes?"

"Not tonight, okay?"

"Not tonight what?"

Slow, unsure words. Plaintive. "Not tonight. You know."

"For what?"

"For the stuff."

"What stuff?"

"You know. The . . ." the child's voice cracked. The child did not want to give it a name.

"What stuff?"

Her tone cowering. "The messing around stuff."

She hesitated.

"It hurts."

Bargaining. "I caught supper. So not tonight. That's fair."

The doctor, still as ice, whispered to Virgil, "I took a chance here."

His voice on the tape. "Do you mean the touching stuff?"

"Uh-huh. I caught the fish. So that's fair, okay?"

"Okay. That's fair."

"Stop it," Virgil said.

Dr. Lowe laid a finger on the pause button.

"I can't believe this. Her father? She never said a word about this to me."

"That's common."

"Jesus." Virgil stood. "Jesus. Did her father really do that?"

"I can't say for certain, of course. She thinks he did. That's what matters. It might help explain her blackouts and the amnesiac barriers. Sexual abuse at a young age can be a root cause for a multiple personality syndrome like Ellen's. There could be others, of course."

"Multiple personality? What . . . ?"

Dr. Lowe answered with his finger. He raised the chalk tip, then pushed it down on fast-forward, only for a moment, then pressed play.

He lifted the finger from the button liltingly, a conductor to his orchestra.

". . . Both your parents are dead, yes?"

"Yes."

"When did they die?"

"My mama passed when I was twelve. They said she had a heart attack but I know it was from drinking. And maybe she got some kind of disease too, no one ever said. But she went ugly. I don't know about my old man. I was long gone by the time he kicked."

The doctor paused the recording. Virgil pitched to the desk to lean his hands on either side of the cassette machine; he dropped his head to look straight down onto it like a man spitting into a well.

"That's not right. Her parents died—"

The doctor interrupted, "In an auto accident on Seven Mile Bridge almost nine years ago. Yes, I know."

"That's . . ." Virgil hoisted his head to the psychiatrist's knowing smile, ". . . that's not Ellen."

Dr. Lowe slipped his finger to the pause button. He pressed and released to roll the tape.

"Yes," he said again, grinning with white teeth, tiny bleached sheets hung on a line, "I know."

"Who are you? Do you have a name?"

"'Course I have a name."

"What is it?"

"It's not my real name."

"Tell me anyway."

"This was always one of my favorite ones."

"Tell me and that's what I'll call you."

"You won't laugh?"

"I won't."

"Alright. It's bee sting."

"And that," said the psychiatrist, mashing the stop button, "is where your wonderfully peculiar wife fell asleep."

Beatrice twiddled her thumbs.

Ellen twiddled hers.

Beatrice fixed her eyes on the floating image. She sat on a ray of light.

Ellen gazed into the aquarium seated on a deep blue sofa amid the clouds in the sky blue waiting room.

Ellen mumbled to herself, wondering what Virgil and the doctor were talking about for so long.

Beatrice wondered the same.

Beatrice worried about what she might have said lying on the doctor's couch, fogged by the drug dripping into Ellen's arm.

Ellen worried the same.

Ellen looked down into her lap. Beatrice looked down into Ellen's lap.

The doctor's office door opened.

Dr. Lowe filled the doorway.

"Please come in."

Ellen took the chair next to Virgil. The doctor settled behind his blobby desk.

Beatrice twirled a finger in her hair. "What did I tell him?" she asked the image.

"What did I tell you?" Ellen asked the doctor.

The psychiatrist lifted a palm. "Don't worry

about that right now. You did wonderfully under hypnosis."

"Am I crazy?" Ellen glanced to Virgil. "Am I?"

Virgil looked for the doctor to answer.

"We don't use the word 'crazy,'" Dr. Lowe corrected. "You have a condition I will call a recurrent interictal dissociative seizure."

"Oh, God," Ellen threw up her hands, "God."

"Ellen? Settle down. Listen to me. I want to ask you a question."

She brought down her hands, limp, instantly aggravated. "Fine. What?"

"What does the term 'bee sting' mean to you?"

"Is this one of those free-association things?"

"If you want it to be. Alright."

"Doctor, honestly, I'm a little too upset right now to play games. Can we do it later?"

"Let's just do this one for right now. It's important."

"Alright, fine. Bee sting." Ellen put her hand to her forehead. "I don't know. Itching? Swelling? Is that right?"

Dr. Lowe gave no response. Ellen lost patience, wanting to give some answer to generate a reply. "What?" she insisted. "Wasp? Hornet? What do you want from me?"

Virgil met the doctor's eyes. Dr. Lowe arched his brows, dropped them, then turned back on Ellen.

"Let's move on. Tell me, please. When did your parents die?"

"What has that got to do with it?"

Dr. Lowe inclined his head to wait.

"Eight years ago," she said, still irritable. "An accident on Seven Mile Bridge. I told you that before."

"Now. Please stay calm when I ask you this next question."

Virgil said in a tone of petition, "Ellen. Please."

The doctor continued. "Did your father ever abuse you sexually?"

Ellen's eyes snapped shut, held fast then shot open.

On the path to the light, Beatrice covered her own eyes with her hands.

Ellen shot from the snowman chair and moved behind it, shielding herself from Dr. Lowe and Virgil.

"Did I say that? Did I say my father abused me? Tell me I didn't."

"Ellen, sit down."

She bellowed. "Damn it, tell me! Did I?"

"Yes."

"Well he never! Never! You understand? Never!"

Beatrice groaned. "Oh, man. Shit shit shit."

Dr. Lowe said, "We understand. Now please bring yourself under control and sit down so we can continue."

Virgil stood. He slipped beside Ellen to guide her back into the chair. She shook him off like a child that has hurt itself and wants to be left alone to ache. She sat untouched.

"Ellen, I'm going to prescribe a course of action

that ought to give us a clearer picture of where to go from here. Please listen to me. Under hypnosis you manifested a personality separate from your normal state. The human brain is a complex set of wires and sometimes they simply get crossed. It's our job to uncross them, that's all. Don't get upset, but maybe your father did abuse you and you've repressed it. Maybe he didn't. It's also possible that you've developed some form of temporal lobe epilepsy. No matter. We'll learn in due time. For now, these are the things I want us to do."

Beatrice listened with growing dread to the fusillade of tests Dr. Lowe had in mind for Ellen. EEG exams, the sensitivity of which could be increased by sleep deprivation or special electrodes placed in the base of the skull or run up through the nostrils into the brain. A lumbar puncture to tap fluid from the top of the spinal column. He suggested they consider electro-convulsive therapy, better known as shock therapy. Also psychotropic drugs. Haldol, an anti-psychotic, for Ellen in case she was not suffering a split personality but was in fact hallucinatory. Klonopin to target Ellen's seizures. Prozac for Ellen's depression. Xanax for Virgil, a boost to help him through the coming ordeal.

Beatrice quavered. Though she was in the light which cast no shadow, she felt a pall.

Beatrice forecast the inevitable, arriving in Ellen's body during one of Lowe's tests, electrodes up her nose, anti-psychotics in her veins, restraining straps, nurses, cold hands, beeping machines. Beatrice was afraid of needles, drugs, curtained enclosures, medical terms, TVs mounted from the ceiling, bedpans, charts, Jell-O mold on a plate, water in a jug. She had not forgotten her own recent death surrounded by all that. She would be encircled by it all again if Ellen succumbed to Dr. Lowe.

"And," said the psychiatrist, "I want to recommend a voluntary committal so we can put you under full-time observation. There'll be group therapy. Daily sedation, of course. Periodic evaluations. You can choose a private ward or a public psychiatric hospital. The latter would be cheaper but I wouldn't recommend it."

Ellen's eyes blurred, blinking from tears.

Behind Beatrice, a voice.

"She's fucked."

Beatrice spun to the figure who spoke.

The man standing there might have been God. He was short, ancient, droopy, a creased face. Shining eyes that might have been the light that ignited the stars. Powerful hands that might have raised mountains and flung out oceans. Floppy ears to gather in the hosannas of the universe.

He spit the shell of a sunflower seed at Beatrice. It landed on her leg.

She brushed off the wet, split bits. Quickly she glanced back to the floating image of Dr. Lowe. It was gone.

"Don't worry, sister," he said, "our chat isn't gonna take place in life time. You won't miss a second of your little game."

Everything about him was wrinkled, his robe, his phlegmy voice. He sat slowly, wrinkling himself to the floor of the light.

"Like I said," he rasped again, "she's fucked. And you're the one who fucked her."

"Ex*cuse* me?" Beatrice took a haughty tone; even for God, good manners should prevail. "To *whom* do I have the pleasure of addressing?"

He catapulted another sunflower seed into his jowls, chomped once and spit again, this time missing her knee by inches.

"Call me Coach."

"And whom, may I inquire, do you coach?"

The old spirit looked away from her in disgust, then back.

"*Whom*," he lampooned Beatrice's tone, butterflying his hands in a mocking, girly way, "*did* I coach, ya nitwit. I'm dead. So're you, in case you mighta forgot."

"Alright. Who did you coach?"

"Oh, for pete's sake! Who do you think?"

"Earth?"

"No! Who the hell do you think I am?"

"You're not God."

"No, but He couldn't have won a lot more games than me."

"I give up."

He slapped his knees.

"Jesus wept, girl. I coached the New York Yankees!"

5

"THE Yankees again?"

"Yep. The Yankees again."

"What is this? Why do you guys keep bothering me?"

"As I understand it, you've already had that explained to you."

"And as I already said, you guys don't mean anything to me."

"Who did? Nobody, that's who."

Beatrice thinned her lips.

"Ha!" The Coach licked a finger and scribed an invisible slash in the air. "Gotcha! Here, have a seed."

"No thank you."

He bopped her lightly in the shoulder with his fist of seeds, prodding. She looked away.

"Suit yourself. Look, you need someone to talk to. I'm the Coach so they reckoned I ought to come see if I couldn't help you out of the jam you're in."

"Go away."

"Can't. Not till I make my pitch."

"I'm not listening."

"That's not my problem."

Beatrice sighed and faced him, reluctance staining her face. "So why'd you get sent? I'm sure there were lots of other Yankees."

"Are you askin' why me? You mean to say you're askin' why—" Indignant, he loaded another seed, bit, and spit. "—me? Shoot. You're right. I ain't nobody. I only coached the damn New York Yanks to ten pennants and seven World Series Championships, five of 'em in a row, mind you, in just twelve seasons. I know that don't make much of a hill of beans compared to the excitin' life you lived. So excuse the hell out of me, sister. There ain't much I could tell a big wheel like you."

She shrugged. "So congratulations. You had a great life. You want me to applaud?"

"No thanks. I've had me enough applause."

"Good."

"Though I did make one slip-up."

Beatrice sighed. "I guess I'm supposed to ask you what it was?"

"That'd be good."

"Okay. What was it?"

"I coached the Mets for two years."

"Whatever."

"Even so, I figured I'd take a whack at you. Get you fired up on your feet and ready to charge right up the path into the light and move on. You know. Coach you into it."

"Fine. I got time. Take your shot. Coach."

"Good girl." He pointed up the way to the glow. Just gazing at it Beatrice sensed the welcome, like the warmth of a hearth.

"See that yonder? When you're done with your life, you go back there. You remember all your past lives. You admit all your mistakes, you put together all your wisdoms. Up there you're a by-God angel!"

He jabbed the crooked finger at her. "But sittin' right here, hangin' on like some barnacle between life and death, what are you? You given that any thought? In case you haven't, I'll tell you what you are. No offense but you're a piece of spinach stuck in Heaven's front teeth. You're a stubborn, spiteful, lonely ghost, an ex–butt shaker who had a few bad breaks early on, then screwed up the rest of her life and now wants to slam the barn door after the mule is gone."

He rattled his fistful of sunflower seeds. Some spilled from his grip and rolled, gray spots on the ray of light.

"Your whole time down there you dodged love like it was the dadburn plague. You had your shots. You know it's true."

"Kiss my ass."

"I would, sister, but I ain't got the fifty bucks."

Smiling, the Coach paused to enjoy the feel, if not the crack, of a solid hit. He marked up another slash in the air.

He asked, "How 'bout that fella in Dallas wanted to marry you?"

"He was a pimp. And a lawyer."

"Oh, pshaw! He wanted to mend his ways. But no. He wouldn't do for Ms. Bea Sting! You was too high and mighty. And there was that time in Baton Rouge when you was seventeen. What was that boy's name? Bob."

"That was my cousin."

"Second cousin. Done all the time in Loozy-anna. But no. You was too good for him too. Mike in Miami."

"A cop."

"A helluva good man."

"He arrested me."

"Five times. Hated to do it every time. He told you so. Anyway, you get the point. What about your family?"

"Like I told the last Yankee, I don't want to talk about it."

"Yeah, well, this Yankee ain't gonna talk about just what *you* want to talk about. Now what about your family? When are you gonna stop blamin' them for the life you led? So your mama died when you was twelve. You're all drippy over how tough your own life was, how about some sympathy for hers too, for the pain she felt instead of blamin' her for leaving you so quick."

"She was a drunk."

"Probably. But she cared about you, sure enough."

"I don't remember."

"That's convenient. And when are you gonna forgive your daddy?"

Beatrice spread her arms. "Forgive him? Forgive that son of a bitch?"

She started to stand but the Coach put out his hands to signal her to stay seated on the path. He didn't want to deal with Beatrice on her feet.

She wailed. "He started knocking on my door when I was ten. What'd you want me to do? Shoot the bastard when he came into my room? Mama died and I put up with it for three more years until I couldn't take it anymore and I ran away. Alright? You tell me what else I could've done?"

The Coach rubbed his chin, deepening the wrinkles of his cheeks, his skin so rubbery and loose his face took on a clown's rictus.

"Sweetheart, I ain't sayin' you had no easy choices. Runnin' away from your daddy mighta been for the best, who knows. What I'm climbin' on you about is how you kept on runnin'. Runnin' from your heart your whole dang life. Never let anyone catch up to you, never let tenderness lay a glove on you. You bartered love, sold it, despised it, ducked it, when all the time it was just waitin' for you to pull up and rest for a bit. I know your mama died hard and your daddy messed with you but twenty and thirty years later you were still carryin' them two things like scars from a whippin'. No ma'am, we all got to step up and take responsibility for our happiness just as much as we do for our sadness. But you never did, pure and simple. Sad, sad, sad is all you ever were. And now look at you. Pitiful. Sittin' here on your beam of light, whinin' all of a sudden about how much you want love in life."

The Coach tossed another seed into his mouth.

"That ain't how it works. You're supposed to do the work before you die, sister."

Beatrice held out a flat, empty hand.

"Let me get this straight," she said. "Tearing me a new asshole is supposed to make me want to follow you into the light? Did this approach work with the Yankees? You're some coach."

"Damn right it worked. And it ought to work with you too. You need a new asshole. That's what you get up there, you dang fool! Up there you get a brand-new everything! You want love? Come with me. You'll get it. More'n you can imagine."

"I want to be loved down there. That's where I failed. Just like you said."

"Down there?" The Coach pushed his tongue at a seed stuck to his lower lip. "That's the bush leagues. I'm talkin' about the Show. The Big Time!" He pointed again up the way to the glory, the radiance. "I'm talkin' about that!"

The Coach pulled in his arms which, in their flailing, had twisted his robe. He straightened himself as best he could then got flustered and continued.

"Look, sister. What I'm telling you is the truth. It's what we all do when we finish life. But no. You got a different idea. You got to mess with the rules. You got to sit here jerkin' around with that woman down there."

"What did you mean when you said she was fucked and I was the one fucking her?"

"Did you hear what that doctor has in store for her? Spinal fluid taps and drugs and the nuthouse? All because of you and your meddling. You are sending that woman into hell. And that's not something you have the right to do."

"Then why don't you stop me? If I'm breaking all the rules, why don't *they* stop me? Why am I getting zapped in and out of her like I have been? Why do I watch everything through her eyes? Who is she to me? What's the link? You're the Coach. You run the team. Tell me what's going on?"

"Nothing I can do if you won't come into the light with me."

"I can't. I deserve another chance."

The Coach sputtered. "Who are you . . ."

He turned from her and glared behind him up the path to the light; he lifted his hand back to Beatrice, as if to entreat the light, "See this? See what you're asking me to put up with here?"

He finished his thought and looked down at her. "Who are you to say what you deserve? What you deserve, sister, is what you're being offered. Heaven."

She said nothing.

"Then," the Coach said, "I can't help you."

"Can't or won't?"

"All the same."

The Coach rose, quicker than he had sat. His robe fell in cleaner folds than before, he appeared younger preparing to return himself into the light.

"The only thing I can do is tell you what I would do in your shoes. I'd stop. Right now, on a dime. I'd stand up and follow me if I was you."

"And if I stay here?"

"Then you'd best tell Virgil what's going on."

"Why?"

"Well, first of all, that was your A material last night in the motel. You were damn good. Better'n you ever were for pay, I'll say that."

"You watched?"

"Honey, we watch everything. Even you."

"Well, what's wrong with me giving him a good time. She sure as hell hasn't done it for him in a while."

"Just how do you know that?"

She made a pinched face.

"It used to be my job to know, okay? Come on, what's so bad about me letting old Virgil get laid? It might do their marriage some good."

"Well, it might, you silly ass, if it'd been his wife he was jumpin' around on the mattress with. But it wasn't. It was *you*. A pro! He was just thinking it was his wife." The Coach lowered his voice, "He was just hopin'."

"So."

Exasperated, the Coach looked away as though following the flight of a moth darting around his head. He brought his eyes back to bear on her.

"So? You liked it! You laid there squirming on your back dreamin' about what it would be like to have all this oohin' and cooin' and la-de-da for yourself."

Beatrice covered her gasp with her hands. "You can read my thoughts?"

"For the love of Mike, sister, I can read your dang face! You were grinning like you just stole home plate! You got this idea stuck in your skull that you want love on Earth and you figure this might be just the unsuspecting fella to give it to you. There's just one big problem."

"And that is?"

"You're gonna have to take him away from his wife." The Coach raised a finger. "You're pulling these two people apart. Sure as shootin' that's what you're doin'."

"They were already apart when I got there."

"Whoa, sister. That ain't your call to make. Love's a damn difficult thing to spot sometimes, like a good curveball. You think it's comin' right down the pipe, you take a good cut and then, whuff, there she goes a foot off the plate and you're standin' there twisted up like a pretzel and looking like a dumb shit. Besides, what do you know? What makes you think you're qualified to tell whether or not those two ain't in some kind of love or other? You couldn't spot love if it stood up in your soup. Maybe their love is just hibernating. Maybe it's just takin' a break."

"And maybe not," Beatrice obstinately said. "Look, I won't be the first woman to take away somebody's husband."

"You'd be the first dead one."

She pursed her lips.

"Look here," the Coach said. "You got one

choice if you're gonna hang around out here on the path and that is you got to tell Virgil. It's his life. It's his decision what to do about you if you won't go away."

"He won't believe me."

"It's still his decision. Let him make it."

The Coach was right, she thought. Besides, if Beatrice really wanted Virgil to fall for her, he had to know. It wouldn't work otherwise. Both times in bed when he'd called her the endearment "Ellie," it had evicted Beatrice right back up here. She'd have to find a way to ease him into it.

"But isn't telling him against the rules too?"

The Coach pinched his face back at her. "Can't say." He took a step back. "Beatrice?"

"Yeah, Coach?"

"Come with me. We love you."

"Thanks but no."

He sighed. "Well, they warned me you was stubborn. I guess I believe it now."

He took another step back. The light seemed nearer as if it had taken a stride forward.

"Coach?"

"Yes?"

"Give me a break with the Yankees, okay?"

"I'll see what I can do."

"One more thing?"

"Yes?"

"Is there really a plan?"

"Yes, Beatrice, there's a plan. . . ."

She said the rest with him, ". . . There always is."

The Coach turned fully to the light and in silhouette lifted his arms in a way to suggest he was politely asking the light to dance.

"And no matter what you do," he said, rising to his toes, shuffling his feet, turning at the shoulders, "you're always a part of it."

The spilled sunflower seeds where the Coach had sat faded and disappeared. Beatrice's floating image of life reappeared. Inside it Dr. Lowe said again, "The latter would be cheaper but I wouldn't recommend it."

Beatrice rotated for a moment to check in with the vision.

Satisfied she had lost no part of the goings-on, she turned her eyes to the light where the Coach had waltzed away.

The many green islands of the Keys are sewn together by a black tarmac ribbon over oyster white bridges. On the map they describe a connect-the-dots whip at the tip of Florida, snapping westward and upside-down. They are hardpan coral peaks battered by sun, wind and Atlantic and Gulf hurricanes. The people who call them home cling to them like anemones, pride is their spiny stickum. The people are typically hard-nosed and leather tanned, jocular and insular; the islands are isolated and the inhabitants, who call themselves "conchs" after the drab crabs who live in pastel shells, are seasoned to it. They are aware that they are on their own. Conchs are tough bones Nature cannot chew through.

Ellen, a native, knew the names of all the cays. She reveled usually in telling Virgil which one was next on their infrequent drives to Miami, and then again in reverse on the way back home; names which slip off the tongue as tropical names often do—Largo, Tavernier, Matecumbe, Vaca, Marathon, Bahia Honda, Cudjoe, then as you approach the terminus, the blander English trader names, Big Coppitt, Stock Island, Key West.

Ellen had stayed close-lipped since leaving Homestead on the mainland and they had sped out onto the sapphire waters beneath Highway 1. She did not say, "Largo," the first island, but stared out the window for an hour, not as though she were going home but as if leaving forever. Virgil told her everything would be alright, Dr. Lowe had more tests to do and something simple would surely turn up as the answer so don't worry. Ellen responded with breaths and nods.

On Islamorada, Virgil stopped at the Coral Grill Restaurant and Bowling Center, Ellen's favorite eatery in the Keys. The Coral Grill featured a nightly buffet: shrimp thick as thumbs, soft roast beef and chicken for which no knife was needed, big-game fish hooked in waters one mile away, au gratin potatoes, steaming asparagus, pale sweet pastas, a dessert tray not of cafeteria cheap cakes but the good stuff, fluffy and creamy. Ellen seemed cheered. She loaded her plate with grilled pompano, prawns, potato salad, buttered green beans and breads.

"Virgil," she said at the table, fitting in a fork-

ful of fish, "thank you. It has been one awful day.
I feel better."

"Good." Virgil concentrated on his roast beef.

Ellen wiped her mouth and laid the napkin on
the table. "Now, it may not be the best time to talk
about this, but I can't think of when there will be a
good time because this is all happening so fast. So."

"I don't think we have to do this."

"We have to consider the store."

"I'm not sure that's what I'm worrying about
right now."

"Well, you'd best start. If I'm going to be sick,
if I'm going to be in and out of hospitals and
loony bins until I can beat this, then you've got to
run things."

"Ellen, you're not going to any loony bins.
Stop this."

"Virgil, you're not the one who missed Plantation Key entirely on the drive down. I am. It was
just gone. We were on Tavernier and now here we
are in Islamorada. Plantation Key is in between
them. Always has been. Fifteen, twenty minutes of
my life. Poof. Missing. This isn't happening to
you. It's happening to me. I don't know what it is
but I do know it's not simple. It isn't going to go
away just with a pill or some group therapy session.
Now honestly, when have you ever known me not
to buck up and take on a problem head on?"

"Never."

"Thank you. I'm calling Dr. Lowe tomorrow
to make arrangements to check myself into one of
those psychiatric wards he was talking about.

Then I'll call the insurance and see how much they're willing to pay for all this. After that, you and I need to discuss how much we can afford because even though I would prefer a private hospital, I don't want to get myself cured just to come home and find out we're ruined financially. Life will go on after this, Virgil. It always does."

"I think you're moving a bit fast."

"I didn't want you to know this but the blackouts are getting longer. Do you want me to wait until you're dealing with the crazy me for whole days and weeks? No, it's got to be tomorrow. It's settled. Now, we have to talk about the business. You're going to have to run it while I'm away, you know that. That means more hours. More responsibilities. That means keeping a closer eye and a tighter rein on Woody."

Virgil pushed his fork at some spinach leaves on his plate. Low-fat Thousand Island dressing and the guts of a last tomato slice formed a pinkish gore.

Ellen stood with her plate held out in both hands. "I'm going for seconds. When I get back, we'll discuss the particulars. There are some accounts I need you to pay special attention to. Alright? Can I bring you some more shrimp?"

"I'm fine."

"Yes, you are," she said, swiveling for the burgeoning buffet tables. "You're the lucky one."

Virgil finished his iced tea. For a time he rubbed his fingertips coated with the cold sweat from the glass into his eye sockets.

"Fuck," he spoke into his palm. "Fuck."

"Virgil?"

He lifted his head out of his hands.

She said, "You look tired."

"I am, a little."

Her plate of seconds was a portion of cottage cheese and a small mound of fresh fruits.

"Can I get you some fruit? Pineapple is good for a headache."

"No. I'm fine."

She settled slowly into her chair. She arranged the napkin prettily in her lap. "I always hear you saying that. You're fine. Are you, Virgil? Are you fine?"

He nodded.

"It's just that you don't ever ask for much. You're always fine. What do you want, Virgil? What about you? Ask for it."

"You don't have to do this. I'm—"

"Fine," she answered for him, "yes, I know."

She leaned over to scrape some fruit onto his plate.

"Eat some. I can't finish it."

She forked a pear slice and put it in her mouth. She bit only half and laid the fork down.

"What do you want from me, Virgil? You're a good man. You should have what you want. Tell me."

"Nothing."

"You want lots of things. You want me to lose weight. You want me to be a better lover, more like we've been the last couple days. You want me to think less about the store and more about our marriage. You might even want me to give you a divorce."

Virgil gaped. "No. I . . . we . . ."

She continued. "This whole sickness thing came at a bad time for you, didn't it? Yeah, I've been watching, you were getting antsy. You're still a good-looking man, got your education, and here you are trapped with an overweight workaholic chick you never bargained for. You were getting no sex at all for a long time and you started figuring maybe you'd like to get yourself a little something on the side or maybe even slip out of this marriage altogether. You could make it on your own, though sometimes you like to act like you couldn't. Then all of a sudden we start having a little electricity in the sack, you get your hopes up again and then, wham, I up and get this storm brewing in my head and you don't know what to think, leave me or stay. Except you can't leave me with this going on because it's not the sort of thing Virgil would do. No, sir. Virgil is loyal. You had some misfortune in your life and I helped you out of it. You'll do the same for me. You'll make sure I'm okay, and until I am you'll forget all about the things that you want for yourself out of this marriage. You'll just suffer along quietly until ol' Ellen gets better, and who knows how long that could take. And once she's better, you've still got no guarantee that things will improve between the two of you. Well, I don't want you to forget about the things you want, Virgil. I want us to keep having a good time together, great times even. I promise I'll get better fast. I promise to work on the weight. I promise we'll keep having fun in bed, whenever we can. And we'll spend less time at the store. Hell, if they can train dogs we can train Woody. He's not so bad. If he can sell cocaine, he can sell a paintbrush. Woody can spell us once in a while, can't he?"

Virgil held his head cocked to one side in disbelief. "I guess so."

"Good. And I'm sorry I've waited so long to tell you all this. You know what? Tomorrow, let's close the shop and hang out at the beach. I love the beach."

Virgil brightened. "I know. I wondered why we stopped going."

"Yeah, me too. And let's take Woody. He'll be fun."

"But you said tomorrow you were checking into a psych ward."

"Did I say that?"

Virgil nodded.

She snapped her fingers. "Damn! I'll tell you, Virgil, this is getting really weird. I must have blacked out again. Why would I say that? Sweetie, that must have been the crazy me talking again. No, no, that plan's off. Forget it. You and I can whip this thing, the two of us. And look, Virgil, honey, no matter what I might say about checking myself into a nuthouse, you stop me. Okay? Do not let me leave you."

She lifted the rest of the pear slice and followed it with a dainty scoop of cottage cheese.

"Ellen?"

"Uh-huh?"

"You're eating left-handed."

She set the fork down fast. It rang her alarm on the plate.

The two stared at each other like two sides of a mirror, separate but tied, one not moving until the other moved.

Virgil raised his hand slowly in a timid greeting. She raised hers back, the reflection.

Virgil waited. She waited.

He spoke.

"Who are you?"

No answer. She licked her lips.

"You're not Ellen. Who are you?"

Again no answer.

"Are you 'bee sting'?"

She lifted the fork to dig up a small mound of wet curds. Chewing, she said, "It's spelled with an 'a.'"

"What is? 'Stang?' 'Bee stang?'"

She giggled. "No, you goof. Try again."

"The 'bee.' You mean B-E-A?"

She closed her lips around another forkful of cottage cheese. She held the fork still, as if deciding whether or not to swallow, her eyes locked at an odd distance. Then, with a suddenness that surprised Virgil, she snapped out of the pause and pulled the fork from her mouth and gagged. Bits of cottage cheese clung to her tongue; it looked diseased and spotted.

She grabbed for her water glass and gulped.

"Aaak," she made a show of it, "I hate cottage cheese."

Virgil gave her a lopsided, quizzical gaze while she took in the riddles around her: the unfamiliar food on her plate, the fork in the wrong hand, the conundrum of fractured time.

"Oh, Jesus," she said, shaking her head. "Jesus, this has got to stop." She pointed at Virgil, as if he were the one who had stolen her time.

"There," she wielded the pointing finger, "you see? You *see*?"

Under a full moon, flowing beneath the bridges linking the Keys, the tides are strong. Here the Gulf of Mexico and the Atlantic Ocean merge and swap waters like lovers. Always under such a moon the catwalks of the bridges glow with the kerosene lamps of shrimpers who cast flotation nets to snare the clouds of sea meat dragged out of the grass into the swift current. Hauling in their nets, they shine flashlights down into them to see the red-dot eyes of the squirming shrimp. They boil their catch alive in pots of bay seasoning on Bunsen burners and sip beer from coolers. Virgil was one set of headlights speeding past them. The blue butane fires, yellow lanterns, stars above the fretted waters, he drove through the many dim lights and the silent night, only wind whispering over his windows, only tires rubbing the road, only Ellen's arms strait-jacketed around herself and her closed eyes for company.

Seven Mile Bridge arched ahead. During the

day, its crest held the most beautiful blue view in the Keys, of turquoise glass in all directions broken by spatters of clouds, sandbar bottoms and scattered wooded reefs. At night, because there was nothing to see but murky waters and moon dapples, Seven Mile Bridge was a fright, it was high enough to leap from and die.

Approaching the apex of the bridge, she said without releasing her arms from herself, "Please stop the car."

"I can't. There's no shoulder up here."

"Stop the car. Just for a minute."

He pulled as far to the right as he could; traffic slid around him, some honked. She reached into the backseat for the bunch of flowers he'd presented her upon leaving the hospital. She slipped out of the narrow gap between her open door and the concrete bridge.

She stood at the railing, staring out over the dark Gulf. Virgil turned on the car's flashers then clambered out. He stood beside her.

"What are you doing?"

She divided the bouquet into parts. She cast out one clump of long-stemmed daisies. They dropped from sight the moment after she opened her hand as though the darkness were more hungry for the blooms than the water far below.

"That's for the dead," she said gazing down.

Carefully, thoughtfully, she separated another bunch.

"And that," she said, flinging the flowers with a left-handed toss, grunting with the effort she put into the heave, "that's for the living. Like you, Virgil."

She did not throw the remaining handful of flowers but let them tumble from her fingers one at a time. They followed one another into the night like parachutists.

These she did not dedicate. Virgil asked for whom they were meant.

"Those," she said without meeting his eyes, "are for me."

Virgil took her arm and gently tugged her around to face him.

"Bea?" he asked. "With an 'a'?"

She smiled and patted his chest.

"Get in the car, Virgil. You don't want to be standing out here on the bridge when Ellen gets back."

6

HE tried to drive without looking at the road.

"Watch the highway," she chided. "I didn't turn green. My head's not spinning around, is it?"

"No."

She flicked a finger at the windshield. "Then watch where you're going."

Virgil put his eyes forward but stole furtive glimpses at her, his head jerking like a barn owl's.

"Who are you?"

"I told you. Bea. Beatrice, actually. But call me Bea."

"Are you my wife?"

"Is your wife's name Bea?"

"No."

She leaned against the door and tucked a leg under her. "Then I'm not your wife."

Virgil was driving thirty miles per hour down the back slope of Seven Mile Bridge.

"You're gonna cause an accident." She swung her hand at the road. "Speed up!"

He stepped on the accelerator.

"Look. This is going to be hard for you to believe. I barely believe it myself. I'm trying to ease us both into this. Now stay with me, okay? Don't drive off the bridge when I tell you."

Virgil squeezed his hands on the wheel. He glanced once at her then stared at the road.

"Okay." He swallowed. "Go ahead."

"You're okay?"

He nodded.

"Okay." She bit her lower lip. "Listen to me. Whatever you do, don't let Ellen put herself in a mental hospital. She's not a lunatic."

This was Ellen's voice. Ellen's lips moving with the words, Ellen's leg curled under Ellen's rear. Referring to herself as "Ellen."

"No offense . . . uh . . . Bea, but Ellen sounds crazy."

"She's not."

"Then what is she?"

"Virgil?"

"Yes?"

"Hold on."

"I'm holding."

A dark, silent moment hung in the car as if from a noose. "Her body's being possessed. By me. I'm dead."

Virgil swerved to avoid the side of the bridge.

"Damn it!" she huffed through gnashed teeth. The tires squealed.

"Ahhhhhhh!" she screamed. Then a moment later, she said, "Oh, shut up."

"I got it, I got it," said Virgil, "don't holler like that."

"I didn't. The second one was your wife."

"Ellen?"

"She's gone right now."

"Gone where?"

"I don't know."

"You don't know?"

"Virgil, look, you're going simple on me. Do us both a favor. Be quiet and let me explain. I don't know how long I'll be in this time so let me get it all out. Okay? And keep your eyes on the road. If we have an accident, it won't be me that gets killed."

He nodded tensely. He clutched the wheel, leaning to the steering column like a near-sighted codger.

She inhaled through her nose, releasing the breath with the words.

"I died two days ago in St. Joseph's Hospital in Key West. Since then, and I swear I do not know why, I've been zooming in and out of your wife at the strangest times."

He looked at her; she gestured again for him to turn his head back to the road.

"There's no rhyme or reason to when I come and go. None I can figure, anyway. But the facts are these: I'm here now, I'll be gone any second, and I reckon I'll be back."

The bridge stretched one more mile over silvered waters to the solid ground of Key West. The nearing of the city, the relative calm in Ellen's tone despite her insanity, the woman's nonthreatening posture against the door, all worked to lighten his grip on the wheel. He sat back in the seat.

"Ellen?"

"Still Bea, Virg."

"Okay. Bea?"

"Yeah?"

"Where . . . uh . . . where are you?"

She answered quietly, "I'm right here."

"No. I mean . . ." He trod lightly; he didn't know exactly what he was doing asking her questions. Maybe he could elicit some more delusional information the doctors might later deem useful. He was keeping her distracted until he could get Ellen home where she would snap out of it. He was proving to her that he was harmless and a friend like some cautious missionary who's happened upon his first cannibals. "I mean, where are you when you aren't . . . uh . . . you know . . . here?"

She said it with confidence, loyal to the notion, as if it were very, very true. "I'm in the light."

"You're in Heaven?"

"No." She inclined her head, sad. "Just the light."

He looked at her. His wife's long blond lashes were down.

The bridge ended. He drove in silence while the island's buildings grew on all sides.

Finally, he asked, "Aren't you supposed to go to the light?"

She spoke quickly. "No, you're not."

Surprised, for he was sure all the pop books on the topic were explicit—you die and you're supposed to go to the light—he asked, "Why not?"

"Because," she insisted, "we live down that street. Don't you know where you are? Take a right. A *right*."

Virgil hauled on the steering wheel to make the turn in time.

"My stars," she gushed around clamped teeth.

Peevishly, Ellen put a hand to her breast to monitor a mock heart attack.

Ellen flipped open a suitcase on the bed. It lay there splayed wide, a leather mouth the size and gray of a hippo's jowls. The thing even had a red lining for the gums and tongue. Ellen folded garments neatly and fed the maw while Virgil fidgeted in the rocker beside the bed.

Ferrying clothes from the dresser to the suitcase, Ellen prattled. "I'm mostly taking underwear. I don't think I'll have much call for pretty dresses there except when you come to visit. I'll bet they make us wear those ugly blue gowns with the tie string in the back. Ugh, I can just see us, a bunch of crazy women sitting around trying to talk to each other about our feelings and such when all we can really think about is how awful we look. The one good thing, you know, is I'll be able to drop some of this weight you've been on me about. I'm sure the food will be just dreadful."

Virgil read her anxious chatter, neat busy hands, her brave face. She appeared excited, even eager, over the prospect of a stay in a mental hospital. What did she think was going to happen? The hardships and stigma, the curtailments on her freedom that were so uncomfortable for Virgil to contemplate, seemed to fill Ellen with song like birds flocking in a tree. She chirped about how much better she was going to feel, how slim she would be again, how happy and productive would be their relationship again when she got out. It didn't faze her to be crazy; craziness was like some Girl Scout badge to show how hard she'd worked, she'd dedicated everything to her business and her marriage. Something in her head had just given out under the wear and tear. Now all she needed was a tune-up, like a car. Tighten this, lube that, replace this, and snap!

She closed the suitcase. "When I get out, Virgil, you are going to be so pleased with me."

She put a warm hand on his cheek.

He realized his silence in the face of her remark was a tacit statement that he was unhappy with her now. She knew this and pressed the hand to his cheek, smiling down at him. He wanted to tell her to stay home with him, keep every promise she'd made him yesterday in the restaurant, get better at his side instead of in a hospital, lose weight, work less, have more sex and fun, but these were things her other personality had promised and she didn't know what she'd said, how wonderful it all sounded. And he couldn't tell her, just as he couldn't say how badly he needed these things not from a delusion but from his wife.

He covered her hand with his and held it against his cheek. "You're going to be fine again, Ellen."

"Yes, I am." She nodded firmly, the strong Key West vigor in her eyes, of storms and sunny days ahead. "Now, carry that downstairs. I'm going to take my shower. Then we'll spend our last night together for a while."

An hour later, Ellen lay growling in her sleep. Some breathing mechanism in her was always out of alignment when she slept, no matter how she rolled or contorted. Her hair was clammy from the shower, the smell of conditioner was acrid to Virgil's nose on the pillows. He got out of bed.

He sat in his rocker and propped his feet on the mattress. The full moon projected a pearlescent square through the window onto the bedspread. He watched the clock change hours. Outside, palm fronds riffled on the trades and the few early pedestrian foot-clicks waxed and faded on the sidewalk; their echoes of aloneness became huge when they entered the bedroom and Virgil on his vigil felt akin in his own isolation. The box of moonlight crept along Ellen's covered form until it slid up the headboard and he fell asleep in the chair.

He had a dream, another one of the dreams of longing excellence, but this time the instrument at his command was not one of music or strange erotomaniacal women, it was his wife. She was not the puffy Ellen who lay before him in the real bed but was instead an idealized image of the young woman he'd first met four years ago; Ellen's dream body was a sharpened shape of bronze, shoulders and waist chiseled, her belly button a taut thimble to fill with saliva and sweat. He touched the dream-Ellen and his fingertips and tongue brought hunger to everything, she was afire, he smelled her rich vapors, the odor of her burning jungle, she was lush and feral and hot and she wanted him.

He opened his eyes. Daylight in the room. Steam from a cup of black coffee curled under his nose.

"Hello," she said, holding the mug. She looked into his lap and twittered. "And good morning to you too, sir."

Virgil yanked his feet from the bed. He closed the gap in his boxer shorts, tucking himself in.

He cleared his throat, mumbled quickly, "Morning," took the coffee and rocked back so she would retreat.

Virgil sipped and stretched his stiff ankles and knees. Ellen sat on the edge of the bed. It wasn't Ellen, the peculiar racy smile told him so.

She spoke. "She knew you weren't in bed with her. She woke up twice in the night and saw you just sitting there and didn't do a damn thing about it. That is some shit, Virgil. Your last night together in bed and she just lets you sleep in a rocker."

Virgil kept the coffee held under his nose; he spoke with his lips behind the dark warmth of the cup. "Good morning, Bea."

She smiled and nodded grandly.

To bridge the silence, he continued. "You're up awful early."

Her smile widened. She pointed to his lap. "So're you."

He lowered the cup, a fig leaf to hide his embarrassment. "So," he cleared his throat again, "what can I do for you?"

She sat up sharply. Her smile fell.

"Aw, Virg, don't treat me like that. I'm not some traveling salesman from the beyond dropping by to sell you something. I'm just a poor dead chick who's trying to figure things out. Same as you, except you're not dead."

"Uh-huh." He waited; she just looked at him. "What are you trying to figure out?"

"Lots of stuff. Like why I'm here talking to you. Why Ellen's the one I'm stuck inside. Why I come and go at the most ridiculous times. And there's other things that aren't my business, but I wonder about 'em all the same."

A quiet alarm buzzed inside Virgil to remind him that he was conversing with his wife's psychosis. But even if she was an alternate personality, she seemed personable. He sipped, good strong coffee, glue to hold a frayed morning together.

"Like what?"

"Like, for instance, how a guy like you ended

up so unhappy. I know how it happened to me, but not you."

"Let's not talk about me."

"Yeah," she laughed, "that's right, I forgot. I'm the interesting one. I'm the one who's a delusion."

She skidded backward, jamming her legs under the covers. She fluffed a pillow and lay back.

"Just in case your wife shows up. I don't want to freak her out this morning. You can tell her she just woke up."

"That's smart."

"Yeah. I'm not too bad. Anyway, let's look at what we've got here. I'm dead and unhappy."

"You're not dead."

"Can you be sure about that?"

"Of course."

"Ah," she lifted her left hand, her tone musical, inscrutable, "we'll see about that. Anyway," she repeated, "I'm dead and unhappy. You're alive and unhappy."

"I didn't say that."

"Trust me, honey, I can spot 'em. You're unhappy. What happened to you?"

"Nothing."

"Then why does Ellen keep mentioning some accident you had? Why were you living at Woody's halfway house when you and her met? That's work release, Virg. I know about this stuff. You did time."

"I did time."

"For what?"

"I killed a woman. It was an accident. I was drinking."

"What'd you serve?"

"Four years. Out of ten."

"You must have been a good boy inside."

"Good enough."

"And Ellen took you in. Gave you a job. Gave you some respectability back. And you were grateful."

"Yes."

"Seemed like the thing to do for a con just getting back on his feet."

"We were in love."

"Were?"

Virgil owed no reply to a delusion.

She asked, "How about now?"

He paused, then said, "How about it?"

"Looks like you've stopped being so grateful." She raised a hand off her stomach. "Look, thanks for telling me about the accident. I appreciate that. I know about tough breaks."

He waited again. He said, "What about you? You said you were unhappy. About what?"

"Oh, no no," she said, "we'll do me another time. For now, let's just agree that we've got things in common. Neither of us has ended up where we'd hoped we would. Me, especially, seeing as how I'm dead.

"So," she continued, her tone cheerier, "we're both looking for something other than what we got. Me up there, you down here. Then suddenly, with no explanation, boom, I'm here. I could have ended up inside a nun or some farm girl in Iowa but I'm here, in your house, in your wife. What does that tell us?"

"I don't know."

She smacked her lips. "Me neither. I keep getting told up there that there's a plan. That's it. Then they act like they don't know what the plan is."

She paused to point a finger to the ceiling. She said with intrigue, "But I think they do."

Virgil set his coffee on the floor.

"That's enough." He worked his hands in front of him like he was waving off traffic. "Snap out of it. Ellen? Do you hear me?"

"Virgil, you snap out of it. She doesn't hear you. Get that through your head. Ellen doesn't remember anything that happens when I'm inside her."

Virgil stood. "Stop that! You're not inside her. You're Ellen. Cut it out! Ellen?"

She sat up on the bed. "Listen to me."

He put his hands on his hips. He looked out the window; no answers there, just the normal world that had lately turned so unearthly. He dropped himself back into the rocker, elbows on his knees, poised to spring again to his feet.

"Look at you," she said, "like you're mad at me or something."

"I don't need this, Ellen."

"Bea, babe. It's Bea. Look, aren't you even curious what the big cosmic plan is? Why all this is happening to you and me? I sure am. Come on, you must be."

He sat stonily.

She wheedled. "A little?"

No response. She continued.

"Look, if you let Ellen leave here today, this is all over. She's gone and I'm gone with her. So before she goes, I only have one thing to ask. Give me a little time to prove what I'm saying is so. If I can't convince you, then you can zip her up in a baggy and ship both of us off to the funny farm. What the hell, maybe I'll meet a nice doctor. But right now I like you and I want to stay around. Virgil, maybe the plan they keep talking about up there in the light isn't just for me. Maybe it's for you too. You know? Maybe I was picked for you."

Virgil blinked at Bea's admission.

"You like me?"

"Yeah. What's not to like? I've seen plenty of you."

"How?"

"Here's the way it works. Even when I'm not here inside Ellen, I'm up there watching and listening to everything she does. I'm with her non-stop. It's a trip."

Virgil sat back. The rocker creaked his confusion.

"Come on, Virg, let me hang around. We'll figure it out together. Maybe have some fun along the way."

He stood. "No."

He put out both hands to stop her from getting up. "Just lie there, just . . . just close your eyes, let her wake up." He went to the bedroom door. "I need to . . ."

He glared at Ellen. Bea. "Don't . . ."

He hurried from the room, speaking to the flying steps, "Just . . ."

Ellen looked at the clock. She pulled back the covers and jumped out of bed.

"Oh hell, the morning's half gone." She stripped off her nightgown to pull on jeans and a sweatshirt. She called downstairs for Virgil who did not answer.

She put her hair up in a loose bun and rumbled down the steps. Coffee was made; it was too strong and she ran tap water to cut it. She drank the cup, poured another, doused it with more water and took the mug to her desk to sit with the phone book open.

Ellen called their family insurance agent. She told him in a straightforward manner that she intended to commit herself to a psychiatric facility.

"It's been coming on for some time, I expect," she said.

He was surprised and expressed his regrets over her troubles.

"Oh, I'll be alright," she said, "just need to catch my breath, that's all."

The agent asked if this action were being taken on the advice of a physician; it would make it easier for him to secure benefits. It was, she answered,

Dr. John Lowe in Miami. She would call Dr. Lowe's office and have them fax to the agent the particulars of her condition and the doctor's recommendations. She would like to have all the details wrapped up this morning, she said. She'd already set her mind and had a bag packed by the door. He promised to call back as soon as he got the fax and could contact his underwriter in Chicago.

Ellen called Dr. Lowe's office next and gave them the agent's name and fax number. She told them as well that she had a bag packed by the door and was ready to go as soon as Virgil returned to drive her to St. Joseph's where she would check in to the psychiatric wing and begin those tests the doctor had mentioned. She wanted this thing licked and lickety-split, she quipped to the nurse. Then she would like to have Dr. Lowe find her a spot in a nice private facility in Miami near him so he could keep an eye on her progress. The nurse flattered Ellen's desire for recovery, added that Dr. Lowe was the most brilliant and wonderful man in his field, sighed dreamily, and said she'd get right on it.

Ellen changed into a denim smock over a cream blouse with blue canvas flats. She brushed out her hair and left the bathroom.

In the kitchen, she poured more coffee and diluted it again. She reached into the refrigerator for two eggs, butter and white bread. She closed the door, then reached back inside for one more egg.

"Great," Beatrice flung at the image, "fucking great! Look at this. Four cups of coffee. Butter. White flour and three fried eggs. That's not nutrition, that's a loaded gun."

Slathering jelly on the toast—"Sugar!" bellowed Beatrice, "Ah, you're killin' me!" Then she laughed at the sorry pun—Ellen in the image asked aloud, "Wonder where he is." Beatrice, now in the role of viewer of a quiz show playing along at home with the TV, answered, "He went out for a walk. We scared the shit out of him." Ellen munched the toast and flipped the eggs just for a second, to eat them runny. "Ugh," Beatrice grimaced, watching the yolk stream yellow tar over the china plate. Beatrice looked up the glowing path to the light. She pointed back to the hovering vision. "I hope you guys are watching this," she called out, "because bad eating habits is how half of you croaked."

Ellen finished breakfast, ran water on the dishes and left them in the sink. Upstairs she brushed her teeth. She returned to her desk and sat gazing into the hallway at her suitcase waiting by the door.

She crossed her legs and flexed the toes of the lifted leg to make the canvas shoe bounce against her heel.

A pen in her hand. She set it down. Her brow in her hand. The suitcase in the hall. She straightened a paperclip.

The phone rang. It rang again. One more time. Then Beatrice heard the phone with Ellen's ears and answered it with Ellen's hand.

"Hello? Yes, yes," she sang to the insurance agent, "that's wonderful. Thank you so much. That's very quick service. But I'll tell you what. I've changed my mind for right now. Oh, you know how these things go, they always look better if you just wait them out. I won't be leaving after all, I've decided I'm going to beat this thing here at home with Virgil. No, no, I feel wonderful but, honestly, you never know when it'll come on again. That's right, go ahead and cancel everything right now. If we need it, we'll call you first thing. Yes, I'll phone the doctor straight away. Thank you so much. I'll tell Virgil how wonderful you've been. Bye now."

Quickly Beatrice fumbled through Ellen's desk for the Miami phone book. She dialed Dr. Lowe's office and canceled arrangements there with the sweet nurse. The woman sounded touched by Ellen's courage to go it alone with her husband.

Beatrice slammed down the phone.

"Phew." She wiped her forehead in pretend exhaustion for finishing before Ellen regained control.

Beatrice carried Ellen's suitcase upstairs, tossed it on the bed and unpacked. Tucking panties into a drawer, she heard the front door open. Virgil padded up the steps, hesitance in his sneakers' stride.

He poked his head in. She did not face him but continued stowing clothes.

"Did you have a nice walk, dear?"

"Yes."

"Did you clear your head?"

"What are you doing?"

She closed the emptied valise. Snap snap. Then turned.

"Don't you mean *who* is doing?"

"Bea?"

"Bingo."

"Where's Ellen?"

"She's not here right now. May I take a message?"

Virgil glanced at his feet, the only things that made sense for him, the only things that could get him out of this situation. He looked down the steps to the open front door.

"Come in," Beatrice invited. "C'mon, sit down. Let's talk a little more. Poor baby."

She took his arm and pulled him to his rocker beside the bed.

"Go ahead," she said, bouncing back on the bed—Ellen's butt landed harder than she anticipated and she lost her balance, graceless, she'd have to pay more attention—"ask me anything. I'll tell you whatever you want to know."

Virgil gazed long at her face, inspecting; Beatrice waited. "Where's Ellen?"

"I don't know."

"I mean, where does she go when you're in her?"

"I really don't know, Virgil." Beatrice indicated the air around her.

"Tell her I want her back. We can work things out. I can't take this."

Beatrice leaned her hands on her knees. "Do you, Virgil? Do you really want her back? Be honest."

"Yes."

"I don't believe you. I think you only want her back because like you just said you don't think you can take this. But how much longer can you take what you had before? A wife who changed on you without warning to where now you wake up in a house where you get treated like a mutt she took in from the pound, giving you scraps of affection tossed in a bowl on the floor? Here, Virgil, have a little affection. That's enough, boy, I'm the only one around here who gets to overeat. Now guard the house, guard the store, watch Woody, fetch my slippers, sleep by the bed. Is that what you thought love would be, Virg? That why you married her in the first place? To be a cocker spaniel husband?"

He worked his jaw, like a man testing it after a punch.

"It's not her fault," he said. "She's been trying." Virgil pulled his eyes away from hers. "No, you're wrong. We were straightening things out."

She laughed. "What? You mean the sex?"

She watched Virgil take this in. He bit his lip. She could tell that he saw what was coming.

"Honey," she slapped her thighs, still laughing, "I hate to tell you but that wasn't 'Ellie.'"

He worked his hands on the arms of the rocker.

She nodded. "Yeah, babe. That was me."

He blinked, calculating, following a speeding and dodging channel of realization. He muttered, "Are you telling me that I . . ."

"Yes," she said kindly, "you did."

He breathed hard through his nose. He looked up now. "With . . ."

"With me. Yes. Bea Sting."

"But it . . . I . . ." He shook his head, showed his lower teeth.

Beatrice watched, fascinated. Here was a man dizzied by dervishes of conflict and emotion: disbelief blurred by a creeping suspicion that this was really happening, embarrassment tinged with uncertainty as to what exactly to be embarrassed about, dashed hopes at what looked like a setback to renewed intimacy with his wife, anger at being tricked, amazement that he might actually have been tricked by what he believed was only a hallucination—all of it mixed up with the fact that it had indeed been great damn sex, and to get more of it, he had to consider sleeping with Bea again, but he couldn't do that because Bea wasn't his wife, although, wait a minute, he could sleep with Bea because Bea was a delusion of Ellen's, but . . .

She was moved by his genuine consternation. He honestly does want to patch things up with his wife, she thought. He's a little upset, sure. That's because this is a sweet guy.

"Yes, cutey," she said, leaning to touch his knee, "you did the horizontal mambo with another woman." She waved her hand, erasing his act out of the air. "But it's okay, you didn't know you were doing it."

Still shaking his head in little tremors, Virgil said, "I don't believe this."

"Fine. Don't believe. When Ellen gets back, see if you can get her to try some of those tricks you and me did. Then talk to me."

"You're not real. You're just something in Ellen's head."

Beatrice thrust out a hip and ran her hands down Ellen's fleshy ribs and waist, the same seductive game-show-hostess move she liked to use at the beginning of her private dances.

"Oh, honey, trust me. I'm real. And I am not just in this head. I'm in the whole body."

She laughed again, cheering the room; she knew how to work her old charm, even in this ungainly framework. But Virgil was not warmed by her.

"I'm not listening to you."

Beatrice sat composed on the bed. "Oh." She sighed, still beaming allure at him because she detected that he wanted to be allured. "But just maybe you ought to. Think of it this way. What if I'm exactly what you claim I am, just another personality from somewhere deep inside Ellen's head? Then maybe I'm telling you the truth, what Ellen really thinks but can't tell you face-to-face unless she invents some wacko make-believe character named Bea Sting. Maybe I got all the right in the world to screw your brains out and do whatever because maybe I'm really just your wife, just like you say, but she's gotten so rigid and cold she can't do it anymore as Ellen, she has to come on to you as someone else, someone safe, someone dead. Or . . ."

She framed her face between her hands to mimic a television picture; she tilted her head at him and gave him a staged, toothy smile, Miss Dead America.

"Maybe I'm exactly who I say I am. Bea Sting."

"You can't be."

"Why?"

"Because it's too incredible."

Beatrice stopped her playfulness. She leaned to Virgil again and reached for both his hands. He shied but let her take them.

Quietly, knowingly, she said, "Trust me. It's not."

They sat together. She trailed her thumb over his knuckles.

"Virgil, you need to know. I canceled all her plans to go to the hospital. I called everyone and said we were putting it off. Now, when she gets back, she's still going to want to go. Please. Please don't let her. Not until I can convince you."

"Ellen, you need to go."

Ignoring his plea to the wife who was not there, Beatrice said, "And if she goes, I promise you I'll walk her right out the front door first chance I get. I'll ask 'em real nice and they'll call me a taxi. Virgil, give me one shot."

He took back his hands and put them on the armrests. He rocked back.

"And if I wanted to stop her how would I do it?" he asked. "What do I do when she finds out everything's been canceled? She'll just call everybody again and go her way. It's a voluntary committal. If she wants to go, she can go. It has nothing to do with me."

"Tell her what you really think the truth is. That she canceled everything herself. That her other personality didn't want to go. That it wanted to stay at home and try to work things out first with her loving husband. That you agreed."

"How are you going to prove to me you're dead?"

"I can only think of one way."

Beatrice stood. She tried hard to beam some of the light of Heaven out of Ellen's eyes, she wanted to sheathe this body in it—an aureole, a flame—the way her guides had done so Virgil could marvel as she had, so Virgil could witness her own soul inside Ellen. But she could not. The light was not here in the realm of life.

He asked, "Why are you doing this?"

Beatrice pushed on Virgil's nose. He crossed his eyes and glowered.

She lowered the hand and stood bolt upright, cocksure like a bullfighter on TV.

"Why are you letting me?"

7

"I DON'T want to be here. Why do I have to be here?"

"It's just an errand. I told you. We won't be long."

"You realize I'm supposed to be in the hospital right now."

"You agreed to try it at home for a little while. Just until we see if this thing is going to go away on its own."

"I didn't agree. My other personality canceled all my arrangements. She agreed."

"You agreed too. We talked about this, Ellen. You and me. Remember?"

"I'm confused. This whole thing. I'm sick. This is no place to bring a sick woman."

"Only for a minute."

"I'll wait in the car."

"No, we talked about this. We said you'd stay right by me for a few days. Alright?"

Virgil pulled into a space reserved for visitors to the sheriff's office. Ellen did not get out of her side; he walked around the car to open her door and coax her out.

"Ellen, I have to do this. It's the sister of a guy I knew in jail. I promised."

Getting out of the car, she complained, "Why can't he come and do this himself?"

"Because he's still locked up. Look, he called and asked me." He closed Ellen's door and locked it. "All they need from me is an ID. I knew her back in high school. A quick look and that's it. Five minutes."

Holding Ellen by the crook of her elbow, like leading an elephant by the trunk, Virgil took her up the steps through the front door. He asked at a desk for the morgue and was shown the way down a mucous-green linoleum floor, a tunnel of a hall shrouded in official shadows and repeating heel-clicks, antique wooden doors with worn knobs and rippled-glass panes, all of which ate at Ellen's shaky reserve, communicated in nervous shudders through her arm cupped in his grip.

She said, "I've never seen a dead body before."

"Neither have I."

"I don't want to do this."

"Neither do I and you're not making it any easier."

The door marked MORGUE was at the far, dark end of the corridor. Its textured glass pane was alight from inside. Virgil opened the door and found a corner office with two windows open, sunshine and air capering about a desk where a thick-set blond deputy sat listening to earphones and scribbling on paperwork. The man pulled down the earphones with the robust stiffness of a serious weight lifter.

"What can I do for you?"

"We're here to identify a, uh, a body."

"Which one? We got a bunch." The deputy's accent was thick, northeastern, maybe Boston. He had the ruddy busted face of an Irish saloon fighter. He shuffled on the desk for a form. His brown sheriff's jersey looked as though it might split at the biceps.

Virgil answered. "A woman who went by the name of Bea Sting."

Ellen jerked her arm from Virgil's clutch.

"Who? Bea what?"

The deputy gave a faraway smile.

"Yeah. Ol' Bea. Shame what happened. We're gonna miss her around the station."

Virgil widened his eyes at the deputy.

"You . . . um . . . you knew her?"

"Well, yeah." The man swiveled his head to Ellen, then back to Virgil. "No offense to the lady here," he said, boosting his eyebrows, "but it looks to me like you did too."

Ellen took a stance closer to Virgil's side.

"Exactly what," she asked prudishly, "are you implying about my husband?"

The deputy grinned. "Nothin', ma'am. Nothin' whatsoever." He slid a register across the counter.

"You have to sign in before I can take the two of you's downstairs."

Virgil scribbled his and Ellen's names while the deputy walked from behind his desk. The man was squat, a hydrant. He had the proper form now in his mitt.

"So you'll be claiming the body?"

Ellen tugged on Virgil's arm. "What does he mean? Are you claiming this woman's body?"

Virgil addressed the deputy, "I just want to look and be sure it's her."

"Oh," the deputy waved the paper for them to follow, "it's Bea."

Virgil followed the slab of the deputy's back downstairs, towing Ellen, who hissed, "Bea Sting. What kind of a name is that?" Virgil expected a stench of formaldehyde to rise from the basement or some rotting smells but the air was fresh and recycled, the stairs well-lit. The deputy hummed whatever song he'd had interrupted and jounced down the treads in time to the tune. The steps ended in a large pale room with a gray painted concrete floor, incandescent lights humming louder than the deputy. Three walls were filled with square drawers arranged in rows, each drawer finished in shiny refrigerator white.

"It's cold," said Ellen.

"Ma'am, trust me," the deputy said, "you don't want it hot down here. She's right over there."

He rapped a knuckle against one cooler door, chest high in the wall. "Ol' Bea. You know I hear she used to really be somethin' a few years back. Up in Miami."

"What," Ellen asked, chilly as the room, "did she used to be, if you don't mind?"

The deputy shrugged, struck dumb. Respect for the departed is what his shrug meant.

Virgil stood opposite him while he pulled the long tray open. The sliding corpse, covered in a blank sheet, was accompanied by a breath of mist as though it were a giant pallid tongue sticking out of a frigid mouth. The deputy lifted the cloth carefully from the face. He folded it down just below the neck.

Ellen turned away and walked to the far corner of the room. The deputy took one step back from the tray, graciously, to give Virgil a private audience with the cadaver.

Looking at the corpse's face, Virgil felt that eerie sensation you get when the phone rings and before you pick it up, out of the blue, you know who's calling.

His balance tilted; he leaned against the tray. His mind raced to the single rose, red and forsaken by him on the lobby sofa. He saw Bea Sting, this woman on the slab, her blood, red and forsaken on the hot concrete sidewalk, one arm reaching to him across a crimson creeping spill.

The skin drained of life, waxy and colorless, did not hide her beauty, as in a black-and-white photograph. Death did not rob her of her high cheekbones and daring square chin, slim nose, deep sockets—dark sockets, eyes shut like vaults—full lips that though blue cradled a smirk. Virgil, not believing even as he did it that he would ever touch a dead body, laid his hand on the cool moon brow and smoothed the brown hair.

Ellen thinks she's Bea Sting, his almost Fedora from Top Hat? How the hell?

How did Ellen find out? She must have known about his appointment at the Ramada somehow. Woody told her. She must have followed him there. She stayed behind when he left. Went into the lobby. Saw the rose. Saw the beautiful woman pick it up. Watched her wait, then saw her go outside and be murdered. Saw Virgil leap out of his car and run up to her. The shock—double shock, her husband cheating on her, or at least intending to cheat but losing his nerve, and then the shooting right in front of her—was too much for her. Just like Dr. Lowe said. She's taken on a separate personality, a personality she's invented, of the woman that her husband must have desired more than her. A woman her husband sneaked off to meet.

The deputy spoke. "Told you she was somethin'."

"Yes," Virgil nodded, not taking his eyes from the corpse, "you did."

"You believe that? She must've been forty at least. Man oh man."

Virgil couldn't help himself when the deputy lifted the sheet just a little for him to peek under it. The first thing he saw was a neat perforation in her chest, then two more holes, little cold black volcanoes. Virgil could tell nothing of the story of this body's life, the life that had taken decades to occur, because it was buried and silent in the stiff white flesh. But there in the three craters was the wholeness of her end, the end he witnessed. The tale was quick, violent and complete.

He nodded, instinctively solemn. Then, inwardly embarrassed, he allowed himself to see her breasts.

"Holy . . ."

He caught himself. He looked up at the grinning deputy. The man, the hulk, stepped up to the tray to screen Ellen's view for Virgil.

Virgil whispered, "Jesus."

The deputy poked his finger into the sheet. The breasts had not flattened into pies as they should for a woman lying on her back, especially deceased, but stood proud and white as wedding cake.

The deputy whispered back, "Good work that guy didn't shoot these."

The deputy jabbed the dead breasts again to make them jiggle. He whispered again, "Like fuckin' Jell-O molds."

Virgil was repulsed by the deputy's necrophilic glee but could not help himself in joining the man in admiration. He fought the urge to look further down the body and lost to it; he lifted the sheet inches more to catch a look at the flat belly, trim hips, dark pubis.

The deputy glanced at Ellen, who was pacing along the far wall with her arms crossed.

He lowered his voice. "This guy shot her. Dusted her outside the Ramada Inn. We're still lookin' for the fat son of a bitch. We know who he is, we just gotta find him.''

"Jesus,'' Virgil whispered back. Then he asked, "Why'd the guy shoot her?''

The deputy spoke in a hush, as though out of respect for the dead, but Virgil knew it was to keep Ellen from hearing. "She was a pro. He was one of her johns. She'd jilted him earlier that afternoon. She calls Top Hat and tells them about it. Then she settles down at the Ramada to wait for her seven o'clock john. But that guy stands her up, and while she's waitin' for a taxi, this fat fuck comes back in a limo and catches up with her on the sidewalk outside the motel. He makes a play for her and she shuts him down. So he got pissed off and popped a coupla' caps in her. Right on the sidewalk. You believe that crazy motherfucker, wastin' a beauty like this? Fuckin' goon. She wasn't bothering no one, she was just goin' home.''

The deputy replaced the cloth neatly just below the shoulders to give her the classic look of wearing a white off-the-shoulder gown. Virgil was saddened looking at the corpse, feeling the link that was almost between them in life and the curious connection that had grown instead after her death. She was captivating indeed; Virgil tried to animate her to imagine what she must have been like, how an evening with her as his Fedora would have gone.

"Have you two had enough?''

Virgil looked up past the deputy. Ellen had her arms crossed.

"I want to leave."

"Come over here," he said. "Take a look. She's beautiful."

"Nobody dead is beautiful. I want to go."

The deputy moved aside. Ellen sighed and walked to the cadaver. Unblinking, she looked down onto the face on the tray.

Ellen stared for several moments, apparently struck numb by something in the quiet gray face. She stood motionless, then softened, her shoulders slumped. Ellen ran a hand across the cheek the way a mother's hand sweeps away a child's tear.

Virgil waited. Then he prodded. "Well?"

At his voice, Ellen hardened again. She pulled away from the body on the slab. Her face was a scold.

"Well what? She was a tramp." She turned to the deputy. "Isn't that right?"

The deputy shrugged his meaty shoulders again. "Not for me to say, ma'am."

"Well, it's not for you to be copping a feel on a dead woman either. Virgil, claim this body or not, but we're leaving."

The deputy slid shut the drawer. It sealed with a final puff of fog.

The deputy led them up the stairs. Over his shoulder, he said to Ellen in a soft-pedaling voice, "Look, lady, I was just checking the condition of a cadaver. It's part of my job. Sometimes we gotta hold these bodies a long time."

"Deputy, I'd rather not hear anything more about you holding those bodies."

The deputy sighed, bested.

She finished with him. "Just please get us out of here as quickly as possible."

"Yes, ma'am."

In the office, the deputy sat. From a drawer he pulled out a cardboard box and laid it on his desk.

"I got her personal effects here. This is all she had on her."

He opened the box to show a small purse, a wallet, a watch, makeup, a hairbrush, long black earrings, two opal rings, several silver bangles and a tarnished silver locket. Virgil took up the wallet to look for the woman's ID but found no credit cards or driver's license, only two folded fifty dollar bills. Ellen, oddly fascinated, ran her fingers over Bea's jewelry.

The deputy spread his paperwork on the table. His pen was poised.

"I need your names."

Quickly, Virgil put down the wallet. He backed away from the desk, pulling Ellen with him.

He opened the door. "I'll have the brother contact you."

He pushed Ellen into the hall. Virgil said, "Thank you," and followed her.

Outside in the parking lot, when Virgil had straightened from unlocking her car door, Ellen slapped him hard with an open hand in the chest.

"Why did you make me go in there? Who was that woman? You tell me right now what's going on."

Ellen's face dropped. She said, "Oh . . ." Her

jaw fell. "Oh my God. That's what Dr. Lowe asked me."

She leaned against the car.

"He asked if the words 'bee sting' meant anything to me. That was her name."

Her hand clasped to her forehead. She stayed for a moment in that posture, wood still, mouth agape, staring at the ground.

Slowly, she brought the hand down, made a fist—not the regular female fist but a good one, thumb lapped over the balled fingers—and slugged Virgil in the chin.

"You son of a bitch! Why'd you haul me in there?"

Staggered, Virgil scrambled backward, holding his jaw. "Jesus." He touched his lips gingerly to check for blood. "I thought you needed to see it."

"See it?" she thundered. "Why would a woman want to see her own dead body! I looked like hell!"

"You poked me."

"The deputy poked you."

"Same thing. You let that jerk do it."

"Did you see the size of that guy? How do you propose I could've stopped him?"

"A gentleman would've found a way. You're no gentleman. You looked under the sheet."

"It was a dead body."

She stuck out her lower lip. Virgil looked away from traffic to see her pout.

"It was my body," she said. "It was a good body. Just wasn't bullet-proof."

He agreed. "It certainly was a good body."

She punched him in the shoulder, again with the well-made fist. "What an asshole you are."

Virgil took a hand off the wheel to rub the arm to appease her, to show she had scored.

"Thank you," she said, smiling.

"You hungry?"

He realized he was speaking to Beatrice, addressing himself absently, easily, to her, the self-described spirit.

"Do ghosts eat?"

She cocked the fist for another sock at him; Virgil recoiled and held up a hand.

She barked in play, "Don't mess with me." She pulled the hand down. "I'm not speaking to you anymore until you tell me why you took Ellen in there."

The mention of his wife's name from his wife's mouth rekindled the spookiness of his situation.

"That was a nasty thing to do," she continued, "you knew I was watching. You knew I'd see myself. You said you'd go alone. Can't I trust you?"

Virgil pulled into the lot of a seafood restaurant and parked. He shut the car down then turned to Ellen. Beatrice.

"I'm sorry if it upset you but I had to do it."

"You lied to me."

"Oh, excuse me if I lied to you. You claim to be a dead woman sitting in the light who shoots in and out of my wife's body but you're ticked off because I told a lie."

"I don't claim to be a dead woman. I am. You saw me."

"All I saw was a refrigerated corpse with some bullshit name of Bea Sting."

"It wasn't a bullshit name. It was my stage name. All your actresses and dancers have them."

"How about your escorts and hookers?"

Ellen made the fist. She demanded, "What is that supposed to mean?"

Virgil had had enough of being clubbed. He snatched down her fist and held it. They glared, face-to-face.

"It means what it says. Bea Sting was an escort. With Top Hat Escort Service."

"How do you know that?"

Virgil pressed on. "Bea Sting got shot Monday night at the Ramada by a guy she'd turned down. Bea Sting was a hooker."

"Not anymore! I was an exotic dancer."

"Whatever."

"Look, the fat fuck who shot me wanted me to turn a trick and I wouldn't do it. I was not that guy's whore! I was just a dancer and, yes, a professional escort. And just how do you know about that? I never saw you when I was alive."

Beatrice tried to shake her hand free from Virgil's grip but he held her tight.

He yanked her wrist. "I was your seven o'clock Fedora."

Her hand relaxed in his mitt. Virgil had to support its weight.

"You?"

"Yes. Me."

She blinked, examining Virgil's face. "Black hair," she murmured. "Nice jawline." She glanced at his pants. "Pleated khakis."

She leaned her head out to look down at his feet.

"Oh my God. Hofheimer loafers."

With her free hand she swung at him, many times. Virgil jerked on the arm he held and struggled to snatch the other flailing one. She fought to free the wrist in his clasp to hit him with that too.

"You walked out on me!"

He protected his face. She went for his body.

"Damn it, calm down. I said I was sorry."

"Sorry my ass," she shouted with the flurry, "you got me shot! What's the matter, wasn't I good enough for you?"

She got him in the ribs.

Virgil pulled her one arm down hard and thrust his open hand under her chin and shoved her back. He had never before laid a hand on Ellen in anger. It wasn't anger now, it was frustration and fear. He pinned the back of her head against the window.

"Stop it! That's enough. I did not walk out on you."

She spoke—squawked, he was still pressing on her throat: "You did too walk out on me."

Her free hand went down into her lap. He let her off the window and released her arm.

She swallowed and said, "I waited."

"I got cold feet."

"Cold feet."

"Yeah. It was the wrong thing to do. So I put the rose on the sofa and left."

"Thanks. I was the wrong thing to do."

"That's not what I mean. I never saw you. I left before you came into the lobby."

"You didn't see me?"

"No. I left the rose on the sofa for you. You got it."

Again, he was talking to Beatrice. He let it go. It was simpler to just call her Bea when she was acting like Bea and he was running low on patience and control right now.

She rubbed her windpipe and calculated.

After a moment, she said, reluctant and placating, "I got done up real nice for you too."

He said nothing.

"It was a gorgeous rose." She frowned wanly. "Getting killed sucked, though."

That was enough for Virgil. He was impatient with her wandering off the topic and upset with himself that he had laid a rough hand on her. He wanted to get back to reality, to the point, why he'd taken his wife to the morgue.

He said, "Look, *Ellen*. I took you into the morgue because *you* needed to be shocked out of whatever delusion you're locked into. For some reason, you think you're Bea Sting. You're not. You're my wife. Ellen. Do you hear me? Stop it right now."

"I'm not Ellen and I'm not a delusion."

Virgil lowered his voice. "Listen. Maybe Woody let it drop that I was going to the Ramada

that night. You followed me. You saw me go in
with the rose, you saw me leave. Then you must
have seen Bea Sting pick it up and you put two
and two together. You watched her get shot and
then saw me jump out of the car. It freaked you
out, something in your head snapped and now
you've identified with her, you're becoming her, I
don't know why, maybe like you said, to please
me, to get my attention. Maybe it's because she
was slim and attractive and loose and in some part
of your brain you wanted to be her after you saw
me go to meet her. I don't know, I'm not a shrink,
I can't tell how this happened. But it has and
you've got to stop it, Ellen. Stop it."

She shook her head slowly, rejecting it all.

He said, "Maybe like Dr. Lowe said it has
something to do with your father abusing you . . ."

Again she pulled her arm back. This time Virgil did not bring his hands up to defend himself or
stop her. She could hit him if she wanted.

He continued, ". . . maybe it didn't. Maybe it's
because you know we're having some problems in
our marriage and we never talk about them. That
could be my fault. Then seeing me go to the
Ramada kicked you over the edge. But you had to
go with me to see her in the morgue. You had to
see that Bea Sting was dead so you can stop this."

She lowered her hand. "Stop what, Virgil?
What am I doing that you want stopped so badly?"

"That's not the point. It's got nothing to do
with what I want. This isn't normal. You turn into
this Bea Sting creature and all of a sudden you . . .

you drop all your inhibitions, you go around acting like a . . . a . . ."

"Woman?"

"No!" Flustered, Virgil thrust his palms at her.
"Jesus, look at you. You try to punch my lights
out, you holler at me, Ellen would never hit anybody, she'd never holler at me. But you . . ."

She lifted a hand to interrupt him. She spread
the fingers to count on them, starting at the pinky.
"I make you laugh. I make you talk. I make your
dick hard. Those are also things Ellen wasn't
doing. Virgil, smell the coffee. You were deader
than me before I came into your life and you
know it. That's why you called Top Hat and went
to the Ramada in the first place." She finished at
the thumb. "I make you alive!"

"This isn't," he repeated, "about me."

She fished in her pocket and held up by its
long silver strand Bea Sting's locket, pilfered from
the box the deputy kept of the corpse's personal
belongings.

"What is it about, Virgil? Tell me, because I
sure as shit do not know."

He reached for the locket; she swung it away
from his grasp.

"That's Bea's."

"Right. It's mine. Ellen grabbed it."

She pulled the locket in and stroked it with her
thumb. She pressed a tiny release; it sprang open.
Where there was room for two small pictures
there was nothing, just the backward insides of an
empty silver heart.

"Something's going on here, Virgil."

Virgil felt shovelfuls of confusion land on him. He lowered his hand and shook his head.

She pocketed the locket.

Virgil pointed. "We've got to take that back to the morgue."

"No. I'm going to let her keep it."

"Let who?"

"Ellen."

Virgil sighed. At the sound, she bowed her head, sorrowful, and mumbled, "Oh shit."

"What?"

"You still don't believe me."

Virgil matched her quietness. "Come on." He wanted to reach to her by saying her name but could not bring himself to call her Bea and was not sure she would appreciate Ellen.

He spoke softly. "Come on, look at it from my perspective. What are my two choices?"

He pulled in his hands to make a scale as if weighing two different melons. "Over here we have: You've got a malfunction in your brain or some multiple personality disorder which a million other people have. Both common. A reasonable explanation. Or," he raised the second hand to measure its load, "over here: You've been taken over by a spirit from beyond the grave."

He lowered his hands and made a scrunched face, an attempt at sardonic comedy. "Gee," he said, "tough one."

She rubbed the wrist where Virgil had grabbed her.

"I can tell you things. Things only I would know. Bea would know. I can still prove I'm her."

He shook his head. He waited.

Then he said simply, "You have to go to the hospital."

"Virgil?"

"Yes, Ellen?"

"It's still Bea."

"Alright. Yes, Bea?"

"Will you give me one more chance? Just one and if it doesn't work, if they won't help me, then it's okay. You can bundle Ellen and me off to the hospital. Just like you said."

She took his hand. "Come on. Buy me dinner and I'll tell you my idea, okay? I know I'm a few days late but I came a real long way to keep my Fedora with you."

Virgil creased his brow.

She opened her car door. "Let's go inside. Ghosts don't eat. But Ellen damn sure does."

The waiter removed the plates. When he brought back the check, she watched him set it down. Then, when the waiter's hand withdrew, her eyes did not follow, frozen in place the way he'd seen her do before.

"Anything else, folks?" the waiter asked.

In a moment she looked up and asked the boy for a plastic bag filled with ice cubes.

When he was gone, she flexed her left hand.

"Hi," she said.

"Hi."

"What did I do?"

"You punched me."

"With my left hand?"

"Yes."

"Where?"

Virgil pointed to his jaw, right side, slightly swollen.

Ellen asked, "Does it hurt?"

He shrugged.

"How long this time?"

"About an hour and a half."

Ellen smacked her lips, trying to taste something. "What did I have for dinner?"

"Baked fish. Steamed vegetables. Salad. Hold the French fries."

The waiter returned with the ice pack.

"I'll have a piece of apple pie, please."

Virgil inhaled and held his tongue.

"That was the longest one yet," she said. "They're getting longer. Every time."

"I know."

"Why did you take me to the morgue? Who was Bea Sting?"

Virgil explained how Bea Sting was an escort and dancer with Top Hat. How she had been shot by a spurned john in the lobby of the Ramada Monday night. Again he hoped that, faced with the truth, the delusion in her head might break down and scurry away like roaches in a kitchen when the lights are turned on. But this time in his explanation he did not mention that he was the date Bea Sting had been waiting for that night at the Ramada. He wanted to see if Ellen would remember following him there and admit it.

"No," Ellen said when he was finished, shifting the ice pack. He saw she was neither shocked nor tearfully relieved of her burden; she was irked. "I never laid eyes on that woman before in my life. I never even heard of her until Dr. Lowe asked me about her stupid name. Why on earth would I be taking on the personality of a cheap thing like her? She couldn't be more unlike me than the man in the moon. Some topless dancer shimmying around for money. What kind of idea is that? The very notion of me having that hussy as some ideal in my head, Virgil, suggesting that I might somehow want to be like her. What does that say about your opinion of me?"

The apple pie slice was set before her. She took her left hand from under the ice pack to check the soreness. The knuckles would not bend well. She sucked through her teeth at a jolt of pain.

"So you just sat here and had dinner with me while I was Bea Sting?"

"Yes."

"You just sat here and had dinner with a whore? Just like that? Well, Virgil, I never thought I'd see the day."

"You didn't."

Ellen shifted in her seat.

"Did you tell her what you told me? About why you took me to the morgue? To scare her out of me?"

"Yes."

"And what did Bea Sting have to say?"

"She's the one who punched me."

"Well, good for her at least."

Ellen rattled her head at some absolute thought, her mind being made up.

"Well, it didn't work, Virgil. That's all. Not only am I gone for longer periods each time but now I'm getting violent. I won't have this. I won't have myself beating on my husband like some fishwife and parading around town thinking I'm a prostitute."

"You're not a prostitute. Not anymore, apparently. You're an exotic dancer."

"Oh, not anymore? How noble. Is that what she was, then, an exotic dancer? Okay, an exotic dancer named Bea Sting. That's lovely."

She plunged the fork into the pie.

"So that's what's wrong with me. For a reason I cannot fathom, I think I'm some sexpot dancer named Bea Sting. Oh, that's . . . that's rich. Now are you sure it was Bea Sting who popped you in the jaw? Or did I become Joe Louis too while I was gone? Who's next, Einstein? I could figure out the universe, I'm sure he's had a few more insights about it since he's been dead. I know, next time I'll be a car salesman, we need a new minivan. I can get us a deal."

"Ellen, calm down. Eat your dessert."

Around a mouthful of apples and crust, she sputtered, "That's ridiculous. A dancer."

She clanged the fork on the plate and held out

her hands. She looked down at herself in the restaurant booth, surveying her front, then up to Virgil's eyes.

"Why would I possibly identify with a dancer? Do I look like a dancer to you?"

Virgil paused. Tired, he couldn't help himself, he said, "You used to."

"Oh thanks a lot. That's just what I need to hear from my husband right now. Recriminations and accusations when I'm as sick as I am. I'm going to the hospital. Tomorrow. I can't take another day of this."

Virgil rose to pay at the counter.

"It'll have to wait until lunch," he told her. "I've got something I have to do in the morning."

"What is it this time? A field trip to the cemetery? Are we digging up more bodies for me to see?"

He turned away. "Ellen, you're not making this any easier."

She called after him, sarcastic and oblivious to the fact that they were in public. "Oh I see, that's my job, to make this easier for you. Maybe it'd be easier for both of us if I just let you have Bea Sting all the time."

Virgil, on his way to the cash register, wouldn't allow himself to consider that.

She spoke even more loudly.

"You two could dance all you wanted."

8

HE sat upright before sunup. He listened to her sleepy mumbles for traces of Bea; he found himself wondering if delusions or ghosts slept.

There remained at least another hour before dawn. Virgil's thoughts darted about his open eyes, they chased him like mosquitoes into his clothes and out of the house. He walked past folded morning newspapers on porches, down Duval in front of hushed shops and turned on Angela. He walked to the cemetery and followed the wrought-iron perimeter, the many headstones inside so mute and final—the color of moon and bones—and he puzzled about the finality they hinted at with their beginning and ending dates driven into granite. The darkness about him seemed absolute but in an hour it too would begin to blush into a day that would be full and gleaming, not a trace of darkness left, only to chase itself again into another night and on into day, what

really ends? He padded down Front Street to a
view of the Atlantic, the ocean makes the clouds
make the ocean, the seed makes the grass makes
the seed, what escapes the circle? Anything? The
stars? He searched them, pondering, and walked
back to the house.

By now the sun was flicking off the street
lamps. She was awake, the kitchen light on. He
entered the house. She was in the shower. Coffee
burbled on the counter. It was weak. Ellen.

He showered quickly in the guest bathroom,
changed and scribbled a note saying he would
catch breakfast out. He had an errand to run and
would be back in around two hours.

Virgil remembered painting the steps. Four years
ago, during the four months he'd lived here on
Virginia Street, he'd been told to paint them
twice, neither time because they needed it. Climbing them now he wondered how many coats these
steps bore from other hands, how deep lay the
wood beneath a decade of layers of sorry labor.

The big green Victorian with the wraparound
porch and two slate gables was a prison. The
black wrought-iron fence was the perimeter. The
grass, shrubs and palms made up the prison yard.
The front door was the prison gate. Every inch of
the place was neat, squared away.

He went inside. A sturdy and stern matron
greeted him from the desk. He signed in a visitors'
register and asked to see Woody.

The boy was brought out from the dining hall.

Though he came and went from here to the shop on Duval Street six days a week, Woody, like the rest of the two dozen inmates, was watched and regulated. His bed was checked four times a night. He signed in and signed out to go to work. He did chores around the grounds on Sundays. One evening a week he had an escorted shopping trip. That was last night. He met Virgil in a new pair of blue jeans.

"These okay?" Woody asked, patting his stiff thighs.

"They're good."

"Thanks for the cash."

"Don't worry about it. Let's go out on the porch."

Woody sat next to Virgil on the steps and clomped his sneakers on the first tread.

"Man," Woody said, "I been here just two months and already I've painted these fuckers twice."

"You're going to break my record."

Woody spit. "So. What's up? The shop's been closed for two days. I been stuck here doing laundry, man. You don't call and give me no explanation. You can't do this to me without telling me what's up."

Woody spit again. "How's Ellen?"

"She's fine. Why do you ask?"

"Like, the last I time I saw you guys she was screaming about what was she doing in the bathroom. Next thing I know you close up the shop, send me back here to Alcatraz and I don't hear shit for two days. So I asked what's up with Ellen. Tell me what you think I did, man. You didn't just drop by to shoot the breeze. You firing me or something? What's with that look? I told you, I got you cold."

"You ratted me out, Woody."

The boy sat bolt upright as though a dagger had been rammed between his shoulder blades. "Me? I ratted you out?"

"You told Ellen."

"About what?"

"About the Ramada."

"No way, man."

"She knows."

Woody jumped to his feet to testify his disbelief at Virgil's accusation. His voice rose; he paced, his hands flapped like the wings of a mad goose.

"No way, no fucking way I would rat you to Ellen! I don't care if you tie my tongue to the back of a fucking Buick and drag me down the fucking highway," Woody's voice echoed on the quiet breakfast street, "I would never tell a goddamn thing you tell me. If you don't trust me, fine! I quit!"

The front door opened. The matron poked her head out and glared at Woody. He shut down immediately. The door closed.

"Sit down, Woody."

"No way. Fuck you."

"Sit down."

Woody took his place again next to Virgil.

"Why would you ask me that, man? I would never do that to you. We're brothers."

Now Virgil spit.

Woody said, "So she knows. How'd she find out if it wasn't me? Which it wasn't."

"I don't know."

"What'd she do?"

"She freaked."

"I bet, man. I've seen people freak."

"No. Not like that. I mean she's flipped out in the head. She's started getting blackouts. Like that one you saw where she went into the bathroom then forgot how she got there and started screaming."

"Wow."

"Only now the blackouts are getting longer. They're lasting hours at a time."

"Man."

"We've been to doctors, they can't figure out what's wrong. One said it's a multiple personality disorder."

"Like she's two people?"

"Yes."

"That is too cool."

"She wants to check into a mental institution this afternoon."

"Whatever." Woody patted Virgil's knee sagely. "Chicks get crazy once in a while, you know. Maybe it'll be good for her to get some time off. E's pretty intense."

"Maybe. I don't think so. I've been telling her to stay at home. She'll get better. It'll go away."

Woody spit again, dotting the sidewalk. "I don't know, man. The human brain is a mother-fucker."

"She'll be okay."

"What should I do if I'm around when she has one? Like, do what?"

"Just act normal. Actually, she's pretty okay when she's gone. I mean, you know, having a blackout. You'll like her."

"That's cool."

Woody paused. He changed his mind. "That's fucked up."

"Maybe so."

"What are you gonna do?"

Virgil nodded, pursing his lips, compiling a response. "I don't know, Wood. I don't know what's gonna happen."

Virgil stood.

"The shop'll be open today. I'll be in after lunch. Give Ellen some room. Stay in the back, okay?"

"What if she freaks while I'm there? Can I, like, talk to her and shit?"

"If she talks to you."

"Oh, wow. Do I, like, call her Ellen?"

"Yes. I gotta go."

Woody stood also.

Virgil put his hand on the boy's narrow shoul-der. "This could get a little strange, Woody."

The boy shrugged. Virgil felt the spindly clav-icle rise.

Woody said expansively, "Everything is strange,

Virg. Everything is fucked. Don't trust it if it ain't fucked."

"You're just a kid. How did you get this way? Was it drugs?"

"Man, it wasn't the drugs. They were just for kicks and cash."

"Then what?"

Woody lifted his arms to encompass the seen world, Key West and beyond, then turned his head to the morning sky to take in the unseen as well.

He said, "Look around you."

Woody leveled his gaze to give Virgil a look of bemusement, as though Virgil—an ex-con himself and so one who should have known what Woody was telling him—was in fact the last person to learn that absolutely nothing made sense and Woody found that funny.

Virgil left him there with his arms out, seer-like, wondering who was right: Beatrice, who claimed there was a plan revealed to no one on Earth, or Woody, who believed that everyone except Virgil knew there was no plan at all.

"You are Virgil."

Fatima said his name with drama as if it had just come to her in a divination. But she knew it because he had a 10 A.M. appointment at her house on Eaton Street.

She wore silver hoop earrings and a black wrap dress fringed with maroon cord. She was as tall as Virgil and broader. With her bulbous belly and breasts, Fatima filled the doorway like a bull in an alley.

"Yes," he said. "Good morning."

She stepped aside to let him into her foyer, closing the door behind him. Virgil turned sideways to avoid her breasts. The walls were burgundy, the wallpaper was ribbed like corduroy. Old steps, they looked rickety, rippled up to an unlit level. A framed picture of John F. Kennedy hung beneath a glowing sconce.

"Here is my card."

The card read: "Fatima Tugsal, Psychic Consultant, Palmist, Auras Read, Spiritual Medium, All Questions Answered, Past Present Future, A Div. of Tugsal Co."

Fatima, divining again, answered a question out of the air.

"My mother and three sisters are all psychics in Jacksonville and Daytona. My brother in Miami Beach, he is an accountant." She shrugged and turned down the corners of her mouth. "Pah. Business." She measured Virgil with her gaze. "You. You do not look like a man who has come to Fatima for business. No." She shook her head; wild ringlets like black ivy swayed. "Not business. Come."

She slid back a pocket door to reveal a parlor that shut out the bright morning. No light from outside slipped past high velvet curtains; the room was lit only by a Tiffany lamp on a cluttered desk and a shy candle on the mantel. Old, scroll-armed furniture was covered in a thick wine-colored fab-

ric, the oriental carpet was skinned. The room
had a gloomy depth to it as though there were a
cavern beneath the threadbare rug; this was a
room where much happened in darkness, the way
it does behind closed eyes. In the center were two
facing chairs, plush and pillowed. The walls were
festooned with framed famous faces. Virgil recognized immediately Churchill, Yitzhak Rabin, Lin-
coln, Buddha, Keats, Madame Curie, Lindbergh,
Hemingway, Laurence Olivier, Sitting Bull, Joan
of Arc, Robert Frost, Indira Gandhi, Ayn Rand,
Haile Selassie, Howard Hughes, Lawrence of
Arabia. Fatima touched his wrist.

"Tea?"

"What? Oh, no. Thank you."

Again, Fatima and the unasked question.

"The rule is, first, they must be dead. Second,
they must have possessed great souls. I collect
them. Great souls. They are my friends. They are
my guides."

Virgil did not reply. Fatima did not ask questions or invite comments. She gave answers.

"Technically," she said, settling into one of the
chairs, gesturing Virgil into the other, "I am a
Turk. Ethnically, my family are gypsies. We have
great power in our blood."

She waved a large hand.

"It surprises you that I say this about myself.
Why? Would you prefer me to approach the spirit
world humbly on your behalf? Hat in hand,
pleading like a waif? No, Mr. Virgil. The spirits
do not listen to waifs. They will ignore a weak

voice in the fields of Heaven. One must be strong to congress with the souls there, to be heard amidst the sounds of their joy. They have left the plane of earth behind and to have them come back, even for a short visit, one must add to their joy. I, Mr. Virgil, am joyful. And I am strong. So Fatima speaks only with the best." She regally swept her hand around her gallery of souls. "As you can see."

Virgil peered into the recesses of the Tiffany lamp's throw: Peering back at him were Alfred Hitchcock, Plato, General MacArthur, Jack London, Malcolm X, Edison, da Vinci.

"You are familiar with my price structure as we discussed on the phone."

Virgil tightened his lips and opened his hands in his lap.

"Good. I should remind you before we begin that the other psychic services I provide, though less expensive, can often be more reliable than attempting to contact a particular soul. I cannot guarantee I shall be able to reach your friend, what is her name?"

"Bea. Bea Sting."

"Yes. Thank you. Bea Sting is a rare name. A name they should recognize in Heaven."

"Actually, she said to tell you that she's not in Heaven proper. She's only in the light."

"You have spoken with her?"

"Yes."

Fatima rolled her shoulders and laced her fingers.

"Hmpf. Mr. Virgil, if *you* have spoken with her, you do not need Fatima."

Quickly, Virgil said, "Well, no, I haven't actually spoken with her. Those are just the, uh, signs I've gotten. You know. Nothing definite."

She eyed him.

"Fatima does not enjoy games, Mr. Virgil."

"No, ma'am."

"She is in the light."

"Yes."

"She has only recently died."

"Yes."

"She is not happy, Mr. Virgil. She must go into the light. But, perhaps since she is not yet joyful, her ears are not yet filled with the songs of the spirit world. Perhaps she will hear our call. Perhaps we can help her go into the light. Let me see your left hand."

"No, thanks. I don't . . ."

"I must know who you are, Mr. Virgil, if I am going to beseech the spirit world for you. Don't worry, it is included in the price."

Virgil proffered the hand.

Fatima rubbed a thumb roughly over his palm. She touched a thick fingertip to her rouged cheek and pulled down so Virgil saw the red capillaries on the underside of her eyeball.

She said, "You are a quiet man, Mr. Virgil. You run like a river, very deep and without much noise. You flow within banks. You prefer your strength to be contained within another's. You do not change directions easily."

She lifted her gaze from the lines of his hand.

"But I see you will change."

Virgil felt the crowd watching from their perches on the shadowy walls, a jury. Fatima's reading seemed somehow public.

"Mr. Virgil, right now you do not have a great soul. You know this. It is not your fault, of course. It is extraordinary luck to have a great soul. But greatness is not a trait. It is a result. Great souls can be made."

Fatima collapsed her arched brows. She released his hand.

"Tell me about Bea Sting."

Virgil took a moment to compose his reply. He was disheartened by the news of his soul; the gathering on Fatima's walls—Cervantes, Chiang Kai-shek, Susan B. Anthony, Leonard Bernstein, Crazy Horse—turned up their noses at him.

"Did you love her? It is easier to contact a soul if it is a loved one. It gives them a firmer hold in this world."

"No. We, um, I never . . ."

"What else, Mr. Virgil? What was her profession?"

"She was a professional escort. And a dancer."

"What kind of dancer?"

"I think, in bars."

"A stripper, Mr. Virgil?"

"I believe so. Yes."

Fatima glanced away from him to the men and women, the tiered chorus of the celebrated and consecrated. He followed her eyes to Gertrude

Stein, St. Francis of Assisi, Eisenhower, Monet, Dante. She sighed, perhaps to excuse the insult to their company.

She laid one hand on the slant of her bust, the other over her stomach. The white backs of her hands were adrift on the black expanse of her dress.

"You understand I must enter into a trance state to communicate with the spirit world."

"Yes."

"Regardless of what happens in this room, do not become frightened, Mr. Virgil. Do not stand. Do not make any sudden or unexpected moves. And most important, do not speak unless the spirit speaking through me addresses you directly. I do not know who my guide will be. Though, to be frank, I suspect it will not be one of the caliber I am familiar with. You understand."

"Yes."

"Finally, I remind you I cannot guarantee success. I have never attempted to contact a . . . such an individual as your Bea Sting. And I have never spoken with a spirit who has not gone fully into the light. I do not know if it can be done. You accept this?"

"Yes."

Fatima nodded. She stood and crossed to her desk where she picked up a micro-cassette recorder. Back in her chair, she clicked it to record and laid the machine in her lap.

Fatima closed her eyes and relaxed her neck; her head and hair lolled back. She turned over her wrists on the chair arms so her palms faced up; she looked like a woman waiting to catch something big that would be dropped down to her.

She hummed in a quiet soprano, then swung to a low register with startling control, then to a middle range warble as if she were a radio and someone was twisting the dial searching for a station. She did this for several minutes, scanning the spirit world's frequencies. Virgil sat still, moving only his eyes.

Except for the humming and frequent twitches of her fingers, Fatima might have gone to sleep in the chair. Waiting, Virgil dodged his head a little to test himself on more of the eminent dead faces in the audience.

Ellen packed the suitcase again and set it near the front door. She fried her eggs and ate them reading the morning newspaper. Beatrice read the paper along with her, except that Ellen's eyes scanned the words and pictures faster than Beatrice could keep up.

Ellen flipped past a department store ad for women's undergarments. Beatrice shouted, "No, no, go back! Go back!" Ellen folded the section shut and set the paper on the kitchen table beside her coffee and bacon strips.

From the distance behind her—distance was not something Beatrice considered where she sat on the path to the light because the light was everywhere and she knew she could reach it with a wish, with one step to it—there came a holler.

"He's gone!"

Beatrice turned.

A brown head bobbed like it was running fast toward her. She saw hands pumping and feet all in a blur, all chestnut.

Another shout. "They're not gonna get him!"

The head sank, the hands lifted, one foot stretched while the other tucked itself under and the collection of swirling running brown slid right up to Beatrice.

He sat up and threw out his arms.

"Safe!"

He stood to brush his white raiment free of pretend dirt.

Beatrice sighed.

"Don't tell me. Another ball player."

He held out his hands out in a pleased "ta-da" stance.

She asked, "A Yankee?"

Handsome brown spirit. Teeth perfect as his gown. Eyes with energy, like two young blackbirds. Even under the robe Beatrice could see he was bow-legged, lumpy with muscles.

"No," he answered. "Brooklyn Dodgers originally. But Coach just traded for me. He said you wanted a break from the Yanks. Can't blame you, I never liked 'em. How about my entrance? Coach always liked my speed."

"How is Coach?"

"He's good. Happy. What do you think? He's in Heaven."

She turned to glance at her floating image.

Ellen's hands cleared the breakfast table.

The guide spoke behind her. "Don't worry. She's sulking around waiting for Virgil, just like you."

He bounced from foot to foot as if on embers, ready to jump. He seemed to sizzle. His voice carried a sibilance like a fuse burning.

"So Bea. Are you ready to go?"

Beatrice looked up at him. "That's it? That's your whole approach? 'You ready to go?'"

"Yeah. What's wrong with it?"

"It's not what I'd call convincing."

"Well then, are you ready to go pretty please?" There was something powerful about this spirit, straining and condescending, as though he had to try hard to stay in human form and not explode like a nova. He was harnessed and it was taxing him.

He shoved his open hands out side-by-side as if ushering her through a door. "After you."

Beatrice shook her head.

Insistent, he nodded.

She shook her head again.

He glared at her. "You really ought to come with me."

Beatrice folded her arms. "I was hoping you might've come to help me."

"Getting you to come with me *is* helping you. Look at you. Sitting here by yourself, messing around with that woman, even messing with the plan for all I know. Come on, let's go. I'll walk so you can keep up."

Beatrice uncrossed her arms. "You know I'm not going."

"Yeah. I know."

"So why're you here?"

The guide stilled his shifting feet. He held up a hand to Beatrice's floating image. The vision, a view of Ellen's closet, was replaced by a display like one shot with a video camera, none of Ellen's darting glances but focused and composed. A dim room. One lamp. One flickering candle. Pictures hung in rows on every bit of wall space.

In the image sat Virgil, hands in lap, patient as ever. In the chair in front of him, a massive woman appeared to be asleep.

The guide pointed a cinnamon finger.

"They're looking for you. Just like you wanted."

Beatrice caught her breath, excited. The guide lowered himself beside her.

"Nobody up here likes that woman," he muttered. "She's gotten too big for her britches." He snickered suddenly. "And when you get too big for those britches, you are *big*."

"What are we going to do?"

The guide eased his giggle into a grin, the crack in his face like a white slice hacked out of a tree trunk, so broad it threatened to topple the top half of his head.

"Well, Beatrice, my dear. You're the one likes to mess with people." He clapped his hands. "So let's mess with 'em."

Fatima's song halted its parabolas and settled into an eerie alto drone. Without lifting her head from the back of the chair, she hummed louder. Her bosom—Virgil was surprised to see it could get larger—swelled.

She quieted. She froze.

She raised one foot and brought it down on the carpet.

Boom.

She tapped the toes of the other foot. Twice quickly.

Ba-ba.

Again the first foot. Down hard.

Boom.

Again.

Ba-ba. Boom.

Ba-ba-boom. Ba-ba-boom.

Fatima opened her eyes and lifted her head. She jerked her face to Virgil. Her feet beat out the rhythm once more—*boom, ba-ba-boom*—then quit.

Then she said it. "*Boom, bop-ba-boom, bop-ba-boom, bop-ba-boom . . .*" She heaved from the chair as if she were a puppet whose strings had been taken up. She peaked an eyebrow beguilingly at Virgil. The cassette recorder spilled from her lap, its little red record light still glowing on the carpet. She intoned, "*Boom-bop-ba-boom,*" and every time she said "*boom*" with billowed lips she took a deliberate step toward the center of the room. She put her hands on her hips—"*boom, bop-ba-boom*"—and lengthened her swagger, dragging the top of each foot behind her across the carpet, walking away from Virgil's popped eyes and dropped jaw.

At the edge of the rug, by the Tiffany lamp, she whirled, arms cast out to Virgil to invite him inside their embrace—*"boom, bop-ba-boom"*—and shimmied her beefy shoulders and great chest, the invitation seemed more like a beckon into a gyrating washing machine than into a woman's arms. Virgil kept his seat, weighed into it by Fatima's odd lewd dance as surely as if the big woman had plopped onto his lap.

With her arms held out, Fatima began to swing her head, sending the inky loops of her hair into orbit until they fell over her face, her vermilion lips visible through the coily curtain like a fire at night. Fatima turned sideways, springing her heft onto one leg. The other gam she lifted gracefully. Slowly, she grasped her black wraparound dress and tugged to reveal a jet stocking, slim ankle and a cannonball calf. She tugged the hem higher, above the knee and mid-thigh, and straightened the exposed leg to touch the toes down gently, at the rhythmic *"boom"* point, in a step toward Virgil.

With Fatima approaching, pulsing *"boom, bop-ba-boom, bop-ba-boom,"* Virgil climbed the back of the chair. Fatima stopped her teasing promenade inches from his shoulder. She hooked her thumbs in the silk scarf about her waist and shoved it down into a ring around her shoes. Her hands disappeared under a fold of the dress. She drew a

secret string and held the dress open in silken
ebony wings. Virgil gaped at her black slip, black
bra and cascades of white skin and paunch, her
fat-bound navel buckled shut like a boxer's eye.

She rotated to face away from him, her hips
now grinding in time to her *"boom-bop-ba-boom."*
She dropped the entire outfit in a heap at her feet.
She leaned over, put her hands on her knees and
wigwagged her wide tail under Virgil's nose.

She said, "Bzzzzzzz."

Virgil could not retreat further into his chair
without tipping it over or leaping out of it.

Her rear rocked left, right, then left, described
a clockwise circle, then counterclockwise, and
suddenly stopped in position. Virgil looked at it,
then beyond her backside to the portraits on the
walls who had not changed their expressions.

Fatima stood erect, still turned away from him,
facing the faces on the walls. Her chin dipped
sluggishly, her hair rose up her shoulder blades
while she looked down at herself.

She muttered, "What the . . ."

Her back expanded, her lungs inflated.

She whirled on Virgil. He braced for her
scream.

Instead, Fatima held up a finger. "Excuse me
a moment."

Her voice was calm. It seemed to Virgil huskier
than before and surprisingly cavalier for her situation.

She reached to the floor for her clothes and
was confused putting the wrap back on, not find-

ing the tie that held the front closed. She secured
the silk scarf around her waist with a shoelace
knot, leaving two dangling bows under her belly.

She spoke. "You know, that woman has
absolutely no respect for the rules. You understand what I mean? None."

She pushed her hair out of her face and
plopped in the chair opposite Virgil.

"That was totally unnecessary. Dropping the
lady's clothes like that. I told her she could get in
for a minute or two just to say hello to you, you
know, to make her point, but no, she had to go
and do this . . . this bullshit."

She picked the cassette recorder off the floor
and dropped it in her lap. Fatima's physicalness
had changed, carrying now a different and spe-
cific kind of grace, her voice and hands moved
with a jaunty ease, her legs crossed at the ankles,
slouching. It was athletic.

"We're not supposed to do that sort of thing.
It gives us a bad reputation, you know, like we're
poltergeists or something. It makes y'all scared of
us. Anyway. I'm here now. I kicked her butt out.
So what can I do for you?"

Virgil did not release the pressure of his back
against the chair.

"Relax. Come on, I've got things under control. Ease off it. There you go."

Virgil slid his rear more onto the chair's cushion but remained stiff. His hands clutched the
chair arms as if the chair—his only oasis in this
swirling room of silent staring heads and shadows

and the mercurial macabre swaps in Fatima—
might turn against him next and he needed to grip
it to tame it.

Fatima said, "So. Tell me. You believe her
now?"

Virgil was lost. "I . . . um . . . who?"

"Bea Sting, man! You believe she's dead now?
Because she damn sure is. That's why you came
here, right?"

Virgil said nothing.

"So, are you convinced? I mean, she wasn't
supposed to do that and all, but that *was* one heck
of a dance she put on. Fatima couldn't have done
that on her own. No, sir."

Tentatively, Virgil leaned forward to touch
Fatima's knee, like touching an electric wire that
might or might not be live.

"Fatima? Wake up. That's enough."

She jerked the knee from under his fingertips.
"Hands off, pal. Fatima's not in right now."

Virgil recoiled.

"Look, I can see you're not convinced yet. So
go ahead while I'm here. Ask me some questions.
But don't ask too many. I'm not enjoying this. It's
like being covered in white mud."

Virgil looked at the whirring recorder in her lap.

"Let me speak with Bea."

"No." Fatima waved the request off. "No way.
I'm not letting her back in. She's liable to run out
the door and flash a cop or something. Bea's
crazy." Fatima laughed. "She's funny, but she's
crazy. You talk to me."

"Who are you?" He jutted his nose at the walls. "Are you one of them?"

She issued a rich, rasping cackle. "Who, them? No, man, I'm not hanging on ol' Fatty-ma's wall."

"Then you're not a great soul?"

"Hey, hey, watch it now. I don't know about *that*. I'll leave it to you to decide if I was great. Listen here. I played four sports at UCLA. I was the first black man ever to play major league baseball. I took the Brooklyn Dodgers to six World Series in ten years. We finally beat the damn Yankees in '55. I was the first black man inducted into the Baseball Hall of Fame. I've still got people naming their babies after me."

Fatima cracked her knuckles. "So I don't know. You tell me. Was I great?"

Virgil nodded.

"Yeah, well, you know what? The truth is it really doesn't matter. That was just one life. I was worthless in about six or seven others. Listen. It's not us in Heaven who say a soul is great or poor, good or bad, this or that. It's *you* folks, man, that crap goes on only down here. Living is what makes a soul different. Dying makes us all the same."

"Where are you?"

"I'm on the path to the light."

"Are you with Bea?"

"Of course I am. That's the point."

"Why hasn't she gone into the light? Can you tell me?"

"Simple. It's because she's one stubborn white woman, that's why."

Virgil smiled. That rang true.

He began, "Look . . ." Then Virgil paused.

Fatima tickled the air impatiently with two plump fingers to draw out the rest of what Virgil wanted to say.

He pressed ahead. "Look, I have to use the phone for a moment. Can you wait right there?"

"You need to make a phone call? Right now?"

"It's . . . Bea knows what I'm doing. Will you hold on, just a sec?"

"Sure. Whatever. Go."

Virgil moved quickly to Fatima's desk. He dialed the shop, Ellen answered.

He spoke quietly. "It's me. I thought I'd bring lunch back to the store. What would you like?"

He waited while she answered. Fatima paid no attention, busy checking out the backs of her hands.

"Okay. That's fine. No, nothing's wrong. I'll take care of it. See you in a little while. Bye."

He hung up and returned to his chair.

He asked Fatima, "Do you know what she wants me to get for lunch?"

"Pal, I'm an angel. Not a mind reader."

"Ask Bea. If she's watching everything through Ellen's eyes like she says she is, she'll have heard what Ellen just said."

Virgil swallowed. "Ask her."

Fatima raised her palms. "Be right back."

The big woman twitched as if goosed by the seat cushion.

She looked somewhere over Virgil's head first, her gaze unshifting, then met his eyes.

"Mr. Virgil, how are we doing?"

"Very well."

Fatima ran her hands quickly over her disheveled dress and the awkwardly tied scarf at her waist.

"Something very strange. Did I . . . ?"

Virgil nodded.

She churned her hands as if to shake something sticky off them. Irritably, she began to rearrange her dress.

"*Oy yoy yoy*, this is what results when you converse with the lower spirits. I warned you, Mr. Virgil, what might happen. That is why I only communicate with—"

She jerked again, froze and unfroze and barked at herself, "Oh shut up, woman!"

Virgil jerked, too.

"Alright, I'm back," she said. "I got it."

Virgil hesitated.

"Alright." He took a breath, a leap, not onto a path of light but a course leading deeper into obscurity. He could not predict or pretend to know what lay ahead if Fatima got this right.

He asked, "What does Ellen want me to get for lunch?"

Fatima laughed loudly. "Reservations!"

Virgil found himself on his feet. He found air in his lungs and could not empty them. He backed away from the chairs, from giggling, jiggling Fatima.

"You think you're slick," Fatima brayed. "Her last lunch before the nuthouse, she wants you to take her to the yacht club. Ha! I got you, man. You're out!" And Fatima jerked a thumb in the air to show Virgil he'd been caught and called out.

"Oh my God," Virgil heard his voice. "Oh my God."

He backed across the carpet, bumping into the desk. He put his hands out to keep the Tiffany lamp from tumbling. He fumbled with his wallet and left a fifty on the blotter.

In the middle of the room, Fatima crossed her legs, ankle over knee. Smiling ingenuously, glad to see him go, she waved Virgil out the door.

Retreating, groping behind him for the doorknob, Virgil's shoulder grazed the wall. Mao Tse-tung, Robert Mitchum and Houdini tilted their heads.

9

VIRGIL left the medium's house. He absently wandered down Eaton Street, then west toward the ocean. Walking, he could conjure up nothing—from limitless time and boundless space to his own aimless footsteps—that minutes ago had not been changed.

Everything he saw on his way—the culture of man, the bright pallet of Nature, the walking hard souls of people and beasts—bore the sudden imprint of the Eternal the way a cheek wears a slap. The world, existence, the universe—where did it stop, was there any word now for what he lived in?—had been sheared of all its familiarity and common mysteries and given a new structure so that he did not recognize any of it.

At the western tip of the island he came to the walls of Fort Zachary Taylor, immense and stoic, over a hundred years old, each sooted stone the size of a balled-up man. He put his back against the fort and slumped facing the Atlantic.

Virgil shut his eyelids and let the sun dawdle on his cheeks without thinking, just listening to the little waves worrying at the island.

At last he turned from what he did not know—which was almost everything he believed and understood before, swept away by the one fact that Beatrice was really dead, that in fact she was in, or near, Heaven and all that this implied. God and his angels were no longer a hazy article of faith, an appealing memory from Sunday sermons, a difficult leap and desire of the heart and mind across logic and skepticism; no, God and his angels had actually come to him. Beatrice was Virgil's personal burning bush, and he tried to focus on what he should do. Actually *do*.

Was he supposed to sit and contemplate for the rest of his life like a monk? Spend his remaining years coming up with answers and insights based on what had been revealed to him and then spread those insights around to mankind like some gallant Jesus? Had he been chosen to bear a message to humanity? No, Beatrice would have been visited upon someone else with a better manner about them, less brusque, more spiritual and eloquent than he, if that was what was being asked from Above. Virgil was repressed and horny. An ex-con. These were not the traits of a prophet.

Or maybe he was wrong; maybe there was nothing left for him to do in life now that he knew that Fatima was right, that this earthly plane, this rock, was just a stepping stone. He was supposed to commit suicide, to rush off the rock to learn the rest of the answers and partake in the joy at the next level. Yes?

No. That didn't match up either. If they wanted him dead, they wouldn't have sent Bea Sting. They would have sent Al Capone or Attila the Hun or waited until he stepped off the curb and sent a bus.

Why him? Why choose a loser who in his life had taken a life? A former CPA who had forfeited his freedom and forgotten his future? A man who'd sat by and watched his marriage founder?

He questioned the waters, the biggest thing he could see, more immense even than the sky. He assumed for some reason that this was where the ear of the Eternal was. He asked if he'd been chosen because he knew what it was like to have everything and then have nothing? And then to do nothing to change his lot, to keep on choosing nothing? Was it because he'd been broken and humbled? Was it because he was longing? Because he was empty?

That was it. Virgil had hit on it. A king, a lover, a happy man, would not listen so closely to Heaven as would a wretch. Just like Fatima said, you need to speak loudly when the ears you are trying to reach are clogged with joy. But when they are not, unhappy ears will hear even a whisper, a moan. Virgil was selected because of his longing. He'd been drained. And because he was empty, he could be filled.

Filled with what?

He was supposed to perform some role. Beatrice had spoken of a plan. A plan that might involve him. Obviously, it did. He would find out what his part was, why Beatrice had been sent.

Virgil stood. He put his hands on the fortress wall. It was peaceful, as stones are. He walked to Duval Street like Adam through Eden, flesh of the Garden itself, newly confident and convinced that he belonged to the Eternal.

Ellen did not see him when he came in the back door of the shop. Woody did and Virgil gave him the shush signal. He moved where he could watch Ellen without being seen and knew immediately that this was indeed Ellen, the way she busied herself with some unfinished framing and her bossy tone calling Woody to get the vacuum out.

"How's she been?" Virgil asked the boy quietly.

Woody kept a flat face. "You know. She's been Ellen."

Woody fetched the vacuum and Virgil watched from the back. Ellen moved with surety in her work. She had always been the perfect cog for her life since Virgil had first met her, she fit and moved smoothly inside the machine of her days. Four years ago Virgil had been plugged into her machine, had become a flywheel in her life, though it had never been his design to do so. It just happened, like so much just happened and you wake up late one day to find it is not your hands on the machine after all but its hands on you.

Now everything had been irretrievably changed

for Virgil. Ellen had been changed too and, like Virgil before, she did not even know it. She'd become part of the plan, the unexplained and unfolding scheme of the Almighty. Ellen was now the one who was the unwitting sprocket. Virgil's life was the machine. And Beatrice was the key that started it all.

"Ellen?"

She dropped her scissors at his voice. "My goodness, Virgil, you gave me a start."

"Sorry. I came in the back way."

"I was beginning to wonder where you'd gotten to. You just up and left me to wait for you here. It's a half hour past lunchtime. Did you get all your chores done?"

"Yes."

"Where have you been? Why did you come in the back?"

"I was taking a walk. Thinking some things over."

"Heavens, Virgil, you haven't changed your mind again."

She leaned her softness against the counter. "We discussed this. We agreed I should go into the hospital today. The sooner I go in, the sooner I'll come out and we can get on with our lives. Now can we go to our lunch? You made the reservations, I hope."

What she'd said—"getting on with their lives"—was impossible for Virgil now. Their lives were things so transformed that they could not be gotten on with.

He said, "I don't want you to go to the hospital. I want you to stay at home with me. I think it's for the best."

She sucked in a sharp breath. "Why? When I want to go to the hospital, when my doctors tell me it's what I should do, why do you want me home?"

Virgil did not know yet what the plan required of him; nonetheless, he figured that anything he did must further it. After all, this whole ball of wax came from God. God certainly knew in advance what Virgil was going to do and must therefore be relying on him to do it.

Virgil was set loose into a spree of correct choices. So Virgil lied.

"Ellen, I'm sure it's just some temporary thing. It'll go away on its own. And when it does this week or next I don't want you sitting in some psychiatric ward where you can't convince the doctors that you're alright and just come home. Give it a few more days and let's see what happens."

"But Dr. Lowe thinks I should have more tests. I might have epilepsy or brain cancer or I don't know what."

Virgil knew it wasn't any of those and all of mankind's medical exams would find nothing so he said, "Honey, you can have any tests you think you need. Anything at all. You just say the word. I'll even set them up for you."

"But what about that dead Bea person? I can't keep acting like I'm her for hours every day, maybe even longer. Virgil, she sounds so unsavory. What about the shop?"

He lied about Bea Sting. "Ellen, it's not as bad as all that. Really, you only pretended to be her once or twice. And even then you were fine, you didn't do anything out of the ordinary. Okay, you punched me yesterday, but I deserved it for taking you to that morgue. Honestly, I don't even notice it anymore when you have your lapses. You've been acting totally normal. Totally. Especially at the store. Ask Woody. I just think you're having some blackouts and don't remember little parts of your day, that's all. It's probably stress."

"What about you? Isn't it hard on you having to keep an eye on me every minute?"

He lied about himself. Even as the words formed on his tongue, they felt more to him like making a wish than a lie. "No, not at all. You're my wife. It's my job to stand by you no matter what it takes. Besides, I'll really miss you if you go to the hospital. I need you beside me. I can't run the shop by myself. The house will be really empty. We can handle this thing together. I love you."

When he was done, tears welled in Ellen's eyes. "I'm afraid, Virgil. For my health. You're not the one with a runaway brain, I am. And it really frightens me."

Virgil took her in his arms. He kissed her salty cheek. He talked to the blue and shining eyes.

"I know, honey, I know. It's just for a couple more days. Like I said, I'll watch over you like a hawk and if I see it get any worse, we'll rush you right to the hospital. I promise, okay?"

She nodded, squeezing his waist. She blinked and forced a smile. "I have my doubts but if you say this is the way you want it, okay. A few more days."

Ellen backed out of his loose hug, sniffling. "Well, right now what I think we both need is a good lunch."

"That's probably a good idea."

"Will you stay at the shop while I go home?"

"Sure." Virgil hadn't called the yacht club. He'd do it while she was gone.

Ellen said, "I want to change for lunch."

She headed for the door and opened it. Virgil stepped quickly to her. He turned her by the shoulders and looked into her eyes. He spoke—intensely, like a movie vampire mesmerizing his prey—past Ellen to the circuitry of her soul which he knew she shared with another spirit.

Slowly he said, "That's *good*. I want you to change *soon*. *Come* to me after you *have* changed."

Ellen cocked her head, puzzled, moving back a pace onto the sidewalk.

"I will, Virgil, I will. Goodness sakes."

At the house, Ellen fielded a phone call from a friend in the Junior League who'd heard from the wife of Ellen's insurance agent that she was feeling poorly. "Oh, I know how you feel," the friend said, "wouldn't we all just like to go bat-shit once in a while? Well, I say good for you, Ellen. It can get to be too much, can't it? Sometimes I think I'd like to just tell the world that it drives me up a wall and to leave me alone for a while. But we can't, can we. We're women, we're supposed to be stronger. It's not fair but then what is? Well, you keep me posted. I just might come join you."

Ellen changed into a dark skirt for lunch then went into the bathroom to wash her face and brush her hair out of the ponytail. She propped her hands on the sink and leaned close to the mirror, almost touching her nose to the glass.

Ellen's eyes filled the image before Beatrice. The woman rapped on her forehead with her knuckles, as though softly on a door.

"Whatever you are in there," Ellen whispered, "leave me alone. I don't like this."

During lunch at the yacht club, Virgil hung on Ellen's words, staring at her face and hands. After lunch, back at the shop, he hovered and watched her keenly from behind corners. Ellen lost her patience once and snapped at him, "Go about your business! My goodness, leave a person to do her work."

Soothed after the outburst, she approached and said, "I appreciate you keeping an eye on me but it's making me antsy, like you're expecting something from me. So could we just pretend things are normal?" He nodded but stayed at her side. She whirled on him. "Shoo!"

Virgil behaved like a young suitor waiting for his girl to finish dressing upstairs, making half-hearted attempts to focus his attention elsewhere, anxious to call her name up the steps. Beatrice enjoyed watching him stew. She believed that whoever was running the plan must have been enjoying it too for she was not sent into Ellen all afternoon.

At six o'clock, Woody had just left and Ellen stood at the counter tucking the day's monies into a bank deposit sack. She scribbled entries into the shop's register. Suddenly, Beatrice—who had never balanced a checkbook in her life—set down Ellen's pencil and put her chin in her hand to watch Virgil sweeping up filings and dust in the framing room.

She'd gotten his message that morning—"I want you to change *soon. Come* to me."—dropped like a note in a bottle into the waters of Ellen's eyes. He believed her now. He was waiting for her, waiting all day. He looked covertly up at her from his broom, back down to his work, up again.

She sneaked three twenties out of the sack, folding them into a pocket of Ellen's dress.

"Virgil?"

"Hmmm?"

"You bought lunch. Let me take you to dinner tonight. I want lobster at the Key West Grille."

He leaned the broom against the wall and walked over.

"Shouldn't we stay in? How do you feel?"

"Like lobster."

Virgil backed up several steps from her. He dug his hand into his pocket. Quietly, he said, "Alright," and quickly tossed his keys.

She caught them, left-handed.

He stood motionless, his arm outstretched from

the toss. The shop was unmarked by sound; the jangling keys snatched out of the air seemed to take all other sound with them into her catching palm.

Virgil opened his mouth, closed it, licked his lips, and said, *"Boom."*

She smiled at his cleverness. She answered with the rest of her ditty from Fatima's parlor. *"Ba-ba-boom."*

He said, "Hi."

Beatrice set his keys on the counter. She walked in front of him, moving until her breasts graced his chest. He lowered his arm to drape it across her shoulders. The other arm circled her waist. She stood inside his loose embrace. The man seemed stunned. She nuzzled his cheek.

"Hi," she said.

She wanted his arms to draw her inward—it would have been a sign of her growing sway over him—but his arms did not. He held her the way a man holds something he has stolen, tightly enough to control it but without conviction that it is his, knowing it might be reclaimed from him at any moment. Even so, she breathed deeply against him.

"I don't know what I'm doing," he whispered.

She smiled into his shirt. "It's not your fault. It's a limitation."

"What?"

"The living. Even the sort-of living like me. We're not allowed to know what we're doing."

"The plan?"

"Uh-huh."

His arms did tighten. She felt his jaw work, his mouth in her hair.

"I don't care, I've got to know. Who am I holding? Are you an angel? Are you real? Have I gone crazy too? What are you, Bea?"

She leaned back to see the question in his eyes. The ring of his arms supported her. "I'm a woman."

She kissed him gently on the mouth.

She broke free of his arms. He was left in mid-kiss, stumbling forward, confounded by the sudden lack of her.

"Virgil, cool your jets."

He opened his eyes. "What? Bea? What?"

"Do you want to do this?"

"Do what? Kiss? Yes."

"No, you jerk, not just kiss. Not just jump in the sack either. I mean this."

Virgil spread his hands. "This what, Bea? What are we doing?"

"This. The hugging and quiet little kisses. Lobster dinner and candlelight. You know . . ." She mimicked Virgil, deepening her voice almost to a yawn, "*Come* to me."

She extended her hand and waved it back and forth, taking in both of them and all of the unexplored and unexplained that lay between them.

"This this."

Beatrice sat on the stool behind the cash register.

"Because," she said, "I want to. With you. Do you know, Virgil? You were the last thing I saw

dying on that sidewalk. You, and your voice. I . . .
I felt something when I heard your voice. I want
to know what that feeling was. I want to find out
the rest of it."

She shrugged. "But I got to tell you we don't
exactly have what you could call an easy row to
hoe in front of us. You know? I mean," she made
a sympathetic face for the prospects of their des-
tinies, the couple made up of the quick and the
phantom, "look at us."

Beatrice pressed her point further, wanting all
cards on the table. "You know my situation. I
don't know when I'm going to be here day or
night or how long each time. I don't know what's
going to happen to me or you. I mean, I look
ahead at our future and, frankly, it's a dilemma."

Virgil stuck his tongue into his lower lip.
Again, she saw that he knew what was coming.

"And besides," she said because it was time to
say it, "you're married."

He paused and showed his lower teeth again.
This was his thinking face; she was learning him.

"Yes. I am."

"And? I got the very strong impression you
wanted things to get better between you and
Ellen. How does that affect you and me? And vice
versa?"

"I don't know," he said. Beatrice grimaced. He
sped up his words at the face she made, before
she could say something. "I'm being honest here.
This is new territory for me." He put his hands in
his pockets. "Ah, shit."

He looked at her, Beatrice, the spirit looking back at him out of Ellen's body.

"I guess I'm going to have an affair on my wife."

Virgil shook his head at the prospect. He lowered his glance and murmured "hmm" to himself.

He looked up and offered Beatrice a small, unsure smile.

"It's kind of already started, hasn't it?"

Beatrice shrugged her shoulders in a sort of sympathetic "oops" gesture.

She gave him a moment of silence to hang the realization of infidelity up on the walls inside himself, in the private room she knew was inside every man, gave him a space to back away and look at it, make sure it was straight, make sure it matched the room.

When he looked up, she said, "It's not too late. We've only known each other a couple of days, we can still back out. You can settle in again with old reliable Ellen. I'll bake her an apple pie. I'll leave it in the fridge then I'll just disappear. You won't ever know I was here."

He nodded. "Yes," he said. "We've only known each other a couple of days."

"That's not very long."

"No it's not. But you were sent to me, we both know that now. I've got to know what that means somehow. So, yes, even though it's been just a short while, I know something."

"And what is that?"

"I know I want more of you too."

She laughed in nervous relief. She took him into her arms and squeezed hard. His arms tightened around her in response.

"Oh yes," she whispered, "this is what I missed. This is why I couldn't go into the light. Just this, right here."

At the beginning of their lobster dinner, Beatrice slipped the waiter the sixty dollars she'd taken from the store's cash bag.

Virgil saw the transfer and asked, "Where did you get that?"

"I took it from the shop."

"Bea." He searched for words. "We're not supposed to steal from the business."

"Well, I just couldn't stand the thought that right in the middle of dinner your wife might show up and start gagging and bitching about the food and you'd get stuck paying the tab. She probably hates lobster."

Virgil smiled. "She does."

"And I wanted to take you out to dinner. So I had to pinch some cash out of the bag to do it."

"Don't do it anymore, okay?"

She shrugged. "Hate the sin. Love the sinner."

Waiting for the food to arrive, Beatrice and Virgil sipped red wine. He began to talk about himself. He told about his past in Virginia—private schools, summer camps in the Blue Ridge Mountains, and college at the University of Florida. His father, a high school principal, had died ten years ago from lung cancer, a smoker; his mother was in a home up north, Alzheimer's. No brothers or sisters. Then, without her asking, he told her about the killing.

"It was a Saturday when we went out."

Beatrice set down her wineglass.

"It was sunny. Late October, you know, when the rest of the country is heading into fall but in South Florida we're real smug about our weather. Bugs are gone. Days are shorter but still hot. I went skiing with three buddies from the firm. I was the designated driver. I was only going to have a few beers. Stay straight, let the rest of them party. How's that for irony?"

Beatrice nodded.

"It's funny how small a thing it was. I'm hauling one of my friends behind the boat, we're taking a tight turn to get up some speed for him, then the hull thumped and the prop kicked up for a second, like I'd gone over a speed bump. I didn't even think about it until my buddy let go of the rope, yelling at us. I turned to pick him up and I remember . . . I just remember her arm. Her arm floating in the water. And my first thought was, How could this be? It was a little bump. But there was this arm floating on its own and this guy screaming at the top of his lungs. Twenty feet away there was a patch of water the color of iodine and in the middle of it, white, I remember how white she was even surrounded by all that bloody water. The girl sank, blood pouring out of cuts and stripes all over her. And I remember thinking to myself how it was such a little moment. So small. This girl had just died an awful death and there was nothing to mark it, no rising music, no clap of thunder, no crowd. Nothing. Just more sunshine. The water was rocking real gentle. Just four drunk buddies, one of us who wouldn't stop screaming."

Virgil and Beatrice both looked down at the white table linen as though it were a campfire, as if this were where the oracle lay drawing Virgil's tale from him.

Beatrice fingered the stem of her glass. "What'd you do?" she asked.

With disgust, Virgil repeated, "What'd I do?"

He licked his lips. "I stood there, watching her go down, and my only thought was, How can I get away from this? Not thinking that I'd just killed a human being but how can I figure a way out of it. I said to my friend in the water, 'Get in the boat.' And they all looked at me, you know, in horror, and that's when I knew I was alone. They hadn't done this thing. I had."

"That's terrible."

"No, Bea, they were right. The other two guys in the boat dove in after the girl and tried to bring her up. I stayed on board. I was the killer, the one who was driving. I wasn't allowed in the water. They couldn't find her, she'd sunk too far. Another boat came by and called the Coast Guard. Their divers went down after the body. They checked my blood alcohol. I got arrested and I went to jail."

Beatrice said only, "Virgil."

He took up his red wine to conclude his story. But he held it and could not take his eyes from it.

"Every day I see that water. And every day I wish I'd dived into it to try and save her. Every day I wish I'd never told my buddy to get in the boat. The law convicted me because I had a couple of beers in my system, Bea. But that's not what I was guilty of."

Then he told her of prison and all the barren time he'd had to feel over and over again the boat chop the girl, nights and days that became as brackish and baleful as the ocean around her savaged sinking body. Four years spent that way. Then Ellen.

Virgil sipped his wine to end his turn. They sat hand-in-hand for a while, the candle between them a small sun holding their two worlds in gravity and orbit. When the lobster arrived Virgil perked up and pulled her plate in front of him to crack the shell and prepare the meat for her.

Beatrice took this as her cue and gave Virgil her own truths. The things she'd done with her life weren't hard to say to him. She was dead. They were done. Texas. Miami. Key West. The dancing, the strangers, money tossed on disheveled sheets, promises tossed with the money but worth so much less to her callous secret heart. Her death, quick and disagreeable as deaths go; inevitable, she believed, death waiting for her not in ambush but as a family legacy. Her mother died young herself. They'd shared the same heart, it seemed, both doomed to be unhappy and stopped young.

He asked gently, "What about your father?"

Beatrice stuck a knuckle in her eye.

He prompted. "That was you under hypnosis in Dr. Lowe's office. Wasn't it?"

She nodded.

"I'm really sorry," he said.

She sniffed. "Oh, the old bastard just couldn't keep his hands off me." She gave a brave laugh. "I guess I was just too pretty even back then."

"I'm sorry."

Virgil waited. She put all her fingers on her forehead and pinched as if to drag off a mask.

"Well," she dropped her hands, gaining composure now behind a sniff and another valiant smile, "we know there's at least one son of a bitch in Heaven."

Virgil smiled. "Probably just that one. And he only got in because he helped make you."

The flush cooled from her face. Beatrice shoved away the orange wreckage of the lobster.

"Well, that's it. No more rich foods." She slapped her hip. "Old Ellen here's going on a diet."

Virgil ran a finger down his chin.

Beatrice picked a remnant of meat from the lobster's gouged frame. She wiped her hands and looked at the watch on Ellen's wrist.

"It's almost ten," she said. "That's four hours. That's the longest one yet."

She sucked her fingers. "Virgil, don't you get it? Don't you feel it?"

"Feel what?"

"Haven't you noticed that the more you and I . . . you know . . . get to know each other, the longer I stay in Ellen's body?"

"It does seem to be working that way."

"So if you and I keep on going like we are . . ."

Beatrice pushed her hands across the table at Virgil. She worked the fingers slowly like two tarantulas stepping over the linen. Her face took on a queer, wide-eyed look.

"Look," she said, suddenly breathless, "I know this might sound harsh, but if you and I are falling for each other, then maybe that's the way things are supposed to work. Maybe that's what the big plan is. Love wins out. That's probably what Heaven wants here on earth, Virgil, that's why I was sent to you."

She squeezed his hands.

"Can't you feel it?"

"Feel what?"

"Fate. Kismet. I don't know. The plan."

She squeezed again.

"I feel it, Virgil. You can too. Just give yourself up to it."

Virgil paused, as though trying to siphon some of the urgency from her voice.

"What do you think will happen to Ellen? To her soul?"

"I don't know. Probably it'll go back to Heaven."

She lifted one palm to shoulder height with the other still touching him, a woman swearing not on a Bible but on her new lover's hand.

"Look," she said, "I can only tell you how I feel. We both have souls. What about them? Don't our souls deserve happiness in this life?

Virgil, think about it. We were brought together. You and me, across distance, time, dimensions, odds, I can't even guess what stood between us. But here we are. We've been matched up twice, first by Top Hat and then by Heaven. So if not even death could keep us apart, how can we let life separate us now?"

Beatrice stood. She took a deep breath like a woman about to jump off of something high and risky. She pulled up on Virgil's hand. He too rose out of his seat.

She said, "Only one way to find out."

Hand-in-hand and without words they walked to Whitehead Street. The night around them was motionless, without others on the sidewalks or breeze in the palms; a gust or a car with headlights or even some tourists window shopping after hours would have given them company and so would have helped distract her from the flutter in her chest and the sense that Virgil's hand was holding hers only loosely and seemed damp. At the front door, nervous, Virgil dropped the keys sliding them into the lock.

Inside, she stood in the foyer under the chandelier, arms crossed. Virgil leaned against the wall.

Beatrice put a hand to her breast. "That was a lovely dinner." She said this as a way of assuring him that here on the precipice she was still firmly Beatrice.

Without flair, without a trace of dance, she unbuttoned Ellen's blouse. She unbelted her skirt, unsnapped the bra, peeled down the panties. She

let them molt from her, fall into a collapsed pile at
her feet. Beatrice walked out of them, Venus out
of her clam shell, naked, another woman's flesh
between her and Virgil but closer now. The gen-
erated heat was all Beatrice's. She moved to him
and pressed him to the wall to give him all of her
heat.

He opened and shut to her hothouse warmth,
surrounded her slowly with a raised leg and his
two arms, curled his head over hers and pulled
her in, Venus flytrap. They stood together for
minutes, sharing the solitude of two expectant,
burdened hearts.

Virgil dropped the leg and pushed her back.
He put his fingers to work on the buttons of his
own shirt.

Beatrice tackled him there in the hall, laughing,
and wrestled off Virgil's clothes.

Straddling him on her knees, she took him
inside her and orgasmed at once.

"Ahhh," she laughed, "ahhh God! Virgil, God!
Roll me over!"

She bailed onto her shoulder and Virgil rolled
with her. He put his hands on the hardwood floor.
Beatrice lay on the bed of Ellen's spilled clothes.

When he came she came with him. In the
moment, blind and bursting, Beatrice felt her soul
soar out of the body but not alone, there was Virgil too; like two thunderbolts, they flashed and
struck the same ground at once and were spent.

10

THE grandfather clock pealed midnight.

They lay naked under the blanket, she with her head on his shoulder. Virgil felt her rustle. She put her hand between her legs.

Furiously, she kicked back the blanket and clicked on her lamp. So it was Ellen who had heard the grandfather clock toll.

"This is sick," she said. "I can't tell you how disgusting this is."

He propped himself on his elbows, irritated, like a man who has set his clock radio to awaken him to classical music and is instead jolted out of bed to heavy metal.

"Ellen, calm down."

"Calm down? I'm married to a man who takes advantage of his wife while she's blacked out? What are you, some kind of necrophiliac?"

"Ellen."

"Virgil, I'll tell you right now, you're the one who's sick in this house."

"Ellen."

"The last thing I remember is doing the books at the store and now I wake up sore six hours later to find out you've been having an orgy with me the whole time."

"Not the whole time," he grumbled. "We went to dinner first."

"Oh, don't you talk smart with me, mister sicko."

She sank into the rocker beneath the window. "What are you doing to me?"

He pulled back the bedding to sit on the edge of the mattress facing her. The fragrances of sex, funky and dank, wafted up with his sweep of the blanket.

"I'm not doing anything to you," he said. "You're my wife. What's wrong with sex between a man and his wife?"

"But it's not *me* you're doing it with. It's someone else."

She slapped the arms of the chair. "It's that Bea Sting woman again, isn't it?"

"No."

Virgil was dismayed that the lie he had just told and the one he was about to tell were coming to him so easily, water from a tap. That's what he was becoming, he had to admit: an adulterer. A spigot of lies and deceptions in the face of a woman who had never harmed him or fooled him, whose body he could still embrace but whose soul he now could lie to. He felt a small chunk of him-self—of his old self (of his own soul?)—shearing off, like an iceberg in unaccustomed warm waters.

"We talked about this before. You've only acted like you were someone else a couple of times, that's all. Come on, tonight I never even knew you were having a blackout until right now when you told me. We worked all day together, we went out for a nice dinner, then we came home and, yes, we made love. Yes, several times. Like we used to do and, frankly, like we should never have stopped doing. And what's wrong with that? A man enjoying his wife?"

Ellen stared at him, slack-jawed. "How was it?"

"How was what?"

"You know."

"It was . . . I don't know. What do you want me to say?"

"Say what it was, Virgil. How would you describe having sex with me while I was uncon-scious?"

"Problem-free, I guess."

She nodded, grim. "It was her."

Quickly, Virgil pounded the lie down harder. It was a nail that was not in all the way, was not holding. He was amazed at the strength he could command.

"Ellen, you're being paranoid. Bea Sting has nothing to do with you or anybody else. She's dead. I can't believe I'm hearing this."

"Women know these things, Virgil."

"Are you," he mocked a gasp, "are you accusing me of having an affair? With *who*, for God's sake?"

"With my other personality. During my blackouts."

"With Bea Sting?"

"Yes."

Virgil yanked away the sheet and reached to the floor for his underpants. Putting them on, he huffed, offended.

"I can't believe this. I share a wonderful, sexy evening with my wife, who at midnight suddenly decides to tell me that I have actually, all that time, been with another woman."

She nodded again, studying him.

He headed for the door. "I can't sleep now. You've got me too upset. Let me know when you get this idea out of your head and I'll come back upstairs."

Calmly, she said, "Tomorrow I'm going to the mental hospital."

He turned in the hall. "No."

"You can't stop me. It's a voluntary committal. I don't need your permission."

He returned to the corner of the bed, speaking while he walked. His tone became supplicating.

"Ellen, please believe me. You're not turning into anyone else. Not Bea Sting, not Jackie O, nobody. You're fine, you're Ellen, all day long. All that's happening to you is a couple of times a day you lose your memory of what you'd been doing for the last several hours."

"Six hours this time."

"Yes, six, alright. But, sweetheart, you don't need a mental ward. You don't need to be locked up away from your home and business and husband. Look, how about this? We can get you some more of those tests at St. Joseph's that Dr. Lowe talked about. They sounded awful but if that's what you want, you can start tomorrow."

"No. That's not what I want."

"Okay. Good."

She leaned the rocker back. Chin up, shoulders arranged squarely in the chair, she was a naked judge. She pronounced: "I know why you don't want me to go to the mental ward. You don't want me to take her away from you."

He stood. He shuffled as though in leg shackles past the foot of the bed to the bedroom door.

"Ellen, Bea Sting is dead."

"That doesn't seem to stop her."

He left the room and trod numbly down the steps.

"That woman's in my head," she called after him. "I want her out."

Virgil stood in his underpants at the bottom of the staircase in the tangled dark of the big house. He gazed up the stairs to the dimly glowing room where not Beatrice but Ellen sat in the light.

Virgil made a cup of instant coffee. He took it in front of the television but did not turn it on. He drank his coffee and thought about going back out into the night. It was Key West, the smallest city in America that never slept.

Instead, he climbed the unlit stairs and slipped back into bed.

She reached her hand through the darkness. He took it. She put her head on his chest, settling it down with a deep sigh like a spaceship landing. Virgil did not know who would step out of the ship, Ellen or Bea.

He stared up into the iron black.

"Virgil?" A moving jaw on his chest, the capsule was opening.

"Yes?"

"Can we talk for a minute?"

"Yes."

"I've been trying to see all this from your viewpoint."

He closed his eyes.

She said, "Why you don't want me to go to the hospital."

"Uh-huh."

"I can see your side of it a little. We haven't exactly been the model couple for the past year or so, have we?"

"Hard to say."

"Well, you don't have to say it for it to be true. It is and we both know it."

"Alright."

"Now, you tell me that I'm acting normally during those periods when I say I can't remember. Truth be told, Virgil, from the looks of things I'm not acting normally at all. I'm acting better than normal. You've said we laugh more, I eat cottage cheese and fruits, which are better for me. You said we had a romantic dinner tonight. We make love, which . . . well, that's good to be doing that. Married people should be doing that. And to be honest, you're right. You and I had sort of forgotten for a while to be doing that, hadn't we?"

"Yes."

"Well, it's true and we have to face up to it. Nobody's fault. So, from where you sit, you've got it pretty good actually. I've been making you a pretty good wife the past few days. I even socked you in the kisser, which I can't condone but you did deserve it, you admitted that."

"It was a good shot, too."

"So you've said. Left-handed at that. Well, with all this in mind, I can understand why you wouldn't want your wife trundling off to an insane asylum just right now. You'd have to start working more hours at the shop and you'd have to say good-bye for a while to all this newfound fun and sex and fisticuffs."

"That's not exactly how I look at it."

"You don't need to take a defensive tone. I'm simply trying to fathom your reasons for keeping me out of the hospital. And I can see that you do have some reasons. In some respects they're even good ones. We're behaving the way we're supposed to. Like we love each other. Now, all I have to do is agree to pay the price for us having such a good time."

"What price?"

"I have to agree to not remember any of it."

He sat up; the color was sucked from her face,

grayed from the throw of a dying moon.

She completed the thought: "At least until this condition goes away by itself or I get fed up with it and take myself off to the hospital anyway. And I can't say how long until either one of those happens."

He let go her hand.

"Ellen, we can get you some more tests, like we talked about."

She sat up to match him and turned on the lamp. The warming bulb seemed to imbue the rumpled bed, the walls, the yellow air with the rising fever of their words.

"I told you I don't want more tests."

"Then what do you want?"

"I want," she said evenly, "for you to swear to God that what you've said is true. That I'm not Bea Sting or any other split personality. That it's me."

"I swear," he said, bobbing his head when he spoke as if the words in his mouth were solid and he had to shake them out like pills from a bottle— he could swear to God, God had sent Beatrice, clearly He was behind all this—"to God."

Her eyes held on him for a moment, detectors, sensors. Then they blinked and crinkled. "Good," she said, patting him on the knee, "good. That's all I ever wanted was for whatever problems you and I might have in our marriage to stay between the two of us. We can work them out, the two of us. I couldn't bear the thought of another woman. Even if I was that other woman. That sounds so silly, doesn't it?"

She turned off the lamp. She slid under the covers, Virgil did the same. He lay, eyes closed, listening to Ellen's breathing, hearing her moan first then snore, waiting for a change in her like a seaman taking the measure of the ocean, eyeing the fickle clouds, minding the wind's musings, heeding the whitecaps.

Beatrice watched Ellen waken. Virgil was already out of bed, downstairs, probably reading the paper over coffee. Ellen showered and dressed and went down to eat. Beatrice endured the routine, the too many cups of too-weak coffee, the gooey-eyed eggs, bacon, toast and jelly.

She waited for her turn in Ellen through the sunny stroll to the store beside Virgil, opening the door, straightening the workbench. Ellen called the bank, restocked some brushes while mumbling about Woody's lateness, greeted a customer, sent the man cheerily out the door, told Woody he was late. She watched Ellen's treachery which she had expected to come in some form. When her time arrived in Ellen at mid-morning, Ellen was busy punching numbers into a calculator at the counter. Beatrice lowered the poised, now alive fingers to the small plastic keys, typed in one million dollars, hit total and then approached Virgil with her finger crossing her lips, shushing him in pantomime.

He said, "What?"

She waved him off, conveying "Don't speak."

He furrowed his brow. She pointed to herself,

mouthed the word "Bea" and waved hello. He smiled broadly and waved back. This time he copied her and mouthed the silent question: "What?"

Beatrice reached in the pocket of Ellen's skirt and pulled out a small cassette recorder. From her other pocket she produced two already full tapes.

Virgil's mouth dropped open, speechlessly displaying that he was speechless.

Beatrice spoke. "Virgil?"

He didn't answer; she gestured for him to say something. "Uh, yeah? Yeah, *Ellen*?"

Beatrice lofted her eyebrows at him. She motioned him to play it cool.

"Watch the store," she said, eyes lit up, "I've got to take a huge shit." Virgil threw his hands to his head. Beatrice walked the recorder to the bathroom, swished her dress to make the sound of lifting it and closed the recorder in the room, leaving the door slightly ajar.

"That ought to hold her," she quietly said coming back to Virgil. They moved to the far end of the store from the bathroom.

"What was that?" he hissed, pointing back to the toilet. "She was taping our conversations. She doesn't trust me."

"Virgil, I hate to bust your bubble but you're not the world's cleverest liar."

"But she believed me."

"She said she believed you. That doesn't mean she does. And obviously she doesn't."

"I had to lie. I didn't have any choice."

She kindly patted his chest. "Yes you did. Excuse me."

Beatrice tiptoed to the bathroom door and opened it with stealth. She reached her head in and sighed loudly once. She slipped the door shut again.

"Look," Virgil said, "I've been thinking some things over and this just convinces me even more what we have to do."

He sat on the stool behind the counter, exasperation in his body. He looked to see that Woody was busy with his boxes and brooms in the back.

"Bea, I swore to her last night that she wasn't turning into you during her blackouts. Did you hear me tell her that?"

"Of course."

"You know if she finds out you're here, she'll haul both of you off to a psych ward somewhere. There's no other way around it. You're going to have to start acting more the way Ellen would. That's it. So starting now I've got to teach you about the shop. How to frame, managing the books, the names of regular customers. We'll have to avoid her friends for a while. I'll have to let Woody go."

"No."

"No what? Bea. Please."

"No. You're not going to turn me into Ellen. I'm not going to be your bookkeeper, your boss and your housemate. You've already had one of those. If for some reason you think you need another, you can have the old one back. She's in the bathroom."

"Fine." He surrendered, hands up. "Then we're nailed, because I can't keep fighting Ellen every damn day about going to the hospital."

"Oh, Virgil, wise up." Beatrice spread his knees on the stool and stepped between them. "Your wife never had the slightest intention of going to any mental hospital. She was just using that as a way to suck sympathy from you and anybody else within earshot. Doctors, her friends, that insurance guy, she was eating the attention up with a spoon. You never talked her out of going, she let you talk her out of it. She had you telling her how much you needed her: 'Oh, honey, don't leave me alone in that big bad store and this big empty house.' Virgil, she was loving it. She pushed all your buttons and she's still pushing them. Believe me on this one. I used to push buttons for a living."

He looked hurt.

Beatrice put her hand on his cheek.

She crept back to the bathroom, opened the door and stepped inside. She took the listening recorder inside.

"Uhhhn," she groaned, grinning madly out the door to Virgil.

"Phew." She heaved a sigh. "Oh, my gracious."

She flushed, washed her hands, and came out carrying the recorder.

"Oh, goodness," she patted her gut satisfactorily, "that would've definitely killed a lesser woman."

Beatrice raised a finger to Virgil for silence.

She held up the recorder and said, "Virgil. I did some thinking while I was on the pot. I want to show you something. Here. Look what I have done. I'm ashamed of myself. I was secretly recording us this morning in case I might have another blackout. That's because I didn't trust you to be straight with me. I thought you might be lying to me about that vile Bea Sting critter. But I have decided not to give in to my own deceitful nature and to trust you completely. You are a good man, Virgil, better than I deserve, and I am going to do everything I can to be worthy of you. Now come over here and fuck me against the cash register till we both sing opera."

With that, Beatrice held the tape recorder high like the severed head of an enemy and clicked it off.

Turning to Virgil, she said, "Let's get something straight right now. I didn't live and die just to come back to earth and have to hide who I was. Do you understand?"

"I think so."

"If your wife doesn't like the way I behave, what can she do about it? I don't think we have to give in to Ellen's petty threats. Do you?"

"No."

"Good." She tossed the inert recorder onto the countertop. "When she hears this, she's going to know something's up. But that's alright. We'll just have to weather it, whatever she does next. Besides, how is she going to hide anything from me?"

"I don't know."

"And even if she does go to a mental hospital, it's only a voluntary committal. She'll check in. I'll check her out. She'll check back in. I'll check out. They'll stop taking her pretty quick."

"I guess so."

"Alright. That's settled. Now, stay right there."

Virgil sat on the stool. Beatrice walked to the back. She called for Woody.

"Yeah?"

The boy came out carrying a bottle of window cleaner. Beatrice took it from him.

"Go to lunch."

"It's only ten thirty."

"Go."

Woody looked past Beatrice's shoulder at Virgil. He shrugged.

Beatrice dug into Ellen's skirt pocket, found a ten dollar bill and gave it to the kid.

"Go."

"Okay. Cool. When do you want me back?"

"One o'clock."

Woody looked past her shoulder to Virgil on the stool. He called over, "Man, see. If you were my age, you'd need till like three."

Virgil flatly said, "Go, Woody."

Beatrice added, "Now."

"Cool."

Woody walked away. He turned back and shook a fist at Virgil, solidarity. "Yeah, Virg. Go for it."

She followed him to the front door. When Woody was gone, she threw the dead bolt and flipped over the plastic sign from OPEN to CLOSED.

She moved back to Virgil. She pulled him off the stool and backed him against the cash register. She puckered and slowly he pushed his lips through the curtain of her hair.

"Repeat after me," she whispered.

"What?"

"Figaro. Figaro. Figaro."

11

BEATRICE stayed through the work day. Virgil convinced her to begin learning about the workings of the store, not just to mimic Ellen for the sake of appearances but so that he wouldn't have to do everything himself.

He showed her the rudiments of operating the cash register. He walked her through the aisles of art supplies, showed her how to measure and cut mats and frames.

"I got an artistic eye," she told him. "I did my own choreography and designed a lot of my own outfits. I can do this."

When Woody came back a little after one o'clock, Beatrice had a talk with him about girls. She told him he smelled very nice today and that women like that in a man, women are very sensitive and things like smells, textures, and sounds move them. She told Woody to remember this and she would give him more information about women gradually as she deemed him ready to understand it.

When she was finished, Woody smiled at her. "You're having one of those blackouts, aren't you?"

"What blackouts, Woody?"

The boy indicated Virgil, seated at the register. "The ones Virgil told me about."

"Well, if Virgil told you, it must be so."

"This is so excellent."

Beatrice thanked Woody and told him to go into the gallery to dust frames and change a light-bulb that was out.

He hesitated. "You're not still my boss, are you?"

"Don't test me."

Woody obeyed and went into the gallery.

In the afternoon, they let Woody go an hour early, after Virgil warned him not to mention Ellen's blackouts to her again, even if she was in the middle of one. "It'll only make things worse," he said with no further explanation. Despite a look of keen curiosity, Woody agreed.

At six Virgil and Beatrice closed the shop and walked home hand-in-hand, greeting other retreating shopkeepers on the sidewalk. Beatrice whispered to Virgil, "I like this."

Virgil identified one man who said to them "good evening" as the Cubano butcher, Leoncio. Beatrice tugged Virgil around and towed him back up the sidewalk to Leoncio.

"*Con permiso, señor,*" she said in her Texas

Spanish, *"me encantaría por favor carne de ternero. Es para mi enamorado aquí."* She tugged Virgil's hand excitedly when Leoncio bowed his big brown head, uttered *"Sí, señora, sí,"* and led them the half block to his *carneceria.* He unlocked the door and picked for her the best veal shanks in the glass counter.

On the way to Whitehead Street, Beatrice carried the veal in Leoncio's wax butcher bag with both hands like a purse filled with cash. She hugged Virgil's arm and did not speak but breathed deeply the departing sun that gave jewel facets and tinsel to Key West's old sailors' and merchants' homes.

Beatrice ignited the kitchen: burners, oven, salsa music, candles. Life and light flocked to the room. Virgil stood in the doorway for the first few minutes of her performance. She did a dance step at the sink, she twirled make-believe pixie dust across the pots and counters. He went upstairs to his habit of showering off the day.

In the shower, he was too happy, so he worried about being caught. He envisioned his wife barging in the front door, catching Beatrice in her kitchen, cooking for her husband, bellowing, "How *dare* you! Get *out!*" Then he looked with his mind's eye below his dripping feet down into the real kitchen and there was his sprite singing and prancing. His fear vanished, boiled into the shower's steam and out by the humming fan.

It was seven o'clock now. Beatrice had been present for more than eight hours this time.

When he came down, the dining room table was set with silver, china and red wine in goblets, the room lit only by a candelabra. Beatrice barred his way into the kitchen, though the smells hooked him by the nose and drew him.

"Sit down," she said, pointing to a seat at the table. "Dinner is served. And when we're finished, I want you to take me out dancing."

Before the first bite, the aroma of the food began to work on Virgil. He saw himself spending the evening in, sated and still, not twisting in a Key West disco.

"Smells great," he said. "But I don't know about dancing. On weeknights, we always used to . . ."

She stretched her lips. She put two fists on her hips.

He said quickly, "I'll take you dancing."

"Just sit."

Virgil slid into his chair. The candles and china and silverware gleamed, the room was dim and diced by glints of light. Beatrice went into smooth action. She put a heaping portion in front of him, then a smaller version at her own place. She sat primly.

"Osso bucco with risotto alla Milanese. Asparagus and my special Dallas spicy hollandaise."

Virgil stared down at his plate while Beatrice spread her napkin over her lap.

She said, "Eat."

Virgil raised a finger with a thought. "Right back." He rose and went to the kitchen. He took a bottle of ketchup from the refrigerator.

Beatrice watched him, fork in hand, head still, eyes following. At the table, Virgil glopped a heaping of ketchup on his plate.

"Virgil?"

"Yes?" He looked up from slicing a wedge of the osso bucco.

"That's veal."

"I know."

"That's ketchup."

"I put ketchup on everything."

"She didn't mind?"

"No."

Beatrice sighed. "Fine. Eat."

He smiled and smacked his lips in exaggerated anticipation. Beatrice held her posture, fork pointing up, shoulders square, eyes on him. Virgil skidded the meat through the ketchup and slid it into his mouth. He squinted.

Chewing, he said, "Oh, yeah."

She sliced a dainty bit of the veal and put it in her mouth. "Oh," she murmured. "I can cook, can't I?"

"Bea?"

"Mmm hmm?"

"Why were you so unhappy?"

"Aw, Virg."

"I want to know. We've talked about me, now I want to know about you. How does that happen? I mean, look at all the things you could do. You could cook, you were beautiful, you were sexy, smart, funny. I'm guessing you were a good dancer."

She threw a comic grimace at him.

"Why didn't things work out for you? Tell me."

She sipped the wine. Her fork clinked on the side of her plate when she set it down.

"What can I tell you?" she said. "It's all a myth. Beauty. Money. A little fame. Being a good cook. Even being a good lay. No matter how much you think each of these things matters, they all add up to zero when it's over. Your money won't sit next to you in a pile in a hospital room and take your hand when you're dying. Your boyfriends are all gone because that's what boyfriends do. Your looks mean nothing if all they're good for is to get the tits on your corpse one last poke by some horny deputy. It's a sham."

She raised a finger at Heaven.

"And they know it. You know what they do? They make us come down here and start from scratch each time, little drooling babies without a clue. Then we spend our whole lives trying to figure out how to be happy and most of us get it wrong, we wind up grabbing a hold of money or whatever else makes us feel good and we call that happiness. Then, at the last minute, right before we close our eyes, we start to figure it out. We look around and we finally see that the only thing that ever meant something to us was love. Not the car, not the vacation home, the portfolio, the nice ass, all the stuff we thought was so great. And, poof, next minute you're dead, you're in the light, you're an angel, and suddenly you understand everything clear as a bell. A dollar short and a day late, as far as I'm concerned. Then, after you hang around up there for a while—and this is the part that really rankles me—they send you back down here to start over again. Blank as a stone. Why can't they let us remember just that one thing? Why can't we be born with just that one piece of knowledge the way baby whales are born knowing how to swim? That love is the only thing that matters. Think about how perfect the world would be. But no, they don't want that for some reason."

She picked up her fork but did not spear food with it. She brandished it, her angry trident.

"They got me, Virgil. I was just another one who found out the truth on her dying day. And when I got to that day I was alone. I had no one next to my bed. No one waiting for me at home or pacing by the phone for word about me. I was left to freeze in a fucking morgue with no one to claim me. And all I had in Heaven to meet me was strangers. So I said to them, 'Fuck you, you didn't warn me. You set me up, let me live my whole life wrong and *now* you tell me.' I figured that wasn't fair. So I refused to play fair back. I didn't go into the light like they want me to and I won't go until I get my fair shot. I don't care how many ballplayers they send me."

Virgil blinked.

"What?"

"Never mind."

"What ballplayers? You mean like the one who got into Fatima?"

Beatrice lowered the fork and plowed up some asparagus. "Why? You jealous?"

He did not answer. Beatrice lifted the bottle of wine and filled his glass.

"I don't want a Yankee or an angel, Virgil," she said sweetly. "I want you."

"Yankees? New York Yankees?"

"Don't ask," she said, shaking her head. "Now, finish the dinner I made especially for you. And then, because it's a weeknight, we can stay in."

Virgil lowered his gaze.

"But that doesn't mean," she said, tucking a bit of osso bucco into her grin, "that we're not gonna dance."

Like a train that stops at a station in the middle of the night and switches locomotives, with none of the sleeping passengers aware of the new engine and crew, Beatrice moved to the light during sleep and Ellen returned to her body.

Ellen awoke before Virgil, naked. A bottle of aloe skin lotion was on the night table beside her head. She smelled her hands and shoulders, clucked her tongue in disgust and slipped out of the disheveled bed. She crept to her closet to check the pockets of the skirt she'd worn the night before. Beatrice had put the micro-recorder back in the skirt and Ellen found it there. Ellen took the device into the bathroom, closed the door and sat on the toilet seat listening to the tape at low volume.

When she was done, she stood and looked into

the mirror, deep into her own eyes. Beatrice examined Ellen's face also, searching for the fear that ought to be there after hearing her strange behavior and admission on the tape, after losing almost an entire day to black memory. But Beatrice saw no dripping tear or stripe of fear. Beatrice saw what Ellen saw, determination.

Beatrice in the light said, "Uh-oh."

Ellen dressed quietly in jeans and a blouse. She went downstairs to the kitchen to toast an English muffin. In the dining room, she saw the stumps of candles and two wine-stained goblets. She growled while she dumped the glasses in the sink.

Ellen munched the muffin in quiet anger. She went upstairs to the bedroom, picked up a tennis shoe and fired it at Virgil.

He snorted and jumped up in bed.

"What? What?" he said, glancing around.

"I'm going out."

"Um . . . okay."

"It's Ellen."

He sharpened at that. "I know. Of course it's Ellen. You're Ellen. That's who you are."

"Oh, just stop it. I'm taking the car."

"Where you going? Wait," he began to climb out of bed, fumbling on the floor beside the bed for his underwear, "I'll go with you."

"No. Have your breakfast and go open the shop."

He called after her but she was down the steps and out the front door.

She drove to a small industrial park near the airport with a view of the runways and entered a drab little building past a peeling wooden placard that read: JACOB BRUMFELD, PRIVATE INVESTIGATOR, CRIMINAL, CIVIL, PERSONAL, PROCESS SERVER.

Beatrice in the light said again, "Uh-oh."

Coffee gurgled in the corner beneath a plaque and several framed references to Jacob Brumfeld's former status as a Special Agent of the FBI. A secretary's desk was scattered with notes, files, Rolodex cards and a calendar. Coffee rings stained a lot of the papers. Apparently there was no secretary; this was just Jacob Brumfeld's second desk. A water cooler let go with a big bubble.

Jacob Brumfeld called out through the open door to his office. His chair scraped the floor.

"Hello? Who's there?"

Jacob Brumfeld was short and thick. He was bald on top, the remainder of his rim of hair clipped back to gray bristles. He wore a starched white shirt rolled up to the elbows, dark plain tie and wing tips. The chest, hands and wrists of Jacob Brumfeld looked abnormally powerful.

"Yes? Miss . . . ?"

"We've met," Ellen said quickly, "at a Chamber meeting. I run the art supply store down on—"

"Duval Street," Jacob Brumfeld said. "Ellen."

"That's right."

"You're husband's the ex-con. Manslaughter."

"Why, yes."

"Sorry." Jacob Brumfeld indicated a chair at the empty desk. "I tend to categorize people. Bad habit. Too many years in this line of work."

Ellen sat. "I suppose that's understandable."

"Coffee?" he asked.

"Thank you."

Jacob Brumfeld poured two, both cups bearing the eagle logos of some federal association, and sat.

"What can I do for you, Ellen?"

"I want to hire you to do an investigation for me."

"Who?" Jacob Brumfeld lowered his eyebrows, serious.

"Me."

His brows bobbed back up.

"You want me to investigate you."

"Yes."

Jacob Brumfeld sipped his coffee. He nodded to himself.

Ellen said, "I can't tell you why."

"It's not my job to know why," he said. "If I asked why before I took every job, I'd never take another one." He sipped his coffee.

Ellen rubbed her palms together. Jacob Brumfeld looked into his coffee.

"What do you want?" he asked. "Background check, polygraph, search out some long lost relatives, adoption records, security check?"

"I want you to follow me."

"Surveillance."

"Yes. On me."

"On you."

"Yes."

Jacob Brumfeld nodded again.

"You need a bodyguard? Someone giving you trouble?" He paused. "You're an attractive woman, someone stalking you?"

Ellen batted her eyes. She looked into her lap, embarrassed. "No. Thank you."

Brumfeld continued. "Your husband giving you a hard time over something?"

She lifted her eyes and smiled at him, entertained. "Mr. Brumfeld, you're asking a lot of questions."

"Sorry. Notice I didn't ask why."

"No, you didn't."

"And please. Call me Jacob."

"Alright, Jacob. I just want you to follow me. I want to know exactly what it is I do."

He twisted his head and repeated. "What it is you do."

"Yes."

He waited, then said, "That's a first."

"I'm sure."

She reached into her purse for her checkbook.

"Here's a check for two thousand dollars. I don't want to know how much surveillance that will buy me. Just do it. Twenty-four hours a day. You can photograph me, record me, videotape me, I don't care."

She tore off the check and handed it to him.

"I'd cash that this morning," she said. "Don't ask me why."

With what looked like his blunt brand of clowning, Jacob Brumfeld waved off the notion.

He folded the check into his shirt pocket.

"I want you to bring me full reports every day, at a time and place of your choosing. Don't tell me where or when. I want everything: pictures, tapes, everything. You keep copies."

"Alright."

"Now, Jacob. It's very important that you agree to a few more things."

"And they are?"

"If I call you or speak to you at all and tell you to stop, do not do it. If my husband demands you to quit, do not do it. Under no circumstances are you to stop watching me, no matter what you hear from this moment on. Do you understand?"

"Yes and no."

"That will have to do. Also, do not do the surveillance yourself. I'll be looking out for you and I'll try to avoid you. Have someone else do it."

"You want me to watch you, but you'll be trying to avoid me."

"Yes."

He sipped more coffee. He tapped the mug with his fingertips. Jacob Brumfeld thought a lot before he spoke.

"If I've got to hire someone, it'll cost more."

"And I will pay it. I'll give you another check for a thousand dollars when we're finished."

"Okay."

"One last thing."

"Take your time."

"I want you and only you to bring me the reports and whatever else you have. And this is most important. Do not give them to me unless I tell you the password."

"The password."

"Jacob, don't you think I know how strange this must sound?"

"No. I don't."

Ellen took a quick taste of the coffee. She stood. "Here's the password."

She turned away from Jacob Brumfeld. She held her hand behind her back where he could see it but not her.

Ellen asked Jacob Brumfeld, "See this number?"

Beatrice lifted her head and mumbled, "Yes indeed. Ol' Ellen's catching on."

Jacob Brumfeld said, "Yes."

Ellen said, "Multiply it by this number."

"Okay."

"Subtract this."

"Yes. Alright."

"And multiply again by this. Do you have it?"

"Yes."

She turned to him. "Good. I don't care what measures you have to take. Anything you have to do."

Jacob Brumfeld pulled open a drawer. He removed a form with carbons attached.

"You'll have to sign a waiver. Take a seat for a few minutes so we can fill it in."

Ellen took the papers from him, a pen from the desk, and signed at the bottom.

"There," she said, straightening, "you fill it in for me. I have to go now."

Ellen tugged on her shoulder bag and turned for the door. The water cooler burped a good-bye bubble.

Jacob Brumfeld stood. "You know . . ."

Ellen stopped in the doorway.

Jacob Brumfeld said, "If ever I was going to ask a client why, this would be the time."

Ellen drove directly to the store and parked in the back. She pushed open the rear door and strode inside. She saw Woody first.

She nodded to the boy and kept walking. He raised a hand from his broom.

"Virgil," she said, walking up to him, "you may as well know. You'll find out anyway."

Virgil said, "Good morning."

Ignoring his salutation, she reached into her purse for the micro-cassette recorder. She held it up and shook it at him while she spoke, punctuating certain words with a rattle of the machine.

"Since I don't seem to be able to *keep* anything from you. Since I apparently have a sudden *streak* of guilt about trying to take some measures to figure out on my own what's going on with me, *not to mention* a fixation on sex and what sounded like a serious *intestinal* problem. And since I can assume that during my next blackout, when I again become the good and honest Ellen, I will tell you at the first opportunity what I, the *evil* Ellen, did this morning."

Virgil took his listening post on the stool.

"I'm all ears. Ellen."

"I have hired a private detective named Jacob Brumfeld. I am having myself followed. Twenty-four hours a day. He has already been paid so he will not stop, even if it's me telling him to stop. I am going to get to the bottom of this, Virgil. With or without your help."

"Aren't you taking this to an extreme?"

She took one step closer to him, then stopped herself.

"You know I'm not stupid, Virgil." She tossed the recorder on the counter with a clatter. "And you also know I'm not *this*."

"Ellen?"

But she was gone into the back, beyond Woody's cowed wave good-bye, and in the car, spinning out of the lot.

She drove to Whitehead Street. Pulling up in front of the house, she mumbled, "Just hold off a while longer."

Ellen scrambled around the house, filling a straw basket with cheese and crackers, bottled water, a paperback book and sunglasses. She grabbed a beach chair from the backyard and her floppy straw hat. Lastly, she took from her desk a yellow legal pad and a pen.

She drove thirty minutes north on US 1 to Bahia Honda State Park. She found a desolate stretch of beach and rolled up her pants legs. She set her chair and straw basket in the sand. Sandpipers skittled along the edge of the foam, gulls mingled and squawked. Ellen tugged down the brim of her big hat.

She took out the pad and pen. For many minutes she gazed at the empty page; the pen point dove at the paper a dozen times like one of the crying, soaring gulls but pulled up each time in a scared, false landing.

At last Ellen touched pen to page and wrote. Beatrice read along.

Dear You,

Imagine how that feels. To not even know how to address a letter to yourself. Do you know? Take a guess. It feels like hell.

I have questions. Who are you? Virgil says you're me but you and I both know that's not true. Are you Bea Sting? If you are, how did you get into my head? I never knew any Bea Sting when you were alive, never even heard of you. How could that be?

If you're not Bea Sting, who are you? Why do you betray me every chance you get? Why are you fighting me? If you're just a part of my brain, even a haywire part, then why do I feel like you're my opposite and my enemy? Again, how could that be?

Look, you. Me. You know about the detective. You know he's going to catch you and tell me exactly what or who you are. Then you know I'll do whatever I have to do to beat you. Hospital, drugs, therapy, operations, I don't care if you cancel every medical appointment I make, I'll stay after you.

*Finally, and I know I have no right to
ask this of you but I will anyway, do me one
favor. Don't make a fool out of me. Fight
fair. My family has lived in Key West for
over fifty years, my parents earned their good
name and I've worked hard to keep it. Don't
shame me out of that. Don't make me a
laughingstock.*

*It's clear that Virgil likes a great many
things about you. I can be those things, too.
Let me work it out with him. He deserves to
have me, his wife, beside him. He is more
complex than you know.*

*He's my husband. And that store is my
birthright.*

Go away.

Ellen

She tore the sheet from the pad and rolled it
into a scroll. She gripped the paper in her left
hand and eased her head back against the beach
chair.

She sat like that for hours, in the stretching sun
of morning, looking out under the big brim of her
straw hat. She watched the doilies of surf draw
and withdraw on the sand. Intermittently, feet and
knees of solo strollers or couples ambled by; she
never once glanced up to say hello, but kept her
gaze and hat slouched down like some stoic Western gunfighter.

Beatrice sat in a light that was neither cool nor
warming and wanted to feel the sun Ellen felt. She

was aware of Ellen being watched; she knew a
tentacle of Jacob Brumfeld must be somewhere
nearby. She grew restless. Tapping her fingers,
she became aware of time passing.

Sea foam slid about Ellen's ankles in lace slippers. The rising tide chased her higher in the
sand, she moved the beach chair and basket to
recamp above the water's reach. She took off the
straw hat to wipe sweat from her brow. She laid
cheese slices over crackers and ate them. Never
for a moment did she release the yellow scroll in
the mailbox of her left hand.

Ellen read her paperback. Beatrice did not like
novels and did not recognize any of the characters, coming in as she did in the middle of the
story. The afternoon warmed and wore on and
Ellen's hold on her body seemed strong, or rather
Beatrice's claim to it appeared weakened, out here
away from Virgil.

Hours passed. Morning became afternoon.
Beatrice waited, staring at the black drapery of
Ellen's closed eyelids.

Finally, and as always without warning or reason, Beatrice felt the sand between her toes and
the lowering sun on her arms. She was thirsty,
dripping sweat beneath the T-shirt and long
pants. How could Ellen sit like this for so long, so
still, hot and parched, clutching the rolled-up
note?

Beatrice tossed the paperback into the basket
without marking Ellen's place and dredged up the
bottled water for a swig. She tugged out the tail of

the shirt tucked into the jeans and knotted it above the waist. Beatrice unfurled the letter, reread it, then reached for the legal pad and pen. She wrote:

Ellen,

I know how you feel. I've got questions too. More questions than you have. Maybe that's because I know more about what's going on than you do.

Funny how it works that way. The more I find out, the more I learn how much more I don't know. It's like being lost in a jungle and you climb the tallest tree to see where you are. And all you see from up there is just how big the jungle is that you're lost in.

Take my advice. Be glad you're the only one in this mess who doesn't know what's going on. That makes you the only one who's innocent.

You're right about your family name. I promise, I'll watch it. And that was nice work with the detective.

Also you're right, I will stop you from going into a hospital. You can forget it.

Thanks for the compliment. There's a lot of things about you that Virgil can't let go of either. But just like you said: I can do them too.

I can't go away. I don't think I'm supposed to. In fact, it looks like I'm staying longer each time. That's because Virgil doesn't want me to go away. I don't think Heaven wants me to go, either. There's a plan.

That must hurt. Well. It hurts.

There are no answers, Ellen. Not yet anyway. So you may as well stop asking. I have.

Sorry.

Me

She rolled the page and stuck it in her right hand. She didn't know when Ellen would get it, she was just following some procedure that seemed to have been established between them. Clutching the note, Beatrice packed up the chair and basket, glad to be in action again, and headed for the car.

She loaded everything into the trunk, slammed the lid and fished out the keys to drive into the setting sun back to Key West.

She put the key in the ignition, turned it and froze.

The starter made a terrific grinding noise. Beatrice heard it, but could do nothing about it for it was not her hand holding the key.

Ellen let go. The car started and idled.

"Damn it!" Beatrice said in the light. She'd had less than ten minutes in Ellen this time.

Ellen looked around. She read the crushed page in her right hand.

When she was finished, she folded the paper and stuffed it in a pocket. She yanked the rear-view mirror around to see into her own eyes.

Beatrice looked too. In the mirror were a pair of narrowed orbs, grim, two blue armies massing.

Ellen muttered, "Mmm hmm."

She drove to Key West, naming the keys and bridges as she went.

12

THE big house on Whitehead Street seemed to Virgil unsettled, in the path of something.

The house was filled with Ellen's things, brown antiques and lacy touches, modest fabrics and yard-sale dolls, and nowhere did he see evidence of himself. No painting he'd favored at the gallery, no knickknack noticed around town and brought home. No memento from his life before they'd met. Rugs, chairs, candlesticks, lamps and tables all predated him at Whitehead Street. What impression had he made in his own home? Had he tried and given so little, he wondered? Was he in fact here? Had he left no track at all in this house, nor back at the shop, were his tracks even in Ellen? She'd made room for him in her heart and her bed and livelihood, but it was up to a man to spread out, to plant flags and flowers and build entrenchments in a woman's life, to inhabit her and shelter her. Where was this to be seen by Virgil's hand in this house?

He opened the refrigerator and some cabinets and made himself a sandwich. The kitchen noises he made clashed openly with the gloomy air in the house. Virgil's tramping about the kitchen made more unsettled noises, strikes, clicks and scrapes, with the close-in echoes of a dungeon.

He finished the sandwich with munches and swallows and tossed the drained soda can in the recycling bin with the clang of a tin cymbal.

He encountered her the way a man happens upon a snake, he recoiled onto his back foot. She was in the parlor where he went intending to sit in the gathering dark and wait.

She said, "Hi."

"Hi."

She patted the sofa cushion beside her. "Come and sit with me."

She watched him sit, unblinking. She held out her hand to him.

"It's my hand, Virgil. It's not hers. Please hold it."

He linked fingers with hers. She placed their hands in her lap and turned to look out the window to Whitehead Street. She watched—and with her, Virgil thought, Beatrice watches—the full night drape over Key West, the guest inns release their tourists, the trees rest from a day of breezes.

"Do you remember," she asked, "when we first met?"

"Of course."

Ellen put her free hand to the glass pane, her fingertips touching it like a dear face.

"You were a sight."

For a half hour she did not speak more. They did not turn on any lights in the house but sat with twined hands, letting the walls grow darker than the street and the studded sky over Key West. Virgil gazed into the night, into the house and at his quiet wife.

Beatrice waits, he thought. I wait.

She knows I'm holding hands with Ellen.

Something betrayed him. Something in his hand linked to Ellen's, something that only wives know of their husbands.

Without facing him, Ellen asked, "Is she watching? Does she know we're sitting here holding hands, you and me?"

He composed answers immediately. Standard responses now, all of them: Who? Bea Sting? When will you let that drop, Ellen? You are not Bea Sting. And so on, all lies, all stone walls. But he was not in a mood to lie. He'd enjoyed the peace of Ellen's hand and her breathing, the sweeping night and shadows hiding all flaws in both of them, just the junction of hands and night and the familiar. Ellen had dashed it. He paid her roughly.

"Maybe you should tell me. Is your detective watching? Is that why we sat in the window, so the son of a bitch could keep an eye on us here holding hands?"

A wretched righteousness filled him and he

stood, breaking the bond of their fingers.

A noise came from outside the front door, a hollow thump as if someone had kicked over one of the plastic trash bins standing beside the street for morning pickup.

Virgil leaped for the door. Outside, one of the green Dumpsters lay on its side. Virgil looked both ways on the street. A black figure tore across lawns.

Virgil shouted. "Get back here!"

The runner was gone. Virgil did not give chase. He went back inside the house. Ellen's slow footsteps shuffling up the dark stairwell came down to him like the sounds of a shovel digging a grave.

Ellen closed the bedroom door, signaling Virgil to spend the night in the guest room. There he lay awake for hours like a man on guard. He sensed predators and pitfalls: Jacob Brumfeld prowling about the house and the trash cans, Ellen's climbing suspicions and percolating anger, his own foolhardiness and skulking bad luck, Beatrice's damn-the-consequences attitude, even God and His eternal sneaky silence about the plan.

In the morning he rose late to voices and the smell of coffee from the kitchen. He slid on a shirt and jeans and walked downstairs. They'd started without him. Just as well, he thought.

At the foot of the steps he looked through the hall into the kitchen. Jacob Brumfeld sat at the Formica breakfast table, dressed in a starched white shirt and tie, gray slacks, black tassel shoes.

A shrub of hair on the backs of his wrists stuck out from under his cuffs. His wide back and shoulders were probably hairy too. A jackal with a shaved head. Perfect, thought Virgil, remembering his restless night.

Virgil went to sit in the parlor. The morning sun diced slats through the partially pulled blinds; ballerinas of dust twirled in the beams. He placed himself far from the kitchen, hearing only snatches of Ellen's voice rising and falling and Brumfeld's low growl.

After a while Virgil heard nothing. The big house was like a giant clock tower, ponderous and mum in those moments approaching the hour, when massive hands would slip into place and the tolling begin.

Ellen entered the room.

"Ellen," he greeted her flatly, still holding to his indignation of the night before.

"Virgil."

She sat opposite him. There was color in her cheeks and nose. She'd cried or blushed or gotten angry in front of Jacob Brumfeld or all three.

"Where's your detective?" he asked.

"Waiting in his car."

"Going somewhere?"

"In a minute."

"You want me to come too?"

"No."

Ellen dropped her head. Her hair curtained her face; her chest shook.

"He's told me some things."

"Like what?"

"I don't want to go into them right now. I just wanted to give you something."

"What."

"He fished this out of one of our garbage cans yesterday afternoon."

"You've hired yourself a real winner, Ellen."

She held out a trembling hand. In it, stained and creased, was Fatima Tugsal's business card.

She said, "It looks that way."

Beatrice listened at the breakfast table while Ellen gave Jacob Brumfeld the right password number—forty-four—then created a new secret number behind her back.

Jacob Brumfeld laid out for Ellen his facts.

He was a farmer of information. In one day on the job, he'd planted seeds—snoops, interviews, police contacts, hidden infrared cameras, high-powered microphones, even a confidential source—then harvested his first crop of facts and brought them to market. He made no hypotheses about what was going on; if he had any notions, he kept them to himself. He'd been hired by Ellen only to build a connect-the-dots picture of herself and that is what he did.

He spoke to Ellen in a monotone, appearing to keep something back, not information but something private in his own breast; perhaps, Beatrice guessed, watching the detective's face through Ellen's glances, there was a tinge of attraction for Ellen brewing under that brute hide. Jacob Brumfeld explained to Ellen first how Virgil had contacted Top Hat Escort Service for a Fedora. He translated what a Fedora was. Not a hooker, he specified. A dancer. Professional companionship. Beatrice appreciated that. Ellen asked if sex with a Fedora was common and Jacob Brumfeld said no, typically it was not. It was up to the girl, and that also was true.

Virgil had gone to meet the Fedora at 7 P.M. at the Ramada Inn on Roosevelt. He entered the lobby on time carrying one red rose, the signal for The Fedora. He exited the lobby five minutes after the hour, reason unknown, leaving the rose behind on a sofa.

The Fedora entered the lobby two minutes later. She'd stayed in the motel following an afternoon appointment, a private dance; Jacob Brumfeld also explained to Ellen what that was. That appointment had turned sour after the john got out of line up in the room. The Fedora waited in the motel lobby for her seven o'clock john, then asked the young male clerk to call her a taxi. She exited the Ramada to wait for the taxi on the curb next to the parking lot, carrying the rose with her. Minutes later, the jilted guy from the afternoon arrived in a white stretch limo. The woman resisted his advances and he shot the woman three times in the chest with a .45 automatic. She died ten hours later after emergency surgery.

The following afternoon, Virgil drove Ellen to Miami for a series of medical tests. Dr. Kithathanon and Dr. Lowe.

Two days later, Ellen and Virgil went to the City Morgue to identify the body of the murdered Top Hat escort.

Bea Sting.

The next morning Virgil visited a local spiritualist, Fatima Tugsal, a woman with a short criminal record from eight years ago in Atlantic City for petty theft, card-sharking and confidence scams.

Jacob Brumfeld described Ellen's trip to the beach yesterday, what she was wearing. He ventured one departure, mentioning that she ought to be more careful next time at the beach and take along some good sun block to protect her nice skin. He cleared his throat and returned to his details. She was observed writing on a notepad once with her right hand, then again with her left. The two notes had not been found and Ellen would not produce them. He covered briefly last evening's quiet hand-holding in front of the living room window, Ellen and Virgil sleeping in separate rooms. And finally, he said, gathering his notes and not looking at her, no reports of Virgil and her encountering each other throughout the night.

Ellen sat through it all like a defendant on trial. She accepted Jacob Brumfeld's simple manly kindnesses, the way he saved her from embarrassment with a firm voice, without judgment, without making eye contact when referring to sex. Ellen only listened to the damning words, hands flat on the table, whispering requests to Jacob

Brumfeld for explanations, staring at the photos and transcripts. She drew hard breaths while the evidence built, littering the Formica with pages of transcripts and photos. During Jacob Brumfeld's presentation Ellen added nothing to his medley of facts, as if she wanted to see where he would lead on his own, to see if the detective, if he ever proffered a conclusion, might arrive at the same place she did.

Beatrice watched Ellen straggle out of the kitchen into the parlor where Virgil waited. She sensed in Ellen's hesitance and Virgil's removed tone that a schism had opened between them. Listening, she hoped Virgil would tell her right then, with Jacob Brumfeld in the house to hear and catalog it, that he did not love her anymore. That he loved Bea Sting. But Virgil did not.

Ellen and the detective did not speak in the car.

Jacob Brumfeld parked in front of Fatima's old house on Eaton Street. He put on his suit coat and straightened his tie while Ellen got out. He knocked on Fatima's door.

The medium answered, dressed all in black and dangling silver. Beatrice thought of a horse tacked out for a parade.

She waved a hand. Bangles rang. "You are Detective Jacob Brumfeld."

"Yes." He indicated Ellen. "And this is . . ."

"Your client. I know."

Ellen put out her hand. "Ellen."

"Come in."

In the hall, Fatima handed them each her card. "You want to ask me questions."

Jacob Brumfeld said, "Yes."

Fatima opened the parlor door. "In here is where all questions are answered."

Ellen took in the convocation of colorless faces on the walls. Judging from her racing peeks about the room, Beatrice in the light could tell that Ellen was spooked.

Ellen and Jacob Brumfeld sat in plush chairs opposite Fatima in the middle of the dark room, lit only by the Tiffany lamp and the one candle.

Fatima crossed her hands over her large breast, a dramatic posture of burial.

"You want to know about a client of mine. A Mr. Virgil."

"Yes," Jacob Brumfeld said. "I discussed this with you on the phone. You said—"

She interrupted him again. "The one thing I have discovered in my dealings with the afterlife, Mr. Brumfeld, is that those things which we come to believe are true and immutable we inevitably learn are merely shifting shapes, not reality at all but images, shadow play. We cannot rely on what we see or hear or touch in life. In other words, Mr. Brumfeld, things change."

Ellen said to Jacob Brumfeld, "Virgil called her."

Unabashed, Fatima said, "Mr. Virgil has requested that our dealings remain confidential. Yes."

Jacob Brumfeld reached under his jacket to his

belt. He unsnapped a small leather sheath, opened it and held up his credentials to Fatima.

"I'm a former Special Agent of the FBI and a licensed private investigator. If I learn of evidence of a crime, I am bound by law to report it to the police. I will tell you right now that I can have you subpoenaed by this time tomorrow. I suggest that if you have nothing to hide then you do not hide it."

"What crime? There's been no crime. I've done nothing wrong."

Jacob Brumfeld clipped the leather case back onto his belt. "Maybe. Maybe not."

"I'll pay you," Ellen said.

Fatima huffed. "This is not right."

"I'll make it right," Ellen said. "Mr. Brumfeld, may I see you in the hall?"

"Yes. Excuse us."

· Ellen led him into the hall, shutting the door to the parlor.

"Could you really do that?" she asked the detective. "Subpoena her?

"No." He shrugged. "You did tell me to do whatever I had to."

"Do you pull that trick often, Mr. Brumfeld?"

"Jacob."

"Jacob, do you break the rules whenever you're stymied?"

"No. That was just another first in what is becoming a disturbingly long list for me."

"Thank you. But I think I ought to talk to her alone now."

Jacob Brumfeld's face went pained at being left out of the info loop and he opened his mouth to campaign against it. But his jaw closed and he relented.

"Good instinct. I'll wait here in the hall."

Ellen patted the barrel of his shoulder. She said, "Good instinct."

He asked, "You'll give me a report?"

Ellen said nothing and stepped inside the parlor to Fatima. She closed the door behind her.

She sat. "I apologize. He's a necessary evil."

"It's sad," Fatima nodded, "when evil becomes necessary."

Ellen gazed around the room. "Impressive."

"Thank you. They are my spirit guides."

"I see."

"You must understand I cannot speak openly of confidential matters involving the spirit world. They trust me to be discreet. That is one of the reasons why I am honored by them as a spiritual gateway."

"I understand."

"Thank you."

"I understand many things, Fatima."

The medium rolled her eyes.

Ellen said, "I understand about your police record in Atlantic City."

The medium's eyes went big on Ellen, then shifted quickly to her walls of portraits as if to beg them, "Don't listen to her. She's making that up."

From the pocket of her skirt Ellen pulled her gold credit card. She held up the plastic between two fingers and flashed it to reflect what little light there was in the room.

"I understand that Mr. Brumfeld offered you two hundred dollars over the phone to speak with us. What was my husband's offer to keep quiet?"

Fatima swallowed. "Four hundred."

Ellen reached out the card. "Make it five. Ring it up."

Fatima drew the card in, covering it quickly in her paws as if to hide her gleaming perfidy from the gray eyes on the walls.

The medium bustled to her desk to make a credit card imprint. She returned to her chair and handed Ellen the slip and a pen. Ellen signed, then laid the receipt in her lap.

"Tell me what happened."

Fatima laced her fingers over her belly, her composure regained. She put her chin up and spoke with dignity, not at all betraying a trust in front of the many great and dead but giving a reading, this time not of the future but simply the past.

"Mr. Virgil came to me and asked me to contact a spirit."

"Bea Sting."

"Yes. How did you know?"

Ellen ignored the question.

"What happened?"

"I informed your husband that I was unaccustomed to dealing with such spirits. I am more familiar with a host of departed souls of a more lofty station."

"Fatima?"

"Yes?"

"I don't have time or patience. Something happened in here that Virgil doesn't want me to find out about. Tell me what it was for my five hundred dollars or I'll have Brumfeld ask you for free."

Fatima unwound her fingers. She reared her head even higher and said proudly, imperious, for all those on the walls to recall.

"She came."

"Fatima."

"Say and do what you like, madam, but I made contact with the spirit of Bea Sting. Mr. Virgil said that she has not gone all the way into the light. Her soul is near it, waiting, deciding whether to move on. I called her and I received her into my body. And this I can prove."

Ellen tapped the credit card receipt in her lap.

"Then prove it."

From the floor beside her chair, Fatima produced a micro-cassette recorder. She held it the way Ellen had flourished the credit card, turning it, displaying it.

"This," Fatima said, "cannot leave here. You may listen to it for your money. You cannot have it or copy it. What is on this tape represents the most incredible experience of my life. But outside this room it is worthless. Even dangerous, for it will surely be called a forgery and a hoax. Perhaps even as your Mr. Brumfeld suggests it might be used as evidence against me by the authorities to show that I have not learned my lessons. But I have. This tape shows that I have the gift. Truly. For she did come to me. She and another. You will see."

Fatima pushed the play button and laid the device in the lap of her skirt.

Ellen leaned across and picked it up.

Fatima reciprocated, reaching over to take the credit card slip from Ellen. She tucked it inside her bodice.

The tape began with Fatima's operatic hum. Ellen looked at the recorder then glared impatiently at Fatima. The medium said, "Wait. Listen."

The small speaker played the sounds of Fatima's possession. Bea Sting's striptease leitmotif of *"boom-bop-ba-boom"* was followed by the raucous laughs of the ballplayer spirit, the shamed questions of Fatima returning to her body only for confused moments, Virgil's own startled questions, his phone call to Ellen, then his stumble out the door while the ghost guide cackled quietly.

When it was done, Ellen rewound the tape and listened to it again. She stopped at several places and backed it up to listen intently: Fatima purring "Bzzzzzz"; the guide's references to the medium as "Fatty-ma" and "white mud"—Ellen looked up and caught Fatima in her chair grimacing; Virgil's remark that Bea Sting was "watching everything through Ellen's eyes"; and Virgil's phone call home to Ellen for lunch, the ballplayer's howling answer, "Reservations!" and Virgil's astounded response, "Oh my God, oh my God."

Ellen handed the recorder over to Fatima.

"Thank you." Her voice was shot through with exhaustion.

Ellen stood.

Fatima said, "Please. You will tell no one of this."

"Don't worry. And I expect the same from you."

"Of course."

Fatima stood also. She said, "She was here. Bea Sting was here."

"Yes. She was here."

"Miss Ellen?"

"What?"

"You seem troubled."

"No. I'm relieved. I know what to do now."

The medium's eyes snagged at Ellen's throat.

"What is this?"

Ellen looked down. "It's a locket."

Fatima stepped forward, reaching. Ellen leaned back but let the woman approach.

Gently, Fatima put the silver heart between her thumb and forefinger.

"This heart. It is empty?"

"There are no pictures inside it, no."

"It feels empty."

Fatima stroked her thumb over the locket, wincing as though a low voltage had flowed out of it into her.

"This is hers, did you know that?"

"Yes."

"Why do you wear it?"

Ellen answered quietly, confused, "I don't know." Then she took Fatima's hand from the locket and stepped away. She said again, now with irritation, "I don't know. It doesn't matter."

Fatima smiled. "Everything matters."

The medium shook her ringlets. Her voice was again continental and imperious. "Perhaps you would like me to call Bea Sting back. You could speak with her directly. She was here once. I can summon her again. Or perhaps the guide."

"Fatima."

"Yes?"

"She's here now. She's listening to every word we say."

"I know. Bea Sting is your angel." Fatima beamed. "You are so lucky."

Ellen sighed. "No, you idiot. She's trying to steal my husband."

Ellen closed the door on Fatima's gaping mouth.

Jacob Brumfeld drove her home. In the car, he asked what happened in Fatima's parlor.

Ellen did not speak.

At the house on Whitehead Street, she turned to him. "Thank you, Jacob. That's it. Call off your dogs. Is there money left over?"

"Yes."

"You can keep it."

He nodded. "I appreciate it."

She got out of the car.

Jacob Brumfeld rolled down the passenger side window. "Ellen?"

"Yes?"

"Look. I've never done this before. Not in twenty years in the Bureau and six more as a PI. Every time I was told to I've walked away from cases. But this time I've got to ask."

"I can't tell you anything, Jacob."

He raised both hands and rattled them, in pantomime as though on Ellen's shoulders, to jar something from her.

"That's it? Nothing else? You just walk away and leave me in the dark like this? No more information?"

"No, Jacob. No more information."

He stared at her, glum, weaned too soon.

She put her foot hard on the first porch step.

"Ellen?"

"Yes?"

"Something stinks."

"I know."

A charged sort of peace settled over Virgil when he put the phone down from bribing Fatima. When Ellen had left the house she'd looked wounded and determined and Jacob Brumfeld had looked dogged and persuasive. Virgil could not stop what he knew would happen: Ellen and Brumfeld would make Fatima a better offer and Fatima would blab. Virgil was without alternatives. So, like a chess king in check, he made the only move open to him and went to the shop.

He found Woody there waiting on the curb. The boy was convulsing under a set of headphones, tapping his sneakers and drumming on his knees. From twenty feet away Virgil heard the squall emanating from the headphones as though Woody were listening to the recorded sounds of a sawmill.

"Woody." The boy with puffed cheeks did not hear him approach. "Woody!"

Woody looked up. He stopped the tape player and doffed the headphones.

"Virg. S'up?"

"That a new Walkman?"

"Yeah. Bought it last night."

Woody gathered the cord and player and tucked it all in his jacket.

Virgil asked, "Wasn't that a little loud?"

"Yeah."

"It's going to ruin your hearing one of these days."

"So?"

Virgil nodded. Another man resolved to his destiny. He unlocked the shop door.

The two of them went to their silent morning routines. Virgil made coffee. Woody cruised the aisles searching for merchandise that needed replenishing.

While the coffee brewed Virgil watched the boy's crew-cut head weave among the maze of shelves.

"Woody?"

The boy kept walking, head down, a hound on a scent. "Yeah?"

"You believe in angels?"

"I don't know. Why?"

Virgil shrugged though Woody did not see it. "Just wondering."

Woody's head disappeared when he bent to check a stock number.

Virgil said into the shop, "You believe in Heaven?"

The unseen voice. "I don't know."

Virgil waited for the boy's head to pop up again. He asked, "But what if you knew for a fact that there was a Heaven and life after death. What would that do to your beliefs?"

Woody stared numbly. He said, "Maybe you're not listening to me, Virg. *What* beliefs?"

Woody finished his rounds. He brought his clipboard to the stool where Virgil waited for the coffee to brew out.

Woody asked, "Something's up. Gimme the 4-1-1."

"I think I have to let you go."

Woody set his jaw. "Why? Because I said I didn't know if I believed in Heaven? Man, you don't even want to *think* about that lawsuit."

"That's got nothing to do with it. It's just . . . it's just Ellen and me. I don't know what's going on with us. I'm afraid it's going to get weird and I don't want you in the middle of it."

"That's cool. I know how you guys are. I can deal with weird."

"I don't think you want to deal with this one."

"You're firing me?"

"I'll give you two weeks pay. If Ellen and I get

things straight, I'll bring you back if you haven't got another job already."

"Man, they'll send me back to the farm."

"I'm sorry."

"Does E know about this?"

"She'll agree with me."

"I want to talk to her myself. This sucks."

"I don't want you here when she gets back. I can't explain it to you. Maybe sometime. But right now you've got to go."

Woody grabbed his backpack and stood in front of Virgil with his hand out, his face ornery. Virgil opened a drawer, took up the store's checkbook and scribbled out the boy's severance.

Writing, he said, "I have to do this. I don't know any other way."

Woody snatched the check from Virgil's hand. "This is about her blackouts, isn't it?"

"Yes. It is."

"It's bigger than that. Something's fucked up and you're not telling me."

"That's correct."

Woody held out the check. "Dude. If there's trouble, you know me, I'm solid. We're brothers."

"Yes we are, Woody. That's why you have to leave for a while."

"You need me around. You're too bummed all the time. I'm good for you. Straightening me out and shit is the only fun you have. Let me hang."

"No."

The boy nodded. Slowly, he pulled out his

headphones, spread the pads wide and slipped them over his ears. He clicked the play button on the tape deck. Muffled screeching bolted from his head. He turned for the door.

Virgil said, "Stay in touch."

Without turning, Woody said, "What?"

Virgil did not repeat himself. Woody opened the door, stepped into the untrammeled light of Key West, became a silhouette and was gone.

Virgil stared at the door. The sound of its closing hung like gun smoke in the big room. That was hard. Woody would definitely be sent back to the juvy farm if he didn't have a job to keep him in work release. Woody would feel betrayed. Woody could wind up on the streets again. Yes, yes, all that and more, Virgil thought, but he did not believe that the plan required Woody's involvement. The boy was a bystander, nothing more, and as such might be hurt or warped far worse if he were somehow caught up in this collision between worlds, Heaven and Earth. Woody could be spared.

Virgil left the CLOSED sign facing the street. He sat on his stool and waited for her return. He did not drink the coffee but left it heating to perfume the air. The aroma made the store and gallery seem less still, less brooding.

He wondered who would open the door. These last few days he'd wondered that a lot, who would he work with during the day, have dinner with, talk with, sleep with? This morning he wished it would be his wife who turned the knob on the shop door. If she's gone to see Fatima, then she knows about Bea Sting. It was time to get it all out in the open.

An hour later it was Ellen who entered the shop. She announced herself the moment the door closed behind her, not in any way other than how she said his name.

"Virgil."

"Ellen."

"We need to talk."

"Yes," he said, "we do."

"Where's Woody?"

"I sent him off. I fired him. He didn't need to be involved in this. Where's your detective?"

"I fired him too."

"Does he know?"

"No. I want this to stay between us."

"I agree."

She said, "Between the three of us."

That was the signal, the green light. It surprised Virgil that she moved into the fray so quickly, but that was Ellen. To the point.

He cleared his throat.

She stopped him. "Virgil?"

"Yes?"

"I never know how much time I have, so do me this one favor."

"Yes?"

"Just talk to me. No stories or lies. Just you and me and our little eavesdropper and what we're going to do from here. Okay?"

"Okay."

He swallowed. "You've always been good to me, Ellen. I admit that right off."

Ellen pushed her hair behind her ears. She moved in front of him, the counter between them. The sun cut squares on the floor at her back.

She said, "I can take her away from you."

"What?"

"I can take her away. So far away she'll never get back. I can strand her somewhere in some awful place on the planet with no money, no identification. I could make it so she can never get back to you. And if she tried or if you came after her I could take her away farther. I could keep her away from you until she's gone for good. I know she can hear me. So I'm telling you both, right now, I could do it."

Virgil stood. "Ellen."

She calmly said, "Sit down, Virgil. I'm not going to do that."

Virgil folded again onto the stool.

Ellen glared. "Top Hat," she said.

Virgil waited.

"Top Hat Escort Service. You knew Bea Sting while she was alive. You were the one she was waiting for at the Ramada the night she was killed."

"I didn't stay."

"Thank you. I know that. But it doesn't make up for my having to hear about it from Jacob Brumfeld."

Virgil paused. Brumfeld. How did he find out about the Ramada?

He said, "I didn't know her. It was the only time I ever did anything like that."

Ellen laid her hand to her forehead. She spoke to the shining floor.

"Why, Virgil? Why did you go to a call girl? Are things between us so bad that you had a need for that?"

Virgil inhaled to answer, not knowing what he would say, but certain the words were pent up behind his teeth and lips like a pool waiting to be undammed, the words would flow; he opened his mouth but she continued and he caught himself leaning forward on the stool, he put his hands on the counter and pushed himself back, so anxious was he to finally speak.

"Why did you lie to me about her?" she asked. "You told me she was just a delusion, you let me go to those doctors and make a fool of myself. She's real, Virgil, she's a ghost inside me. You knew this. Why didn't you tell me?"

He waited. A tear welled in her eye; she stifled it with a knuckle.

"Why are you having an affair on me, Virgil? You're my husband."

"Yes," he said, "I am. And you're my wife."

"Alright," she said, snuffling, fighting more tears, "I suppose I ought to listen now."

Virgil left a moment unfilled before he began, an overture of silence that had been the running theme of his discontent for years.

"Ellen," he spoke standing to go wherever the words might wash him, "when we first met, it was clear we needed each other. We filled up a lot of holes between us. You were crushed at your parents' death. I remember it like it was yesterday. All of a sudden you were left alone, your parents and the store had been your life. You needed someone to take care of, so you could mend your heart by using it and get on with your life. Fine. Me, I was a fresh ex-convict with no family, one suit, all my money spent on lawyers. You were the answer to my prayers. A home, a wife, a job, you gave me back my name, all at once. And because we clung so tightly to each other in the first two or three years we didn't even think about doing much more than just fixing the other person. It was pretty intense. I guess that made us think we were in love and maybe we were. I thought I was anyway."

She scrunched her eyes and her hands shifted in her lap as though she'd considered reaching for him and pulled back.

"I was, Virgil. I am."

He continued, in full torrent now, the river Fatima had told him he was, flooding the banks, over Ellen, over her nervous, wanting hands and sad, wanting, beautiful face.

"Over time, my needs changed, Ellen. Yours didn't but mine did. Right now, four years after we first met, you still need exactly who you perceive me to be, the quiet man around the house and the store, the ex-con you took in and did a good turn for. The quiet guy on the mattress next to you every night. Great. Good for you. But what about me? I'm not the ex-con anymore. I'm not, look at me. But I still work at your shop, live in your big house, eat at your table. I still go to sleep quiet on the mattress next to you."

He moved to the window and pointed outside.

"When I was in prison, they took everything away from me, my freedom, sunshine, my career. You gave all that back to me, Ellen. Thank you. I mean that."

He lowered his finger. He put it to his chest.

"But the one thing you haven't given back to me is my identity. I'm still living in a six-by-ten cell. I'm still not a man."

Ellen nodded.

"And she does that for you? Bea Sting?"

"Yes. She makes me feel special. Me. Not the husband Virgil or the employee Virgil or the ex-con Virgil but me. The whole man."

Ellen lowered her eyes and chuckled.

"What," Virgil asked, "do you find so funny?"

Ellen quit the rueful snicker. "Nothing. There's a lot to weep about here and I just thought I'd have myself a little laugh when I got the chance."

"And?"

"And, Virgil, do I have to remind you that making men feel special was Bea Sting's profession? She used to do it, if I'm not mistaken, by the hour."

Virgil felt an urge well up to defend Beatrice, tell Ellen that Beatrice wasn't what she might seem from her line of work, cognizant that Beatrice was watching and listening and certainly expecting him to stand up for her. But he let Ellen's remark go unchallenged; something far inside him stung, as if some mark had been bull's-eyed, and he would not acknowledge it.

He returned to his stool behind the counter. Ellen was close, her hand flat on the countertop. He kept his own hands in his lap to leave the counter surface to her. He looked at the flesh and veins on the back of her hand, knew well every line and texture of the hand.

"So what," he asked, "are you going to do? You say you're not going to leave. You going to throw me out?"

"No."

"Then what?"

"Virgil, in a normal world, I would demand you stop seeing this other woman and we'd get to work putting our lives back together. But I don't seem to have that option. For all I know she—Bea, dear, are you listening? Of course you are. She could slip into me before I finish my next sentence. And no, I'm not going to drag her away from you to Siberia."

"Why not?"

"Because, you ridiculous fool, I love you. You are my husband. I will not beat a hasty retreat from this marriage because of a dead woman who refuses to go into the light like she should."

Ellen turned her hand over, face up on the counter, an invitation. He laid his hand in hers and felt the fit. In the same instant he felt the clash, the stain, of his unhappiness.

"Virgil," she said, tightening her grip around his palm, "listen. If I've made mistakes, if I've overlooked things about you, I can make that right. If there's a place inside you I can't go right now, you can show me the way in. And if there's ways that Bea Sting makes you feel better about yourself as a man, more alive, more important, sexier even, I can learn those ways." Ellen paused, thinly smiled. "Well, some of them anyway. Hopefully, enough."

She pulled her hand from his. Again, that something inside him that always acted of its own volition squeezed now to try holding on to her hand, but she slid out, fingertips last.

"Virgil, let's be totally honest with each other. You know it's not for anyone else to make you feel special in this world. That's something you have to do for yourself. I can help, and perhaps I ought to have helped a lot more than I have. What with all the guilt and such you feel about killing that poor woman in the water eight years ago and going to jail and whatever else you never tell me about. But in the end, it's your own responsibility to take care that you are at peace with who and what you are. Alright. But you need to hear this from me, dear, your wife, because you certainly won't hear it from her while she's trying to make you feel so good."

Ellen stepped back.

"Now, I want you," she said, "to figure out what it is you want. And who you want it from. Then you need to choose. As quickly as you can."

She joined her hands in front of her. She looked like a choir singer, head up, chest out.

"I know what I'm risking, here, Virgil, don't think I don't. If I lose you to Bea Sting, I lose my soul's place in this body. Don't look so shocked, you have figured out that's the way it works. Bea knows, so I'm sure you do too. I just want you to be aware that I'm willing to take that risk."

She stepped back again, a ghostly smooth tread in reverse toward the shop's front door.

"Bea Sting," she said, looking up now at the shop ceiling, drifting back still, "you do what you have to do and so will I. But no matter what happens, no matter which of us disappears, you remember I am his wife. You will never be."

Ellen stopped backing up. She leveled her gaze at Virgil.

"And that, I believe with all my heart, is Heaven's plan."

Then Ellen, spinning on her heel, went out the door.

The instant Ellen closed the front door, Woody came in through the back.

"This is so cool," the boy said, scanning the ceiling. "You mean, she's, like, up there?"

"Yes."

"Doing what?"

"I don't know. Waiting. Watching."

Woody brought his eyes down to Virgil. "Does she have wings? You know, a harp and shit?"

"I don't know. Woody?"

"Yeah?"

"Let's take a walk."

Virgil locked the front and back doors to the store. He and Woody walked down Duval into the heart of Old Town Key West. It was already late enough in the morning for the tourists' kids to start getting ice cream. Rented bicycles swam in the human stream, old folks rang the tinny bells on wobbling handlebars. T-shirts and beach towels hung as banners outside shops. Cars prowled for parking, shoppers hunted for souvenirs. Like a wood stove, Key West crackled and stretched itself to the rising heat. Virgil walked next to Woody silently, taking in the earthly routine of it all and any anger he felt at the boy's double dealing dissipated.

But to teach Woody a lesson, he said, "The first thing I want to hear out of your mouth is an apology. Then you can tell me what you thought you were doing."

"I'm sorry."

"No one likes a rat. You should've learned that at the farm."

Woody lowered his head. "I was gonna tell you. You know, at some point."

"How much did he give you to be his informant?"

"A hundred for the stuff about you going to the Ramada. Another hundred if I came up with something else good."

Woody kicked at a stone. It skittered and ricocheted against an alley wall.

"This," the boy said, "is really good."

"What did he tell you?"

"He said I'd be helping you guys out."

"That figures."

"He said E was in some kind of trouble but she couldn't tell him what it was. And since I worked for you I was in a good position to help keep an eye on you both."

"And why not make a few bucks in the process."

"The dude was in the FBI. Those guys scare me. I mean, fuck. He was convincing."

"I'm sure."

"I'm sorry. I thought I was doing a good thing."

"Yeah. I know."

"Am I still fired?"

"No."

"What about Brumfeld?"

"Ellen said she's done with him. So are you. You tell no one. I mean it. Understand?"

"Yeah. Sure."

"I'll give you the extra hundred to make up for it."

"That's alright," the boy said. "I'll just keep the severance pay."

They turned east and walked hands in pockets to the marina, called Land's End. There, long halyards clanged against naked masts. The working grumbles of men and machines came from the bowels of hulls. The ocean pitched up whitecaps beyond the ripples of the harbor; the wind plucked the strings of the stays and dangling lines.

The boy asked, "So this is the real shit? Ellen's not just loony tunes?"

"This is the real shit," Virgil answered. "Bea's dead. She comes and goes inside Ellen."

Woody whistled. "You were right. This is pretty weird stuff."

Virgil watched a pelican land on the pier.

Woody said, "Look. I don't know a lot about this sort of thing. I mean, you know, I never went to Sunday school much. But the whole time I was listening to you and E, you know, I was saying to myself, Fuck! This is excellent. I mean, this makes a lot of sense out of a bunch of crap in this world that before just never made sense. You know?"

Virgil knew but did not say it.

"And you know me, man. I'm, like, a moron, so if it made sense to me I figured, whoa, this is worth looking into. You know, life and death, man, this is the best! Turns out they're connected. There's really angels and Heaven and the light and all that. So, look, Virg, if you tell me this isn't bogus, then I believe it. That's why I walked into the shop. I wanted you to tell me if it was true."

Virgil patted the boy's chest.

Woody stopped walking.

"So," the boy said, "I want to help."

"You've helped enough already."

"Do you know what you're gonna do?"

Virgil ran his hands through his hair and took a deep sniff of salty air and impossibility.

"What can I do? I can't let things keep going

the way they are, switching between Ellen and Bea with no way of telling who's who or when I'll be with one or the other. I love Ellen, and I'm breaking her heart. But there's something about Bea I just can't let go of."

Virgil narrowed his eyes to cast them over the water, the noon sun cutting the horizon sharp as scissors, the world sloping away at the blue edges, so vast, and Virgil wanted the world not to be so big right now but smaller, something he could handle, every step he took not so momentous as to involve God and souls and adultery and loyalty and love. Could he just take a baby step, please?

"What can I do?" Virgil repeated. "Ellen says she wants me to make up my mind fast, to figure out what I want and choose. It's not fair to her to drag this out."

He raised his hands but as if there was too much weight in them dropped them before they rose higher than his waist. Was the plan really for him to decide whether or not to exile Ellen's soul from her body so he could be with Beatrice? Could he do that? Would God ask him to do that? In exchange for what?

Virgil shook his head in slow turns and dropped his chin to his chest, giving his head the look of something being screwed down.

"If I could just . . . see Bea when I wanted, you know, at least know when she was coming. Call her. Like any other woman. I could spend time with her and get to know more about her. Figure out what it is they want from me. Figure out what it is about her that makes me nuts. Make up my fucking mind."

Woody's face took on the pinch of a thought.

"That's what E said she wanted, right? You to figure it out."

"Yeah. So?"

"And you said you need to have Bea around more so you can do that."

Virgil turned away. "Woody, don't start."

The boy laid a thin arm on Virgil's shoulder. "I got an idea."

"No," Virgil said, shrugging the arm off, "no, I don't want to hear any more crazy suggestions out of your head. Now's not the time."

Slowly, Woody tugged him around. The boy's lips were taut, his brows knitted.

"Virg?"

Virgil tilted his head in a long, patient blink. "What, Woody?"

"I been thinking while you were talking."

Virgil began an exasperated sigh, but looking at the boy's face, knowing he was sincere in his way, dropped it.

"About what?"

"Normally I'm full of shit."

"Normally."

The boy swung his brow deliberately as if what he was about to say was as large and pendulous as storm clouds.

"Not this time. I know a guy."

13

ELLEN walked home from the shop.

At first she put her head down and muttered to keep from drawing attention to herself. She quietly implored Beatrice to leave her alone. She said she understood how lonely it must be for Beatrice to be dead after what had probably been an unhappy life but why did she have to rob Ellen? Why not somebody else? Wouldn't she rather go find someone rich with a better body and a younger husband? She asked again for Bea Sting to let Virgil and her work things out between themselves, there was plenty of good left for them to build on, why did Beatrice have to come after Virgil, of all men? Crossing Southard Street, Ellen began to heat up with the sun and her voice climbed a notch into an harangue on the immorality of stealing another person's body and husband.

One woman approaching up the sidewalk

greeted her, singing, "Ellen, I saw you and your husband at The Grille the other night."

Ellen said to the sidewalk, "It wasn't me."

The woman stopped and laughed, "Why, of course it was you. That husband of yours was doting on you to beat the band. Why, I thought he was going to fall out of his chair just listening to you talk."

Like a brace of quail flying out of the brush, Ellen's hands and head went skyward. She spun at the woman.

"It wasn't *me*!"

The woman put her back against a wall and let Ellen pass.

Arriving at Whitehead Street, she paced the house, careening from room to room. Neither her feet nor her hands would settle. She yanked shut curtains to blind the house, glared at her reflection in mirrors. She picked up objects and set them down, as if reasserting her ownership over her own house by touching things, like an animal covering the scent of another.

Beatrice watched it all like someone trapped on an out-of-control carnival ride. She wanted to get off but couldn't; she wanted to shout at whoever was overseeing the ride, "Hey! Stop this thing!" Beatrice took no joy from Ellen's pain and grew tired from her stumbling about and mumbling but soon the woman's misery became something she found she could endure. Even so, she was relieved when Ellen, finally exhausted, collapsed on the parlor sofa.

The day passed into late afternoon and Beatrice was not sent into Ellen's body. Ellen's despair seemed to be a match for Beatrice's impatience. The two sat in their respective lights—one golden, one shuttered—in stalemate.

Beatrice gazed at the plaster ceiling of the Whitehead Street parlor, cockeyed and bleary through Ellen's eyes.

Beatrice said to no one, "Damn. I don't know what to do."

A voice issued from behind her. "Of course not. That's because you are in hell."

Beatrice did not jump or whirl at the words. She'd been expecting another one.

Slowly she turned.

The angel said, "Do you know what hell is?"

Where the Coach had been all rumples and the other two guides were absolute beauty and youth in brown and white, this angel was a collection of circles. His face was pie-shaped, his eyes were rings, each nostril a cave, the ears on his great head like wheels on a toy truck. Each finger was thick as a roll of coins. The biggest circle was the globe of his belly pushing out his robe. But he was not pudgy; he was a round study in power.

"Hell," he said, "is knowing you're in hell."

Beatrice waited. The angel looked down on her.

She asked, "You're going to explain that to me, aren't you?"

"Of course."

He brought two meaty palms up to frame his idea.

"Now you take a fellow, he's hitting .300. Having a marvelous season. Then for no good reason, because there never is, he starts to hit the ball right at people. He's tagging it good, mind you, but right at the other team and he's making outs. He's stranding runners. His average starts to dip a little, then a lot, and things don't get any better. Now if you leave this fellow alone, let him work it out, give him a pat on the rump now and then, you let him stay in the lineup, he's going to keep hacking away at it, trying his best and he'll stay on an even keel. Pretty soon he's hitting them where they're not again and you've got yourself your .300 hitter back."

The big spirit paused to see if Beatrice had any questions. She did not. Instead she goaded the parable, saying, "But?"

He liked that. He smiled.

"But you tell that same fellow he's in a slump, you focus his attention on it, and he'll take twice as long to get his swing back. He's going to press. He'll stay up late worrying. He'll monkey with his mechanics. He'll ask everybody he knows what they think is the matter with him. He's going to be smack dab in the middle of hell. When he didn't even know that's where he was until somebody told him so."

The guide lifted a tufted finger.

"Now the moral is—"

"You a Yankee?"

The finger wilted. "Don't you want to hear the moral?"

"In a minute. You another Yankee?"

He was put off his rhythm by her detour.

"Say, you promise we can come back to the moral? It's a good one."

"Sure."

"Alright. Then yes. You might say I was *the* Yankee."

"That's a little bold, isn't it?"

"It's not a brag if it's a fact."

"So how come we're back to Yankees?"

"You remember what happened when Coach sent that Dodger last time. We all saw the hash he made of things. The word is you've got to be kept on a short leash."

"Says who?"

The guide chuckled. His stomach shook and it seemed to rule his whole, the rest of him jollied with it.

"It's common knowledge, dear. Anyway, the moral."

"How many home runs did you hit?"

"Quite a few. Anyway, the moral."

"You real famous?"

"You don't get more famous. Beatrice?"

"Okay. The moral. Do me a favor?"

"Yes?"

"Just apply it to me right off. Don't make me wait through a couple of versions until I figure out what you're talking about. I've got a lot to think about already. Just give me the stripped-down model, okay?"

"Deal."

The guide folded his legs under him and sat with a grace bigger even than his body. Beatrice was not surprised to see him move like that; she'd admired the ease in both motion and word of all her angels. She felt a twinge at not knowing when she would be one of them.

He said again, "You are in hell."

Beatrice pointed to the light streaming at the end of the path. "I don't think so."

The guide crossed his arms over his barrel chest. "Trust me. It doesn't matter where you're sitting. Hell isn't what's under your fanny."

He jabbed a finger at his heart.

"This is where hell is. Right here's where you keep it, right here close, where you keep your soul. And you, Beatrice, are definitely in hell."

She regarded him quietly. She said, "You're doing it."

"Doing what?"

"You're doing that angel thing where I have to wait and figure out for myself what you're saying to me. I asked you to just tell me straight out."

"I'm trying. Patience, Beatrice."

She clamped her lips tight.

He said, "You did something you weren't supposed to do."

"What."

"Let's take a look at the life you just finished. It was one big swing and a miss. Swing and a miss. And then, for some reason, you just stopped swinging, period. It's odd. You figure anybody, even the worst hitter, is going to make a little contact now and then before he's done. Foul a few off, at least. But you? Nothing."

"Look," she said, barely restraining herself, "cut the baseball crap. Just tell me."

He crossed his legs, Buddha-like.

"You're getting edgy," he said.

She crossed her own arms.

He continued in measured tones. She could see the concentration on his face to mete it out plain and simple.

"Alright. Here it is, as clear as I can say it. You weren't supposed to know that your life had been so bad. You weren't supposed to even think about your life until you'd arrived here and entered the light. Then you'd have been able to look back on it the way the rest of us do, with some insight and prudence. You would have seen it in the context of all your other lives as well as in the context of life itself. You'd have had us to support you until you got a handle on it. But when you plopped yourself down here on the path, refusing to move like some mule, you looked back at your life before you were ready to understand or accept it. You found out your life had been one long slump."

Beatrice hung her head.

The guide shifted to his knees. He reached out to lift her chin and smooth back her hair from her face

"Poor thing. You had so little go right in your time. Then you died and before we could get you

into the light, you figured out what you shouldn't
have. Now you're sitting here on your lonesome
where we can't help you, trying to make sense out
of everything. I came to tell you the only thing
that I could, that no one can make sense out of life
while they're still living it. It wasn't designed to
make sense. It has another purpose altogether."

He sat back on his haunches. "Look at you.
Your swing is off. Your timing is gone. Your confidence is shot. You're beginning to fidget, Beatrice. You were tapping your fingers. You're
bringing bits of life back up here with you where
they don't belong. Time. Impatience. Suspicion.
Hope."

He indicated behind her to the floating image.
She turned to look through Ellen's eyes, which
were fixed on the parlor ceiling. Another weary
lament was rolling like cigarette smoke from
Ellen's lips.

He said, "That's the path to hell."

He pointed again to the light. "That's Heaven."

The guide stood.

"I want you to come with me, Beatrice. It's not
going to get any easier for you." Again he indicated the floating image. "Or for them if you stay
here."

He held his hand down to her. "Come into the
light. Let all this hurt end."

She looked up at him, his white girth. He
could hold her, she thought, he could wrap up the
hell in her heart so tightly she'd never again feel its
spines or be suffocated anymore by its fumes. All

the angels could do that for her, they were waiting to do that for her.

But, she hoped and believed, so was Virgil.

"I don't know what to do."

"Then trust me. Trust the light."

"Virgil needs me."

"Needing," the angel said, "is the easy half of life. Not needing is the other half."

Beatrice said again, "I don't know what to do."

She reached for his hand. He reached back.

He pulled up.

She pulled down.

She brought his knuckles to her lips and kissed them.

"I love you," she said. "I love all of you. Thank you."

Beatrice let the hand go.

The guide stepped back.

"Well, that's something," he said with a gratified chortle, "that's getting a piece of the ball, at least."

Beatrice said, "Don't give up on me."

He shook his head. "We won't."

The angel walked away several paces. He planted his bare feet and raised an arm to point one finger toward the light, gazing where he pointed. Then he brought his hands in tight and went into a stance, holding a phantom bat at his shoulder. He waited, staring down some object with almost malice in his mien. He wiggled his behind a few times, grew still, then swung. His feet twisted, his hips pivoted, the swing was so mighty he collapsed into it and he became a white brilliant ball that sailed in an arc away up the path and, to Beatrice's amazed eyes, over the light.

Key West is a heart. It is engulfed in warm waters. It is linked to the body of America by thin, tenuous and busy lines. It is hot and beating bright, it is dark and brooding. In the heart is the soul and in the soul there is mystery. And in the mystery of Key West lie many intents.

Virgil stood on a ragtag street. He took in the rundown houses, the cars—some rusting, some waxed—parked beside scalded yards and noisy children playing with cans and sticks. Eight days ago Virgil would not have let Woody bring him into this poor Latino neighborhood of saints, Key lime–pie bakeries, tortilla shops and small, peeling, wooden homes. This was the Carib sector. The old-timers here, mostly Catholics, spoke of the fortune-tellers of Havana, Nassau, Kingston and Port-au-Prince. They told their children and grandchildren of the spirits who lived in the cathedrals of the banana trees on the blue water plantations. They spoke of charms and hexes and voodoo.

Eight days ago Virgil would not even have raised an eyebrow at Woody's descriptions of black magic at the hands of an old man from Haiti, the father of a boy he'd known at the juvy farm. Virgil would have told Woody of the rumors of weird rituals emanating out of these streets into Key West like a quaking in the heart and said "No," and he would have been able to mean it.

"No."

"Yes."

"No."

"Will you just chill?" Woody climbed out of the car. "Come on. Just see the guy."

"It's too spooky."

Woody gave the exasperated cough. "Spooky? With what you've got going on, how can you honestly call *anything* spooky?"

Woody walked around to the driver's side of the car. He leaned his elbow in the open window.

"Dude. Look. Between the two of us, we've seen a lot, haven't we? A lot of life, some death, some strange shit. But we don't know it all." The boy's voice was calm, mature, compelling. Some old archetype inside Woody was speaking, some ancient seeker, humble being. "What we know is like this"—he snapped his fingers—"compared to the knowledge that's out there. This guy in this garage might be a fake piece of shit or he might be someone we should talk to. He might know things, he might be able to do things. But, whichever, there is no way anything ever again is spooky. So just let's get out of the car and check it out."

Virgil balked. Woody rolled his eyes.

Eight days ago, Virgil would not have knocked on this corrugated metal garage door or opened it at the call of "Enter."

Inside, candle flames made the room shiver. The walls were clotted with drying herbs bound in sheaves, primitive drums with stretched speckled skins, gourd rattles, feathers and plumes, colored liquids in glass bottles, dozens of earthenware jugs. The floor was bare dirt. Against one wall sat a large stone covered in candles, beads, small flags, coins and costume jewelry. Between the dirt floor and bare rafters a thick wooden beam stood. Palm fronds had been strewn across the rafters to make the beam appear to be a tree trunk. Papier-mâché bananas drooped in ripe yellow bunches.

A shallow hole had been dug, wide and broad like a barbecue pit. On top of a straw mat in the hole lay a short, fat black man with eyes closed. Around the hole, a checkerboard pattern of corn-meal had been meticulously poured out. Beside the man in the hole stood three pint jars of water and three pints of red wine. The mat and the man had been sprinkled with sesame seeds. A wooden stake was driven into the ground at one end of the mat, a bronze crucifix at the other. Twenty-one candles in three companies of seven stood glowing along the lip of the hole. Between the fat man's legs a bound red rooster clucked unhappily.

Luis don Pedro Thiebaux opened a white sheet and spread it over the man's legs and the chicken. He sprinkled the linen with salt, then clapped his hands over his work.

"Jean, I be back in a little while," he said into the hole. "Just relax, mon. If de chicken squirm too much, give him a squeeze."

Don Pedro turned to Virgil. He was medium height with slender shoulders under a cardinal jacket. He wore a white shirt and an amulet that caught the candlelight and broke it into blinking red facets. His arms swung bent at the elbows and his walk was nimble, that John Wayne man's gait where the feet follow a line, like walking on a rail. His face hung a goatee, his dark eyes did not waver.

He put out his hand. The nails on each finger were over an inch long, curling downward in little hard yellow waterfalls. Virgil slid his hand carefully into don Pedro's. The hand was huge, the palm vivid pink; the effect was that the hand itself was a separate creature with talons.

Don Pedro said, "You be Virgil. Welcome."

He found Woody over Virgil's shoulder. "And you de boy who look out for my son Baltazar at the juvenile farm. T'ank you."

He announced to them both, "I am Luis don Pedro. Please. We go outside to talk and let poor Jean rest."

In the driveway, in the light of afternoon, Virgil realized that don Pedro looked better by candle and shadow. His face was pocked and his teeth and eyes were the color of cigarette tar. His sport coat was haggard at the sleeves, the amulet was cheesy. His goatee and hair were greying and needed brushing. But the hand that touched Virgil's elbow was genuinely unsettling.

"Jean Claude," don Pedro said, indicating with a backward glance the man in the hole inside the garage, "don' know what wrong wit' him. He tired all de time. Headaches. Always a bad mood." Don Pedro shoveled a fingernail into his goatee.

"Difficult to tell. I wan' him to lose weight. But his wife t'inks it because he unhappy wit' her. Who can tell? So."

He put his two giant palms together; the nails made a thicket of thorns.

"We got time to talk before I go back in. In one hour I take de rooster from 'tween his legs and put it in a black box. Tonight I gon' bury it down by de ocean."

Virgil said his first words to don Pedro.

"Alive? You bury it alive?"

"Yes. De *loa* Marinette take away Jean's sickness in de rooster. De bird mus' be alive or Marinette will no' accept it. It no' de rooster's flesh dat carry away de illness. It de spirit."

Woody muttered, "Cool."

Don Pedro continued. "Dat what voodoo do. It bring together de *loas* of de spirit world and people. T'rough voodoo, we speak wit' dem, walk wit' dem, dance wit' dem. I heal wit' dem."

Virgil looked at the side of the garage. "Will it work?"

Don Pedro showed his buttery teeth.

"Only sometimes in voodoo we tell de *loas* what to do. De rest of de time, we ask."

He spoke to Woody, whose eyes were wide.

"De gateway 'tween de two worlds has got many keys. Prayers, food, cigars, charms, de *vévé* you saw on de ground around de hole, de rhythm of drums, sometimes de life of an animal. Dere be many *loas* and each got his own appetites."

Virgil opened his mouth to speak. Don Pedro

held up a long finger to stop him. Virgil looked at the creamy underside of the nail.

Don Pedro said, "De one t'ing all de spirits ask is belief. Dey will no' come for curiosity seekers. Dey come only for de faithful and de humble."

Inside the garage the rooster squawked. Jean grumbled, *"Merde."*

Don Pedro shouted, "Jean, relax!"

He dripped his next words slowly, like rain, turning slatted eyes at Virgil.

"No' many whites believe in voodoo. It ask too much of dem. Why you here?"

Before Virgil could answer, don Pedro pivoted to Woody. "Do you believe?"

The boy snapped to attention as though don Pedro's look had scorched him. "Me? Oh, yeah, man. I got no problem with voodoo. You know, why not? Geez, I mean, the stuff I've seen already—"

Don Pedro interrupted. "Baltazar told me you talk too much. And you, Virgil? Why you no' in a church or a doctor's couch? Why you come to Luis don Pedro Thiebaux?"

"I have spoken to a *loa*."

"You?"

"Yes."

"Really?"

"Me too," chimed in Woody.

"Are you a necromancer?"

"No," Virgil answered. "Just a man. Just a believer."

Don Pedro's face pulled back like a turtle's.

Even while his mouth twisted down, his eyes brewed surprise and suspicion.

"My wife," Virgil said. "A spirit has come. She speaks to me through her."

Virgil noticed that he was unintentionally speaking in the formal but broken pattern of don Pedro.

"Woody tells me your son says you are a man of great knowledge. I've come for your help."

"Help for you or for de *loa*?"

"Both."

"And no help for de wife?"

Virgil said nothing.

Don Pedro nodded, sizing up Virgil.

"What time you got?" don Pedro asked.

Virgil looked at his watch. "One forty."

"I mus' go inside. Fat Jean will t'ink I deserted him. I can no' have that." Don Pedro winked at Virgil and stage whispered in a poor attempt to keep Woody from hearing. "I sleep wit' his aunt."

He gestured for Virgil and Woody to follow.

Inside the garage, the chicken had twisted the sheet about itself; a band clipping one of its wings had come undone and the bird was flapping out of kilter. Jean lay as still as he could but things in the hole were in disarray. He'd bumped one of the jars of rainwater, spilling it and making a mud slick under the mat. All the salt and sesame seeds had fallen from him. Only the cornmeal *vévé* around the pit was untouched and this don Pedro trod on while he kneeled to soothe and retie the rooster. He stroked Jean's hair.

"Jean, *ami*, how you feel?"

"Hungry."

"I t'ink Marinette taking lots into dis chicken."

"It don' feel like it."

"You gon' be fine."

Don Pedro pointed to a clay basin filled with water. He told Woody, "Bring me dat."

Woody fetched the pot. Don Pedro cupped water in his hands and flung it in Jean's face.

Jean spluttered. Don Pedro repeated the drenching ten times. The spray put out a few of the candles beside the hole. Jean lay under the deluge blinking, gasping in disappointment each time don Pedro scooped into the water.

When the basin was empty, don Pedro said into the hole, "Got to chase de *mal* out de head too, mon."

Jean dug his knuckles into his eye sockets.

Don Pedro asked, "You hungry now?"

Jean shook his dripping head. "No."

From a burlap sack don Pedro dug another handful of sesame seeds and sprinkled them over Jean as if seasoning a big burger.

Reaching down into the pit, don Pedro fanned out his hand and laid it across Jean's broad, round face. The man's mouth, nose and eyes disappeared behind the sinews and claws of don Pedro's clutch. Jean's body relaxed, though Virgil thought he might have kicked or gagged instead. But Jean lay still, the hand a mask over his features. Don Pedro closed his own eyes and turned his face slowly down to his hand into the hole. He mumbled something mellifluous, pidgin French, his voice bottomless and beautiful.

When he opened his lids and lifted his hand away, something had been sucked out of Jean; the man's eyes were rolled back in his head, the whites showed like dice, his mouth hung open and his tongue lapped over his lower teeth. He was breathing but so barely that Virgil looked twice to be sure. His arms and legs lay like logs; even the chicken was still.

Woody whispered, "Holy shit."

Don Pedro said to them, "Let's go upstairs and talk 'bout you' *loa*."

Ellen lifted her head.

She staggered into the kitchen and put the coffee maker to work. While it burbled, she went back into the parlor, raised the blinds and sat on the window seat. She closed her eyes, bathing in the flooding sunlight. The light was so bright the darkness behind her lids turned blood-red and veined.

She went out the front door to stand on the steps. A neighbor lady wheeling a pram said good morning. Ellen waved meekly. The lady stopped and Ellen walked down to see the baby. During the conversation Ellen bent to the grass and grabbed a handful of blades. She held these to her nose and breathed their broken perfume. The lady wheeled on. Ellen took off her shoes and walked barefoot around the outside of the house, touching her fingers to its old boards, peeling the

places where it needed painting, pruning a branch
from a shrub that had grown too gangly. She
picked up the garden hose and sprayed pigeon
guano off a windowsill.

Inside, Ellen poured coffee. She carried the
cup back into the bright parlor. She pulled a
photo album from a drawer and spread it across
her knees, turning pages slowly and doting on old
Polaroids of her mother and father, of gone and
forgotten family cars, vacations, pets. Ellen had
been a slim child, pigtailed and serious even at
Christmas. She never smiled, Beatrice noticed,
following Ellen's fingertips tracing over plastic
shrouded faces. She never smiled and meant it. I
smiled all the time and never meant it.

Ellen's history rolled in gentle waves under her
hands, page drifting after page, years pressed flat
like calendars. Beatrice knew what Ellen was
doing: She was taking her ghost on a tour. See
what you're stealing from me, each lingering look
at a photo said. Each glance at an antique from
her parents' time in the house, each acknowledg-
ment of plants, light, keepsakes, was an appeal.
These photos are mine, Ellen was saying, this
mom and dad, this house, that shop, that neighbor woman and her baby carriage and our short
chat, this sofa, the stains on this sofa, all are mine
and can never be yours. You haven't lived this
life, so even if you can wrest from me my body
you will have won nothing, nothing but a trophy.

Ellen turned more pages, sipping coffee. She
took out two small photos of herself, one as a child,

one as an adult, and cut out the heads. These she stuck inside the silver heart locket, one on each side so that the two faces of Ellen looked at each other through the dark of the closed heart. Beatrice thought there was something strange about Ellen's affinity for the locket, the only souvenir Beatrice had of her mother, but she was oddly glad that the long empty thing had some pictures in it now. Ellen sighed and shut her faces in the locket and closed the album. She held the book tight to her and leaned back against the cushions. Beatrice waited for Ellen to resume her plays on Beatrice's sympathy or attacks on her morals but Ellen said nothing, choosing instead, like a good movie director, to let action and images speak for her.

Following Ellen's eyes around the room, almost hearing the woman's thoughts, Beatrice wrestled with her own remorse and obvious selfishness. Ellen's appeal to let Virgil come back to her, to let Ellen as Virgil's wife provide what he needed, was heart-wrenching. Her gamble with her soul was brave. And Beatrice's last spirit guide had been the most compelling of them all; he'd shown Beatrice that she was cracking under the strain of worry and waiting. All of this had made her want to go on with the big guide into the light, to end the hurt like he'd said, both hers and Ellen's. She wanted to finally view and understand her other lives. She wanted to find her peace.

But Beatrice was not experienced with empathy for women and she knew it. She found her resolve slowly hardening by Ellen's dumb show of precious memories. Beatrice looked at the sunlight and furnishings through Ellen's eyes and thought: At least you got to live in this bright house. You got to be in those pictures. You had those parents and those cute cats and Christmases and new Chryslers in the driveway. You had that nice neighbor lady and her darling baby to talk to, green grass to smell, a new garden hose to spray, a respectable business and a good-looking husband, and I didn't.

Beatrice had danced for creeps and fucked creeps, spent her whole adult life hunkering in a trench of smut and not striding around a fine old house on Whitehead Street and a clean gallery and art supply store on Duval. Beatrice had not worn one ribbon in her hair, ever, while Ellen's album was full of pictures of the little girl's unsmiling head, pigtails adorned lovingly with ribbons and bright plastic barrettes, her face stoic behind milk mustaches and ice cream smears. Beatrice had worn her mother's locket for thirty years and had left the thing unfilled the whole time and now Ellen comes along and puts her own pictures in it. Then, at the end of her life in a parking lot Beatrice had taken three lead slugs in the chest to pay her for her life like coins tossed to her and even then she'd crossed the barriers of Heaven and earth just to get back this far.

She wanted to be loved in life and wanted everything good and proper that came with it. What was she willing to do to get it?

Again, she said, "I don't know what to do," and her voice sounded to her ears pitiful. She turned her head over her shoulder to look up the path as though this might be the phrase to summon another guide, a Yankee, a Met, a Dallas Cowboy, whatever, she wouldn't care, she would welcome him, just one more to sit with, maybe the next angel would be the one to talk her into the light.

But there was none, only on all sides of her the perfect stillness of perfection, which must be still to stay that way.

Luis don Pedro Thiebaux offered Virgil and Woody tea.

Woody took a seat on the edge of one of the two cots in the room and said, "Sure." Virgil hesitated, thinking of all the herbs and oddities hanging in the candle-lit garage below and the ritual being endured by fat wet Jean Claude in the grave with a chicken between his legs. Virgil was afraid don Pedro might make some kind of tea out of *Macbeth*, eye of newt and wing of bat.

Quickly, Virgil took in the living space that don Pedro had shared with his son until Baltazar had got himself sent off to the juvy farm at age thirteen for slashing a switchblade across the arm of the landlord when the man came to collect late rent and began to berate don Pedro. The upstairs single room was sparsely furnished. A soiled hook rug and two flimsy cots covered the raw floorboards. A large clay pot with a piece of plywood on top served as a bedside table. A makeshift kitchen with greasy shelves filled one corner, a battered desk and two chairs stood in another. A porcelain toilet and sink jutted from a wall. Everything in the room, poorly illuminated from the one small and very high window, was dingy, the Cordovan color of tea. The room was a bowl where air, light, furniture and people steeped and turned brown.

"Virgil?" don Pedro asked, reaching for a canister. "Tea?"

"What kind do you have?"

"Earl Grey."

"Yes."

Virgil sat in the desk chair.

Behind don Pedro's back, Woody took the opportunity to raise his eyebrows and wiggle his fingers at Virgil. His lips sang silently, "Woooo, woooo."

Don Pedro brought the tea. He sat opposite Woody on the other bed.

Handing the cup to Virgil, don Pedro said, "Yes. I know what it like to have a wife of powerful *connaissance*. I be a strong *oungan*. But my Mathilda, she was an even stronger *mambo*. Such a wife can make a mon wonder if God Himself may no' be a mon."

Virgil put the steaming tea on the desk. "It's not my wife who's powerful, don Pedro. It's the spirit who comes into her."

Don Pedro shook his frizzy head. "No, no, no, never t'ink dat, mon. You' wife, what's her name?"

"Ellen."

"Ellen is no *bosalle*, Virgil, she no beginner. Somet'ing 'bout her soul has drawn de *loa* to her. No no, mon, dis Ellen got power."

Don Pedro sipped his tea. The china cup was invisible behind his hands.

"You see, God does no' allow us to speak wit' Him direct. He send instead his *loas*. Dese are spirits of de dead who have stayed on earth 'cause of strong *connaissance*. You and me, Virgil, Woody, we all got *loas* to watch over us and protect us. What de name of you' wife's *loa*?"

"Bea."

"Dat a good strong name. You' wife been called to de service of de *loa* Bea. She been mounted. Woody?"

"Yeah?"

"Go downstairs. Sit quiet wit' Jean Claude. Keep de chicken calm."

Woody opened his mouth.

Don Pedro said firmly, "Dis be talk among men." When Woody had clomped hangdog down the stairs, don Pedro poured himself fresh hot tea. Over his shoulder he said to Virgil, "People afraid of voodoo. But don' need to be. Voodoo just like what you believe in, Christians, Jews. Only we don' believe de spirits so far away as you do."

Don Pedro sat on the edge of his bed. "Tell me what you seen."

Virgil covered everything, from his call to Top Hat Escort Service and Beatrice's murder after an exotic dance at the Ramada to Ellen's first short blackouts a week ago and the doctors in Miami, to the morgue, Fatima, Jacob Brumfeld, Woody. He described how Beatrice was on the path to the light, told the *oungan* about God, the ballplayers, the plan. How Beatrice watched everything through Ellen's senses. How Ellen had no recollections of Beatrice's stays in her body. He brought don Pedro current up to that morning in the shop with Ellen, her plea for him to end his affair with the spirit Beatrice. That Ellen knew what was at stake: keeping her soul joined to her body.

The tea in their cups cooled. Don Pedro said nothing but listened with slight moves of his head as if to hear sounds other than the ones Virgil was making. When Virgil was done, don Pedro put his hands together. His nails clacked.

"So what you sayin' is you wan' be wit' dis *loa.*"

"I think I need to be able to be with her. Yes."

Don Pedro waited for more.

Virgil added, "I think I'm supposed to be with her."

"You t'ink?"

Virgil turned defensive. "I think that might be the plan. Yes."

Don Pedro bobbed his head. "Den you know de mind of God."

Don Pedro's nodding became a slow, ominous shake, like a tree agitated by a harsh wind.

"Whew, Virgil. You must got plenty *connaissance* you'self, mon."

Virgil let his jaw hang. "What is that supposed to imply?"

Don Pedro was suddenly comradely, jolly: "Come on, mon. You say you know de Bea for what, a week? You married to de Ellen for four years. So what you t'ink it . . ." Don Pedro raised his eyebrows and lifted his nose, a comic snooty pose, ". . . imply?"

Virgil did not answer. Don Pedro reined himself in.

"Tell me, mon. Would you have fallen so much for de Bea if she were no' dead and inside you' wife? What if you jus' met her at de motel alive like you was supposed to? Would you still be so crazy for her? Or would she just be what she was? What you call her? An escort? An exotic dancer?"

Virgil swirled the chilled tea in his cup. "I'm not sure that's any of your business."

Don Pedro laughed again. He said, "You no' sure 'bout a lot. But dat's okay. You don' need to be. You say you wan' be wit' de *loa* . . ." Don Pedro blew through his lips to make a flubbering sound like a horse. "I got no t'ing to say. Except maybe dat you blinded by somethin', mon. It you' wife you wan' be wit."

Then don Pedro seemed to get an idea. He screwed up his lips, narrowed his eyes as if peering into a closet and leaned toward Virgil. He extended one long finger which, because of its curling nail, pointed not at Virgil's face but at his feet.

He lowered his voice. "Hey. You sleep wit' dis *loa*?"

Virgil opened his teeth and took a long blink. Then he blew through his own lips and made almost the same horsy sound.

Exasperated, he asked, "Does that matter?"

"*Ay yi yi,*" don Pedro trilled, his hands up beside his ears, celebratory, "you did! Oh, mon, I tell you, dere is much, much *connaissance* here. You slept wit' a *loa*? Ho! I envy you, mon. All I ever go' to do was dance wit' dem. But you? *Whooop-ahh!*"

Virgil waited through the sorcerer's mirth.

Don Pedro rose and put the cups of tea in the sink. He was careless with them and they clattered, the way Ellen handled dishes.

"Look, mon," don Pedro spoke from the other side of the room, staying in the shadows there. His voice was dropped an octave. "I know what you wan' from me."

Virgil stood also. "What is that, don Pedro?"

A cloud scudded in front of the sun. The light from the high window dimmed. The room seemed to incline its head. Don Pedro grew darker. In that moment and for the first time, Virgil sensed what don Pedro really was: even standing there in a shabby room wearing an outlandish secondhand jacket and a toy amulet, like a tiger in a zoo don Pedro did not need his jungle trees and sugar cane around him. His true nature—even here in a Caribbean ghetto of Key West—was unscathed and shining right now; don Pedro was in truth a creature of the hidden world and hidden knowledge and his eyes and barbed hands transported Virgil away from the dirty hook rug on the floor and thin cots and his cheap costume clothes, across more than an ocean and more than the flung stars but across borders of power and cause and effect, to the night drums and thrumming chants, disjointed dances and bonfires of the voodoo rituals of supplication for the spirits who came always when demanded and often when asked.

Quietly, don Pedro said, "You wan' me to help you' *loa* to come."

The *oungan* waited and while he did so touched the fingernails of his thumbs and pinkies together one at a time, a ghastly rendition of the old children's rhyme, *The Itsy-Bitsy Spider*.

Finally he said, "What you wan' me to do is evil."

Then don Pedro sat on the bed. The springs squeaked. "I would no' help a mon do somet'ing I t'ought to be evil."

Don Pedro turned his face away from Virgil.

Virgil moved for the steps to leave. The sun had not come back to the room.

Behind him, don Pedro spoke. "But I would help a *loa*."

Don Pedro laughed again, a deep chortle like the sound of burning.

14

THIS arrival into Ellen was the easiest. There was no jolt of suddenness, no disconcert of slipping into the body to find an open mouth in the middle of a sentence or some posture Beatrice had to maintain to keep from staggering, no object she must tighten her hand around to keep from dropping. There was no mood Beatrice brought with her that was a reversal of Ellen's. This time, Beatrice slouched on the sofa in Ellen's body and quietly continued to look at the parlor ceiling without even a blink in the transition. The body was cooled and breathing deeply, sad, sad Beatrice felt in the bones and brow. Worried. Scared. Something else, too. Strong. Beatrice fingered her mother's silver locket hung around Ellen's neck and remembered her own life and the anguish and strength that carried her through it.

Beatrice could not sit this way for long. She had, her whole life, buried woe and depression

beneath activity like a dog with a bone to save
until some other time, scratching over sadness a
mound of anything else.

After ten minutes she sat up on the sofa. She
quickened her breathing.

"Alright. That'll do."

Beatrice rose and walked toward the kitchen.
In the foyer, she stopped and looked back into the
parlor, beyond it into the dining room, back to the
kitchen and the foyer where she stood. All of it
was done in dark fabrics, yellowed wallpapers
and Formica, gilded framed mirrors, turn-of-the-
century oak antiques with heavy legs like old
charwomen. The big house seemed crippled and
dying, unable to jump or run, the thick furnishings and drabness were hobbles on its legs. It
needed life breathed in, the rooms filled with
cooking smells and flowers. Paint the antiques,
strip the walls, make it a lively place for parties
and light.

Beatrice strode to the kitchen and found the
legal pad. She took up a pen and at the table
wrote:

Ellen,

    *You know why it never bothered me to
have other women's men attracted to me? To
dance for them and turn them on, go out
with them, even sleep with them when I felt
like it or the money was right?*

    *To tell you the truth, it's because I figure
those women gave their men to me. It made*

me kind of mad sometimes. It was plain as
day they weren't taking care of their
husbands and boyfriends the way they should
have. Whatever form that should have taken
in all those thousands of households over the
years—sex, back rubs, good meals, a gesture
of support, even a gentle word—they weren't
doing it. That was my job. I was good at it.
Men don't have but so many different tastes
and needs. One woman can handle them all
if she has a mind to. But too many women
just don't, or won't, or forget to, like you.
And that's where I came in.

And you know what else? I bet I saved a
few marriages along the way. Gave the men
a break, a little trip to Paris before they went
back down on the farm. And some of them
went back and told their wives they wanted a
little more of Paris in their lives, told their
women to cherish them a little more, give
them a thrill now and then, whereas before
me maybe they wouldn't have.

Yes, and maybe I ruined a few marriages,
too. But those I ruined would have been
targets for someone or something else, like a
weak-swimming fish in a school of sharks. I
don't feel bad about being one of the sharks.
We serve a purpose.

But let's talk about you for a minute.
You got guts, some serious cojones. You got
smarts. You got good bones and pretty features
hidden under a lazy streak. You also have a

*sensitive, needy side. Why do you keep all
that from Virgil? Why won't you take
anything from the man, let him be a whole
man for you, like he said he wants to be? It
would help you be a whole woman for him.*

*What are you scared of? Me? I'm just
death, Ellen, you got to face me or whoever
handles that up here sooner or later. No, I
think you're scared of life. Look at your
house, it's a shrine to your parents, dead
eight years now. Look at yourself, shut off
from anything like passion or joy, resisting
the slightest giving and sharing with your
husband other than chores. You let yourself
grow overweight to keep the demands on you
as low as possible. When was the last time
you had your hair done? Got all dolled up
for him? You are closed as a coffin, and
that's given Virgil nowhere to lay his love for
you, nowhere until he found me.*

*I'm warning you, Ellen. If I want to, I
can keep him. And if I do keep him, I'm not
going to feel bad about that either.*

*Okay. I'm tired of this moping around. I
bet you are too. We need a girls' day out.*

Bea Sting

Beatrice rolled the yellow page into a scroll and
again clutched it in her right hand for delivery.
Upstairs she rooted in the closet for Ellen's sneakers and took a pair of white socks from a drawer.
She threw them into Ellen's handbag, grabbed the

keys to the Volvo and locked the front door behind her.

She drove out of the neighborhood to Roosevelt, to her old gym, Shape U, in the same mall as the Winn Dixie, enjoying the warm sun on her arm slung out the car window. Beatrice was jaunty, wearing sunglasses and driving fast. She had set something in motion, not knowing what. Even so it was liberating to think of closure and to drive under a blue heaven and a white light.

At the gym she used Ellen's credit card to buy a guest pass and a leotard, size large, jet black with a hot pink top and thong bottom. In the locker room, after snapping the outfit into place, she checked herself in the mirror and, viewing her rear, clucked her tongue.

"Mm mm mm," she muttered to the unaware Ellen. "Like two pigs wrasslin' in a sack."

To the pulse of throbbing techno music, Beatrice walked across the carpeted gym floor. There were only women working out right now in the early afternoon, some Beatrice recognized. A few nice figures on these housewives, she thought. Her own shape used to be the best in the building; she'd reveled in being older than these other afternoon women but firmer, her waist slimmer, butt higher, and breasts fuller, the crown on her curves. She knew she was more desired than they, no matter who they were married to, even imagining that she'd probably danced for most of their men. Now Ellen's body chafed against the tights, even in a size large, especially in the crotch and armpits. Beatrice knew the others were looking at her. Maybe they recognized Ellen from the art supply store.

Clutching the yellow note to Ellen, Beatrice sauntered past a few women on their machines or floor mats and made no eye contact. She moved silently to her old nemesis, the stair stepper by the large silk dieffenbachia, where she used to sweat until she saw the drops fly onto the leaves.

She touched the machine's LCD monitor face. "I'm baa-aack."

She draped her towel over the black bar, punched in a mountainous program, guessed at Ellen's weight and started.

Within a minute, sweat beaded over her lip. Even before the red dots mounted much on the monitor her legs burned, lactic acid on fire front and back. She pressed on, grunting with the effort.

"What's the matter, Ellen?" she said through teeth gritted. "Can't keep up?"

She continued like this for thirty minutes, enduring pain and exhaustion that soaked the dieffenbachia, which though fake looked happy dripping in a tropical rain. She pushed herself past scorching muscles with short bursts of pep talk, all aimed at Ellen. The legal page in her right mitt grew wrinkled and wet, but the ballpoint ink did not run so Beatrice clutched the paper hard and ignored it while she bore down.

When she was finished, she stepped down and almost fell backward. Her legs were rubbery and felt stuffed with springs. Drenched and flushed, she toweled off, never letting go of the note, and walked toward the locker room on knees she fought to keep from buckling. Now, in a leotard dark with the dousing of her workout, she nodded and matched eyes with the smiling women around her.

In the shower, Beatrice held the rolled note high in a Statue of Liberty pose. She dressed quickly and tossed the sweaty clothes into the handbag.

The walk to the Volvo across the parking lot was radiant, the air sweet and her legs sore and satisfying.

"What do you want to do next?" Beatrice asked the missing soul. "I think we should play hooky a little longer. Any arguments? No? Sure?" She nodded, closing herself in the Volvo. "Okay, then."

She drove to a beauty salon on Angel Street, a swanky one she could never afford, but Ellen's good civic reputation and Visa opened new doors. She asked at the reception desk beside a real dieffenbachia and a towering flowering cactus for "the works."

Beatrice was seated by a smooth, slim-wristed man and given a fruit juice to sip. In moments her shoes were removed and her feet set to soak in a tub of warm, bubbly green liquid.

The salon hummed around her with chat and music, the sounds of running water and hair dryers, womblike noises to her closed eyes and receding thoughts. She relaxed in the chair and did not speak to the women who came to work on her face and feet except to say hello or thank you. Her legs ached and she considered a massage after the beauty salon.

For an hour she let them pamper the body. She stayed far inside it, avoiding conversation, opening the eyes only to approve of nail polish hues or greet a different beautician at her side before sinking again into the cushioned seat, to float on hushed, generic compliments about Ellen's skin, hair, features and coloring. At a depth beneath the lowered lids, Beatrice tried to slide aside a little, make some room on the couch of Ellen's fanny for Ellen's soul, somehow, to come sit beside her in the darkness and join her in the flesh they shared, to enjoy along with Beatrice the fingertip graces and slippery appliqués of the salon. She tried to sense company, would have liked it if she'd felt it; it would have been intimate, an embrace closer than anything she'd ever experienced, their two girls' hearts and souls together, sisters in the body, not caged but coupled.

When a manicurist tried to slip the rumpled yellow sheet out of the right hand to dip the nails, Beatrice raised her head. She tightened her grip on the page. In that instant, she lost her hold on the body.

On the path to the light, with a bittersweet swell in her own chest, Beatrice wanted to mist up. But she could not. She did smile, the other half of what was swirling around inside her, while she watched Ellen stare at the toenails she'd had painted a red so deep it seemed black.

"What is that?" asked Ellen in a careful voice.

"It's called 'Vamp,'" said the beautician. "It's

the hottest color. It's the one you picked."

Ellen nodded. "Uh-huh."

She paused. "Why do my legs hurt?"

The beautician shook her head. "I didn't know they did. Can I get you something?"

Ellen licked her lips. "Just give me a moment to myself, please."

The girl walked off with a swish. Ellen read the damp letter in her right hand.

When she was done, she folded the paper up and slipped it into her pocket. She beckoned the girl back.

"Did I make a hair appointment too, or was it just nails today?"

The beautician blinked her long, real lashes.

"Everything. You asked for the works."

"Does that include makeup?"

"Of course."

"Well," Ellen said, taking in her image in the big wall mirror, "well, well, well."

"Yes?" the girl prodded.

"Well, that's very nice."

Ellen shifted her gaze back to her toes, the nails like ten drops of dried blood.

"For a shark."

Ellen laid her head back and closed her eyes. Beatrice looked into the same darkness, butted against the same shut eyelids she'd hidden behind only minutes before, and believed she felt Ellen reach to her.

Though they sat alone in the room, don Pedro talked to Virgil in clandestine tones, glancing left then right, the way a man in a brig speaks to the unseen prisoner in the next cell.

"See, everybody t'ink dey got only one soul. But de trut' is dat everybody got two. First, you got de *gros bon ange*. It come into you at birth as a spark, part of de life flame what shared by all t'ings. It de power what make you alive, make you move and breathe. It you' shadow. When a *loa* come to possess a human body, de *gros bon ange* is what de *loa* mounts and rides. Dat what make you dance wit' de *loa* on you' back."

With his hands don Pedro depicted images of spirits and dances, his long fingers and nails strumming between his face and Virgil's, a puppet show of dark flesh and claws.

"De Ellen?"

"Yes."

"Dat what happening to her. De Bea come and ride her *gros bon ange*."

"You said there were two parts to the soul."

Don Pedro stabbed Virgil's chest with the spear point of a fingernail.

"De other is de *petit bon ange*."

"The good little angel."

"Yes. De *petit bon ange* be you' essence. It travel while you sleep to live in dreams. De *petit bon ange* be all you know and love and fear. When de *loa* come for possession, it leave de body, den come back when de possession over. De *petit bon ange* be like a butterfly."

Don Pedro narrowed his eyes. "It a butterfly dat never die. It you' forever spirit."

He made a sudden motion like snatching a fly out of the air.

"Dat de one can be called by de *oungan*."

Don Pedro released the scary fist. "Dat de *loa* Bea."

Virgil had the sudden sensation of walking through a cave; the further he got from the mouth the darker it grew, the thicker the cobwebs, the sharper the echoes. He knew he wanted to turn back but—in his heart—when he looked behind him for the light to guide his steps out he could not see it, all was black, he'd gone around too many bends and was too far inside to know the path out. So he stepped further on, his unseeing eyes wide-open, his senses prickling, hoping to find the way out by going deeper in.

"Are you saying you can call Bea's spirit?"

"Yeah, mon. If she wan' to come."

Virgil turned his head, as though to hear better. "You're joking."

"I am not funny."

Virgil sent his mind down the stairs where Woody sat with fat hypnotized Jean; he recalled all the macabre equipage of voodoo, the herbs and drums, the dirt floor and the pit dug in it, the cornmeal diagram, guttering candles and bound chicken.

He felt silly and frightened to ask. "Have you done this before?"

Don Pedro laughed with disdain. "Come on,

mon. You t'ink dis happen every day? A *loa* coming back from de dead to take over a mon's wife? You t'ink you can look up in de Yellow Pages for dis kind of t'ing? Come on, mon."

Virgil stood.

Don Pedro pointed at the bed behind Virgil. "Sit down. We jus' talking. Save de standing up for when we gon' do somet'ing."

Virgil sat. The bed squeaked like he'd sat on a bag of rats.

He paused. His swallow in the room was audible.

"But you can do it."

Don Pedro nodded with solemnity. He was purged of brag or extravagance, this was solely a nod of power and cold belief.

After a moment, don Pedro asked, "You wan' me to go on?"

Virgil shifted on the bed, setting off a little screech. "I'm not sure."

"Den stand back up an' walk away."

Don Pedro nodded without smiling. Because don Pedro's eyes could see hidden things, Virgil was wary, he felt clammy, at what the *oungan* could see in him now that was holding him down to the bed, weighing his feet flat to the floor.

Virgil asked, "What's in it for you?"

Don Pedro rattled his head. "Mon oh mon, you don' know, do you? You go' a real *loa* in you' house."

The *oungan* slowed his words, lowered them as if into a well, they almost echoed.

"You go' no idea how powerful dat make you. De *connaissance*, mon. De power."

Virgil took a deep breath.

Don Pedro asked, "You wan' to hear de rest, white mister Virgil wit' de unsure heart?"

Virgil didn't like the challenge in that.

"Tell me."

Don Pedro continued. "Before we can call de *petit bon ange* of de Bea into de body of Ellen, de Ellen *petit bon ange* go' to leave first. We go' to call it out. Once we do dat, her spirit gon' stay near de body for t'ree days, waiting, saying good-bye to de body and de life. Den de Ellen gon' to go onward."

Don Pedro sipped his tea. Virgil stared at the man, the sorcerer.

"And unless God send her back like He did wit' de Bea, once de Ellen *petit bon ange* be gone from de body, she be gone forever. And you, Virgil, will have you' *loa*."

Don Pedro set the teacup on the table beside him. But his lips stayed pursed as though still sipping.

Both men turned their eyes at the sound of a creak from the steps.

Woody's crew-cut head hovered in the stairwell.

The boy's face was stretched in amazement, a gaping trampoline.

"Dude, how do you make Ellen's spirit leave her body?"

Virgil quickly said, "Woody, go back downstairs."

"No way, man," Woody answered. "This is way too radical for me to miss."

"You're not getting involved. Were you listening?"

Woody snorted. "Of course I was. Jean Claude ain't doing much talking."

"How much did you hear?"

The boy's lean frame ascended the rest of the stairs.

"Everything. Big good angels, little good angels. Three days then gone forever. All of it."

Virgil said again, "Go downstairs."

Woody stood on the hook rug between them.

"Virg, look, I got as much right to hear this as you do. I got just as many questions in my head and as much guilt in my heart as you do, maybe more. I got a right to listen, man. I got a right to find out if this is for real."

Virgil rose from the bed. "Woody."

The boy stood his ground. The flesh around his nose grew flushed like he was going to cry. His lips fleered back, baring his teeth.

"No! I can't wait anymore!"

"Wait for what?"

"Christianity," the boy almost spit the word, bending at the waist with the thrust of his answer, jabbing his finger down as though onto a phantom surface in the air, "Judaism, Buddhism, Taoism, Islam, whatever-ism, man, they are all gonna take too long to get to me. I won't last that long, that shit takes years sometimes, even a lifetime. I need to know now, Virgil, now, before I give up and quit looking. Before I live one more day in this bullshit world, I want to know that it's worth the fucking effort I have to put in."

Woody calmed and stepped toward Virgil.

"Look, dude, you know me. You know I got nothing going for me. Nothing. This might be the only shot I ever get at finding out that maybe there's some kind of purpose. So far all I got is your word this is all happening. But if what he's saying really works, if the voodoo master here can pull this off, then I know there is a God and a Heaven and angels and there really is some reason to hope. I've never had hope. Not for a minute, never. And I want it. So I'm staying."

Don Pedro stood also. He tugged on Virgil's arm.

"Mon, let de boy listen. We done not'ing yet. He already heard what we saying. He already know you' wife be a *loa*. What you gon' do? Unring a bell?"

Don Pedro folded back into his chair, his voice creaked with his knees. "It sound to me like de boy here got a better reason for wanting dis dan you. He wan' to know God. I say let him listen."

Again Virgil felt the dark progression into the cave. Before, it had only been him alone wishing for some brand of happiness and release. If he were going to commit sins for that, then little sins. But now there was voodoo and don Pedro and Woody and *loas* and dismissing Ellen's spirit forever and now things were accelerating as though the cave had turned downhill and Virgil was running with a pack into darkness.

Virgil sat on the bed.

Woody asked don Pedro, "Can you really do it?"

"It no' me doin' it. It de spirits. If dey wan' it to work, it will work. If dey don' wan', not'ing we can do. Dis is one of de times when we can no' demand. We go' to ask."

Woody was wired, fascinated. "Alright," he said, pacing. "Okay. What do you need to pull it off on your end?"

"I go' to call de Ellen's *petit bon ange* out de body to make room for de *loa* Bea. So I go' to have some of de Ellen's favorite t'ings. Clothes, perfumes, objects, whatever will help me bring out her *petit bon ange*. I take care of de rest. Den de *loa* can come and stay, if she want."

Woody asked, "You said Ellen's little good angel will hang near her body for three days after she leaves it. Why can't she get back in?"

Don Pedro lowered his hands as though rolling something out of his palms. Then he made a scooping motion with both arms, bringing his arms up to his red chest, crossing them over his cheap amulet.

"We gon' close de gate behind her."

Virgil listened and gave no reactions. He let Woody go with it, let don Pedro continue his ridiculous answers. What these men were proposing to do on his behalf they were only doing for themselves, for the knowledge, the power of *connaissance*. Wicked—and all of it was ugly and blas-

phemous, though Virgil had never in his life until
now worried about blasphemy. Was he really trying to do what Heaven wanted done? Virgil was
aware of corruption, of his own polluting wicked-
ness and selfishness. Would the God of light use
such dark tools, this *oungan* and his voodoo and his
curling hands, the blank, yearning heart of a boy, a
sad and tempting ghost, the death of Ellen? Would
God lead Virgil down this road?

Virgil skipped his senses over the room and the
voices around him and flew away into his memory
like splashing into water. Beneath him the bed
accelerated. Don Pedro's droning, smooth running
voice like a motor. Woody's questions flying in the
room like spray. The light in the attic silted like
seawater through the filthy window. Ellen's death
by black magic talked about like sport. Then under
his feet, suddenly, the speedboat shook again. He
was going too fast, he skipped over the water,
played patty-cake with it, barely touching it. In Virgil's hands, balled fists, the wheel trembled. Before
his eyes, the girl sank again forever into the bloody
current where he'd sent her.

Another body? No, he thought. Please, not
another death.

Not again. I cannot. I will not.

This time, he saw the woman in the water. It
was his wife.

This time, he would stop.

"Woody," he said, "we can't."

"You need money?" Woody asked don Pedro.
"Virgil's got money."

Don Pedro wagged his head. "Dis no' about money."

Virgil stood. The floor was motionless, not speeding, not rocking, not bloody.

"Woody, we're out of here. Don Pedro." Virgil dug into his wallet and left some bills on the bed. He jerked his thumb at the boy.

Don Pedro called to Virgil's back descending the stairs. "Hey, it's okay. I understan'. You t'ink about it, mon. You do de right t'ing. You come back. You stay away. You do de right t'ing."

Virgil did not hear Woody's tread follow him. Without looking, Virgil shouted, "Come on!"

He hurried past Jean Claude, asleep in the dirt pit. Jean Claude snorted at Virgil's bellow and sat up to his elbows. His big belly stopped how far he could rise. Water and mud blotched his shirt. The candles, the *vévé*, the cross and the mat were all knocked askew. The bound chicken lay on its side, exhausted and resigned.

Groggily, Jean Claude asked Virgil hurrying by, "What you wan' me do now?"

Virgil said, "Go home. See your wife."

He shoved open the garage door to stride into the world of light. He was already in the car, his hand on the ignition key, when Woody burst out the door and got in beside him.

"Thanks a fucking lot," was all Woody said, sullen for the ride back to the halfway house.

The sunset is why Hemingway loved Key West. There is a fire in Heaven. There is an ocean of distance—which is freedom for some men—to douse the sky flame into the earthen ash of night-fall. And when the sun completes its dip, there tolls some silent gong in the sand and coral ground, some flare bursts in the bricks and wood, something in the skin of the island tells Key West to break out its other pigments, its dusky, leafy shades and neon glass twists, white linen pants and pearls on gold. Key West under the moon and street lamps is lips and hair and shadowed warmth and it draws passion out like dark wine.

She found him in a street cafe near the shop, sitting at a wrought-iron table for two under an awning. He saw her walking up Duval across the street and did not register at first that it was she. He liked the way she walked, a sundress baring a lot of her, shoulders and some thigh. There was a roundness to her which on the sidewalk, perched on heels, somehow projected plenty. She looked satisfying. And when he saw her tug on the dress to show that it was new and she was unused to it, when she pushed her hair away from her face behind her ears—he thought it looked sexy, a lit-tle unkempt, in front of her face—when she turned an ankle for a moment on an uneven cob-blestone crossing the street to him, he knew this was not Beatrice.

She walked up to the railing. A restaurant palm frond brushed her shoulder. She left it touching her like Eve. She inhaled, gathering her-self in that funny round-eyed way children take a deep drag of air to blow out birthday candles.

"Hello," she said, "Virgil."

"Hello, Ellen. That's a beautiful dress."

Yellow with canary green patterns, the sundress showed she still had a small waist. Her breasts were at eye level for Virgil and he looked straight into them, then quickly down to her hips which now, cocked to one side, gave him again the sense of abundance. He lifted his eyes to her face and there—he caught his breath at an ache he could not trace to its source in himself; it was not sudden but more like an unveiling, as if a sheet had been pulled away from a statue—there was his sunset, the fire in Heaven was in Ellen's face.

15

VIRGIL opened the door. Woody stepped backward on the porch as though a fist might be headed his way.

For a moment the boy bounced on the silence between them. Late afternoon heat beamed at Virgil as though right out of Woody's pores, the boy looked so agitated. Air conditioning ran onto the porch past Virgil's bare legs.

Woody spoke. "You think this is fair?"

"I'm not concerned right now with what you think is fair or not."

"That's nice, man," Woody said, working his jaw as though the punch had in fact come and landed. "What happened to my buddy, my protector Virgil? Huh?"

Virgil looked behind him into the cool house and stepped out to the porch. He shut the door quietly. "Sit down."

Virgil folded on the steps. Behind him, Woody

made some spitting sound, a *ttt*. Woody lagged. Virgil heard the boy's agitated bones jangling, shifting back and forth on the balls of his feet and smelly sneakers. Then Woody sat.

"Look, dude, it's been three days—"

"Shut up." Virgil kept his eyes aimed at the sidewalk leading up to the house. He raised a finger not very high and pointed it at nothing.

"The last time you and I talked you were ready to kill Ellen."

"Man, it's not like that—"

Virgil raised only the finger, not his voice or his eyes.

"I think you'd best take me seriously and shut up."

The boy sighed with the spitting noise again.

"Listen to me, Woody. I heard every word you said at don Pedro's. I want you to know I understand what's going on inside you. I understand what's driving you."

Woody braved an explanation. "Man, it's not about killing Ellen. I like Ellen."

Virgil allowed the interruption. "I understand that too. In fact, the last week and a half I think I've understood more than any man ever in history."

Now Virgil looked at the boy.

"You've been right all along, Wood. I've been just like you. I thought because I'd been in pain, because I'd had some bad luck, because I'd been lonely . . ." Virgil paused and licked his lips, "I was noble somehow. I was deserving. I was owed answers, damn it. Just like you. Then Beatrice came to me, and that meant God Himself had come. That was my answer. That was my forgiveness for the girl I killed eight years ago. So I acted as selfishly and cruelly as I needed to get what I thought was mine by right, what I'd paid for. My happiness. My clean slate. No matter who I had to hurt or betray in the process of getting it."

Virgil put his finger in Woody's collapsed chest.

"That's what you were ready to do, Woody. Just like me, no better, no worse. And you know why I had to stop us? Know what happened to me?"

The boy shook his head. Virgil laid the finger to his own shirt.

"I finally understood the most important thing of all. That I don't know what God's plan is for me. That it's wrong to expect payment for your life, no matter how hard it might seem to be while you're living it. See, I wasn't looking for God's answers, even though I thought I was. I was just inventing the answers myself and believing they were His. So I quit. Right there in don Pedro's attic. I turned away, and I pulled you out with me. And within a couple hours of leaving there, the answers walked right up to me. In a new dress."

Virgil looked into the side of Woody's head. The boy's stiff crew cut, each of the million standing hairs, struck Virgil as a mass of men and women, arms and faces to the sky, reaching, beseeching.

He continued. "So Ellen and I closed the shop

for the last three days. We've been working things out. It's going good. Real good."

The boy nodded. The masses clung and reached up off of a bobbing, tilting world.

Woody blinked. "I'm happy for you."

Virgil waited.

The boy asked, "And what about Bea?"

"I don't know. Maybe since it's been three days without her she's gone on into the light. I hope so."

Woody ran his hand over his pate, brushing down the bristles that gave way, then snapped straight to reach up again. In his head Virgil gave the hairs little screaming voices.

Woody shrugged. "That's it, huh? Thanks, Bea. Thanks, God. It's been great but I don't need you anymore."

"I still need them, Woody. It's just that I'm finding them in Ellen."

Woody stood.

"Yeah, fine. And what about me? It hasn't been just a couple hours. I'm still waiting for my answers. You ever think maybe Bea didn't come just for you but for me too? Maybe I was supposed to learn something, did that thought cross your mind?"

Virgil looked up at the boy rubbing his stubbled chin, more tiny brown souls stretching for salvation, for light out of the darkness inside Woody.

"Bea's gone, Woody."

The boy snorted. "You think so, huh?"

"Yes."

Woody twitched his shoulders. "It's alright, man. Fuck it, it's cool. Invite me in. Let me say hey to Miss E. Congratulate her and shit."

Virgil rose. He laid his hand on the knob of the boy's shoulder.

"Look. I'm sorry. I'm the wrong guy to come to for your answers. I barely got my own. I'm just now learning to trust them. But come on in. Ellen will be glad to see you."

Virgil moved to open the door. He said over his shoulder, "We were thinking about opening the shop again Friday, for the weekend business. We'll pay you for the days off, okay?" He called down the hall to the kitchen, "Ellie? Woody dropped by. Come on out."

Her voice sailed from the kitchen. "Hello, Woody. Sit down. I'll make tea. How are you?"

Woody did not reply.

Virgil pointed at the parlor sofa. "Grab a seat. I'll go help her. You want a sandwich or something?"

Woody said, "No."

Virgil said from the hallway, "Be right back."

When he returned with the tea, with Ellen following carrying a tray of cookies, the door was open. Woody was gone, the air conditioning pouring out to chase after him.

At dusk, Ellen changed. That unheard gong that went off at nightfall in the blood of Key West went off in her also. She excused herself with

dinner simmering in the oven and went upstairs.
During the daylight hours, she was affectionate,
gentle in her competent way. He sat with her in
the parlor with the curtains tied back where they
read books, talked about vacation spots and made
plans to expand the store. She asked questions of
Virgil, not deep probes but innocuous things
such as "What do you think?" and "Do you like
this?" and "Have you ever been there?" They
walked to the beach and on the return perused
furniture stores. Virgil expressed an interest in a
new bed frame, a cherry contemporary. Ellen suggested they consider also the matching bureau.
Then at night, she carried some heat collected
from the sunny day and from the candles on the
supper table with her up the stairs and ten minutes later padded down barefoot in dresses that
made Virgil look her up and down, with her hair
moussed to fall across her cheeks. They ate suppers that were not delicious because Ellen was
not an inventive or knowledgeable cook, but the
fare was light and healthy and out of a cookbook.
Ellen told him she would get better in the kitchen.
Virgil complimented the meals and her effort and
said they should learn together to cook for each
other. After dinner they talked at the table, never
holding hands for very long or brushing bare toes
under the table more than a few times but touching, doing these things. They did not talk about
Beatrice. In the bedroom they were not desper-
ate with each other but welcoming, embracing
warmly and easily, like old friends at the train sta-

tion. Their sex was not spectacular but it was of their mutual making and, as they had done with suppers but this time tacitly, they made an agreement to work together and get better, even to surpass where they had been earlier in their marriage.

The sun was down. Crickets and fireflies were in the yard. Virgil stood in the kitchen pouring a row of crackers onto a tray around a block of cheese. Ellen dressed upstairs. Virgil liked the anticipation, her disappearance, their three-day-old ritual. He set the table and put her cooking pots and pans in the sink to soak.

A knock rapped at the back door. Virgil clicked on the back porch light and opened the door. Jacob Brumfeld stood in the dark.

"Mr. Brumfeld," Virgil said down the wooden steps.

Jacob Brumfeld stood swathed in a black turtleneck and pants. Under the porch light, now crammed with a snow of little moths, Brumfeld's white bald pate seemed to float free like a cold planet in space. He held a manila envelope.

The planet of Jacob Brumfeld's head revolved away from him; Virgil watched the terminator of porch light slide across his features. The detective was following the sound of Ellen hurrying down the steps to the kitchen.

She arrived beside Virgil in the doorway. Virgil stepped back.

"Hello, Jacob," she said.

"Ellen."

"Jacob, we have no more business. Did you come for more money?"

"I'll ignore that question." The man's face stayed blank but that wounded him. He held the envelope out. He dropped it on the bottom step with a flat smack.

"I haven't liked anything I've seen. Not from the moment you hired me. I think you're messed up with some bad people." Jacob Brumfeld's eyes flicked to Virgil and back to her. "And you don't know it. From square one there've been pieces that did not fit. I've done a little surveilling on my own time to make sure you were okay. I still can't make the pieces fit."

Ellen's voice was sympathetic. "That's another first for you, isn't it, Jacob?"

"Yes, ma'am."

"And you don't like firsts, I know that."

Virgil spoke. "Mr. Brumfeld. I'm going to call the police in the morning and tell them that if you follow my wife anymore I'll bring stalking charges against you. You understand?"

Jacob Brumfeld nodded.

Ellen took Virgil's hand. "Jacob, thank you. But please stop following me. I'm fine. Really."

Jacob Brumfeld let his cop face scowl.

"It's not you I've been following. Be careful, Ellen. Good night."

All the photographs were eight-by-ten blowups, black and white, with date and time stamped in the bottom right corner. They'd been taken with a

very powerful lens. The first shots were of Virgil
and Woody talking at the marina three mornings
ago, pelicans perched on the pier behind them.
Dated the same day but two hours later were several photos of Virgil, Woody and don Pedro in
don Pedro's driveway, the *oungan* looking paltry
caught in just one dimension, like a photo of a
carnival sideshow barker in his goatee, tatty jacket
and amulet and carnivore hands. Ellen asked who
don Pedro was.

Virgil said, "Wait."

The last group of pictures were dated that day,
the times were one hour after Woody had visited
Virgil and Ellen late in the afternoon. Woody
walked up don Pedro's driveway, alone. Woody
knocked and entered the garage. Virgil glanced at
his watch: This was three hours ago.

Ellen touched Virgil's hand.

"What's going on?"

Virgil stared at the photo of Woody slipping
inside the garage door and tried to track him
backward from that moment. What had returned
the boy to don Pedro? Woody was upset, clearly
jealous of Virgil's participation with Heaven and
now his growing separate peace with Earth.
Woody was impatient, on fire for his own experience of the eternal. The boy felt abandoned, he'd
come so close to the ugly proof that don Pedro
offered and Virgil had snatched him away.

Proof. Woody was so needy of proof he was
prepared to risk Ellen's soul for it.

Virgil had put a stop to that. Thank God.

But the other half of the equation don Pedro proposed, Virgil had not stopped.

Proof. *Connaissance.*

The return of Beatrice.

Virgil's mind leaped. Ellen sat quietly beside him, patient for his explanation. He pulled his hand out of Ellen's and put it to his head to contain what he suspected. He looked up through the ceiling, to the path to the light.

Three days. The spirit stays near for three days, saying good-bye to the body, to the life.

Virgil last saw Beatrice three days ago.

Beatrice had not yet gone into the light.

Don Pedro knows that. He's using Woody somehow to get to her.

Connaissance. Power.

Virgil pushed the photos into Ellen's lap. He pulled on his sneakers, left by the sofa.

"I've got to go," he said, tying the shoe laces.

Ellen stood when he did. "Let me grab my shoes."

"No."

"Virgil."

"Ellen, please." He pushed a finger down at the photos splayed on the sofa. "Brumfeld was right. There is a bad man involved here. I don't know how bad, but he might be a lot worse than I figured. He's got his hooks into Woody and I've got to go stop it."

"Stop what?"

"Please let me explain when I get back."

"Will I be mad at you when you tell me?"

He smiled quickly. "Probably."

She drew herself close and put her hands over his elbows. Her look was fearless; this was Ellen's strength, doing the right thing.

"I know this is about her somehow. I've been waiting for something to happen. She's in trouble."

"She might be, yes."

Ellen kissed him on the cheek. She stepped back, taking his hands with her to make two raised trestles of their arms. She was pretty.

"Look what she gave me, Virgil."

Ellen let go.

"She needs both of us."

Virgil parked far up the block from don Pedro's driveway. Full night roosted over Key West. Pinpricks of starlight winked low on a horizon swept of clouds. He looked up the street that was tightly packed with wood-frame houses, most of them ramshackle, several gaily painted, garish even though the waning light sapped colors from their facades and bird baths, yard flamingos and wind propellers. No one was out walking, this was the dinner hour. Windows glowed like the stars overhead, this little street of Latin lives its own Milky Way. And none of them in their poor galaxy knew what don Pedro was trying to do here in his ratty garage. Virgil wondered how this street would fill, the silence explode, if just one neighbor woman learned that tonight the *oungan* was trying to steal one of Heaven's souls.

He cut the engine.

"Don't even think," Ellen said, "about telling me to stay here."

They walked side-by-side in the center of the street to stand at the foot of the driveway. The upstairs window to the garage was dark. Below, the dirt floor temple was hidden behind walls without openings. Through those walls came a slow unsettling thrum, a drumbeat, deep as an old hurt. Ellen squeezed Virgil's hand.

He moved in front of her and walked to the garage, his shoes grinding dirt and stones. She followed. He put his palm to the metal door. The rumbling drum inside rattled the door under his fingers, the garage had a pounding heart.

Virgil looked to see that Ellen was at a safe distance. He put his hand to the doorknob.

A whoosh of air like a night bird flying past his ear brought all the stars into his vision and all the suns crashing down onto his neck; Virgil tumbled out of his body and into the world, down to the pebbles of the ground and the stink of beer.

The muscles in his shoulders and neck flashed. Virgil flinched open his eyelids.

Candles flickered all around, on the dirt floor beside him, on top of the large altar stone, in the rafters and palm fronds overhead, on the walls, hanging from cords in midair beneath the fake banana bunches. The room was toasty from the burning. Nearby, flames jigged with the little gust that arose when Woody came to stand over him.

Virgil tried to sit up and found his hands and

feet tethered together with a rough, itching rope. He was trussed like a hog. Woody crouched.

"He didn't hit you too hard, did he?"

Virgil lifted his stinging shoulders out of the dirt to look past the boy's raised heels. Ten feet away through amber light and close, scented fumes Ellen sat on her knees. Her wrists were tied to the central post, the pretend trunk of the banana tree.

Virgil strained at his ropes.

"Ellen!"

Woody laid a hand on Virgil's chest. "She's alright, man, don't freak."

She lifted her head to him. "Virgil. Virgil, I'm alright. Are you okay?"

He snapped his eyes to Woody.

"What the hell have you done? If you hurt her—"

"Nobody gon' get hurt," don Pedro's voice issued from the far side of the garage. "Help him sit up, boy. De mon gon' wan' to see what goin' on. He still got t'ings he can learn."

"Dude," Woody said quietly, "don't kick me or nothing. I'm just gonna slide you up against the wall."

Woody pulled him by the armpits. When Virgil was sitting erect, he saw that the hole where Jean Claude and the chicken had resided three mornings ago had been filled in. The dirt floor was smooth. In a far corner, the *oungan* sat hunched on his shins, a sack of cornmeal beside him. Instead of his red jacket and amulet he wore now a brilliant crimson satin shirt with billowy sleeves, black buttons and a long pointed collar. Out of his lips dribbled a song, sung low, almost sung into the ground, while from between his thumb and fingers trickled a thin yellow flow of grain.

The elaborate pattern he made on the bare floor resembled a weather vane or a signpost, balanced upper and lower by what looked like two pineapples. The cornmeal stream slipped down the nail of his forefinger as though from a chute.

The air in the room purred with the licking candle flames. In a cage beneath the steps, two guinea fowl rustled in a wire cage. They strutted nervously, avoiding each other. Don Pedro stopped his song.

"Dis *vévé* for Legba."

Woody left Virgil's side. He walked to stand near don Pedro.

The *oungan* did not look up. "Go sit at de *maman*. Play."

Woody sat in a folding chair and put a big drum between his knees. He wasted no time. He trilled on the *maman* with his fingertips, beating it like a deep-throated bongo.

Don Pedro stretched his long hand and nails at Woody.

"I tol' you before. Slow rhythm, boy. Papa Legba don' walk fast. Papa don' wan no rap music."

Woody looked contrite. Don Pedro went back to his cornmeal drawing. "We speed it up later for Ghede, okay?"

Woody obeyed and played a dragging dirge on the *maman*.

Virgil had waited long enough. The ropes on him and Ellen made him increasingly anxious, the room was frightening and the situation bizarre. Woody was not his ally. Don Pedro was of a power Virgil could not estimate and this scared him the most.

"Don Pedro, let us go."

The *oungan* made no response.

"Look, let Ellen go, you don't need her." Virgil spoke with increasing urgency, spurred by the ropes and the candles, the drum and don Pedro's intent, indecipherable little song. "I'll stay, I'll watch whatever you want me to. I'll spend the fucking weekend, okay? Just let Ellen go. And Woody. I'll stay."

Don Pedro gave no hint of hearing.

Virgil slammed his back against the wall. The garage shuddered, the bunches of herbs and leaves rustled. "Listen to me, you son of a bitch!"

Woody stopped drumming.

"Who's Legba?"

Ellen's voice was pleasant, conversational. She'd sat bolt upright and smiled at don Pedro, craning her neck to get a look at what the necromancer created in the dirt.

Don Pedro raised up to scoop another fistful of cornmeal. He eased his back and turned to Ellen.

"Legba of de broken foot. He de keeper of de gate. Papa Legba."

"Oh? Is he one of those *loas* you hear so much about?"

Don Pedro nodded. He glanced over at Virgil's still angry face and grinned, approving of this smart woman tied to the pole of the temple.

"He de wisest *loa*. Everybody love Legba. Legba walk wit' a crutch and carry a rucksack. He dress in rags and smoke a pipe wit' fine tobacco. He like de good black cherry. Dat what I got him."

Don Pedro pointed at the altar stone where gifts for Legba—rum, tobacco, plums, money, chocolates—were piled on one side beneath a dozen white candles. On the ground next to the altar sat a large clay pot with a wide mouth, covered with dangling beads of every color. Beside the pot was a brown grocery bag.

Ellen rose from her haunches, sliding her knotted rope up the center beam. She worked herself to her feet and looked over the design at don Pedro's knees.

"That's very lovely. What is it, a *vévé* you called it?"

"Yes, Ellen."

Virgil gritted his teeth at her name on don Pedro's lips. He saw that the lower one of those lips was swollen, like a hive on a dark branch. Someone had smacked him.

The lump on don Pedro's mouth brought Virgil back to his own discomfort, the rear of his head and neck smarted.

"What'd you hit me with, a beer?"

"Yeah, mon. I'm no' gon' wreck my good nails on a hard white head like you."

"How'd you know we were coming?" Virgil sneered. "More magic?"

The *oungan* lifted rheumy eyes from the drawing. He put on a jester's big face and held his fists to his temples, making index fingers into spiky horns.

"Yes! Dat's it, mon! De magic of de Bull."

Don Pedro clapped. "De Schlitz Malt Liquor Bull! I went to de corner market for a quart. I come back and dere you are at my door."

From his seat on the ground, don Pedro re-created the action in the air. "I see you. I sneak up." He swatted one fist down. "Boom! You out wit' de bottle. Den, boom!" He sent a shadow-boxing punch flying and laughed. "De Ellen catch me wit' a good shot. Ho, she almos' knock me out." He clapped his pincer hands again. He cheered at her. "Yes, de Ellen! She go' some power."

Virgil met Ellen's eyes. She shrugged.

Don Pedro held out an arm. "Boy."

Woody came to help don Pedro stand on legs tired from kneeling. The *oungan*, grimacing while he straightened, addressed himself to Ellen, who had shown an interest. Woody, looking small, took his place again on the folding chair.

"Dis *vévé* for another *loa*, maybe you heard of too."

"Oh?" she asked winningly.

He indicated opposite the drawing for Legba, on the other side of the center beam, to another, even more detailed design. This was unmistakably a funeral scene, with caskets and crosses.

Don Pedro waved his talons above it. Virgil thought of a vulture.

The *oungan* pointed next to the altar. On the far crest of the stone lay a second mound of gifts, stacked on a remnant of black velvet: hot peppers, roasted bananas and blackened ears of corn, a tin of salt herring, cigars, a girly magazine, all gathered around a single large black candle.

"De dark gifts for Ghede."

"Ghede," Ellen repeated.

"Death."

Virgil's shoulders suddenly hurt worse. A chill scurried through them.

"Ghede like dirty stories. He like de women too. Lot of people don' want Ghede 'round. Even de other *loas*, dey leave when Ghede show up. Just like people, de *loas* don' wan' to mingle wit' de dead."

Don Pedro dusted off his pants legs.

"Don' worry," and now the necromancer spoke to all of them, to the candles at attention and to the darkness bottled there in the garage which seemed of a special sort, his own private brand, a wiggling, transforming dark which worked like a warped glass so that tawdry don Pedro looked terrifying in it, "tonight I gon' get Papa Legba and Ghede to get along."

Ellen seemed unaffected by the rope binding her hands and don Pedro's galloping, threatening strangeness. Nicely, she asked, "If you don't mind, why do you need them both? Tonight, for instance. What is it you're . . . um . . . going to do?"

The *oungan* smiled again broadly at Virgil. "Mon, I like dis woman. I tol' you, dis de one for you. No' de Bea."

"Oh," Ellen asked, "you know Bea?"

The *oungan* nodded.

"Yes, Ellen. You are for Virgil. I tol' him dat. He know dat."

"Yes, well, thank you." Ellen prodded. "But you were speaking of Bea."

"De Bea is for me." Don Pedro said this without hesitation or qualm, lacking any sense of what instantly made Virgil's mouth go dry, the dirt of the voodoo temple floor seemed coated over Virgil's tongue.

The *oungan's* ears pricked up; he heard some faraway thing, perhaps the dragging foot of coming Legba or the black laughter of Ghede. He said, "Legba gon' open de gate. Den Ghede, nasty ol' Ghede, he de *loa* of death, sure enough. But he also de *loa* of resurrection. He gon' fetch de Bea back from de light to me. He gon' bring her right here. Den Legba gon' close de gate behind her."

"Come where?" Virgil asked, breathing thickly, sounding to his own ears panicky. He wriggled in his ropes. They were tied tight, he was not going to slither out and be a hero. "Where is Bea coming, don Pedro? Bea's gone."

The *oungan* wagged his head.

"No, mon. She no' gone yet. You know dat too."

Don Pedro brightened his look for Virgil. "You gon' get to say hello."

The sorcerer moved beside Woody who was still seated with the silent *maman* between his legs. He laid his hand on the boy; a waxen flow of flesh and nails dribbled down Woody's T-shirt.

Woody looked up the long red arm. Woody, vacant, desolate and forlorn. Woody was to be filled with the *loa* Bea. The boy, a cobwebbed and mostly uninhabited motel for a spirit, a willing chamber where don Pedro could put her, command her.

"See," don Pedro spoke to Virgil, in a voice relating a recipe, "I go' to have a *gros bon ange* to call de *loa* Bea into, some horse for de Bea to ride. De boy here, he *petit bon ange* barely hangin' on. So de Bea can come in dis one real quick, he step aside real easy. So I ask de boy de other day when you bring him if he wan' help de Bea come back. He say sure, no problem." Don Pedro patted Woody's neck.

Virgil said, "You're using him."

Woody attempted an answer but some pressure under don Pedro's hand choked off his words.

"I no' using de boy," don Pedro answered. "I no' using nobody. Everybody get what dey wan' from don Pedro. De boy get his faith, his *connaissance*. You know dat what he wan', somet'ing to believe. You gon' deny him dat? An' you, ol' white Virgil? What you wan' from don Pedro? You come to me and say you wan' be happy, you wan' know you' own mind. I gon' give you dat. I gon' take de

Bea away, you never see her again. You stay wit'
de Ellen, like I say to you t'ree days ago."

Virgil spit, the filth of this business which he
had unknowingly set in motion building on his
tongue.

"And Bea? Does she get what she wants?"

Don Pedro cackled and candle flames moved
away from his breath.

"Dere you go again, white Virgil. You t'inking
you know what de *loas* and all de gods want."

Don Pedro stopped his laugh. He threw a
pointed finger like a knife at Virgil.

"You don't!"

Don Pedro inflated around a deep breath.
Then he moved away from Woody to stand
beside Ellen. He eyed her while continuing to
address Virgil.

"But, now dat you brought me de Ellen, I'm
t'inking—"

"No!" Virgil and Woody both shouted. Don
Pedro answered only Virgil.

"Yesss," he cawed, "yesss, I like dat. Dat tell
me somet'ing, mon."

Don Pedro approached and lowered himself
before Virgil's fastened ankles. Again Virgil
thought of a vulture, now landing to look him over.

Don Pedro nodded, savoring.

"You believe, white Virgil. Yes. You believe I
can do it."

Virgil made no reply.

Don Pedro stood and hovered. "You know de
Bea will come to me because she came to you.

And I wan' her much more, mon. Much more dan you did."

Don Pedro released a call, a screech. "Whoopah!"

He flicked an arm at Woody. "Boy, play de drum."

Woody did not make a move but hunkered over the drum, glaring at don Pedro. The *oungan* ignored the boy's reluctance and continued flapping above Virgil.

"Hear me, mon. You don' know de power a *loa* can give. If I control my own *loa*, I be de greatest *oungan* in all voodoo. It give me almighty *connaissance*. What I can do, you would no' believe. Dey gon' come from Miami. Oh yeah, dey gon' come from Haiti!"

Don Pedro whirled to put his attention back on Ellen. Her pleasant facade, her good cop to Virgil's bad cop routine, was gone. Now she balefully stared at don Pedro. The man showed no sign of reading the disgust on her face.

"First, Papa Legba gon' open de way for de Bea. Ghede gon' bring her to me, straight from de heaven of de dead, straight into dis clay pot. Papa gon' kiss her on de cheek, den he gon' close de way behind her. Den tonight, just for a test, I gon' take de Bea from de pot. And I gon' put her back into you. Nice lady Ellen."

Don Pedro reared up his chin and chest. Ellen recoiled, tied to the stake. He seemed as if he would strike with his head, his beak. He struck with his words.

"After dat, I gon' keep de Bea in de world wit' me. De Bea gon' be my *zombie astral*."

He held that pose, nodding his head slowly, like he was sniffing a wind, about to leap into it.

"Play, boy."

Woody moved only his face, crinkling his nose, a denied child.

He pleaded. "You promised me. I did my side of things, man. I got you what you needed."

Woody's whining broke don Pedro's posture. He turned, nettled. "You don' need de Bea inside you to have you' *connaissance*. You watch her come. It de same."

Woody sullenly repeated, "You promised."

Don Pedro's spat, "I break my promise, boy. Play."

Petulantly, Woody nestled the drum between his legs. With the flats of his hands, he struck the skin slowly, begetting a doleful rhythm.

Boom.
Ba-ba-boom.
Ba-ba-boom.
Ba-ba-boom.

Don Pedro fetched the paper bag. He unloaded items onto a table as though he'd just returned from the market. Out of the sack he pulled a few makeup bottles and brushes. A feather boa, neon green and gaudy. A twenty dollar bill. A bottle of Chanel No. 5. A tin can of mixed fruit in syrup. A bottle of California pinot noir. One perfect long-stemmed rose.

From a drawer don Pedro took a pair of scissors. Ellen did not dodge at all when don Pedro cut a snip of blond hair from the center of her head. This he carefully tied with a black thread and laid with the rest on the table.

"The dead don' wan' feel neglected," don Pedro said, burying his nose in the rose. "Dey jus' like you and me. Dey wan' maybe somet'ing to eat and drink, maybe some gifts when dey drop by. Dat's all. No different."

Lastly he scratched along the bottom of the bag. He lifted out by its chain, dangling it from a nail, Beatrice's silver locket, stolen that afternoon by Woody from Ellen's upstairs dresser while Ellen and Virgil made tea and sandwiches.

When all the things were spread on the table don Pedro passed his hands over them and mumbled some benediction. He lifted from the floor the big clay pot with a wide mouth and set it on the table. Don Pedro stepped to the wall, picking his way carefully through the hundred candles, past Virgil whose rear had begun to itch from the damp dirt floor, and took down three bunches of dried herbs. He set these next to the pot.

He selected one bundle that had broad leaves and shriveled white flowers. He crumbled the bunch between his hands, sprinkling the confetti into the pot. The plant bits released a sweet green bouquet.

"Angelica," don Pedro said. "Pretty smell to draw de Bea's *petit bon ange.*"

When he was done, he put into the pot all the

things Woody had brought, pouring perfume and wine over the lot, then tossing in the bottles. He stuffed several balled sheets of newspaper over them as if wadding a cannon. He carried another cluster of dried herbs to the *vévé* for Papa Legba. Standing over it don Pedro crushed its leaves and small yellow flowers. The candles warmed the smell and wafted it to Virgil's nose with the hint of Chanel No. 5. Licorice.

"Anise for Legba," don Pedro said. "It help de pain in his leg when he comin'."

The last bunch of herbs on the table seemed not so desiccated as the others, with some life still in its veins. Its berries were black and shining, not withered, and the flowers were purple and bell-shaped. Don Pedro picked the bunch up and ferried it to the other *vévé*. This time he did not wring the leaves but kneeled and laid them whole at the foot of the design, as if at a graveside.

"For Ghede," the *oungan* said. "Belladonna."

Virgil recognized it. Nightshade.

In the mesh cage behind the stone altar the guinea hens bumped into each other and scrapped. In a second they backed off. They growled lowly and resumed their doomed pacing.

Don Pedro's goatee hid the top black button of his red satin shirt. He stood from the *vévé* for Ghede in the heart of all the flames and turned his yellow eyes and teeth to where the guinea fowl kept their jerky watch. He stepped through the candles and Woody's slow drumming to the area beneath the steps. He opened the mesh door of

the birdcage and with practiced hands took one
bird out. He set her on the *vévé* for Legba. Immediately the hen began to peck at the cornmeal,
chattering contentedly, scratching away bits of the
design, scattering the leaves of Legba's anise.

Don Pedro took from a shelf a bottle of rum.
He unscrewed the top and sprinkled it over the
feeding chicken and the *vévé*. He set the bottle
down and carved in the air above the bird the sign
of the cross.

He said to Woody, "A little louder."

The boy hit the drum harder and bobbed his
head the way Virgil had seen him do wearing his
earphones.

Don Pedro scooped the chicken up by the
neck. With a deft flick of his wrist he snapped one
of the bird's red wings then the other, then did the
same to both red feet. The chicken squalled but
don Pedro muffled its cry, squeezing its beak
between his fingers. He plucked the down from
the hen, letting the feathers flutter into a pile at
the base of the beam, the trunk of the *faux* banana
tree. When the chicken was bald, don Pedro
rubbed it on all sides of the beam, then laid it
crippled on Legba's *vévé*, the broken chicken now
as unable to move as Virgil. Again don Pedro
sprinkled it with rum. With the neck of the bottle
and the spilling alcohol, he made another sign of
the cross.

Don Pedro took down from the wall an old
sword, heavy and jagged with rust. He grasped it
by its hilt. He began to wave it.

"First east, den west," he said to none of them. "We cuttin' away de material world for de *loas* to come. We clearing de gate for Papa."

To Virgil, don Pedro looked foolish brandishing the sword but it was only a fleeting impulse because Virgil had admitted to himself days ago and now in this grotesque garage more than ever that he was only a pawn and other powers were at play in his life. The *oungan* plied the sword back and forth, hoofing his feet in the dirt, not stiff and old but spry. The shocked hen peeped pitifully. Woody made the drum pulse and don Pedro began to sway and Virgil worried the old man would hit Ellen or Woody with the swinging blade, rusty but still able to do damage.

With a jerk the *oungan* dropped the blade to the ground. Then, his arms flailing fluidly, part swimming, part flying, don Pedro sang in a deep, distracted voice:

"*Ati bon Legba*, open de barrier for me, *ago yeh*!

"*Voudon Legba*, open de barrier, *ago yeh*!

"De *loa* Bea, she gon' come wit' Ghede.

"Let her in.

"Take her into de Ellen body.

"*Ati bon Legba*, stand by de gate! *Ago yeh!*"

Don Pedro's feet stilled. He intoned, "*Ago yeh, ago yeh,*" in time with Woody's beat. Virgil looked at Ellen; her eyes were on the broken chicken. As though instructed by her gaze, don Pedro picked up the bird and twisted its neck around and around as though winding a clock spring until the head tore off in his hands and blood sprayed over the *vévé* and don Pedro's shoes.

The fowl's torso wriggled in don Pedro's hand until it went limp; then he laid the carcass on Legba's scuffed *vévé*.

Don Pedro went to the mesh cage and brought out the second guinea hen. Virgil thought that after seeing what had happened to its mate it might duck the curling mitt groping for its throat but the thing submitted in innocence. Don Pedro held it by the neck as if it were a jug and reached his free hand to the ground for the sword.

The *oungan* said then in a confiding whisper, "Ghede don' care so much about all de carryin' on like Legba. Ghede just wan' his chicken."

Virgil noted that the brown crust on the blade was not rust but dried blood.

Without ceremony, don Pedro laid this chicken across the stone altar and hacked at the neck until the head came off and rolled to lie blinking on the ground. Blood trickled down the altar stone. Again, don Pedro waited for the chicken's body to quit wriggling before he laid it on the *vévé* for Ghede.

Virgil scrabbled in the dirt, pressing his back against the wall. Woody's hands did not rest on the drum skin. Don Pedro moved now without halt, stoked by some dark inspiration. Ellen stood at the center post, her bound hands at shoulder height, revolving around the pole to put as much distance between her and don Pedro as she could. The many candle flames jittered like nervous skin. Nothing in the garage was still.

Don Pedro, with bloody hands, took up a gourd that was encircled with beads. He planted his feet on the *vévé* for Ghede and shook the rattle, chanting *"Ghede ago yeh, Ghede ago yeh!"* He shook the gourd at Ellen. She swung away from him like a gymnast; the banana tree leaves in the rafters rattled. Don Pedro shook the gourd at Woody who looked up and, to some unstated instruction, halted drumming.

A sudden tempest flashed in don Pedro. His torso wrenched. He did not focus his yellow eyes, which were red-rimmed and faraway. With kicking steps growing higher he stomped over both Ghede's and Legba's *vévés*. He did not rattle the beaded gourd in his hands but shook it with the spasms of his whole body. The man's head tossed wildly on his shoulders as though his neck had been pithed.

Virgil was roped and transfixed, unable to do anything to stop this. He was engulfed in guilt, all this was his: don Pedro's jerking body kicking up Ghede's cornmeal with blood spattered shoes, Woody's wide and wild eyes, Ellen's loathing and fear. And what of the damage being done to Virgil's own soul, which Fatima told him was not great to begin with and now must be so cankered and burdened by the sins he'd sent spinning against God and Nature that Heaven would spit him out the moment he hit the path when his life was done, they'd whack him with a baseball bat back to earth and make his next life short and miserable, a gnat to die in someone's earwax. He

didn't know what to do and remembered what
Beatrice had told him, that this, not knowing,
was the greatest limitation and injury of being
alive.

Don Pedro's spell did not last long. He twitched
and jerked two laps around the garage, flinging
himself among the many candles, kicking a few
over in the dirt, and when he had returned to the
spot where he'd begun on Ghede's ruined medal-
lion he heaved a final time, then looked about the
room as if he'd just arrived.

He oriented himself quickly. In the fresh
silence don Pedro dropped slowly to the floor to
his hands and knees, becoming almost catlike to
creep up on Ellen. She stood still and let him
approach. He slid his nose close to her skirt, then
rose up her chest and face. With his eyes only
inches from hers, he gazed, a grizzled jeweler
judging living stones. Don Pedro nodded.

He whispered, as if to Ellen, "Ah, Ghede. You
here. Nasty ol' Ghede. Welcome, mon." She did
nothing to push him away. She was holding her
place firmly and courageously, not like Virgil who
was dumbstruck and helpless. Ellen stood fixed
and erect under don Pedro's crawling eyes and
Virgil loved her for it and took heart for himself.

Don Pedro rocked back from Ellen. She had
punched him earlier that evening. He knew it,
even with her hands tied. He turned for the table
and the big clay pot, the one that held beneath a
stuffing of newspaper those things to draw Beatrice to him. He set the pot on the floor beside

Ellen. From beside the chicken cages under the steps he fetched a bucket of black tar and a brush. He slopped the rim of the pot with the sticky tar, coating also the inside of what looked to be a clay cap for the pot's wide mouth.

Picking up a candle, don Pedro held it high above his head. Woody's sense of voodoo drama was keen or maybe again he was feeling left out. He began another rhythm on the drum.

Don Pedro turned a circle with the candle as though searching the shadows for a stowaway. He called out, "Legba! You here! De Papa is welcome!"

He lowered the candle and his voice. "Look, Papa, I know you don' like dis, 'cause Ghede here too. We invited him. We gon' need you to work wit' him tonight, Papa. Just dis one time, ol' mon, den no more. Okay? I go' plenty in store for you, plenty we gon' do later. But you go' to he'p me now. Den I gon' t'ank you long time."

With that don Pedro put the candle into the mouth of the pot and torched the wadded newspaper. He shoved the paper down into the belly of the pot. In seconds, flames leaped above the lip. Don Pedro spoke louder and the fire climbed out to hear him.

"Yeah," don Pedro wagged his head, "yeah, we heatin' it up! *Ago yeh!* Come on, Papa mon. You take de Bea little angel by de hand and bring her to me. Bring her to de pot! *Ati bon* Legba! *Voudon* Legba! *Ago yeh!*"

Again don Pedro's legs began to bend and

straighten, as if the spitting flames from the pot were beneath his feet.

Don Pedro moved into a corner. He found a shadow and donned it, retiring from the flickering light to shimmy to the missing drum rhythm and wait for the flames in the pot to burn down. Without him in the center, the candles in the room reeled, the hot air and smoke swirled and feathered as though some winged thing were there in the room flying around the center pole where Ellen stood like a windless flag and the pot burned.

After a minute don Pedro stepped out. He said softly, "Yes. T'ank you, Ghede." The big clay pot smoldered. Gray wraiths of smoke clung beneath the rafters and fake banana leaves until they fell up over the lip of the stairwell to congregate in the bedroom upstairs. Don Pedro took up the clay top to the pot and called out, "*Ago yeh*. Papa Legba, close de gate. Den you can go, mon. But you go alone. De Bea little angel stay here! *Ago yeh!*"

With that, he clapped the top over the mouth of the pot, smothering the fumes and last sparks. He twisted the top once to help the wet tar bite.

Don Pedro rubbed the warm sides of the pot with dark satisfaction. He lifted his eyes to Ellen, eyes of anticipation and command.

He said, "Black Ghede. *Voudon* Ghede. Yes, mon."

The *oungan* took his hand from the pot, like an octopus from a rock, and walked to Ellen. He laid the hand over her head, covering it in a cap of nails and veins.

Instantly Ellen's head and chest fell. Her knees buckled. She collapsed to hang from the center pole by her tied wrists.

"Ellen!" Virgil hollered. "Damn it, don Pedro, stop! Ellen!"

Virgil squirmed and only added the thunder of his back hammering against the wall to the tableau of don Pedro and limp Ellen.

Then her feet slid in the dirt beneath her to support her weight and she opened her eyes. She looked out between don Pedro's spread fingers and stood.

The *oungan* took down his hand. He backed away a step.

Her eyes were clear looking around the room, first at don Pedro, then to Woody seated at the drum, then to Virgil, and she winked.

She breathed in deeply through her nose like someone just waking. She turned her gaze back to the boy and in a low voice, a movie star voice, said, "Hi, Woody."

The boy's jaw was already dropped; he exhaled and responded, "Hi."

"Play me something," she said. She motioned as well as she could with bound hands to the *maman* between his knees. "What you were playing before. The slow one."

Woody did not start right up but sat flabbergasted. Don Pedro hissed, "Play, boy."

Woody started as though pinched. The drum began to moan under his palms.

Boom.

Ba-ba-boom.

Ba-ba-boom.

To the rhythm she swirled her hips in a grinding circle. She spread and unspread her knees and did a seductive stroll around the pole, leaning against her rope and throwing back her head—*boom, ba-ba-boom*—like a hot captured slave girl. Don Pedro said, "Yes, yes, yes," and Virgil watched with the slow-motion horror of a car crash. Woody got into it with harder *booms* on the drum and she flung herself around more wildly to the beat. She gave don Pedro a penetrating look and, holding his eyes with hers, gave the center pole a long, lascivious lick.

"So you're don Pedro," she said in her throaty starlet's voice.

Don Pedro motioned Woody to stop playing.

He answered her. "Yes. I am de *oungan* Luis don Pedro Thiebaux. You de Bea."

"I de *loa* Bea," she corrected him, mimicking his accent.

The *oungan* inclined his head in respect. "Welcome."

Woody said again, clambering for attention, "Hi. Hi."

She looked around in a businesslike manner, appraising the herbs, bottles, feathers and candles embedded on the walls. She said, "This is a nice setup you've got here. Everything you need. We ought to be able to work together."

Don Pedro swelled grandly.

Woody, shaking his head in amazement, muttered, "This is so . . ." The magnitude of what he witnessed stultified his description; he settled for another shake of his crew cut.

"Right now," she purred, again making her voice sexy and damp, "I feel like dancing for you. I just looove this body." At that, she giggled. Then a tremor like a wavelength started in her ankles and spread up through her pelvis, arching her breasts and shoulders, shuddering her head to finish it off. Her hair fell over her face.

Don Pedro nodded at Woody to strike up the *maman*.

Over the throbbing drum, she said, "I could really get into this a lot better if you'd untie my hands." She pursed her lips in a half kiss. "Please?"

The *oungan* came near, almost laying his body over hers to undo the knot. He freed her wrists and she stepped back.

"There now, that's worlds better." Immediately she moved to kneel beside Virgil. She spoke sweetly. "I'm going to let this poor man up, don Pedro. Is that okay?"

The *oungan* held out a pink stop sign of a palm. "No."

Ignoring his refusal, working quickly at the knots over Virgil's wrists, she said, "Oh, come on now, you've made your point. I'm here, aren't I? You're powerful, aren't you? There's nothing he can do to you."

In a moment she had the knots loose enough

for Virgil to pick at them and release himself. She turned and rose to put her hands on don Pedro's shoulders.

"Woody," she cooed, "speed it up a bit."

The boy went into his bongo routine. She danced around the *oungan* as she had the center pole, swinging on him, gyrating her hips against his thighs, using the *booms* of the drum to land legs, buttocks and swinging hair against the stiff and proud don Pedro. She kept her eyes joined to his, locking his vision on her. Virgil slipped the rope from his hands and made quick work of the fetters on his feet.

Virgil scrabbled off the ground.

"Okay, that's it! That's fucking it!"

Don Pedro looked from the woman to Virgil. Woody stopped playing.

She backed away from the *oungan* and moved beside Virgil. She wrapped her arm around his waist and squeezed.

"What'd you think?" she spoke normally, not a bimbo now. "Not bad? Not good? How was I?"

He looked into her eyes and saw his sunset, his fire.

"Ellen?"

She feigned shock. "Oh, did you think that was Bea Sting? Virgil, honestly. Did she dance like that for you?" She pulled her arm back and slapped him on the chest. "Tell me she didn't. And that voice. That could not have been how she talked. Oh, please. Honestly." She clucked her tongue.

Ellen stood on her tiptoes to kiss Virgil on the cheek. Don Pedro slipped backward through a shadow to crouch near the large hot clay pot.

Virgil kept his eyes on don Pedro creeping backward. The man looked like a retreating crab. Ellen whispered in Virgil's ear, "I could feel her. She's near. She was fighting, trying to hold back. My God, how awful."

Ellen put her heels down and said again, to herself, "My God." Then she glared at Woody and sighed in deep disappointment. She left Virgil's side and strode to the boy. She lifted him from his seat by the collar of his T-shirt. He resisted, wrestling with her hands on him, squealing, "Miss E? That you?" Ellen almost pulled the shirt over his head, fighting him to his feet. The drum tumbled from between his knees and protested with a bouncing rumble in the dirt.

"Lemme go," the boy whimpered, surrendering, "I ain't shit. Leave me here to rot."

"Shut up, Woody, you little bastard. We'll sort you out when we get you back home." She ignored don Pedro, the *oungan* wrapped around the pot now like some crimson squid with his red-shirted arms, and walked the traitorous boy by the neck behind Virgil, holding his shirt high and out from her like smelly garbage, the boy squinting hard. She turned him, stopped and said simply, "Alright, Virgil."

Virgil whirled on don Pedro. "Let her go, don Pedro."

The *oungan* closed even tighter around the

pot. He skidded in reverse toward the wall, dragging the pot with him.

Virgil said, "Her spirit's not yours, old man. It belongs to God."

Don Pedro wagged his head.

Virgil stepped forward.

"Break the pot."

"No!" The *oungan's* eyes burned black, spittle twinkled on his lips. "No! Dis my *loa*! Legba give her to me. Ghede give her to me."

Virgil picked up the pitted sword from the floor.

"Move away from the pot."

Don Pedro shifted the clay vessel, turning to protect it with his body from the shaft in Virgil's hands. His back came up against the garage wall.

Virgil stepped forward, hefting the sword to prick don Pedro off the pot, then break it.

"Move."

Don Pedro did move, bending down to the foot of the wall, then straightening beside the pot. He faced fully to Virgil holding a pistol.

He jabbed the gun at Virgil, then at Ellen and the boy, as though that action would tack them in place.

"Drop de sword."

Don Pedro flicked the gun, held at his hip, to show Virgil what he wanted him to do. The knuckles on the *oungan's* gun hand were pale.

Virgil let go the sword.

Don Pedro's gun waved like a cobra tasting the air, weaving its one black iris between Virgil, Ellen and Woody.

"You! White Virgil. What you doin', mon?
You such a hypocrite, you know dat? You wanted
de *loa* Bea for you' own. You come to me and say
so. Fine, I t'ink, she come to you, you go' de right.
But den you don' wan' her no more. So, I take her
instead. Same t'ing. But now you say don Pedro
don' get de *loa*? No, mon. I don' t'ink so."

Don Pedro stabbed his free hand at the pot
behind him. "See dis here?" He shook the gun at
them. "See you here? Everything sent by Ghede.
Ghede make all dis happen, don' you know dat?
Ghede bring you here t'ree days ago to tell me
'bout de Bea. Ghede bring me de boy. Ghede lead
me back from de beer store to see you sneakin'
'roun' my door. Ghede gon' protect me no matter
what come."

Ellen moved from behind Virgil. She stood
beside him, squaring her shoulders to the pistol.

"Please," she said, "let her go. Let her go into
the light."

For moments they stood like that, don Pedro
holding them at bay with the gun the way a lion
tamer jabs a chair at his animals. He pawed the
pistol in the air as if to stick them with it instead
of shoot them.

Virgil stepped forward.

He spoke slowly. "I'm going to break the pot,
don Pedro. I'm going to let her soul go."

Don Pedro's whole arm shuddered, wavering
the gun barrel. His nostrils flared. He licked his lips.

"De Bea's soul mine, mon. You worry about
you' own soul."

Virgil took a step.

"I am."

From behind, Woody tugged on Virgil's elbow.

"Careful. The dude's not home."

Virgil pulled his elbow free and took another stride. He held out his hand. He anchored his voice to stop it from quaking along with his nerves.

"Give me the gun, don Pedro. You're not going to shoot me. You have your *loas*. You have Legba and Ghede. They came for you when you called. You already have great *connaissance*."

"No! Dey are no' mine. No' like de Bea. No!"

"Let her go." Two more steps and he could grab the gun.

Virgil leaned to take another pace.

"This is bullshit!"

Woody leaped from behind Virgil and Ellen, shouting and flailing his skinny limbs at the *oungan*.

"Hey, you voodoo dipshit! Why don't you plug me instead? I'm the one you lied to! I'm the one you made an asshole out of! What's left, man? I don't know one fucking thing more than I did when this whole thing started. I'm back to square one. So just shoot me!" The boy pounded his chest like a skinny gorilla. "Go ahead and bring *me* back as your zombie! I'll kick your ass!"

Don Pedro swiveled the pistol at the boy.

Virgil sprang. Don Pedro brought the gun back.

Woody kept shouting. Ellen jumped. Don Pedro fired, he seemed unable to stop the gun, he fired again. Both bullets struck Ellen, who had shoved Virgil aside, in the chest.

Woody landed on don Pedro snarling, tearing
the gun from him, and threw him down. He
jammed one foot on don Pedro's neck and
rammed the gun into his face.

Virgil caught Ellen as she crumpled. She lay in
his lap, his arms and legs encircling her, her
mouth working like a landed fish. The bullets had
struck her lungs, she was drowning in blood.

She lowered her chin to see her wounds, the
two rips in her dress, the spreading red. Her head
fell back in his arms.

"Ah," she gasped, "ah, I can't believe this."
The words were agony.

She clenched her jaw. Her eyes sought out the
clay pot, now unguarded.

She whispered, "Break it."

Without looking away from her, Virgil said,
"Woody."

The boy pulled his jackboot off don Pedro but
not the pistol or his glare. He swung his steel toe
through the clay pot, shattering it. The spinning
shards were sooted on their insides by the fire.
From them, scattered and sharp-edged, were
released the sweet scents of perfume and wine.
The boa, the can of fruit, the bottles, the long rose
stem stripped of its flower, were all blackened by
their ordeal; Bea's little silver locket came to rest
on the *vévé* for Ghede.

"Hold on," Virgil said, his voice catching,
"just hold on." A tear slid down his cheek to land
in Ellen's hair.

Woody lifted don Pedro by the throat and
boosted the yammering, spewing *oungan* to his
feet. He held the gun to don Pedro's head, just as
he'd shown Virgil he'd done years before to a
convenience store clerk. Once you see with the
eyes of God, Woody had said.

"Hold on, Miss E, alright? I'm dialing 911."
Woody spun don Pedro around. "Come on, man,
show me where the phone is. Fast." Woody slung
the slumping *oungan* up the steps.

Crimson foam burbled in the corner of her
mouth. Virgil wiped it away. Tired, as though
wanting sleep, she said, "He's a good kid."

"Yeah," Virgil said, "the best. I'll wring his
neck."

Ellen closed her eyes. A gurgle echoed deep
behind her voice. "Give him a break."

Virgil could not stop it now, he snorted and
cried.

Her eyelids down, Ellen's head slid sideways
against Virgil's thigh.

She breathed, "I'm sorry."

Her mouth did not close with the last word but
hung open. Her body went rigid.

"Ellen, no," Virgil sobbed, "please no."

Virgil looked through tears about the room,
many candles blown or burnt out, hazing the
rafters with the smoke souls of their extinguished
flames. Blood had spread into his pants legs and
shirt sleeves, soaking him, making him feel bathed
in her. Upstairs, Woody urgently gave the dis-
patcher don Pedro's address and shouted, "Bring

an ambulance, stat! Alright, yeah, yeah, I'll hold."
Virgil bent to kiss her forehead. And beneath his
lips, in his lap and hands, she became so heavy,
for Ellen's soul was gone and it is the soul which
lifts us up and makes our bodies light.

Virgil stared into the quiet face. In moments,
she began to feel lighter to him, but he knew it
was only because he—holding his dead wife,
again the woman who had saved him—was so
freighted with despair.

She opened her eyes.

Virgil jerked.

She coughed with a strong squeeze of her
flooding lungs. Virgil, startled and astounded, let
go her shoulders; her head flapped backward. She
grimaced and gritted her teeth. Virgil retightened
his grip on her. His mouth worked, trying to form
a question, "Wh . . . wh . . . ?" She pressed down
her chin to see the twin perforations in her chest.
She coughed again, then dropped her head back
into his arms.

"Ah," she groaned and swallowed, maybe
blood. "Ah, shit." She laughed weakly, but how
could she laugh? "Damn . . . I hate when this happens."

Virgil looked deeply into the wracked, blinking
face.

"Ellen?"

"Guess again."

"Oh my God."

"Correct. Ah," she sucked her teeth, "shit,
Virgil. Why didn't she just let him shoot Woody?"

•

She made another brave effort at laughter but it quickly strangled off.

"Bea." Virgil wagged his head. He sniffled. "Bea. I'm sorry."

"Sorry for what? It was never me, Virgil." She closed her eyes to gather strength to speak. "Admit it. It was always her you were in love with. I used her body. But it was her."

Beatrice mocked a frown. "You just wanted her to be like me. That was nice. But I think . . ." She tightened; something rose, then ebbed inside the body. She waited a moment for it to pass. "I think after a while you'd have wanted me to be more like her."

Virgil whispered, "Maybe you're right."

"Trust me." She poked him in the chest with a heavy hand. A blood dot was left over his heart. "I made my living spotting guys like you."

Beatrice sucked in a babbling breath. There was not much room remaining in Ellen's lungs to hold air.

"I came back to help her hold on. She's strong, Virgil. She loves you. She wants to live."

Beatrice hacked. Down the center of her forehead a thick vein stood out. "And you know, really . . ." She bit her lip. "Ah . . . really, I never did."

Virgil looked down into the twin holes in his wife's chest, hungry and wet like baby birds' mouths.

"Will she make it?"

Beatrice lifted her eyes and gazed up to the

rafters, into the wisps of smoke. Her voice stead-
ied. The swollen vein between her eyes subsided,
taking something from the eyes with it.

"I don't know. You just hold on to her."

Virgil bit his lip.

Woody clomped down the steps dragging don
Pedro by the collar behind him.

"I called the ambulance. Just a couple more
minutes, they'll be here. Hang in there."

Woody let don Pedro go and came to kneel
beside Virgil.

"Hang on, okay, Miss E?"

Trembling, she reached bloodied fingers to
touch his face. Her fingers left two red streaks on
his cheek.

Her voice was waning. "It's Bea, dear."

He shook his head. "No. No way."

The boy glanced up. Virgil met his eyes. He
nodded.

She whispered, "Virgil."

He lowered his ear to her mouth. He listened
then told Woody. "She says she wants you to tell
her if you know now."

The boy touched his cheek and felt the blood
she'd smeared on him. He looked at his damp fingers and ran them down his other cheek to match,
war paint.

Then Woody nodded to her, wincing like he
was about to cry. He turned his head to take in all
of her body, continuing to nod as though tallying
the sad cost of his knowledge and proof, her white
limp legs where dirt clung to the calves, the hips

where blood pooled now in the skirt, the punctures in her chest.

Woody sat back on his haunches.

Virgil said, "Go outside with don Pedro and wait for the cops."

"No." Woody lowered his eyes to his lap. "I'll stay with you."

"Woody."

In Virgil's arms, Beatrice shuddered.

Woody leaned over to touch Beatrice's shoulder. The boy looked to Virgil to be reverent, as though touching a shrine. Woody did as he was told and went outside the garage, hauling don Pedro.

A sigh from her. "Ellen's had a little rest. So I'm going to go now."

Virgil said nothing, certain that words in the face of all that was happening would be cheap and tinny. He nodded and tightened his lips, as though it were him and not Beatrice preparing for the journey.

Beatrice shut her mouth, the effort of talking wrenching her jaw. Then her face went immobile, locked in a distant stare. She drew no breath.

"Good-bye, Bea." Virgil held her tighter.

She was gone. Virgil looked into the fake banana leaves overhead, half expecting to see souls there, hung in bunches—Beatrice, Ellen, ballplayers, little and big good angels.

Then the body flinched. Virgil looked into her face. Her empty gaze was full again and it came back down to Virgil.

A smile spread across her lips, crinkling and brushing away the hurt from dying.

"Virgil," she said, "oh Virgil. I know."

Bea felt buoyant, just for a moment in his arms, the soul in her ascending.

"I know," she said, happy, "the plan."

He stroked her hair.

She released her breath and Virgil felt the body collapse like a bellows.

Virgil wrapped his arms around her. He took one of the still hands in his own. And like that he and the body rested in the ripples of candlelight and time. Outside, Woody paced, wondering out loud where the ambulance was and warning don Pedro not to say one more fucking thing.

Then Virgil jumped. Her fingers were a vise around his thumb. Her other hand dug in the floor, etching lines of pain. Virgil felt her head quiver in his lap, her blood-wet torso heaved. Her mouth spread wide and unleashed a strong gag. She tried to sit up in Virgil's arms.

"It's okay," he said loudly, holding her tight, "it's okay. I'm here. I'm here, Ellen."

She breathed in full gulps, the bullets in her chest were obstacles she fought to clear with each rise of her breast. Her mouth worked, digging air for her lungs like a shovel.

"Ah, ah," she said, laboring to turn her gasps into words, "ah, oh, oh Virgil, Virgil what happened?"

"It's okay, an ambulance is coming. You're going to make it. Hang on. You're going to be fine."

He rearranged her in his lap to make her more comfortable.

"Virgil, I—"

"Rest. Just rest now."

Ellen bore her eyes into him with the penetrating look of the wounded, and Virgil thought he could see behind them her *gros bon ange*, her sturdy and true earth spirit.

"No, wait. I . . . I was gone."

"Yes. For a minute."

"It was her. Bea Sting."

"Yes."

"Virgil? I saw her. I passed her."

Virgil's heart leaped to hear this, to see the ecstasy and life on his badly bleeding wife's face.

"She was beautiful."

"Yes she was.

"I asked her."

"What did you ask?"

"If don Pedro had really captured her soul."

"What did she say?"

Outside, the night was shorn by the wail of a rushing ambulance. Woody shouted through the walls, "Here it comes!"

"What did she say?"

Ellen pressed her husband's hand.

"She said only love can capture a soul. Oh, Virgil."

Her blood was tacky on both their grips. Her blood bonded their hands, squeezing rings about their fingers.

Epilogue

BEATRICE faced the light. It flared for a moment and was too bright. But when she brought up her hand to shield her face, the light, which did not dim, was accepted by her eyes. It shone kindly, the way light is in an opal and a newborn and in a wheat field at dawn and in sea foam at sunset and in the stars over an ocean.

She was alone on the path. No guides came to greet her. The light waited with its eternal patience.

But a gigantic sensation was in her breast; she felt as though she'd entered a tall and perfect library, not a collection of bound books and stale records but of wonderful, brave tales, touching and joyous and tragic and human, all complete and separate yet wound together like the cords of a rope. And all of the tales were her. You are not alone, she thought, with that inside you.

She looked to the light. She spoke. There was

some urge in her to make an introduction of herself, a formality before entering.

"Hi."

She lowered her eyes.

"Okay, I know, I know. I was selfish. It's not about being loved in life, is it? There's no need for that, it's taken care of already. It's about loving. It's about giving and adding, not taking."

Beatrice shuffled her feet and noticed for the first time that she was barefoot; her toes protruded from under the folds of a white robe.

She looked up now. She raised her arms with her eyes. She opened her palms to the light and handed it all over.

"I never loved, did I. Never once."

Beatrice sighed and lowered her arms.

"Crap."

The light glowed like the face of a proud teacher.

Beatrice opened her mouth to say more and in that same instant closed her lips and knew understanding surpassing forgiveness.

She held up her palm and a floating image appeared there. Virgil stood beside a freshly filled-in grave in the old cemetery in Key West surrounded by stately, colorful homes and a fence of black wrought iron. The day was bright; cheerful, oblivious Key West. Virgil looked nice in a new suit. Around his neck hung her silver locket.

A single long red rose rested on the mound of the grave.

Beatrice spoke again.

"I am loved. I was loved. Always."

Beatrice walked toward the light. She enjoyed the silence of the passage, smiling, knowing that silence could not separate her from Virgil, or from her mother and father or her Yankee guides or from the others and others inside her, knowing that none of them had ever really been separated.

In the image floating before her, Virgil moved to sit on the grass. He put don Pedro's deep-throated *maman* drum between his knees and played.

Boom.

Ba-ba-boom.

Ba-ba-boom.

Ba-ba-boom.

Beatrice smiled into the image. Virgil stopped playing suddenly as though someone had laid her hand on top of his to say "No, no, honey. Play something sweet." He looked dumbfounded and left the drum alone.

Beatrice held out her right hand and crooked her left arm as if around a partner's waist. With quick shuffle steps on the path, she twirled. She lifted her arm and spun under it in a smooth jitterbug pirouette.

Then, as if in a dance hall, as if photographers were there to capture the image of the young beauty dancing for all of us who are not dancing, lights flashed.

I wish to thank my agent, Marcy Posner of The William Morris Agency, who pulled a very large rabbit out of a very small hat; my editor, Marjorie Braman of HarperCollins, who provided the hat and thereafter a magic show of editorial wisdom and care; Ellen Hass and Susan and David Morse for their editing and enthusiasm; my writing mentor Pat Hass; and those friends who honor me with their love.